OF
WIND
-AND-
TIDE

ERIN RIHA

Cover design by Ashley Ruggirello

Book design by Ashley Ruggirello

Map by Christopher Winkelaar

Hardcover ISBN: 978-1-942111-78-8

Paperback ISBN: 978-1-942111-77-1

eBook ISBN: 978-1-942111-76-4

REUTS Publications
www.REUTS.com

For all the strong women in my life who told me I could

CHAPTER ONE

$\mathscr{I}$ do not have sea legs. Nor do I have a sea head, sea arms, or a sea nose. But my sea stomach is lying on the floor, and I've just landed in it.

Kern chuckles in that deep, almost lethargic way I've come to hate and shakes his head, mumbling something about dead weight. If there's one thing I've learned over the past few days at sea, it's that you should never trust a captain who takes the height of the waves personally.

"Yeh blathering slop of second-rate soup! Is that the best you've got?" Beck's taunt roars down through the ceiling from the helm above as the ship rocks violently, tossing me against the wall, hard.

"Thanks for nothing," I mumble, but it's a mistake. The physical act of whispering makes me gag, and I heave on the warped deck as another wave bucks the ship, sending me tumbling right back into the mess.

"Girl, you're useless!" Kern says, his mouth clumsy around the words. I look up, and he tosses a rotten-smelling wet rag at me. I catch it and sit back against the wall, wiping my hands and face. It would be so nice to have someone in my corner. At least at the institute, I had Declan to turn to, or Beck. But thinking of Beck, and the way he's avoided me since delivering Declan's letter, makes my stomach twist harder, and I hold the rag to my mouth as I gag.

"I wouldn't do that if I was you," Kern says. He crouches next to me and sighs, tearing the rag from my hands to sop up the contents of my stomach with his short, square fingers. I pull my legs into my chest and bury my face against my knees, but the smell is thick on my filthy oilskin pants, and I stretch them away from me again. Kern sits opposite, stretching his legs at an angle to avoid the disgusting stretch of floor.

"Thank you," I say, rubbing my burning eyes. My back aches, almost as much as my head. The ship pitches again, and I fly into Kern. He catches me around the shoulders before I can knock heads with him, and his wide mouth spreads into a smile.

"You wouldn't have to thank me if you'd stayed where you're supposed to," he says. His tongue is heavy in his mouth, the result of some condition I've only ever encountered once before. There was a girl on the peninsula, the cobbler's daughter, with a similar affliction—same tall forehead, wide nose, heavy speech—but she kept out of the way. She once brought me something I'd dropped, drawing CJ's ire, and when I defended her, it led to a rather unpleasant afternoon. My blood runs cold at the thought of him, and I shudder, curling away from Kern.

"I needed to throw up," I say, sliding back into the wall behind me.

"And you wanted to share?" he asks, crossing his arms over his chest and shaking his head. "Not very nice, Arden. Not nice at all." The ship pitches again, but I catch myself with my legs. My stomach rocks though, and I feel cold sweat line my forehead.

"I need air," I say.

"You know Captain's orders," he says. "You stay down here."

Captain. It's so weird to hear people refer to him with earned respect. They listen to what he says and do whatever he orders. He's not just Beck here. He's Captain. Though, I suppose it's easier to respect his commands when he's actually speaking to you. He spent the first two days in his quarters, recovering from CJ's beating, and then he left, and I've barely seen him since.

I thought I could lay low, could stay below deck and wait it out until the shitstorm around my fake kidnapping and CJ's death had quelled. Now, I'm not so sure. The misery of the last few days has me counting the hours and minutes until I set foot on land. Until I can get back to Declan.

Declan. The good guy with the kind gray eyes and the adoring smile, and roots that stretch deep into the earth. The guy who held me and made me promises among rows of sweet-scented herbs. Who sent me away with a person he doesn't trust because it meant I might be safe. Declan can help me. Declan can fix the broken things.

I just hope he still wants to.

Beck asked me what I wanted to do after Declan's letter, if I wanted to go back, and when I couldn't decide, he apparently made the choice for me.

I don't have allies here. I don't have sea legs. I don't even have Beck's friendship anymore. The closest thing I have is Kern, who has helped me clean up my vomit more times than either of us cares to admit or remember. But there's something unbreakable in a bond like that, and right now, it's all I've got. Even if I don't trust him.

"If you think you can keep your stomach to yourself . . ." he says, and then shakes his head. "It'll be my dick if you get caught. Just so you know." I share a weak smile and press my hand to my heart in gratitude. A girl's got to have allies, and this girl has to start somewhere.

He helps me to my feet. His squat hands are firm and steadying around my arms as I trip over my rubber boots. I guess it's the price I have to pay for living on land my whole life. I've endured my fair share of crappy situations, but never before has the floor literally slipped out from under my feet. Until now. So much for the romantic freedom of a life at sea. It's hard to believe now that I ever imagined myself sailing off into the sunset.

Kern unlatches the door and cold spray whips my face, startling the breath from my lungs. I wipe my face and grab the rail ahead, winding my arms around the thick, galvanized lip. My skin already feels sticky, as more spray splashes onto my cheeks, but the salty fresh air fills my lungs, dissipating my queasiness.

"Stay here," Kern barks into my ear, and then leaves me clinging to the ass-end of the ship. Wind knocks us to the side, hard, but the fresh air is soothing, despite the lick of saltwater, and for the first time in as many days, I'm not vomiting.

I watch the horizon dip and bob, the waves that had felt so violent while below deck less daunting now. There's an ebb and flow to them as they settle, and watching the rise and fall does wonders to calm my stomach and help me find my footing. I don't dare let go of the railing, but after a while, I ease myself into a more upright position, swaying with the ship instead of fighting it. Somewhere above me, Beck controls our route. I don't know how he knows where he's going. My view is limited to where we've been, but I don't see land. Just vast swaths of misty grays and blues almost the exact color of Declan's eyes.

It's hard to believe it's been a week since I saw him. A week ago, we were fighting over things that seem so trite now, standing in the hot sun, kissing in the middle of the lawn. A week ago, he promised to pick me, to keep me safe.

Of course, that meant sending me away with Beck, the boy who saved me from the storm, the kidnapper, the monster. The boy who kissed me good and long, and then took me away to safety. The boy who empowered me to fix what wouldn't heal on its own, and who almost died because of it. The boy I killed for.

The boy who will not look me in the eye.

"Can't follow a simple direction, Capo?" Beck's voice cuts through my thoughts, and a swell of relief and anger rushes me.

"I needed air," I say, my voice a dry creak. I've surely expelled anything that would've kept it functioning properly. His solidness enters the periphery of my vision, his large hands loosely holding the rail with the ease of a true natural. His cheeks and nose are sunburned despite the overcast skies, adding to the damage left by CJ's fists, and his dark hair is a mess of curls made by the sea breeze and saltwater.

"That's the kind of response that gets a man thrown in the brig. You wouldn't do well in the brig." His voice is all business, but I can hear a hint of levity, a glimmer of my friend who also happens to be the captain. Right now, I need my friend.

"Then do it already," I say, pressing my fists into my eyes. I bend my knees to compensate for the swell. Off in the distance, I hear the hungry squawk of a large, stubborn bird. Beck's arm edges closer, brushing against mine, and I try not to lean into the warmth of his spicy orange-and-leather scent.

"What makes you think I would let you quit now?" His voice is low, and the reverberations rattle through my shoulder into my veins, sparking something dim and dulled. Warmth rises in my chest, and I brace myself for another heave, but it doesn't come. I look out to sea and watch a large white-and-gray bird coasting in our wake. It dips into the current and pulls up, clutching a fat silverfish. Then it flaps its long, prehistoric-looking wings and peels out of view. I turn to Beck, but he's gone. I truly am alone at sea.

CHAPTER TWO

*T*he seas are fairly calm in the predawn hours, and I decide to walk around the deck. There's nothing but blue sea and yellow sky along the horizon as I pace across the starboard side. Or at least, I think it's starboard. I don't really know, and there's no one around to ask. It seems as though I have the whole place to myself, and the break from monotony is just what I needed to clear my head.

It's been at least ten days since we made our escape from Rocky Point. Ten days of being stuck below deck, feeling miserable and alone, with nothing to do but peel a few pots of potatoes. But this morning, I need to move. I need to stretch my arms and not hit anything. Tilt my head back and see nothing but sky and clouds — and, apparently, a large black man moving with a commanding stride.

"Don't see you much in these parts," Slick barks from halfway down the deck.

"I needed a change of scenery," I say, but there's a hint of caution in my voice. Will he get me in trouble for this? Beck's made it abundantly clear that I'm to stay below deck at all times — an order his crew never fails to remind me of and one I am plenty sick of hearing. Slick eyes me long and hard before he seems to come to a decision.

"No skin off my ass. Just don't let the boss man catch you. Round here, he's the law."

"Yeah, I know," I say, leaning into the side of the ship. A frown pulls at one side of my mouth. I'm still not used to thinking of Beck the way his crew does. He's not the carefree pirate with the quick, sarcastic barbs anymore. He's responsible for people's lives, including my own, and it's clear he doesn't shoulder that burden lightly. I'd seen glimmers of this side of him before — it's probably one of the reasons Declan was willing to entrust him with my safety — but I still miss the person he was when we were sparring, or alone in his cabin next to the hedge maze.

"Captain fell asleep about an hour ago," Slick says, eyeing me. "He'll be up soon, so you should probably get back down."

"He will?" I ask, unsure if that should surprise me or not.

"Sure," he says, walking past me with a half smile. "Soon . . . midday — it's all relative."

I watch as he disappears around the back of the ship, and then take my time walking around the front, keeping an eye on the bridge for Beck. Aside from Kern, I haven't spent much time with the crew. I don't know if I should trust it, or if I should prepare to be thrown in the brig. All I know is I've been given a chance to breathe freely for a moment, and I'm not about to waste it.

The skies are still dark in the distance when I spot Shaz's wild blond hair standing at attention on the deck. He nods his multiple chins at me, as if he understands what I'm doing. I wonder if Slick spoke to him, or if he just understands. He says nothing as I walk past, and I let it stay that way, continuing my lap.

As the sun rises, more men move across the deck, though nobody loiters for long. As I make my sixth lap, I start to feel useless. I should probably take Slick's advice and head back below deck. My stomach gurgles at the thought, and I grimace.

Someone pushes past me, and I slip into the edge of the ship, grabbing the galvanized railing to steady myself. I look behind me, but whoever it was is gone. A hard, calloused hand squeezes my arm.

"What the hell do you think you're doing?" Beck asks. He drags me to the back of the ship, where he found me several days ago, and when we stop, I get a good look at his face. His left eye is still swollen. His opposite temple is a faded purple, and his nose is obviously broken. But his green eyes are fiery, and he's very much the same Beck.

"I told you to stay out of the way," he says, his words sharp. Off in the distance, I hear what sounds like a whisper of thunder.

"No, you actually didn't," I say. "You didn't say much of anything. You've barely spoken to me at all. I've been left with no instruction and nothing to do except peel potatoes—"

"Who told you to peel potatoes?" he snaps. His bushy brows furrow as his jaw tics. His hair is pulled back into a messy, unwashed knot, and his clothes are rumpled.

"What?"

"You can't just be peeling potatoes."

"Why not?"

"They're my potatoes."

"And you don't want me peeling *your* potatoes?" I glare at him in genuine confusion. I don't know what kind of response I was expecting if I was caught above deck, but this wasn't it.

"Or my rutabagas," he says, letting go of my arm.

"I haven't peeled any rutabagas."

"Well, at least you can follow one instruction then."

My cheeks heat red hot as he just stands there, arms crossed over his chest like armor—but there's a glint to his eye that's familiar. He's enjoying this. I've been vomiting up everything I eat, not sleeping, and can't even take a full breath, and here he is, picking a fight over potato peels.

"I needed something to do!" I say through ground teeth.

"You need to stay below deck."

It's the same thing they've all said, over and over, and I get it. It didn't take long for people to follow us. We launched from the port in Rocky Point in full view of too many sets of eyes who knew what their competition looked like. Our ship—Beck's ship—is fast, though. Really fast. We broke away before I realized we weren't racing anymore. But that doesn't mean I've been afforded even a shred of freedom.

"I can't breathe below deck," I say, my lungs aching. He grinds his jaw into a tight circle. The ship pitches, and I lose my balance. He grabs me around the waist, holding me the exact distance of his forearms away from him.

"What was that?" I ask.

"I imagine it's Shazblister steering us into the middle of the damn sea."

"What? Why?"

"We've been spotted. Or rather, another ship radioed that they saw a pretty brunette who looked a lot like that damn kidnapped candidate from the institute wandering around our deck."

"How?"

"What do you mean, how? Eyes. Binoculars. Sailors know what to look for, Capo. Especially when there's tits involved. Or a bounty." I look behind us, and sure enough, there's a white spot of a boat trailing us in the fog. When did the fog roll in?

"A bounty? From who? CJ's . . . wait—*they're* bounty hunters? How do you know?" Thunder rumbles low and severe, closer than I care to consider.

"I hope they're bounty hunters—that's the least of our worries. Bounty hunters are an obnoxious mosquito compared to the real geldfudgers."

"Who are the real . . ." I can't quite bring myself to repeat his expletive, and amusement quirks the corner of his mouth, there for an instant and gone as soon as he speaks.

"You're an Independent Candidate. There are much more dangerous people who'd like to get their hands on you than a half-wit bounty hunter on a shrimping boat. You didn't really think that inbred crumdudger was responsible for everything, did you? Pickle-brained fella like that didn't seem capable of something as sophisticated as that soap." He looks like he wants to say more, but spares me the more salacious details instead. I'm grateful. Thinking CJ was behind it all was bad enough. The thought that I might still be in that much danger, after everything, is more than my stomach can handle.

"It's just a guess, anyway. Now, do as you're told and get below deck before you get us all killed." His fingers press into my ribs, and I wince slightly at a sore spot. His eyebrows soften for a moment, and he lets out a ragged breath, letting me go, almost pushing me into the door. It reminds me of the day he blocked me against a tree while we were sparring. I shut down, going into the only defense I knew, repeating the mantra that had saved me so many times from the horrors of CJ's "adoration." When I'd opened my eyes again, I saw the same flash of regret in Beck's I see now, as though he had seen what it took to break me and wished he hadn't. He'd built me up after that, but that flash of regret, of pain, is something that remains burned in my memory. It's a look I had hoped never to see again —until today. Then he's gone, and I walk through the door and down to my room.

CHAPTER THREE

I don't last long. The ship bends and bucks, tossing me from side to side on my cot. The echo of rain pelting the deck above is deafening, but not enough to block out the horrific visions that threaten to drown me. So when last night's potatoes seem like they want to resurface, I leave. I open my door as the ship pitches, slamming it from my hand and knocking me backward. I right myself and look out into the galley. Despite the fact that it must be midday, the galley is dark, almost pitch black. The ship bucks again, so severely that I grab the door as it slams shut, pinching my fingers when I don't move fast enough. A current of pain shoots through my hand, and I know I'll be sick all over the floor again if I don't get some air.

I shake out my throbbing fingers and move up the galley toward the door to the deck. Curling my fingers around the latch sends sick burning into the back of my throat, but I squeeze the handle anyway and tug. It swings backward with a thrust, just as another wave rocks the ship, and I nearly topple down the stairs. My aching fingers are still hooked on the handle, though, so I grit my teeth, wincing against the pain, and hoist myself up.

Outside, the world is upside down. The dark, angry rain pelts sideways, and the sea is a blinding torrent of foam and fury. The air is a thick, unnatural gray-green, and as the ship tilts, my sense of what is top and under, right and sideways, is shot. All I know is that if I go back below deck, beneath the waves, I might drown. I pull myself onto the deck, and the frigid rain pelts my face with so much animosity, I forget my aching fingers. My thick wool sweater is soaked in seconds, and water slithers down my oilskin pants into my rubber boots. A wave crashes over the prow, and icy saltwater blinds me. I grab for something to hang on to, but slip and fall, banging my knee into the ship's siding. I try to stand as the vessel lurches, knocking me back down, and I slide on my back along the deck, down, down, down as the ship tilts its battle cry.

A tight hand squeezes my wrist and pulls me up the deck. I can't see who it is, but he pulls me back into the stairwell and I scream, certain I'm either going to suffocate or fall to my demise. Somehow, my rescuer steadies me as we go down the steps, and once we're safely at the bottom, I spin on my heels to face Slick's deep brown gaze.

"Please don't," I say, wiping the water from my stinging eyes.

"Dammit, Arden, stay down there."

"Let me come up. Please. I can't breathe. Ask Beck."

"*Captain* has his hands full right now. He doesn't need some seasick debutante distracting him while he tries to navigate us through a squall we wouldn't be in if it weren't for the bounty on your head." He pulls me down the galley to my cabin door, opens it with a bang, and steers me inside.

"Stop!" I sputter. He shakes his head as the ship lurches too far, and my stomach clenches.

"Just stay down here," he shouts, and then he takes off in

the opposite direction. I stand in my doorframe, familiar panic rising in my throat, constricting my breath. I close my eyes and try to breathe lower, deeper, from my belly. But the boat lunges again, and I stumble, face-first, into the wall, slamming into my cheek. The ache of impact moves through my bones, into my skull. I can't stay here.

I pull myself up the galley, toward the stairs, climbing against the violent rocking motion of the storm. I pause and reach for the door. I don't know where I'm going. Maybe I'll just stand here in the stairwell and get some fresh air. I pull on the door, but it flies open instead. Kern stands there, waiting, on the other side.

"Arden! You know the orders!" he shouts, pushing me back. I slip and my feet go out from under me, but I grab the railing just in time, managing to fall forward instead of back. My shins slam against the creaking wooden steps, and I thump down the stairs. I land at the bottom and slide to port side in a heap.

He lifts me easily, though I don't know how—if anything, he's shorter than me—and carries me to a room I haven't seen before. He pulls something from his pocket, and I realize it's a key.

"I'm sorry. Captain's orders."

My heart pounds in my chest as he opens the door, revealing a tiny cell with no porthole.

"Please, Kern, no—"

"You're a danger!" he shouts, as he drops me onto the tiny cot and slams the door.

"No!" I launch myself at the door, scratching my nails against the wood, finding no handle. The ship tosses me back into the cot, and I slam into the heavy wooden frame square on my back. A wave of nausea pulses upward, and I vomit on my thighs. I close my eyes for a moment once I finish. I don't know why, though. It's not any darker with them open or closed. I reach out and can feel all four walls from where I'm sitting. My lungs feel like they're filling with tar. Each breath is heavier than the last, and my ribs ache with the force of each inhale. I slam my fists into the door and scream, because that's all I know to do. A faint smell of iron and excrement reaches my nose, and I'm instantly transported back to the shed. I can't do anything to stop the vision that swims into my mind's eye: CJ locking me in the shed, blended with his bloodied corpse on the floor in Rocky Point.

I slam my palms against the door, choking on snot and saline. The ship rocks again, and this time, I lose my balance and fly backward, smacking my head on hard wooden beams. Stars flood my vision, the momentary relief of light in the darkness distracting me from the fact I'm going to sleep, and this time, I won't be able to fight back.

CHAPTER FOUR

*C*itrus and salt. They blend together in a way that fermenting hay and horse shit don't. They're bright and fresh and new and safe. They press in gentle fingers along my scalp, through my hair, washing away the smells that suffocated. I curl into the citrus and salt and let the sleep win.

The nightmares don't come. Or if they do, I don't remember them. Everything is murky and dark, and then there's citrus and salt, and it's fine. I'm fine.

When I do wake, it's to his voice. He's yelling at someone, and it's too loud. Too much. He's angry. I pull my knees into my chest and press my face into the pillow. The pillow smells of citrus and leather and salt.

"Arden," he says, pressing fingertips to the base of my neck. I groan something indecipherable into the pillow. The noise hurts.

"Arden, we have to go. I need you to get up." And like that, I'm awake. My eyes open, my head pounds, and I squeeze them shut again, but he pulls a blanket off my body. Somewhere, a door closes.

"How long?" I ask, but it's a reflex. I don't even really know what I'm asking. I roll over, and he's gone. Kern is there instead, biting his lip, nursing a black eye.

"We have to hurry," he says. His voice is stilted, painted with shame and regret. He reaches out a hand for me, but I push myself up on my own, teetering slightly, determined that I will not rely on him.

"Where?" I ask. As if in answer, I hear the squawk of radio noise from the deck. Of course. We're in the captain's quarters. Kern presses a hand to my back, and I jump away from him.

"Do not touch me," I say, too sharply. My head pounds at the base of my skull from the effort.

"Sorry," he mumbles. I push through the door, my fingers stiff on the latch.

It's night. The deck is empty save for Shaz, who shushes me and waves us over to a rope ladder flapping against the side of the ship. It thuds and smacks about halfway down the port side, slapping against the chipped navy paint of the ship wall, sounding hollow and brittle. When I am close enough to lean over and look, my stomach drops. Below—far, far below—in the churning waves, is a tiny rowboat. Slick waves up at me, a stupid grin plastered on his face.

"What am I supposed to do with this?" I ask, and Shaz shoots me a wicked look.

"Dance the tango, obviously," he says, lifting me up. I grab at the rungs just as he sets me on the other side. There's an urgency to his tone, even when he's joking, and I wonder what it was they heard over the radio. "Come on, now. One foot after the other. Don't look down." The wind blows my sticky hair out of my eyes, and the ladder shudders in my grasp.

"We're kind of in a hurry," Kern says, but he doesn't look at me as he waits his turn. I let go of the first rung with one hand and reach for the next. A sliver of reddish-gray wood slices into my palm, but I don't dare let my grip go slack. I slide my foot off a rung and onto the next, and the ladder shifts under its weight. I swing against the ship. It feels wild and terrifying, but I find my balance. Carefully, I shift my other foot, my other hand.

"Great. Good form. Now hurry the fuck up!" Shaz barks. I keep moving, hand-foot, hand-foot. I feel out the sway of the ladder and rebalance. The further I get, the freer the momentum is, pulsing away from the ship and then back like a swing. A really scary swing. But I let myself feel the momentum and move with it, bend with it. I find my rhythm, and after what feels like it should have been more than long enough to reach the rowboat, I look down. I'm at least fifteen feet above the water, and the boat is at least five feet to my right. If I fall, I will either hit the rowboat or the water. Neither option sounds pleasant, but I know without a doubt that I will drown in these waves if I hit them.

"I'll come to you when you're low enough," Slick shouts. "Keep going!" I nod, as if he can see me, and keep climbing down. One rung, then the next, then another, and another. I look back down at him, and he's not far now, getting closer.

"One or two more, then stop," he shouts over the roar of the waves, and I move my hand down a rung, followed by my foot. As I'm lowering my left foot, a swell tilts the ship just far enough that the next wave slaps me, drenching me from the waist down and throwing the rope—with me on it—into the side of the ship. My tender fingers catch between the rung and the ship wall, and violent pain pulses up my arm. I let go and almost lose my footing, quickly grasping at the bar again, crying out at the pain.

"Hang on!" Slick shouts. The rope swings back from the ship again. He catches it, and I slide down. I fall awkwardly into the boat, landing on my scarred hip with a crushing blow that nearly sends me tumbling over the side, upsetting his balance.

"Dammit, Arden! You're going to get us all killed!" he says, righting the rowboat as I pull myself onto the bench. There's a rigidness to his voice that makes me think he's not just angry about my fall. As I settle myself in the rowboat, my hand ghosts over the hard disk pressed against my chest. I reach under my sweater, under the shirt beneath, and feel the smooth metallic edges of Declan's brass compass, strung through a chain around my neck. I untuck it and unclip the solid brass piece. The little arrow fluctuates with our position, but seems to think that north is still in one general direction. I replace it around my neck and grip the sides of the rowboat as we tumble on a swell taller than the boat itself.

"Where are we going? Where are the others?" I ask, frantic for more information.

"Hush, waiting on Kern." Great. The last person I want to die with is the guy who locked me in a cell, any fragile alliance I had thought we'd formed now shattered into dust. Shivers erupt all over my body, and I curl in on myself at the thought, just as another wave rocks the boat too much. I grip the sides, hard, as I breathe deeply—in through the nose, out through the mouth. By the time I look back up at the rope ladder, Kern is halfway down, moving with expert precision and a grace that I don't possess.

"Hold tight!" Slick says to me. I look over my shoulder and see a massive wave closing in on us. He turns the prow of the rowboat into it, and I fold over my legs, grabbing the underside of the bench. The nose of the boat breaks the wave, but my back gets drenched. I look up at the ship. Kern is tangled now in the ladder, his right leg twisted in the rope between two rungs. He hangs by one arm and his trapped leg.

"Incoming!" Slick shouts, but I don't have time to react before the wave slams into us, harder this time. I fall onto my knees and bump into him. He curses and knocks into my temple with the handle of the oar as he steers us around. My head pulses with pain from yet another impact, but as I look back up at Kern, I stop breathing. He hangs upside down by his tangled leg, trying to pull himself up. Shaz shouts down at him; something I can't hear. But when I see him reach into his pocket, I know he's going to die.

"Don't!" I shout and try to stand, but Slick pulls me down, just in time for another icy wave to coat my shoulders. I wipe the water from my face, shivering, and look back up. Kern has cut almost all the way through the rope just above his knee and is at least right side up again, supported by his other foot. But then he cuts all the way through, and the rope around his leg unravels. The rung he's standing on goes flying away, and his foot slips out. He's hanging on to a rung with his left hand only, the knife still in his right, and he's at least twenty feet up. I scream and watch as his too-short body dangles over the pounding waves.

"Kern!" I shout, as Slick rows back away from him.

"What are you doing? We have to get him!" I shout.

"I know! Let me do my job!" I'm shaking with fear as I watch Kern swing into the side of the ship, landing with both feet pressed against the wall. He pushes off, letting go of the ladder, and goes flying backward, diving feet first into the surf. My heart is pounding in my ears, louder somehow than the pound of the waves, and all I can think is that I have to keep my eyes on the water so we can get to him. But Slick is one step ahead of me, and by the time Kern's square head pops up from the water, we're almost within oar's length of him. Slick steers us sideways as the ship leans into a wave, cutting the stance between us while Kern rides the swell.

"Hang tight. This will be rough," Slick shouts over the crashing waves. He reaches an oar out to Kern as he approaches, fighting the stormy surf. Kern grabs the oar, and my lungs scream for air, too constricted by fear to function as they should. A wave smashes into us, plastering the wool of my sweater and heavy flannel of my shirt to my skin as I inhale, choking on the saltwater. The boat starts to tip, and Slick heaves his massive frame away from Kern, from the way we're threatening to capsize. As the boat corrects itself—too much—I lean in the opposite direction. Slick yells something at me as he pulls Kern over the edge of the boat, and we tilt again the other way. I realize too late that I'm the fulcrum here, and I've failed as we start to take on water. I tilt back in the direction Slick is leaning, and Kern climbs in, his hair covering his face.

"You sure know how to make an entrance," Slick says, smacking his shoulder. Kern is breathing hard on the floor of the boat, but he looks happy. Slick rows away, and I look back at the ship.

"What about Shaz?" I ask.

"First mate stays with the ship in the captain's stead," Slick says as he rows.

So, where is Beck? Why would he leave his ship? Where are we all going? Kern is still in a heap on the floor between me and Slick, and I reach out to help him up. He hesitates for a moment, but then takes my hand. I pull him onto the seat next to me. We're both drenched, and soon enough, the shivering starts. Nobody says anything for quite some time, both of us giving Slick room to work. I look at Kern's legs. His right thigh is torn through and bloody.

"Are you okay?" I ask. He nods and laughs.

"I'm fine."

"Should we do something about that?"

"What are we gonna do? Call the medic?" he asks. I shake my head and chuckle. We shiver in silence for a few more minutes as the wind beats at our backs, and I pray for land to appear, just so we can get out of this damned sea breeze.

"I'm sorry, Arden," Kern says, his voice simple and blunt. "We just needed you out of the way. I misunderstood . . ." He stops, and I know what he wants to say: *I didn't know. I didn't know you don't like small spaces . . .*

Which means that now, he does. I wonder who else knows? I look up at Slick's blank face, but his knowing eyes rest on me. Hot tears prick at the corners of my eyes, but I bite the edge of my tongue and swallow them back. I guess they have a right to know. They would need an explanation for why Beck and I were covered in blood, an explanation for who they needed to protect us from. They wouldn't have known, I'm sure, until I didn't follow orders and had to be contained. Beck would have spared them the full details, of that I'm certain.

"If you'd known, would you have done it anyway?" I ask. Slick raises an eyebrow, but says nothing.

"Maybe not such a small room," he says. I snort.

"I'm sorry I put you in that position." He's still, his head slightly cocked, as if it never occurred to him that I would owe him an apology.

"Aw, don't worry about that." He takes a breath and shapes his mouth around words he really means. "I like you, Arden. We all do. You're just terrible cargo." I cough out a laugh, and then can't stop coughing. Chills rock over me in torrents.

"Land ho!" Kern says, and Slick grins.

"Not a moment too soon," Slick says, his energy renewed, pushing us over the breakers with extra effort. By the time we reach the rocky beach, there are two men and four horses waiting for us. Someone in a hood helps me out, and I recognize Perlman's bushy red hair.

"Took you long enough, didn't it?" he says, but his voice is directed over my shoulder at Slick, who now carries the boat over his head.

"Someone had to make a grand entrance," he says, nodding to Kern.

"Show off," Perlman says. Kern grins, his blue eyes sparkling, and I don't think I've ever been so glad to see that face. Wind rolls off the sea, and another wave of chills rolls down my back as my teeth chatter. Perlman waves us toward the horses up the beach.

"All right, enough small talk," he says. "Let's get some fire in our bellies."

CHAPTER FIVE

For my first time on a horse, I've gotta say, I'm not great. I ride with Perlman, which is awkward and uncomfortable against his rickety, awkward frame, but I'm not sure it would've been any better with the other options.

The trail is steep and narrow, flanked by thick trees and vines that swipe at my arms and threaten to dislodge me. The animal doesn't seem too interested in keeping me aboard; I'm not sure Perlman is happy with me either. I'm trying to find a decent balance between holding on to him, trying not to shiver too much to unbalance him, absorbing some of his body heat so I don't freeze to death, and not dripping all over him. Judging by the dark water stains spreading across the back of his jacket, I'm not succeeding.

"Finally," Perlman says, not masking his dissatisfaction with the current situation. When we climb the last bit of trail, a warm, orange light seeps into the forest, leading to a clearing. I almost think I'm seeing things. Set back against a wall of trees is a two-story stone house. The entrance—two beefy wooden doors—is lit with oil lamps, something I haven't seen since I was a child in the peninsula slums. The first-floor windows

23

appear blocked with something, but the faintest hint of orangey-red light creeps into the edges. The second-floor windows are black.

"Whose house is this?" I ask as Perlman dismounts, leaving me with nothing to hang on to. I start to slip, and he quickly grabs my waist, catching me as I fall into his chin.

"Celeste Crookshank's," he says with a grin that looks like the one he gave in the brothel in Rocky Point.

"Give her the respect she deserves!" Kern scolds.

"Sorry, Madame Celeste Crookshank's," Perlman says, but if anything, his grin only gets bigger.

An uncomfortable feeling rushes up my spine, and I shudder.

"Aw, it's not as bad as all that, now. What the prince don't know won't hurt him," Slick says with a hoarse laugh, leaving me behind with the horses. I'm pretty sure they don't want me either. I blush at the thought of Declan seeing me in a place like this. When he sent me away from the dangers of the institute — dangers that had been engineered by more than just CJ, it turns out — I hardly think this is what he had in mind.

"Is Beck here?" I ask, not sure if I really want the answer.

" 'Course he is," Perlman says, nodding his head at Slick. They laugh with a deep, knowing undercurrent that hurts my stomach. There are four other horses tethered with ours, and Kern gets to work watering the ones we brought as Slick, Perlman, and the other nameless member of our party climb the steps. Perlman pulls hard on the door handle, and the sound of clinking glasses and happy customers spills out as he shouts something into the warm light, lowering his hood as he steps inside. A chill grips my shoulders, and I try to shake it off. I stay with Kern, watching him work with the horses.

"You should go in. There's a fire," he says, petting the horse I rode in on.

"I don't think so," I say.

"There is. I swear it. It's big." He keeps his hands trained on the horse, calming it, then reaches into a bag I'm certain he didn't carry down the side of the ship to pull out an apple, feeding it to the docile beast. I reach a tentative hand forward, and the horse jerks away.

"You've made quite the impression," he says with a little snort.

"Would seem so." I step back and shudder into the breeze.

"It's not as bad as all that in there," he says.

"Then why don't you go in?"

"Work to do here," he says, walking next to the horse, rubbing its side. "Go ahead. Celeste will get you something to warm up." I know what that something likely is, and I don't want it. I want to keep my wits about me. But another icy wind bites into my frozen skin, and I relent, climbing the stone steps to pull on the door handle. The door doesn't budge.

"Put your back into it," Kern shouts, not looking up from between the horses. I grip the long wooden handle with both hands and pull, using my whole body. The door finally budges a little, and then all at once, and I almost fall backward. I lean upon the door and look into a large, yellowish-brown, cramped room. Four rows of tables fill the space, all of them nearly full of men, dotted with pretty, overly made up women.

"In or out?" a woman with brassy hair and a raspy voice calls from behind a dark bar.

"What?" I ask.

"In or out? You're letting in a draft fit for Nordania!" she calls, her penciled-in eyebrows shrinking low over her eyes. I pull the door shut as I step inside. For a building made of stone, the space is an exercise in wood tones: blonde wood floors flow beneath medium-orangey oak tables. The bar itself is a beautiful polished mahogany piece that must've taken someone years to carve.

"Who's this?" a man says, looking me up and down from the

closest table away. Chills rush my arms despite the warmth. The woman is suddenly at my side, placing an arm around my shoulders.

"Never you mind, Larry. You wouldn't know what to do with a woman if she fell into your lap."

"This one almost did," he hollers, to the appreciative bellows of his compatriots.

"Almost doesn't count. You know that. How many times have you tried to tell me the same when I come to collect your tab?" she says with a biting laugh. She steers me away from the mean laughter and the prying eyes and turns us toward the bar, leaving me to resume her place on the other side. I look around the room, searching for a familiar face.

The bar sits along the far left side of the room, and a huge stone fireplace rises along the right. A roaring, crackling dry heat that stings my eyes, but wrenches away the cold from my journey, wafts through the space, beckoning with promises of comfort I haven't felt in days. To the left of the fireplace, a cramped staircase hugs the adjacent wall, wrapping behind to disappear, presumably, into the darkened second floor.

"Your friends are over there," she says, nodding at the last table along the back of the room. Slick and Perlman sit along the wall closest to the staircase, facing the crowd of patrons. Next to them, in the corner furthest from the fireplace, Beck sits among his crew, deep in conversation. His eyes don't even lift to see me. I wonder if he even cares I made it. My cheeks flush red, and the woman laughs.

"You'll be warmed up in no time. Let me get something going for you."

"No alcohol, please."

"Well, what do you want then? That's all I got!" she says with that same biting laugh. Something tells me this is the one and only Celeste, and she has very little humor for people who want her warmth, but not her spirits. I look at her and see her fully for the first time. She's middle-aged, with dyed blonde hair. Her straight white teeth are framed in dark, matte lipstick. She looks weathered, weary, and yet her hazel eyes are bright. She purses her dark-painted lips and pulls her cardigan tighter around her shoulders.

"Look, nothing's gonna warm you up faster. What if I slip just a touch of whiskey into a cup of tea? Add lemon? Cloves? Honey?" The tightness in her forehead tells me this is her best offer. I nod and try to work up a grateful smile.

"I'm Celeste, by the way," she says, with a smile that seems more practiced than genuine. She slices into a lemon; I wonder where she got it at this time of year.

"This is your place?" I ask, fiddling with the charm on my bracelet. It's become something of an unconscious habit, the feel of it between my fingers soothing and familiar.

"Yup," she says, placing a hand on her hip and looking around. "Used to be my husband's. Didn't seem right to leave it empty. 'Sides, I like the noise. Helps me think." She presses small, red-brown cloves into a thick slice of lemon with her short, dry fingernails and plops it into a glass of hot water.

"What? Don't trust me?" she asks, and I blush, averting my gaze to look again around the room, taking in the scene. A handful of women in various states of dress are peppered throughout. A brunette has her hands on Beck's shoulders. She's leaning over, nearly spilling the contents of her dress, her mouth dangerously close to his ear as he erupts in laughter. This place seems as though it's in the middle of nowhere. There's certainly not a larger town in the vicinity. How did this girl—and the others—get here? A crawling sensation grounds me as I wonder if any of them are Unchosen, like Neve. Is there a Carla here as well?

The brunette looks up at me as she slides a possessive hand down Beck's chest and casts me a wicked smile. My cheeks flush, and when I look back to my drink, Celeste is replacing the cap on the whiskey. She laughs and shakes her head as she passes me the mug.

"It's just enough to cut the cold." I stare at it for another minute, and her eyes stay trained on me. She leans in, and I look up. Her face is plain, the mask gone, and kindness creeps into her eyes, softening them, showing her true age.

"I've got you. We girls gotta stick together, eh?" My shoulders relax, and the mask snaps back into place as she walks around the bar. I lift the mug to my lips and inhale the scent of lemon, cloves, and so much whiskey that I cough. She snorts and shakes her head, placing her overworked hands on my shoulders. She pushes me between tables to an empty seat across from Perlman, close to the fire.

"Keep an eye on this one, gents," Celeste says, as if she were winking.

"Aw, Celeste, you're killing me! I was keeping my eye on you, don't you know?" Slick says with devastating bravado.

"You know I'm up here, right?" she says with a throaty laugh.

"Celeste, ignore him . . . run away with me!" Perlman says, already slurring his words.

"You wouldn't know what to do with me if I did," she says and walks away despite their protests. The heat from the fireplace is immediate and quickly dries my clothes, but the chill in my bones runs deep. My shoulders vibrate with chill. Perlman reaches across the table and with one long finger, pushes my mug toward me.

"The cold might kill yeh. One drink won't."

"Wow, poetic," Slick says, knocking back the rest of his golden liquor and launching from the table.

"I love poetry," Beck says, eliciting a roar of laughter.

Slick hoists up his pants, smooths out his collar, and moves with a rocking swagger toward the bar. When I look back at

Perlman, he's watching me, his hooded brown eyes focused in a sea of scattered freckles.

"I watched her make the drink. There's not much in it, and besides, Captain's not gonna let anything happen." I look down the table at Beck. He's still laughing with the brunette, his hand tightening on her hip. Something sharp settles in my stomach as I watch them together. He doesn't feel my gaze, doesn't notice me. I want to believe Perlman, want to pretend that Beck still cares, but I'm honestly not so sure anymore. I lift the mug to my lips, hold my breath, and drink deeply. The sweetness of the honey and the tart lemon mellow out the bite of the liquor, and it warms from within as it courses down my throat and into my blood, though it does nothing for the block of ice deep in my chest.

Slick returns with a full glass and a bruised ego.

"Strike out again?" Perlman asks with a shrill laugh. The firelight flickers across his face, making his freckles look as if they're dancing, celebrating Slick's loss.

"Just laying the groundwork. One of these times, I'm gonna wear her down, and she's gonna say yes." Slick straddles the bench seat, his back to Beck and the brunette, and takes a consoling swig of his beer. I drink again, and between it, the fire, and the dull roar of chatter all around me, I do feel warmer. More relaxed.

"How long have you been trying?" I ask. Slick seems surprised by my question.

"Oh, I don't know. On and off for three years?" he says, looking at Perlman for confirmation.

"Don't look at me. I've only been around for two."

"Two years? How old are you?" I ask Perlman. I was certain he was my age, but I can't imagine him coming to a bar like this at fifteen.

"Old enough to navigate the Mittlesee," he says with a bite.

I shrink back in my seat and drink a little more. I'm starting to like it, now that I'm used to the fire of the whiskey.

"He's sixteen," Slick says between sips.

"Eighteen," Perlman barks. "I was sixteen when you met me. I'm eighteen now." Perlman wears the injured mask of a person who's been nursing a chip on his shoulder for at least two years.

"You've been doing this since you were sixteen?" I ask, trying to keep my voice level against the loosening effect of the whiskey. His eyes skate over my face, unfocused, and he nods slowly.

"Yeah."

"I can't imagine that." I set my mug on the table and shrug out of the wool sweater, hanging it over my lap to dry more fully. Between the whiskey and the fire, I'm finally warm enough to be without it.

"Why not?" he asks, his focus sharpening. "Beck's only three years older than me."

"I just mean, being that good at something at that age. Getting to do what you want. Making your own way . . . it's . . ." I trail off, feeling exposed, and bury my face in my mug. When I look back up, his eyes are round with something like wonder.

"Yeah, I guess I'm lucky." He leans in a bit, cautiously, as if deciding whether to ask me a very specific question.

Kern's cold and wet body tumbles onto the bench next to me.

"Guys, we got company."

CHAPTER SIX

I scan the room as I shake off the rainwater he's splattered me with, but there's nobody new. Nothing's changed.

"Who?" Slick says. His voice carries differently, and I realize it's because the entire table has hushed. I look at Beck, and the brunette is nowhere to be seen. His green eyes meet mine, hard.

"Buck McGrath," Kern says, reaching across the table for Slick's beer. He tilts it into his mouth, draining it.

"Hey, man!" Slick says, but the beer is gone, and Kern wipes the foam from his mouth.

"How close?" Beck asks.

"With the horses," he says.

"Who is Buck McGrath?" I ask Perlman, careful to keep my voice low.

"Bounty hunter. Decent one," he says, shrugging one shoulder. I search the room for another exit. Other than the main entrance, there's no other door. If he's out with the horses, then we certainly can't walk out the front. I eye the staircase, but Celeste *tsks* loudly, as if she can read my mind.

31

"You pay to play around here, dear," she says from behind the bar. I take another sip and think. I just need an idea. A way to blend. I'm good at blending. The only other women here move from table to table in dresses and tops with dips and cuts that enhance their curves in ways my flannel work shirt and oilskin pants don't. Beck's brunette from earlier hovers over another man. I can't see his face beyond the distraction of her décolletage and curtain of hair. That might work. Reaching up, I unwrap the elastic from the knot at the top of my head and coax my unruly dark hair down around my face, not certain it's doing me any favors, but hoping it'll at least hide my features from view. Perlman studies me for a moment and then nods, a decision made.

"Over here," he says, a conspiratorial glimmer in his eye. I slip around the table and sit next to him, my back facing the entrance. He bites his lip, and the fire flickers in his eyes. "I'm sorry," he says, and before I can ask what he's sorry for, he places his hands on either side of my collar and rips the fabric down my left shoulder. I lurch backward, away from him, grabbing for the torn fabric as I'm surrounded by male laughter. Anger floods my chest, and I stand. Just as the door behind me swings open.

A calloused hand clamps down on my left wrist, twisting me back and down along the table. I spin behind Beck's back like a ballroom dancer as he tugs me across his lap.

A draft of cool, damp air blasts across the bar, along with a note of uncomfortable quiet that ushers in the newcomers. Beck shifts me slightly to my left so my back is fully toward the bar. The clatter and commotion returns, though with a palpable new tension.

"Keep your eyes on me," Beck says, his voice a soothing whisper. His breath mingles with mine, and where I expect the burn of whiskey, all I smell is spicy orange and something earthy and mellow—tea perhaps? I'm blocking his view of the door, but if he can't see them, maybe they can't see him either. His calloused fingers brush against my cheek, and I jerk. He retracts, and I swear there's just a hint of blush under his beard. But he squares his shoulders and reaches past my cheek into my hair, threading his fingers through my tangled, wild mess of curls. He smoothes it up and over my part, down my neck, and lets it fall into a pool over my collarbone. His fingers run along the frayed edge of my torn collar, and I bite my lip to keep the embarrassment from my face.

"You'll have to forgive Perlman," he says, curling the rough triangle of fabric under itself to make a smooth line. "He doesn't know his way around a woman. Just horses. You should see what he did with his horse's last dress. It was . . . something."

"And you would do better?" A nervous laugh catches in my throat, and his golden-green eyes meet mine.

"Last one I chose made your tits look damn good." I tense and inhale sharply, pulling away from him. His hand drops around my waist, gentle but firm, holding me in place. His thumb slides up and down my lower back, and I glare up at him. "Eyes on me, Capo."

There's a smirk curling into the side of his mouth, and his eyes spark, and suddenly, I understand. The black chiffon dress with the little gold crystals, the one I could have sparred in. "You sent me the dress? Why didn't you say anything?"

He shrugs stiffly, eyes trained somewhere past my shoulder, in the direction of the bar. "Wasn't necessary." The feel of his thumb is soothing, tracing a familiar pattern against my skin, and I sink into it. "I will, however, make sure to punch Perlman's stupid nose." He is warm and solid, and despite the danger, this is the most calm I've felt since we left the capital.

"You know I don't keep track of my clientele," Celeste says, a little too loud.

"We know that's what you say," a booming voice meets hers, and I tilt away from the sound, curling into Beck.

"It's just a yokel, a local bounty hunter. Small potatoes," Beck mumbles. "Like the ones you've been peeling."

"Who are the big potatoes?" I ask, my voice barely a breath. He runs his fingers through my hair, catching on a curl and gently tugging on it until it releases.

"Trouble," he says, coaxing the curl back to life.

"What kind of trouble?"

"International, deep-fried, carnival-barker trouble," he says, placing the curl against the soft skin of my collarbone.

"Now, if you're just gonna bring trouble, you know I can't have any of that. Bad for business," Celeste says.

"Why don't we find somewhere quiet? We never finished that last conversation . . ." a woman's voice says, and the man starts to laugh in a way that sends my skin crawling.

"Where'd ya have in mind?" he asks in an equally unsettling voice. Beck places his palm on my right cheek and turns my face to his, pressing his forehead against mine. My breath catches in my chest, and I hear two sets of footsteps squeak up the staircase behind my head.

"Your hair tastes . . . good," Beck says, spitting strands from his mouth. "Salty."

I muffle an anxious laugh and reach under my mop of hair to pull the strands from his lips. One strand sticks, and I rub it away with my thumb, then let my hand cup his cheek for a moment. His other hand stills, then wraps its way more firmly around my back, holding me against him. I let my hand drift to his chest and feel his heart pumping away—steady, solid. I close my eyes and match my breath with his.

When I open my eyes again, he's watching me, his gaze uncertain, or maybe undecided. I wonder if this is what he looked like inside the panic room, the expression he wore before he kissed me. It was so dark in there, I couldn't see. It was just me and him and his heartbeat, his steady breath. It felt like we were in a world all our own. Like now. The din of the room pulses against us, and I swallow hard around my thumping heart, reality shattering the illusion of memory like a hammer against glass.

"I don't think I'm a very good sailor," I whisper, trying to fill the space so he can't hear my thoughts.

"You're terrible," he says in agreement.

"Thanks," I mumble.

"But you're not a sailor."

"Then what am I?"

"Right now? Dead weight."

"At the risk of repeating myself, *thanks*," I say, rolling my eyes.

"You haven't been taught. You can't be a sailor if you haven't been taught."

"Are you going to teach me?" I ask, slipping my right arm around the back of his neck. His shoulders hitch, and a wry smile settles into his full lips.

"Shit no. I'm the captain. I don't have time for that." His teasing smile crinkles the corners of his eyes.

"So, who then?"

"Kern," he says.

"Kern?"

"Yeah, Kern. You know him?"

"The one who locked me in that tiny room?"

"The brig?" he asks.

"What?"

"The brig. He locked you in the brig."

"Okay then. Yeah. Sure. Him." I close my eyes and let the familiar rise and fall of his breath fill the space for a moment.

"He shouldn't have done that," he whispers, running his thumb up my spine, then down again in a slow, rhythmic pulse, in time with his breath. I shake my forehead against his, but keep my eyes closed.

"So, Kern?" I ask, opening my eyes again. Being this close

to him is disorienting. I want to pull back, leave some space between us, because if I don't, it feels like his eyes might swallow me whole.

"He'll get you shaped up."

"I'm not sure I'm cut out for a life at sea," I say. Now the smile really moves into his eyes, and he relaxes under my touch, allowing me to sink further into him.

"I don't believe that at all, Capo. I think the sea calls to you —the crashing waves; the unpredictable weather; the deepest, scariest blues you've ever seen; the sunsets that'll break your heart. It's unrelenting, unfathomable, unknowable . . . I think you, Arden Thatcher, have saltwater in your soul." From anyone else, I would take this as an insult, but the gentle creases that form around his eyes tell me this is his highest form of compliment. I take a deep breath, and despite the heavy warmth of the smoky wood in the fireplace, I can smell it on him: salt. Salt and leather.

Noise erupts behind us—chair legs sliding along the floor, rowdy laughter, boisterous voices—and he tenses. I dig my fingers into his shoulder. His cheek slips past mine as he lets his forehead fall against my throat, and I drop my face slightly, wrapping my left arm around the back of his neck, concealing his face entirely with my hair, breathing in the sea that lingers on him.

"I don't know about that," I say. "I'm not sure I have a soul." The words are out before I can think of what they mean. Before I know if they're true. He shakes his head into the space between my neck and my shoulder.

"Impossible," he whispers. His words vibrate against my collarbone, low enough that only I can hear.

"How would you know?" I say with a teasing lilt. "I thought you were a soulless pirate." He leans back, exposing his face to the warm firelight, creating space between us, a chasm of cold that I instantly want filled.

"You know that's not true," he says. He closes the space between us, his heat filling the sudden void, inviting me closer. I move in, and our foreheads meet, our noses touch, slip just past each other. His breath catches, and his fingers press into my waist, drawing me closer. When his lips brush mine, it's just for a second, and it's not enough. The tick of his eyelashes against his cheek is the only sound between us. He tilts his face down ever so slightly, his nose slipping past mine, so slowly and too fast, and I don't think. I don't hesitate. I thread my fingers through his thick hair and pull him into my kiss. He is tentative at first, but then his lips part, and his tongue brushes mine as we deepen the kiss. His hand slides up my back, cradling the back of my head, and I wrap my arms tighter around his neck.

A crash shocks us from the moment, and he pulls my head into the crook of his neck. He is out of breath, his chest rising and falling too fast, and the room is too loud. Why is it so loud? I don't dare look, but there are shouts all around us. I hear Kern say something, and a door slams.

"Shit," he says, under his breath.

"I think this one knows something," an ugly voice says.

"I don't know nothing," Kern yells, his voice slower and saggier than usual. I don't think it's from drink—he hasn't been here long enough.

"We have to go," Beck says, his voice hard. I glance over my right shoulder and see a large mass of a man, the one with the ugly voice, standing on the bottom step of the staircase. Kern backs away toward the door, and the man comes down off the step, the brunette from earlier just behind him, one step up.

"I doubt he knows anything, Buck—just look at him," another voice says. "This one don't know his ass from his mouth." More barks of mean laughter echo the first, and I burn, wanting to set them all on fire with my anger at their cruelty.

The girl comes down the stairs and looks at me. Her eyes narrow, and for a moment, I think we're done. Then she whispers something in the man's ear. He smiles at her and takes another step forward. The path to the stairs is now clear, and she gives me another look—a look that seems to say, *go now*. I don't know how two people on the run are supposed to walk up the stairs in the middle of a commotion like this without being spotted.

"Dammit," Beck says again, pressing his forehead into my shoulder.

"Take me upstairs," I say, my voice shaking slightly. He leans back, and his eyes catch a glimpse of the exposed staircase.

"How?" he asks, leaning back into my shoulder. I look back at the girl, and she surreptitiously nods at the staircase. I know how we can get up there, hiding both our faces, but I'm almost embarrassed to say it.

"How?" he growls.

"Throw me over your shoulder," I say, and he leans back, eyebrows arched. His pupils dilate, and his fingers dig into me just enough that I know he's heard.

"Keep your head low," he says. I do, and he swings his feet around the bench, does a spin turn around me, then buries his right shoulder into my stomach and hoists me over it. Bawdy cheers erupt around us, and he slaps my butt, as if in response. I growl at him as a couple more cheers make it clear that our ruse is at least effective. I turn my face toward the wall, and as we approach the stairs, I wait for the ugly man to reach back and grab me by the hair. But we climb unmolested—two, three, four steps, and turn the corner. As we rise past the wall, I catch the eye of the brunette, who gives me an imperceptible nod and then drapes a soothing arm over the increasingly irate man.

Beck tries one door, then another, cursing at each. The third door finally yields. We enter, and the door slams as I propel backward, flopping onto something soft. I don't realize my eyes are closed until I open them and Beck hovers inches from my face. He's breathing too fast, his hands on either side of my shoulders, pinning me. We are frozen like that for another minute. Then he launches away from me, leaving me flattened and flushed against the bed.

I prop myself on my elbows and watch him as he paces the floor of the small bedroom. He smacks his hand hard against the door, and I hear a click, the door locking into place. He goes back to pacing, and I sit up, my hand wandering to my exposed shoulder, cold now without his heat against it. He stops, and his eyes travel up the length of me, and they are not kind.

"No. Stop it!" he says, squeezing his eyes shut, his words frigid and shaky. For a moment, I think he might be talking about getting trapped with the bounty hunters. But then I scoot forward on the bed, and he backs away from me, as if three feet's distance wasn't already enough. My stomach turns inside out, and I wrap my arms around my waist. I don't know what could have changed so quickly. Except, I do. I kissed him. I kissed him, and he kissed me back. It wasn't just me in that kiss. I know it wasn't. But his meaning is clear. The hot sting of embarrassment burns at my eyes, and he turns away from me toward the window.

I pull my knees to my chest and feel the hard edges of Declan's compass. My heart stills, remembering the man who, yes, put me in this position, but who also would not appreciate what just happened downstairs. Who may or may not take me back once he knows what I've done to CJ, never mind that I kissed Beck. Twice. Of course, Beck is right. I need to stop.

"So, what now?" I ask, biting the side of my tongue, hugging my knees to warm up. Something smashes downstairs, followed by the sound of angry voices, and I jump off the bed, running for the door.

"No point, there," he says from the opposite end of the room. And I hear what he means—the arguing voices are getting louder, as if whatever fight they're picking is climbing up the stairs, heading toward us.

I reach for the doorknob to lock the door, but it's missing. There's no lock of any sort on this side.

"There's no lock?"

"Of course not. Haven't you ever been in a brothel before?" he asks.

"You know I haven't," I say, grabbing a high-backed chair from the vanity and propping it under the door handle.

"Yeah, that'll stop them," he says, as he opens the window.

"I suppose you have a more brilliant plan?" I ask. The voices get louder, and I back away from the door.

" 'Course I do, Capo," he says. "Over and out."

CHAPTER SEVEN

"*T*o where?" I ask.

"Anywhere but here," he snaps. I wince at the anger in his words. But there's no time to be sensitive right now. We have to move.

He hoists himself up and slides out the narrow window frame. Then he turns, reaching in to help me, and I stare at his hand. The hand that only minutes ago slipped through my hair. The hand I shouldn't still want to be tracing soothing patterns on my skin. I reach back and twist my hair into a tight knot on top of my head again, wrapping the elastic around it. Then I smack his hand away and pull myself up and through the window on my own.

We're standing on the back roof. It seems original to the building and is covered in dead pine needles. I shut the window while Beck walks gingerly on the slate roof tiles. It seems too steep, too slick for him to be moving so well. A tile slips and crashes to the ground, shattering on impact. For a split second, I think we'll be found out, but there's nothing. No discovery. I peer over the edge—maybe twelve feet down—at the broken pieces below. It's not far, but it's still not a fall I want to make.

Beck reaches the corner of the house and motions me over. I place my feet carefully, keeping my steps as light as possible, and by the time I get to him, he's sliding down the edge of the roof on his knee and hip.

I pause and look around the corner to where Kern is standing with two of the horses, trying to keep them calm. By the time I look back, I can't see Beck at all. "Where . . . ?" I whisper. Then he's on the ground, backing up, looking up at me.

"There's a post down here, about a foot in from the roof. Just slip down and grab it with your legs," he says. Oh, sure. No big deal. Just grab a pole I can't see, twelve feet off the ground, on a slick roof, with my legs. My heart hammers in my ears, and another crash inside—this time on the second floor—startles me. I nearly lose my balance.

"Hurry!" he whisper-yells. I squat down and turn onto my hands and knees, backing toward the edge. Once my legs start to hang over, the panic sets in. There's nothing holding me up here anymore. I try to lift some weight on my right hand, while swinging my left leg down to reach the pole, but the tile I'm leaning into gives and slips out of place.

"Oh!" I cry and fall backward. With nothing to grab on to, my fingers slide over the slick slate tiles; my legs feel nothing but air. Just as my chest reaches the edge, I press my arms into the corner of the roof and stop the momentum, but I still can't feel the pole or any sort of support.

"Stop kicking!" Beck says, and I feel his hands on my ankles. "On the count of three, let go. I'll catch you."

"I can't—" I say, as I slip more, banging my chin into the edge and biting my lip.

"Let go!" he says, and I do, slipping through his arms until he catches me around the waist and lowers me gently from there. There's no time to collect myself, though. I hear a door slam, followed by angry shouts, and Beck practically carries me to the horses, scooping me up onto the largest one. The horse fusses, pounding its feet into the ground, unhappy, as if it knows I'm a terrible rider. But then Beck pulls himself up in front of me, takes the reins from Kern, and we're off.

Angry roars filter through the forest behind us, and I have no doubt the bounty hunters have discovered what they missed. If I thought riding with Perlman was uncomfortable, riding with Beck is on a whole other level. He rides aggressively, a constant battle of wills between horse and master. The horse, for his part, seems to take it in stride, yielding to Beck's harsh driving and, if anything, going faster. I cling to him, curling my fingers around the front of his jacket. Something loud cracks the air around us, and tree bark explodes to our right, the victim of sudden gunfire. I'm so surprised that I let go and nearly fly off. Beck grabs my right wrist and rebalances me, pulling me tight against his back.

"Hold on!" he growls, as if I was deliberately trying to fall off. Long, thin branches and vines whip us from all sides, leaving stinging welts that burn even more in the blistering wind. A thorny vine catches in my hair, ripping what feels like a solid inch from my scalp. I scream in surprise and start to pull my hand back, reaching for my head, but Beck holds it firmly in place.

"Not yet," he grunts, steering the horse to the right as more bark explodes to our left. We're going so fast; the wind around my ears is so loud. I can't even hear whatever it is that's making these trees burst, but I have a pretty good idea what it is. I lean into Beck's back, pressing my forehead into his spine. I flatten my hand against his chest, and he jerks to the left, flinching away from my touch. It's subtle, but just enough to make the horse lose its footing. We stumble down a slope, and Beck leans forward, into the horse, tugging on the reins, getting him back to the previous route. We brush against a tree trunk as we climb, and my leg takes the brunt of it, the rough bark slicing into both fabric and skin. Then we're back on the trail, but we've lost ground, and the tree that just carved into my leg explodes.

"Stop. It," he says, under his breath. But I hear, the slapping sting of rejection renewed. I lean back, away from his body, gripping just his jacket, trying to leave him the space he wants. The wind around us is suffocating, and the rhythm of the hoofbeats is too fast, frenetic. I close my eyes and try to focus on the sound of the wind: constant, unyielding, deafening. If I focus on the wind, there's nothing else to be afraid of.

"Hold on tight," he says, louder this time, contradicting himself. Over his shoulder, I see a river, wide and wild, and Beck is not slowing down. If anything, he's leaning forward, and the horse goes faster, hurtling toward the roar that grows louder by the millisecond.

"Beck . . ." I try to say, but it comes out as a whisper. I squeeze my eyes shut, and the horse leaps. Its hooves hit solid ground, but icy water sprays my aching leg, and he takes off again, surging out of the shallows.

"One more, Hammer," Beck says, to the horse, but I can't help but think it might also be for my benefit. The horse leaps one more time, and his back legs land in the water, soaking my feet in the icy, rushing current. He slides to the left, slipping in the mud and silt, but charges ahead, fighting to regain his footing. I hear a splash behind me and risk a look over my shoulder. Kern struggles on his own horse, but his face is determined, focused as he urges his horse to cross upriver. It's wilder there, but he seems to see a route that I don't. We continue to slip downstream, and I risk a look forward, instantly wishing that I hadn't. Not fifty yards away is a clean, dark line. Without moonlight, it's hard to see much, but the clean line tells me the river doesn't continue, and the roar tells me that this water falls over that edge.

"Beck?" I whimper, and his shoulders harden as he leans into the horse, kicking into its tender flank. He finds purchase, finally, and pulls us onto the river bank—not a moment too soon. The water bursts with gunshots that miss us by mere feet. We move away from the river, and I look back to see Kern make it out just as Buck McGrath and three other men pull up short on the other side. They shout something made indecipherable by our speed as we thunder through the forest, and are soon left behind and out of sight.

"Should be the worst of it," Beck says, his voice hard and clinical, back to being the inaccessible captain.

"Okay," I say. I take a deep breath to iron out my unsteadiness. But he keeps riding hard, and each time I chance a look behind, I can see Kern riding just as hard in our wake. Eventually, the forest thins out, letting in more moonlight, the clouds parting overhead, and we start to climb. Beck eases up on the horse, and by the time we're leveling out, Kern is riding next to us at an easy, steady pace.

"How much farther?" Beck asks, but it's not really a question. His shoulders and back are stiff—too stiff for riding—as though he's uncomfortable and needs to fill the space with something easy and distracting.

"Not far," Kern says. "We crest that hill, and we'll be on the Bluffs." A vague memory of the map in the institute's library surfaces at the name. The Bluffs: a series of plateaus that extend east from the great northern mountain range and hang over the deepest part of the Mittlesee coast. It's steep enough that you can't reach the shore from their peak, and they are difficult to access otherwise. Though I think there might be some towns further to the north, it's a long, treacherous journey any way you go.

"What's in the Bluffs?" I ask.

"My people," Kern says, flashing me a smile that somehow makes his face even wider, his teeth glowing in the moonlight. As we crest the hill, silver grasses dance across a vast plain, and the wind picks up. It rushes at us from both the shadowy mountains far to our left and the roaring waves far over the edge to our right. Beck and Kern pick up the pace, urging the horses to a canter, and we rush across the plain as tall grasses tickle our legs. Beck pulls away from me as the ride gets easier, and I lean back, holding on to just the sides of his jacket.

"There it is," Kern says, taking off in a full gallop. Over Beck's shoulder, I see a white clapboard cottage with black shutters and a stone chimney, nestled into a windblown hillside. It looks cozy and sheltered, the perfect respite for the storm at our backs.

"Finally," Beck says, leaning even further away and picking up the pace. We may be running from a storm, but I think we'll still need shelter from whatever it is that has just erupted between Beck and me.

CHAPTER EIGHT

*O*ur arrival is a blur of kind smiles and hugs and blankets and flannel pajamas. Next thing I know, I'm plummeting from a dream I've already forgotten and don't want to remember. I wipe sweaty hair from my face. But I'm enveloped in soft flannel sheets hinting of sweet, gentle scents: sweet pea and ocean breezes. This might be the most comfortable bed I've ever slept in. Warm, yellow light streams from between blue-and-white gingham curtains.

I pull back the curtain and blink in the brilliant sunlight. Once my eyes adjust, it all makes sense. My room overlooks the ocean far below, and the sun reflecting off the blue-green waves casts an extra slant of brightness to the day. There's nothing but water as far as the eye can see. The bed is steady though, no swaying motion to be felt. It's a bit dizzying to not see any land from my window, and I push back from the edge, sliding my feet to the floor. The floor is made of weathered gray planks, both firm and soft beneath my bare feet. Across from my bed is a stone fireplace where coals still burn dull red.

I stretch, but my left calf screams. Bending over to look, I roll up my long flannel pants and find fresh bandages. I don't remember being patched up, but then, our arrival was such a blur, I don't remember much of any of it. Voices slip beneath the door. I tie my hair into a knot on top of my head, take a deep breath, and open it.

Kern and his mother laugh in a modest, U-shaped kitchen. He's leaning against the shiny, green-tiled counter with a wide, toothy grin. The kitchen is clean, except for some grease splatters on the well-loved cooktop. Kern faces the peninsula, spreading mayonnaise on bread. He layers thin-sliced ham, pickled cucumbers, and cheese, and then passes the sandwich to his mother. She presses it into a cast iron pan on their small, two-burner cooktop as they laugh about something private. A flush of embarrassment rises in my chest—I shouldn't be here. But even if I wanted to retreat, they've spotted me. It's too late.

"Good morning, Arden?" his mother says. She has the same blue eyes as Kern, and her smile is wide, but her face is not the same as his—her nose is small and delicate, her forehead smaller. Whatever Kern's specific affliction is, she is not the carrier. Her voice, her eyes, her posture are full of questions. I hesitate, not sure if I want to answer them.

"Good morning," I say, taking a seat on a yellowed, woven counter stool. They are both dressed for the day in long pants and flannel shirts. I feel underdressed and cross my arms over my chest.

"I'm glad you got some rest, sweetie. Can we make you a sandwich?" she asks, holding up a long, flat slice of pickle. I nod, relieved to answer such a simple question, and smile.

"Get ready for some real grub," Kern says with a wide smile. "No fish today. And no potatoes."

"That sounds wonderful," I say. I don't mind the fish. It reminds me of the peninsula in a weird, comforting way. There's not much I want to remember of my life there with Neve and Carla, but we ate meals together, always fish, and as I watch Kern make lunch with his mother, I long for the girls who were the closest thing I've ever had to family. My heart aches, as I realize I have no idea where they are, and there's little chance I may ever see them again. The last time I saw them, Carla's eyes were filled with happy tears, and Neve swore she would never forgive me for my betrayal. I never had the chance to tell her I didn't want any of it. I may never get to.

"These are the best sandwiches anywhere," Kern says with a grin, snapping me out of my reverie.

"You might be overselling these, Kernan," his mother says, smoothing his unruly hair out of his eyes. He spreads mayonnaise on a slice of dense, brown, seeded bread, and she watches approvingly.

"Nope. Best. Ever."

"How long has it been since you've been home?" I ask Kern. His mother's blue eyes are wide as she watches him, and she brushes a strand of long gray hair from her forehead with the backside of her hand. Between her fingers is a slice of ham, which she then folds in half, and then in half again, placing it on her tongue and chewing.

"I don't know . . . a few months?" he asks, looking at her.

"Try six," she says, and I don't doubt her memory.

"It hasn't been that long," he says.

"It has," she says.

"It's not like you haven't heard from me."

"Marlbury only counts for so much."

"We've been busy, Mom," he says, pointing his knife at me.

"I can see that," she says with a grim smile. My stomach pits at being the most recent source of a mother's worry for her son. And for whatever else I might have brought upon her home.

"I'm sorry, who is Marlbury?" I ask, trying to deflect the conversation from the path I don't want it to go down: me.

"Marlbury? You haven't seen him lurking around?" she asks. I try to run through the faces of the other crew members in my head, but they all blend together into a faceless blur.

"Naw, Mom. Arden's been mostly below deck."

"He's out back now," she says, nodding her head behind her. There's a door to the left of the stove, with a window that looks out into the side of a barn or garage. I didn't think anyone else followed us last night, and I can't imagine who else could have made it here with the weather as it was and no straightforward route to find it.

"When did he get here?" Kern asks, looking behind him as he sets down his knife.

"Early this morning. I'm surprised you didn't hear. He made quite a racket," she says, taking his knife to continue the assembly line. "Don't worry, your father took care of him."

"Oh, good," he says, but he's still distracted, like a kid who knows there's a surprise through the door. He bounces with distracted anticipation, no longer spreading mayonnaise.

"Oh, go on," she says, nodding her head in the direction of the door. He smiles and almost skips to the exit, but then stops. "Wanna come, Arden?" he asks.

"Why don't you give Arden the chance to get some food in her first? And warm clothes—or at least boots—before you make her muck out to the barn?" she says, giving me a knowing wink. Kern looks at me for a moment, the confusion of his next move clear on his face.

"Go ahead," I say, nodding at him. "I'll find you." He doesn't wait for me to change my mind. Kern's mother continues on the sandwiches, turning away from me to face the griddle. She hums to herself, a song that haunts the recesses of the vaguely familiar and long repressed.

"Thank you for having me," I say, interrupting her song. Her shoulders tense, but she nods.

"Of course, sweetheart," she says. "Any friend of Kern's . . ." She doesn't finish the sentence, and I wonder how much Kern has told her, or what she knows on her own. She removes a sandwich from the griddle and puts it on a small, cobalt-blue enamel plate, slicing it down the center with the spatula.

"Go ahead, before it gets cold," she says, setting the plate in front of me.

"Aren't the others hungry?" I ask.

"The others aren't here right now," she says with a wink, and I smile, biting into the greasy sandwich. It's hot, and the cheese burns the roof of my mouth, but the sweet ham and salty cheese blends with the briny pickle. It's perfect. I didn't know I was so hungry until I tasted this.

"So, tell me," she says, and my chewing slows as I reconsider just how much I want to eat this sandwich. It suddenly feels as if we're bartering: a bite for a question. "How does Kern do on Beck's ship? Really?" She doesn't face me, and I wonder if she's granting me the courtesy to construct a decent lie. I'm not sure what Kern has told her, or if she's talked to Beck. Or anyone else. I don't want to lie, but I also don't want to tell her that Kern locked me in the brig. And I really don't want to tell her about his harrowing escape down the rope ladder and dive into a swell. It was heroic, but I can't imagine it would do anything to set her mind at ease.

"Like he said, I didn't go above deck much. Mostly just peeled potatoes and tried to keep from getting sick," I say with a self-deprecating laugh. She turns around, and her forehead creases into four long lines that split upward between her salt and pepper eyebrows.

"Is he doing okay?" she asks. There's a plea in there, for honesty, for compassion for the mother of a boy who isn't expected to make his own way in the world.

"I like Kern," I say, and I feel the honesty in the weight of my words. "He works hard, tries to do the right thing, and I think his crewmates respect him." Her eyebrows narrow as she watches me, but then she presses her lips into a relieved smile.

"Thank you," she says, touching her free hand to her chest.

She turns back to the griddle, and I eat more of my sandwich as the door opens. Kern's father walks in, mid--conversation with Beck, and I put down my sandwich, no longer hungry.

"Thurston, there you are. I was just about to come find you boys." Kern's father leans in to kiss her cheek.

"We was just checking on the grounds, Delia," he says. He's the same height as his wife, and doesn't have the wide forehead like Kern, but his nose is squat and wide, atop a thick, narrow mustache that sits just over his small mouth.

"You see Kern out there?"

"Yeah, he's with Marlbury. He makes such a mess, needs some extra attention today," Thurston says. I look at Beck to see if he'll tell me who Marlbury is, but he keeps his eyes on the floor, avoiding me completely. The room is quiet but for the sound of sizzling sandwiches, the weight of Beck's silence suffocating. I clear my throat and slip off my stool. One thing to be said for me: I can always tell when it's time to leave.

CHAPTER NINE

"She's a Mollymawk," Kern says, toothy grin wide across his face.

"A what?" I ask.

"A Mollymawk. A great sea bird that can be taught to find home. I taught her. She delivers messages," he says, feeding the giant bird a sardine straight from the jar. The bird snaps at the treat like it's a piece of popcorn and caws for more.

"And you named her Marlbury?" I ask, though I don't know why. It's a stupid question. Of course, he's named her Marlbury.

"Obviously. What else should I name her? Cat?" he asks around a wheezing laugh. Kern proudly shows me around the barn/rookery and his piece de resistance, his homing bird, Marlbury. Apparently, Marlbury arrived early in the morning and couldn't get in right away. So Thurston let her in, and then couldn't find the fish fast enough, leaving Marlbury to attack random containers looking for lunch.

"How do you convince a sea bird to make their home on land?" I ask, keeping my distance. Each time I get within about ten feet of the giant white creature, it squawks like I've injured it. Even now, she watches me with shrewd black eyes, like she's got a shiv with my name on it.

"Nah, it's not like that. Her home is where she wants it. She just loves me, she knows I love her, and we always know how to find each other." He tosses her another sardine, and she catches it. "That's the key—always knowing how to find each other." She flaps her wings appreciatively, as if in agreement, while staying perched on the long wooden dowel rod suspended from the ceiling. He smiles up at her, and she eyes him with a graciousness I didn't know was possible from a freakishly large beaked thing.

"So, how did you find each other in the first place?"

"She crashed onto the deck a couple years back," he says, tossing her another sardine and toeing some soiled bark dusk over onto itself. "She was still a little thing then. Probably'd been abandoned for being the runt or something. Her wing was broken," he says, nodding up to her right wing, which she holds stretched out at a slightly crooked angle. "Slick said to throw her back. We had no room on board for a bottomless pit bird who would eat what little fish we got. But I couldn't." He tosses the last sardine in the tin up to her, and she catches it, slipping just a bit and flapping her wings to rebalance on her perch.

"I couldn't just leave her. She needed me. It's nice to be needed, y'know?" he asks. His eyes are trained on her as she bites into the feathers under her good wing, and I see something like paternal pride wash over his square face. A hollowness rises up my chest as I watch him bask in his role as protector. I wonder what it feels like to be necessary.

"So, you trained her to find you?"

"Nah, it's like I said. We just find each other. She flew off one day, and I didn't see her for a few nights. I was sad, but I thought maybe it was just her time to go. And then she found us along a completely different coastline three days later. Then she did it again. Me and Beck started testing it. We weren't real busy at the time. Not like now . . ." he says, looking back at me as if he only just remembered who he was talking to.

"One thing led to another, and now, she can deliver messages if we need her to. She's not the most secret messenger, but she's not real suspicious either. I mean, who sends messages by Mollymawk?" he says with a laugh, throwing his arm up in the air. As if in response, Marlbury flaps both wings and flies in a circle overhead before returning to her perch. She looks back at me and squawks again, her feathers ruffling around her neck.

"I don't think she likes me much," I say, taking a step back, calming her for at least the moment.

"Nah, she just knows you don't like her," he says with a little grin. He picks up a rake and starts combing the wood chips below her perch.

"I don't dislike her," I say, but I take another step back, leaning into the wall. I like the wall. I trust the wall. The wall won't poke my eyes out. She nods her head briefly, as if to say, *I heard that*.

"Like isn't the right word . . . trust. You don't trust her. So she won't trust you. That's the thing with animals. You gotta trust them. They can sense when someone doesn't. And when people don't trust animals, bad things happen. Animals have great instincts, you know." He reaches into his pocket and retrieves what looks like a peanut, flicking it up to Marlbury, who catches it without missing a beat. She swallows it down and continues to eye me suspiciously, as if she knows what I want from her — before even I do.

She could take a message to Declan. Maybe she already has? She could deliver him a note explaining everything, and then bring me a message back. I could find out what he's thinking and put an end to the cacophony of doubt and worry I try and fail to silence every night. But then she squawks at me with an aggressive lunge, and somehow, I doubt she'd help me, even if Kern prodded her.

"I haven't spent much time around animals," I say. *And the humans I've been around haven't been that great either*, I think, but I don't say it.

"People can be jerks. They're unpredictable, and mean, and you don't always know what you're getting with them. But animals . . ." He lifts his forearm, and Marlbury leaves her perch, floating down to his arm. Her talons wrap around his forearm completely, and his expression is soft — no hard edges, no walls. I have no doubt that this man and his albatross trust each other completely. The other night at the tavern, when everyone else went inside the pub, Kern stayed with the horses. They didn't trust me either, but they yielded under his touch. Marlbury floats up from his arm to a ledge up in the belfry.

"Yeh in here, son?" Thurston calls from the open barn doors.

"Yep," Kern calls back to his father, raking with suddenly fast, harried strokes. I smile at Thurston, who nods at me, folding a newspaper into a roll and sticking it in his back pocket. Beck follows, a wry grin on his face at the sight of the large seabird.

"Marlbury, you old girl. How are you?" he calls up to the bird. She lowers herself to flap her wings at Beck, and then resettles on her perch, squawking away.

"If I didn't know any better, I'd say she's unhappy with you," Thurston says.

"Wouldn't be the first girl," Kern says with an asthmatic laugh. My cheeks go hot as Thurston grants me a pitying smile. Beck shakes his head, hands on his hips, and then catches my eye. His smile freezes, and the levity vanishes from his heavy-lidded gaze. He moves a little closer to Kern and sticks a hand into his back pocket.

"She up for another trip?" he asks, his voice lower than

before. Thurston blocks most of my view, but I catch the sight of two pieces of brown paper, rolled into small cylinders just the right size for a bird to carry.

"So, what do you think of this bird?" Thurston asks, closing the distance between me and the other boys, blocking my view of their interaction.

"I think she knows better than to like me," I say. He laughs and shakes his head.

"Same here. Want to go inside? Get something warm to drink?" Thurston asks. I pause for a moment, recalling the last warming beverage I was offered. He smiles and gives me a little nod. "How about some coffee?"

I follow him across the lawn toward the garage. The garage is closed off, and I wonder what's in there. I can't imagine them keeping any kind of transport without a road nearby. The house sits on the edge of the property, overlooking the ocean, and in every other direction, the plateau expands into a sea of tall, yellow-brown grasses, rolling and undulating westward toward a line of purple mountains. The wind roars up from the ocean, down from the mountains, and mingles in every direction, whipping the grasses left and right, up and down. My skin is cold and windburned by the time we reach the house, the dry, fireplace heat a welcome respite.

"The boys still out there?" Delia says, already heating water over the stovetop.

"Yup, but I've had enough of that damned bird," he says, and Delia putters a laugh, turning off the water.

"Tea? Coffee?" she asks over her shoulder to me as I sit at the counter.

"Coffee! It's coffee weather," Thurston says, with a broad smile back at me.

"Let the girl decide for herself," Delia says, lowering her eyebrows at Thurston.

"What'll it be, Arden?" he asks, and they both turn to face

me, waiting for my decision. It's been ages since I've been given a say in anything, even something as trivial as a beverage choice, and I hesitate too long. They cast looks at one another like I might be dumb.

"Coffee, please," I say with a grateful smile. Thurston looks triumphant. Delia is dismissive, but he kisses her temple and crosses behind her, opening an upper cabinet to retrieve three mugs. The newspaper falls to the floor from his back pocket, and he sets the mugs down, picks up the paper, and sets it on the counter in front of me. It rolls open to the front page, where my own face stares back. My pulse races loud in my ears, and I can't stop my fingers from reaching for the thing. When I read its headline, I really wish I hadn't.

CHAPTER TEN

The headline reads: *Devastated Declan determined to find his destiny with deserving debutantes*. There's a photo of me wearing the backward dress, from the night when CJ drugged me. I look angry in the picture, and I can't think of when it would have been taken. The caption says, *The season had all but stalled from the mysterious disappearance and alleged kidnapping of Independent Candidate, Arden Thatcher*. It had? I unfold the paper and see the full bleed of the largest photo: a beautiful shot of Declan, looking every bit the golden boy, with his gray eyes alight and his arm wrapped around Fiona's tiny waist. Her hand rumples his golden-brown hair as she leans back, looking up at him, her fiery red hair cascading down her back. Fiona's fake smile looks downright pretty, and her dress matches his eyes. It's the carefree image of two privileged people in love and is exactly what Siobhan wants people to see. No doubt, this was orchestrated, possibly even by the Espancians who haunt the estate on Fiona's behalf.

But it's not her beauty that packs the punch. I've never seen him smile like that around other people. I've seen that smile myself—in the rooftop gardens, in the hedge maze. When it's just the two of us. Never around others.

I run my fingers along the lines of his smile, as if by touching the grainy, colored image, I can decipher its authenticity, the depth of his joy, or evidence of his deception. A lump grows in my throat, and I fear that if I don't swallow it down, I'll have to answer for feelings I can't explain or handle right now.

"Oh, dear," Delia says, setting a cup of coffee in front of me. I don't look at her. I'm not sure how to without betraying more of myself than I want.

"It is what it is," I say, my voice catching in my throat.

"Oh, come now. It's not real," Thurston says with authority. "She's obviously a viper who knows how to take a pretty photo, and it's been planted in the paper to appease the impatient public." I smile a bit, but I don't really feel it.

"I'm sure you're right," I almost whisper. He knows exactly what he's doing, and it has nothing to do with me. But then, what have I been doing? Running for my life and kissing the boy he's asked to be my protector. Why should I expect that Declan, the man who is actively looking for a wife, would be a saint in a house full of beautiful, sexy, unbroken girls, when I can't even keep my hands to myself around an unwashed pirate with a clear aversion to me? Why shouldn't he prefer any one of these girls who is not a murderess?

"Give us a second, Thur," Delia says, sitting on the stool next to me. She wraps a long arm around my shoulders and pulls me into her side. I let her wrap both arms around me and breathe in the scent of fire smoke and chamomile.

"Tell me something," she says finally, pulling away to lift my chin so I have to face her blue eyes. "Do you want to marry him?" I blink three times and lean away from her hand.

"It is—maybe was . . . my only option." My heart sinks at the realization that it might no longer be an option, and I suck in a rootless breath that does nothing to satiate my increasing pulse.

"Now, that's just not true. You have all the options in the world."

"I don't," I say, but I stop. I don't tell her that I have no home, no family, that my benefactor wants me dead, and I killed my benefactor's son. I don't say that without Declan's help, I might have to spend the rest of my life in hiding, or in jail. Or that I'm not even sure if Declan will believe me or want to help me when he finds out what I've done. Right now, I am utterly alone, and I can't even help myself.

"You are capable of more than you give yourself credit for," she says. "We're pretty isolated here. On purpose, really. Didn't feel the need to interact with humanity on a regular basis once we saw what that humanity thought of our perfect baby boy . . ." She exhales hard, and I hear the pain in her voice, feel the anguish of a mother who doesn't want her child to hurt. "But we still get the news and eat up the updates from the institute like everyone else. You're the favorite. You're his favorite. There's never been anyone like you these past years."

"But I'm not there," I say.

"And whose doing is that?" she asks. "Because it's my understanding that he had a say in it." I nod, but my eyes go back to Fiona's long, slender fingers threaded through his golden waves. I want that to be my hand. I don't want the reminder of what Beck's hand felt like weaving through my hair. I want to be the one there, with Declan, tousling his hair, smelling the mint and basil that is so deeply embedded in his peachy-gold skin, watching him smile and laugh at me in that same way. It should be me in that picture, not Fiona.

"I can't go back, though," I say, shaking my head. "Not now."

"There's always a way," she says, picking up the paper. She folds it neatly, so as not to expose any other pages, and pushes it out of my reach. "And I think you know better than to let a newspaper photo doubt what you know deep down. You know what these newspapers do. They cast you as competitors."

"We are," I say.

"For what?" she asks, her arms folded across each other like a teacher with an obstinate pupil.

"For . . . jobs. Positions—our futures."

"There aren't enough to go around?" It's a silly question. Of course, there are. All the girls who attend the institute are coveted, and placed. There will be a placement for me. That's not the point of this article.

"Fine, for Declan then."

"Is that what you're all doing? Competing for Declan?" she asks.

"Well, no."

"Is that why you went?"

"No," I say. *I went because I was chosen. I went because girls like me go when they're told to, because what other option is there?*

"Then why let a newspaper convince you otherwise? Why compete with these girls? They aren't so different from you, after all. They're in this same experience, just trying to do the best they can." I close my eyes, squeezing them shut, picturing the perfect green of the lawn of the estate on a perfect midsummer afternoon. Even as exposed on that lawn as Declan and I were, I felt safe. Protected. I didn't feel like I was competing with the other women. I don't want to compete with the other women. Not for jobs, not for my future. And certainly not for Declan.

I want him to choose me, to really choose me like he promised. *"It's you, Arden. It's been you since our first conversation . . ."* That's what he said. But what if this thing I've done, killing CJ, kissing Beck—what if it changes everything? What if I've done something that will undo his promise?

"You can't just turn them on, like a transport," Kern says,

pulling me from my thoughts. Beck is standing in front of the door, chewing on an orange peel. I pat my shirt sleeve against my eyes, hoping that neither of them notice.

"Okay, fine. How much longer?"

"How much longer, what?" Delia asks, subtle tension winnowing into her words. I doubt either of the boys notices.

"Beck wants to leave," Kern says.

"Not wants, *needs*. Beck *needs* to leave," Beck says.

"Leave?" I say, before I can stop myself. His eyes meet mine, and for once, he doesn't look away. But they're hard and decisive. Unyielding. Another decision has been made for me.

"We can't stay here and have the whole of Bounty Hunter Nation upend this little hamlet. I mean, where would they sleep? Marlbury won't share a bed. I already asked," he says simply, prying his eyes from mine.

"We?" I ask, more of an accusation than a question. He looks back at me and opens his mouth, but then he winces and all that comes out is:

"Yeah."

"And you, Kern?" Delia asks, holding her breath. I place a light hand on her forearm, and she lays her other hand over mine.

"Nah, you're stuck with me for a stretch," he says. Delia smiles knowingly, but her body relaxes, and she squeezes my hand. I guess this is what it looks like to be missed, to be loved.

"What's that? We're stuck with who?" Thurston says, coming back into the already cramped kitchen.

"Beck and Arden are leaving in the morning, and Kern is staying," Delia says. Thurston's round blue eyes go wide, and a wide smile creeps into his cheeks.

"Well, I won't try talking you out of it. I know there's no point with this fella," Thurston says, clapping Beck on the shoulder.

"You know there's always a way," Beck says with a shrewd grin.

"I don't have that much rum, son," Thurston says with a barking laugh, and the others join in. The conversation continues around me, discussing preparations for the morning, but I can't focus. My eyes drift back and forth between the newspaper that betrayed me and the pirate who saved me, but won't look at me. Who makes decisions on my behalf without even the courtesy of a consultation. As I sit with Delia's hand over mine, anchoring me to this place in time, I can't help but feel like I'm drifting into unknown waters, and only Scio knows what the morning will bring.

CHAPTER ELEVEN

*I*t's dark. Too dark to see anything. I know that if I reach for the walls, they'll close in on me. I keep my arms wrapped around my waist and sit with my legs crisscrossed like a frightened toddler.

"I'm coming, Arden!" Declan calls from outside, his vowels slipping from frantic to lazy. I reach for him and feel the wall inches from my feet. It groans to life, moving closer and closer as a sharp, metallic tang fills my nostrils and filters down into my lungs. Thump-thump, thump-thump. Beck's heartbeat steadies me, and I reach to my right for him.

"No! Stop it!" His voice echoes through the tiny chamber as if through a series of caves and fades to nothing but the crunch-crunch of footsteps growing louder and louder, until they're so loud, I have to cover my ears.

"Atta girl," CJ's voice groans in my ear as the sour stink of horse shit mixes with the ferrous tang of blood. I scream as CJ peels back the skin of my tattoo, centimeter by centimeter, leaving the deeper scar.

"You think this makes you whole? You think this makes you strong? It's just a bandage." His voice is low and slippery, worming its way around my fists, through my fingers and into my ears. "You've sealed me into your skin."

Something wet drips from my palms, slinking down my wrists. I pull them away, and CJ's blood is thick and viscous against my skin. I try to wipe it away, but my skin soaks it up like a sponge. I can feel him seep through my pores, moving into my bloodstream, pumping alive and triumphant. Then I look up, and Declan is there, his gray eyes turning to hard, frigid coals.

"No. Not this. I don't want this." He walks away as CJ's cackle fills the room, and I push back into another wall that moves in to crush me.

I scream, praying for someone to rescue me . . .

—and land hard on the floor, gasping for air.

Silver moonlight falls into my small bedroom in thin shafts. I touch my face and feel slippery wet sweat. My breath is choppy as I push myself off the floor and examine my hands—they're wet, but clean. My nightmare hasn't followed me. I look around the room, pulling the messy, spare blankets and pillow from their perch. I'm shaking, half laughing, half sobbing, searching through the covers as if CJ could be hiding beneath them. I know it's illogical, but I breathe easier seeing there's nothing there. Relief floods my limbs, but the room starts to feel small and suffocating. I reach for the door handle, and when it releases, I let out a breath.

The house creaks with the rush of wind from all directions, but stands solid. Something tells me this house has been here much longer than the humans who inhabit it and will exist long after. The moonlight seems to live in it, bringing the walls and floors, nooks and crannies to life in a way the shadows of the day do not. The wind pushes, and the house shoves back, as if to say, *Is that the best you've got? Ha!*

I smile as my thoughts echo with the sound of Beck taunting the brashness of the waves and inhale another deep gulp of air. The tense coils of nightmare around my chest dissipate, and tension flows out of my limbs as the sweat on my skin cools.

I walk out into the kitchen and stop short. Even in the

moonlight, I can see the green of his eyes, the worried creases that are just starting to take root in his forehead. His mouth is pressed into a grim line, and for a moment, I think he'll stop looking at me, stop seeing me, that he'll turn and walk away. But instead, he retrieves a mug from an upper cabinet, fills it with water, and gives it to me.

"Thanks," I croak. My voice is raw. Clearly, I wasn't just screaming in my dream. Embarrassment creeps into my cheeks, but he nods and leans back against the counter, his arms crossed loosely over his chest. It's too casual. He watches me, and I can't meet his gaze. I'm afraid of what I'll find. When my cup is empty, I hand it back to him. I don't know why I do this; I'm embarrassed as soon as I do. He takes it, refills it, then passes it back to me. I drink again.

"We have a long trip in the morning," he says softly. I wait for the punchline, but it doesn't come. He heard.

"Did I wake you?" I whisper, still not looking at him.

"No," he says, drawing out the vowel into a lie. "Couldn't sleep."

"Guess that makes two of us," I say. The window over the sink rattles, fighting back against the latest punch from the sea below, and we both turn our heads to watch. I want to see it. Or at least get a better view of what the sea is doing. One look at Beck, and I know he wants to be there, too. I can see the thirst in his eyes, a longing to return to the undulating swells that make his feet feel so solid.

"You're going to marry him," he says quietly. It's not a question, but there's a lilt at the end. If I didn't know better, I would think his question is buried under useless emotions like disbelief and hope.

"What?" I ask.

"You are," he says, but his eyebrows raise with the unspoken words: *aren't you?* I shrug, and then nod.

"If he wants," I say. Beck's exhale shakes, catching me off guard, and I set my free hand on the counter.

"Of course, he wants." His words are low enough that only I can hear, as if it's something he doesn't want the house to know he knows.

"He doesn't know everything . . . I've done," I mumble. Beck blushes silvery-blue in the moonlight, and I shake my head violently. "He doesn't know I'm . . . that I've . . . CJ." Even just saying his name invites the tremors back, and I drink the useless water. It flushes away the shudders, grounding me, if not healing the wound forever gaping inside my mind.

"He'll understand," Beck says, soft and decisive.

"Will he, though?" I ask. "What if he doesn't believe—"

"He'll believe," Beck interrupts, turning to me. He is so certain, his eyes so sure. My stomach twists, and I look away.

"But there's also . . . I mean . . ." I blush. I can't help it. There's also the little matter of the kissing.

"No," he says.

"It's—" I say, starting to explain my decision, but he shakes his head.

"We can't do that again," he says. His words aren't harsh. They aren't angry. They're soft and simple and resolute, and they burn in my chest, sending angry, embarrassed flames up my neck.

"I know. You've made yourself perfectly clear," I spit. I don't need to be told twice. He's still as he watches me, an unreadable expression in his eyes, his arms hanging loose now at his sides.

"I have?" he asks, and his normally solid voice is so tenuous, I worry my own breath might blow it away. The house protects it as it hangs in the air. I look at his face, and it's blank, no hint of the perma-smirk I know so well. The light catches on the growing scruff that spreads across his cheeks from a few days of missed shaving. It emphasizes his cheekbones and suits him well. I'm staring, I realize, too long. I shake my head and stare at my feet instead.

"Yes, I heard you. I'll stop," I say, embarrassed that I have to acknowledge his words from the other day. He doesn't say anything, and I keep staring at my pale feet on the gray floorboards, willing the hardwoods to take hold and swallow me whole.

"If we don't leave first thing, it won't take them long to figure out where we are. We're too exposed," he says, as if he's trying to convince me of his plan.

"Yes, I get it," I bite back.

"We can't get distracted. When we get distracted, that's when missteps happen, and if we misstep, then we end up arrested. Or worse."

"I said, I get it," I snap.

"Arden," he says, suddenly inches from me. His hands are on my arms, and I'm shaking, seething with the anger of him being able to touch me so freely after telling me to leave him alone. Furious that I don't push him away. He takes the mug from my hands, setting it on the counter, and places a strong finger under my chin, lifting my face to his.

"You're not hearing me," he says softly, and dammit, I want him to close the distance. "I said *we*." *We*. The word reverberates down my arms and into my legs, locking my knees against each other. This isn't about me. *Not just me*. I press my hands against his chest, and his steady *thump-thump* is wild and chaotic. I bite my tongue and let my forehead fall against his chest. His arms wrap around me, and I inhale slowly, letting him absorb my steadiness. The house shakes in a violent tremor, and then comes to a quick, shimmering stop, seeming to say, *shush!* His heart is back to the steady *thump-thump* I've come to depend on.

"Arden," he whispers into my hair. His breath is so soft, so soothing, I don't want to end this. But I nod and lean back.

"Okay." His shoulders still, and he takes a step back. The space between us feels cavernous, but he needs this space. So do I. He's right. We can't afford a misstep.

"You're gonna have to convince a horse not to throw you tomorrow," he says, the familiar wry cadence back in his voice. "Horses are logical creatures. It's harder to twist their arguments." I fight the smile sparking into the corner of my mouth.

"I don't know. I can be pretty convincing," I say with a chuckle. His shoulders fall, but I don't think the house or the moonlight catches it. Then he squares them again and crosses his heavy arms over his chest.

"I'd like to hear that argument. You going to start by asking why the long face?"

"Ugh, no," I groan, chewing on my bottom lip as I think of a real zinger. "Maybe I'll tell him to stop stalling . . . ?"

"I see what you did there, and it's not okay. I would even go so far as to say it's lame." His mouth hangs open in a goofy grin at his joke, and I stop my laugh.

"Woah," I say, over-enunciating the vowels, and he chuckles. The house moans contentedly with the swell of our laughter and settles into a dull thrum, almost like a steady pulse of its own.

"Better get some rest," he says, not moving. I nod and pick up my half-full cup, holding it against my chest.

"You too," I say, also not moving. Leaving this kitchen feels like something that can't be undone. There's a stasis here that feels comfortable and homey, and I have no doubt we could live together in this space for a long, long time, sheltered from the storm on all fronts. But life doesn't work that way. And when he walks toward me, and the wind howls against the window, the newspaper on the counter rustles, drawing our attention. Together, we face Declan's frozen smile, staring at his newsprint image as though it were alive, and if we move, it might spot us, and we might expose exactly what we're hiding. The house fights back against the wind, roaring into the complacent white noise. Then Beck keeps walking, and I'm alone with a roll of lifeless newsprint and the weight of a one-syllable confession: *we*.

CHAPTER TWELVE

We get off to a rough start in the morning. My horse, a marled, fifteen-hand gelding—or so I'm told—named Sir Squints-a-Lot, is the only horse that will let me ride him, according to Kern, who spent the morning having deep conversations with each and letting them sniff my pillow. Sir Squints-a-Lot took a liking to my scent, he said. He was the only one who didn't buck wildly and try to bust out of his stall. Or he has no sense of smell. Because, when I do finally try to mount him, he's anything but happy. He skitters under my weight, and I clutch at the reins, trying to exert some control. But that only seems to aggravate him more.

"You have to trust him," Kern says, grabbing onto the straps around his face to calm him down. "Trust he's not going to throw you . . . and give him no reason to."

"That makes no sense," I say.

"And you have to trust she's not going to steer you off a cliff, Squinty," Kern says to Sir Squints-a-Lot, who whinnies in protest, but doesn't immediately try to kick me off.

"Why is he called Sir Squints-a-Lot?" I ask, but Kern either doesn't hear me or pretends he doesn't as he leads us out of the stable.

"Just trust him, and don't give him a reason not to trust you," he says again. It still makes no sense, but as we get to riding, I start to understand. When I tense up, the dumb horse does too, ignoring my lead. I try to just follow Beck and pretend I'm calm, but Sir Squints sees through my second-rate subterfuge.

We ride at a trot, unobstructed for a long time, cutting across the great plain, through tall waves of grass that sweep against my boots. Once it's clear I'm not going to tumble from my seat, Beck urges his horse into an easy gallop, and Sir Squints-a-Lot begrudgingly follows. My cheeks and ears hurt from the sharp wind, and I try to keep my eyes on Beck's back. It's easier than what I want to do, which is scan the periphery like a manic meerkat, searching for any threats.

Around midday, Beck looks back over his shoulder, his hair loose and flopping from his small ponytail, and points to the trees. We slow to a canter and turn toward the thin, dark line that lies at the base of the foothills that skirt between the larger mountains to the west and the ocean cliffs to the east. Sir Squints-a-Lot takes the hint and slows without me telling him. He's decided to take my directions as mere suggestions and considers Beck's horse, Hammerhead, the true leader of this journey. Which is just as well, because I don't know what the hell I'm doing, and I figure Hammerhead is as good a leader as anyone.

The tree line looms larger and larger as the sun moves across the horizon, but we don't reach the trees until the sky betrays the first orangey shades of the impending sunset. I'm amazed by how tall they are. We had full, leafy old-growth trees on the peninsula that seemed to weave together, conspiring to keep the sun for themselves. So I'm no stranger to large trees. But none of them ever loomed as large as these. It's as if the trees here were all planted at the same time, and they all sought to be the tallest, ignoring their friends as they selfishly reached for the sun.

Reaching the tree line does two things: it blocks the wind from both the mountains and the coast, but it also blocks the sun. While it's refreshing to not be pelted by the harsh gale, it's also somehow colder as we slow down and enter the shade of the trees. The ground here is looser, redder, and covered with long-dead needles and leaves. The first kisses of autumn are upon us, and nowhere is it more apparent than here in this ancient wood, where the horses' hooves crush a fresh layer of dead leaves and juniper needles, creating a muted, crunchy rhythm that warns of impending cold. We're back to an easy canter when the familiar pangs of hunger poke into my stomach.

"Not much further," Beck calls back, as if he knew what I was thinking. We climb at a decent grade, making it harder to balance and giving Squints and me a new, awkward battle to fight. Soon after we crest the hill, I hear it, and I look up to see the river, running clear and shallow. Beck dismounts and ties Hammerhead to a tree branch, leaving him to drink from the river. Squints drops his head to drink, and I slip awkwardly — but Beck catches me under the arms before I really embarrass myself.

"You okay?" he asks, not letting go. I nod and feel the heat creep into my cheeks at our proximity. He drops me to my feet, but as he walks away, I see the tops of his ears pinken as well.

"I know you've become accustomed to the finer things these days, but how do you feel about camping?" he asks. This is news to me, but as I examine the packs he removes from Hammerhead, I realize he prepared for it. For as much time as I spent staring at the backside of that horse, I'm embarrassed I didn't notice the extra blankets.

"Slept in worse," I say, trying to keep a lightness to my tone, but the weight of my words sinks like a secret tied to a stone. He presses his lips together in a tight, grim nod and tosses me the blankets, pointing to a rocky outcropping about fifty yards up from the river.

"Haven't been bears in these parts since I was a kid. Can't imagine they'd start sniffing around again now," he says, turning back to his horse to remove the rest of the supplies. "Not when there's not even decent meat on you." It's true, the past weeks have not been kind to my figure—between the stress of the attacks at the institute and heaving up everything I ate on his ship, I'm thinner than I should be. Still, the barb seems unnecessary.

"Thanks," I mumble, climbing the hill, trying not to trip on my shaky legs. I've never ridden a horse on my own before and having spent a full day on one has done nothing to make me feel like I've missed out. My hamstrings ache with each climbing step, but I know the spot he meant when I reach it. A solid wall of red rock dips about ten feet into the hillside, creating a sort of cave. The slit towers about fifteen feet high and curves into a dome. It's not huge, but it's enough cover to keep us dry and build a fire. I spread out one of the blankets, setting the other two on top of it, and sit.

All around, in every direction, I see nothing but pink-brown hillsides and golden-green trees. The gentle harmonies of the river and everything around it echo up to me, and I close my eyes, taking in the serenity of the moment. I can just make out Beck's voice as he talks to the horses, though what he's saying is an indecipherable blur. It seems as good a spot as any to hide out the night.

When he finally emerges, he has a stack of dry sticks in his arms, and I take his hint to find more.

I gather a good mound of dried leaves and needles to add to his sticks and get a fire started. And by the time we add some real wood he's splintered from a felled tree near the river, the fire is our only light, and I edge closer to it for its heat.

"I'd like to see your prince charming do that," he says, poking at the little stick pyramid he's set on fire. I think he means it as a joke, but there's a bite to his words. It reminds me of our conversation the night before, and my chest twinges with the pang of loneliness. I miss him, Declan. More than I expected to. He made me feel seen. Understood, even, in his own obtuse way. He promised that we could do things together —big things. Life-changing things. But instead of getting closer to the capital, it feels like we're moving further and further away. I need to find my way back to him. He's constant, and dependable, and I know what to expect with him, even if the one thing I know is to expect the unexpected. I'm still pretty sure he'd need at least a flint to light a campfire, though.

"Did you catch some fish while you were down there? A delicious trout, perhaps? With your bare hands?" I ask, trying to find my way back to our familiar rhythm. We sit with our backs to the cave, facing the fire.

"Wrong time of year for that. And you know I've been on a moisturizing regimen. But I've got something even better," he says with a hint of a joke in his voice. I wait for him to rummage through a bag, and he tosses me something hard and flat, wrapped in paper.

"What is this?" I ask.

"Espancian orange lobster with herbed fig sauce," he deadpans. "Also called, dinner in a bar." I unwrap it and find a square, dense patty made of compressed oats, seeds, and dried fruit. It's really hard.

"Is it edible?" I ask, tapping it with my fingernails. It sounds solid. In answer, he rips his teeth into it, but they get stuck, and his feral chomp turns into an awkward, sawing chew. I take a deep breath and bite into mine. It's a little tough, but it doesn't taste bad, and I can feel it stick to my ribs almost instantly.

"Did you make this?" I ask.

"Nah, Delia's specialty. I've got more for breakfast. Should make it to town by dinner tomorrow, so enjoy these while you can."

The fire crackles, and the river rumbles. It's a companionable silence, tenuous and non-combative for once. I'm not sure I should trust it.

"Do you come to Kern's often?" I ask, listening for his answer over my own too-loud chewing.

"Not as often as she'd like us there," he says around his bar, before swallowing hard. He reaches into a bag and retrieves a canteen, taking a long swig and then passing it over to me. I accept it and sip, choking down the harsh fire of liquor.

"You could've warned me," I say, through coughs.

"Yeah, but you wouldn't have wanted it. Only thing that helps get it down. Nothing like rum to choke down pure nutrition."

"Is that what this is?" I ask. I'm only three bites in, but I already feel finished, as my jaw has already tired of chewing. I take another drink, and it does soothe my aching jaw a bit. I hand it back to Beck, and he accepts, then slides back to his place on the other end of the fire. He chews, and we're silent for a stretch, listening to the upbeat music of the forest: the percussive sap popping; the soprano water trickling; the occasional, syncopated grunt or neigh from the horses. It's peaceful, almost nice. If I forget that we're technically running from the law—and the lawless.

"Where are we going tomorrow?" I ask.

"New Covington," he says. I try to remember the map at the institute. New Covington, from what I remember, is the largest port town on the northern shore. But I have no idea how big. "We need some supplies," he says, as if anticipating my next question. "It's busy enough there that we can blend in. But we'll still need to get in and out quick. If we have people after us, there's likely to be more of them in town." I nod, a chill crawling down my shoulders. He pushes up in one sweeping motion and walks into the cave, returning with a blanket. He hands it down to me, and I mumble my thanks as I unfold and wrap it around me.

"Then where?" I ask. He presses his lips into a low, slow smile.

"I'm going home, to my family's home." I know his family lives on a farm deep in the northern highlands, and I smile, remembering the softness with which he described it before. It was too dark to see his expression in the safe room, but I could hear how much he loved that piece of land. Still, there's something stilted in his face, a hesitancy that I can't quite put my finger on.

"Am I coming with you?"

"Do you want to?" He looks down at me, his expression shuttered.

I hesitate. The truth is, I do. I want to see the red farmhouse, and the barn loft with the amazing views he told me about not so long ago. But it doesn't really make sense. To just hide out somewhere? It must take days to get there, from what he's said, and shouldn't Declan be ready for me to come back sooner than that? I never thought I'd be gone even this long.

He watches me carefully for a moment, and then shrugs, returning to his side of the fire.

"You always have a choice, Capo," he says, words he's spoken before that set something uncomfortable ablaze in my belly.

"Oh, do I?" I mumble beneath my breath.

"Of course. You're an Independent woman, aren't you? You're free to do whatever you damn well please." More words dredged up from the past. His tone is flippant, but his gaze is sharp, and there's something undefinable running beneath the surface of his words. Something that turns the sincerity in them into a poisoned challenge.

The uncomfortable feeling in my stomach grows. "Or you'll make my decisions for me," I mumble and look away.

"You got something you want to say?"

"No. It's nothing."

"It's not nothing, or you wouldn't have mumbled that like you wanted me to hear it." A familiar light sparks in his green eyes, flickering like the embers of the fire between us, and his signature smirk crawls into the side of his mouth.

I exhale and decide to take the bait.

"It just . . . seems like I haven't had a choice in the matter for as long as I've been stuck on your boat, and—"

"Ship."

"What?"

"Ship. We've gone over this, Capo. You pronounced it wrong. And no one has a say on the ship. It's my job to make the decisions. That's how it works."

I stare at him, my mouth hanging slightly open, lost for a comeback. He bites into his bar with his teeth, grinning the whole time. God, he's infuriating.

"So, you were saying?" He gestures with one hand like he's granting me the floor.

I exhale hard through my nose, trying to suppress the frustrated growl growing in my chest. "Never mind."

"No, if you've got something to say, then say it. I don't make your decisions for you. I never have. But it's my job to make decisions when it comes to my crew and my ship. If you don't like them, you don't have to tag along. You're your own person, Capo. You have a choice, you have a voice—and I'm a friggin' poet." He grins, leaning forward, as if baiting me to argue. It's annoying. Obnoxious. And the only thing worse is how hard I have to work to suppress my laugh.

"Don't you—"

"Know it!" he interrupts, letting out a relieved breath. The tension between us melts, and we stare into the fire, settling back into the companionable silence of moments prior.

"So, I get to meet your family?" I ask, returning to the matter at hand.

"Invitation's there, if you want it," he says. "But don't get a big head about it or anything. They're going to meet you, too."

"Will that put them in danger?"

"No," he says, quickly. "It's not an easy passage, and we do a good job masking it. Anyone who follows won't know how to get back." This should make me nervous. I'm going to have to make this trip in the coming days with him—on a horse that wants to kill me. But the nerves don't come. Maybe it's the rum, maybe it's the fire, but I'm excited to meet his family, to find out where this self-proclaimed pirate comes from.

"Do they know we're coming?" I ask, chancing another bite of my bar and immediately regretting it. He shakes his head and stares into the fire, poking at it with a thick, charred stick, coaxing the flames to dance higher still.

"They'll be fine, though," he says, answering a question I hadn't yet thought to ask: whether or not they want us there. He keeps prodding the fire until the flames are fluid and full, and the cave is full of intoxicating warmth.

"Tell me about them," I say, and his eyes lift to mine, like he's trying to decide if I'm just being polite, or if I really want to know. The fire catches the gold flecks in his gaze, making them dance for just a moment. Then he smiles and looks back into the flames.

"They're sea folk stuck on land," he says, prodding at the fire again. "Mom and Dad settled down a few years ago. I can tell Dad misses it, but he misses Mom more, and she'd had enough of it. Or so she says.

"Ammon is my brother. He's older, so he thinks he's

smarter." He stops talking for a minute and rubs his thumb against the left side of his nose. "And then there's Emlyn."

"Who's Emlyn?" I ask, the name sounding vaguely familiar in my mouth.

"Emlyn is Ammon's wife," he says, scratching his beard. There's something off in the way he says her name, as though there's something uncomfortable buried there.

"Okay," I say, feeling a nervous pit spread through my gut. I pull the blanket tighter around me and wonder what Emlyn is to Beck, if there's something he's not telling me about her. Maybe there are unresolved feelings there? It would be awful to watch your brother marry someone you had feelings for. But the way he furrows his brow and stares into the fire, it seems deeper. I don't think it's her he's affected by.

"Will they like me?" I ask, and immediately regret my words. I have no idea why I ask that question. It seems so silly, so trite to worry about whether Beck's family would like me. "Never mind," I say quickly and curl up further under the blanket, wrapping up my meal bar.

"Yes," he says, his voice solid and warm. I don't look at him. I stare at the fire, and the exhaustion of the day sets in, crashing down on me like a crate of bricks. I look to the cave over my far shoulder, and that side of my face is so much colder for having turned away from the flames.

"It doesn't look like rain," he says, all business again. "You can sleep out here. I'll take the first shift." We never even discussed sleeping in shifts, but I suppose it makes sense. I nod and curl onto my side, cocooning myself in the blanket, willing sleep to come quickly.

CHAPTER THIRTEEN

he pretty girl with the dark hair carves out a piece of his shoulder, and the mean girl with the red hair rips out his mouth. The blonde girl plucks out his eyes, and another brunette slices off a piece of his torso. Declan is falling apart in front of me, and I am helpless to stop it.

I scream for help, but Beck does nothing, just stands across the clearing in the woods, leaning back against a tree, telling me that we can't do this, holding two sets of reins while both horses glare at me with suspicious eyes. A hand closes around my neck and another around my mouth, and I taste the sour, iron bite of blood. CJ shoves his fist in my mouth, and I choke on it.

"You'll never get rid of me," he says, physically forcing the cries down my throat. I can't breathe. I convulse, struggling, clawing for scraps of air.

"Arden," he whispers, his words soft on my face. It's not CJ, though. And it's not CJ's fingers in my hair, stroking slowly, rhythmically, soothing the oxygen back into my lungs. I open my eyes and meet Beck's wide, bloodshot gaze. I blink, and the tears fall. He lets them. He sighs, then lets his finger slowly trace the curve of my skull, gently pushing a stray hair back behind my ear. His smell, salt and leather, travels down my nose, blooming in my lungs, reminding me that it was just a dream. That it wasn't real. Beck is real. And he is close, so close, lying on the hard ground next to me. Close enough for me to absorb his calmness. His caress.

"You with me, Capo?" His voice is feather soft against my cheek. He continues to draw soft shapes down my jaw, my neck, my shoulder, and I'm imbued with a warm sense of calm. I blink up at him, and his eyes drop to my lips.

"Beck," I whisper, soft as a prayer, as if saying his name makes *this* real. This safe, little space between the two of us, where things are simple and soft and true. I lean in, inhaling his salty-sweet scent, and lift my lips to his.

He sucks in a breath and jerks back.

"Arden," he says, his voice hard. "We can't."

The spell is broken, the fragile shell around us cracked open to the cold night as he shifts back, away from me. Embarrassment courses hot through my cheeks, and I chew on my tongue, trying to school my expression into a neutral face.

"Hey, it's—"

"I can watch now," I say. His shoulders freeze, and he retracts his hand. We lay there, eye to eye. Silent. I start to rise, and he sits up, too.

"Arden, I know—"

"I'm sorry—"

We say it at the same time, but his words catch me off guard.

"You know what?" I ask. He pushes his lips together, working his jaw in a tight circle.

"I know what it is to end someone," he says softly. I recoil, and his eyes widen in surprise. "I'm just saying, it's not something you're supposed to get over easily. I would worry if you did."

"You don't know me," I say, surprising myself. I wish my

nightmares were just the product of having killed a person. But I know they're so much more than that, and he can never fully understand what it was like to have ended CJ's life. To have felt his blood seep into my clothing, my skin, to try to wash it off me knowing that it would never fully be gone. Just like his horrible, ugly brand I tried to cover up. My hand traces the tattoo, absently, feeling the ridges of his initials—*CJL*—rising beneath the ridges of the new mountain line. I wish that's all the nightmares were—just a product of having killed CJ. Not a symptom of my complete brokenness.

I push myself up and move to the other side of the fire, where I grab a stick and kneel beside what's left of the slow-burning embers. I feel him watching me still, and I ignore it. I swallow down his intrusion, his presumption at what haunts my subconscious. Eventually, I hear him lie down, and when I finally chance a look, his body is steady and still, rising and falling with the rhythm of sleep. I stoke the fire until the sky turns light, and then let it die, watching the embers turn deeper and deeper red, bleeding into the red earth beneath.

CHAPTER FOURTEEN

We don't speak after that. We pack up the camp without a word, clean up the campfire as much as we can, safely, and get the horses prepped for the day. Sir Squints-a-Lot has noticed, but doesn't seem bothered by my silence. Despite the lack of wind and openness, today is a harder day of riding. The terrain we climb becomes rockier as the soil changes from brown to red. Hammerhead is strong and solid on the changing terrain, but Sir Squints-a-Lot is not. He slips and makes missteps, spooking him and me alike. Occasionally, I whisper encouragement and support, but he just chomps at his bit and stares. So mostly, I just hang on and try to trust in the fact that he doesn't want to fall and die any more than I do.

We stop when the sun is straight overhead, or at least it appears to be through the slots between trees. I eat more of Kern's mom's everlasting food bar, and Beck treats the horses to apples and water. I refuse his rum, and he puts it away, untouched.

"It shouldn't be much further," he says. It's the only thing either of us has said.

We continue on through the afternoon, and the terrain levels out as the trees thin. Cool, northern light filters through the clouds, casting the red-bark trees in eerie blues and grays. And then, on the horizon, there's a warm glow of yellow lamplight, like an oasis. We're here. We reach the edge of the tree line, and Beck stops, fumbling with his pack.

"Wrap it around your hair," he says, tossing me a scarf. I want to argue that it's not necessary, but I know he's right. Who knows who might be looking for me here? I twist my braid into a knot at the base of my neck and wrap the long strip of blue-printed muslin around my head and neck. Then we continue into town as the sky starts to cloud over in orangey-blues.

We ride downhill on the main road—a dirt-gravel composite. The street dips down a steep hill to the water, as though it ends there, and if I rode straight ahead, I would be washed up in the current. Just seeing the water, my lungs expand more easily—and a quick look at Beck tells me he feels much the same. The buildings are a quaint mix of shingled cottages and boxy, wood-paneled shops painted in cerulean, canary, hibiscus, and bright white. Seabirds flock in circles over the harbor, which is lined with dozens of commercial and private fishing boats. I don't see Beck's ship, but I see another that looks similar. It's empty and looks like it's seen better days, but it sits anchored, afloat. Seaworthy.

Beck whistles, and Sir Squints-a-Lot follows, nose down, to a corral tucked behind a dingy, white-shingled building. He reaches up to help me down, but I slide off, inelegantly, on my own, catching myself on the ground. I have to wipe the dirt from my hands on the denim pants Kern's mom gave to me, but I smile up at Squints. He stares down at me and snorts, as if to say he'll get me next time. Beck ties up the horses and fills the water trough, then motions for me to follow him. Instead of continuing down the main thoroughfare, though, he ducks down a side alley, and we turn up an even narrower street.

"Here we are," he says. We're in front of a solid black door inlaid on a log building. He cracks the heavy door open and waves me inside. I step in and find myself inside yet another pub, this one smaller than the last and operated by a burly, mustached man behind a small, squat bar. Beck presses his fingertips into my back, but I recoil from his touch. I don't look at him as he sighs and says:

"What? You think I'd get you this far and push you to your death?"

"I don't know. You like to make other decisions on my behalf. So, maybe?" I snap.

"Well, only one way to find out," he growls, giving me a little push toward a table in the back.

It's not a big space, so it doesn't take much to make it to the table. He shakes his head, though, and pulls out a seat for me at the next table over, the one with a straight shot to the bathroom. Or at least, what I assume is the bathroom. I don't argue, though. I don't care enough. I sit with my back to the bar and the front door, and Beck goes to the counter to place an order. I chance a look around and take in the hodgepodge of furniture, no two pieces matching, but rather looking as though they've been collected over time—or whenever they needed another chair. Four people—all men—sit among them, nobody paying mind to anyone else. Day drinkers, committed to their craft.

Beck leans over the bar, deep in conversation with the thick-necked barkeep wearing even thicker eyeglasses. He pours amber liquid into two glasses and pushes them across the bar to Beck, letting the liquid slosh onto the counter. Beck folds a piece of yellowed paper and tucks it in his back pocket, then lifts the glasses. I turn around, so he doesn't catch me watching him.

"Drink up," he says, his voice too loud as he slams the glasses on the table. I look up at him, and he's not watching me. Rather, he's tilting back his glass of whiskey as he falls hard into his seat, smacking his other hand down on the table with a funny crinkling sound. When he pulls his hand back, the yellowed paper is still there. I look up at him, and now, he's watching me.

"You may as well see it now," he says. His flippant amusement masks something deep and nasty, and it sits in my stomach like lead. I take the paper and unfold it, my fingers trembling slightly. I don't know why they do, but when I see what's on it, I start to shake in full. On the left is a picture of Beck—a mug shot. His lip is split, his nose looks to be broken, and he's smirking. On the right is a photo of me. Not just any photo—the one CJ took of me for my institute application. My hair is disheveled, and my eyes challenge the viewer to look away. I look dangerous. It's a far cry from the photo on the cover of the paper and the official pictures from my time as a candidate, but it's a much more familiar face staring back at me. I touch the picture and stare at it in wonder. No matter what I do, no matter the clothes or the makeup or the regular bathing, this is how I will always see myself. Dirty, crazed, kept. I bite on the side of my tongue as I read the words: "*Wanted in connection with suspicious homicide.*"

"They couldn't even find a decent picture of me," he says, pushing back from the table. "At least you look . . . well, persuasive." His words ring hollow in me. It's true. I look like I want to kill the person on the other side of the camera. I did, in fact.

"What is this?" I ask.

"It is what it is," he says. "Stay here for a minute." I nod, but I can't look away from the shell of a girl staring back at me, staring at anyone who has looked at this poster.

"Who did—" I start to ask, but when I look up, Beck is gone. Completely gone. Nowhere to be seen in the bar. I scan the room, but I find myself alone, save for the barkeep and the other three patrons who seem content drinking alone. The door in the back corner moves ever so slightly, as if someone walked through it in a hurry and didn't pull it shut all the way. I roll the wanted flier into a tight cylinder in my fist as I walk to the door and push through.

I'm standing in a dark back alley—I have to squint to see anything—but to my right, I hear voices. The clapboard buildings frame two silhouettes, men identifiable by their posture: a soldier, and a pirate. Or so it would seem. Their voices are low and muffled, their tones terse and their body language curt, not friendly. The soldier gives Beck something flat, then slips back into the shadows. But as he exits the alley, his blue jacket passes under the warm streetlight and something on his arm catches in the light—a gold badge, shaped like a four-pointed star. The Nordanian seal.

I touch the small charm on my bracelet, feeling the edges of the same symbol with the pads of my fingers.

"Can't you ever do anything you're told?" Beck growls, now in my face. My cheeks flush, but I stand my ground and glare back at him.

"Who was that?" I ask, but he takes me by the arm and pushes me back inside and to my seat before returning to his own. He shoves a thick brown envelope inside his jacket and glares at me.

"You gonna drink that?"

"You gonna give me a straight answer?"

"Suit yourself," he says, lifting my glass to his lips and emptying its contents.

"What are we doing here?" I ask. The envelope was the perfect size for a large quantity of money.

"I'm drinking. You're asking too many questions," he says, placing my empty glass on the table with enough force to rattle the other.

"I'm asking questions because you're not telling me anything."

"I'm telling you what you need to know." He crosses his arms over his chest and leans back.

"Great. Another man telling me that I know nothing, that I don't deserve to know what's happening to me, that I don't deserve to make a choice. What happened to all that horseshit you said by the fire?"

"You already made a choice, if my memory serves correctly. Which it does. Should we perhaps talk about that?" he asks, his voice lowering to a lethal whisper. My blood boils, and I want to knock his aloof, piratical ass off his chair. Instead, I say nothing. I seethe and tuck my hair behind my scarf.

"What's the matter, Capo? You don't want to talk?" he says, leaning closer, his face inches from mine. "Fine. But now is not the time to change your mind. So just sit there, shut up, and we'll be on our way soon enough. And remember, it's *me* doing *you* the favor here." He leans in even closer and says through gritted teeth, "*Your Highness.*"

If only I had something to throw at him, like a bottle or an oar or a rusty, mythical trident. There's not even a salt shaker on the table. It's like the bar owner anticipated this and took his side. I cross my arms over my chest while he takes his sweet time at the bar ordering yet more booze.

Something just happened. Something shifted in the atmosphere, and it can't just come down to a shitty wanted poster. He has to have been on one of those before now. I mean, for Scio's sake, he's a pirate! Or so he wants everyone to believe. He looks over his shoulder at me from the bar, his gaze so cold and detached, it's almost lazy. But his posture, the way he holds his tension in his jaw and neck, while leaning against the counter like he's had a few too many . . .

He doesn't get drunk. So who is he trying to fool?

And why did he have to kiss me in the first place? I was perfectly happy with Declan at the institute. It wasn't perfect, but I had never even looked at Beck that way until he kissed me. And then he ignored me. *He kissed me, and then ignored me.* And then we got to the pub in the woods, and he kissed me again. Sure, I made it worse, instigating something I shouldn't have, but he was very much an active participant. So maybe it *was* all a mistake; maybe it can't happen again. Fine. I'll go one step further: it should never have happened at all, and that is all on him. I just want to forget it. Forget everything about him.

Except a small, insignificant, vital, aching part of me doesn't. Not really. Not ever.

"This way. Now," he barks, grabbing my forearm, upsetting the table, and pulling me out through the back door. We go out into the alley, down about halfway, and then duck into another door. This door is different—it's small and shabby, yet sturdy. Heavy, actually. The room beyond is small, dark, and smells faintly of mold and old piss. Movement from the shadowy corner catches my eye. There's a person there, dressed all in black. I back away, and Beck pushes me toward the stranger.

"I don't have all night," Beck says, his words slurred. I'm not sure who the act is for, but it makes me uneasy.

"Beck?" I ask, but it's breathy and small and barely a whisper of sound.

"Easy, Capo," he says softly—and remarkably clearly—against my ear. "I got you." I look up at him, and for a split second, the mask falls, just enough that something small and sincere, and just the tiny bit broken, flashes in his gaze. Then he shuts the door, sealing me in a small space with a stranger. A stranger who smells like earth.

And mint.

"Arden," he says in an all-too-familiar tenor. Slowly, he lowers his hood, and the low lamplight catches on the gold in his tousled hair. He smiles, and his gray eyes practically sparkle.

"Declan?"

CHAPTER FIFTEEN

I hesitate as he removes his black coat completely, setting it on the back of the one lone chair by the rickety table against the wall. I can't process what I'm seeing. Declan is here, in a musty back room, along an alley, in a nothing north coast port town. Something flashes across his face — uncertainty perhaps — and it hits home. It's really him.

I rush him, wrapping my arms around his long neck. His fingers brush over my cheeks, and his thumbs settle into the soft underside of my chin. He looks at me for a long time, as if he too is having trouble believing we're in the same place. Then he kisses me, his mouth warm and sweet. I breathe him in, holding him tight, as though he might turn into the vapor of dreams — or maybe nightmares — if I let go. He pulls back too soon for my liking and wraps me in his arms, holding me tight against his chest.

"God, I've missed you," he whispers into my hair. I can't believe he's here. He still smells faintly of basil and soil, even after spending what was probably several days aboard a ship. The earthiness of his body is a welcome element in the staleness of this crappy room. His golden hair flops over his shining gray eyes, his skin sun-kissed and glowy. He smiles the same easy, joyful smile he's shared with me so many times—the same one I saw in the newspaper. I pull away and punch him in the chest.

"What's that for?" he asks with a wounded chuckle.

"For smiling like that at Fiona," I say. He raises his eyebrows, and I immediately regret my words.

"Are you jealous, Arden?" he asks, looking more than a little pleased. His smile works its way into the corners of his eyes, and his shoulders relax, the uncertainty of earlier dispelled.

"Don't be a jerk," I say, chewing the smile off my bottom lip.

"I don't smile like this at Fiona. I don't smile like this at anyone," he says. "Only you." I study him—the curve of his laugh lines, the crinkles around his eyes. It's true—it's a different brand of smile than even the one from my memory, certainly from the one in the picture. He exhales in a puff and runs his hands up and down my arms. "You saw the paper?"

"It didn't look like you were missing me," I say, feeling a twinge of something ugly at the base of my neck. Is this jealousy? I'm not sure. It feels more like fear. Fear that I might have lost my chance at a future I had only just begun to believe in, that it might go to someone else, someone who doesn't need it. If that's jealousy, then yeah, I'm a little jealous. He slips his arms around my waist and pulls me into him.

"I have been missing you. More than you know. I've also invited photographers to the capital to see how I'm coping, how things are progressing. I do not," he says with a mischievous grin, "invite them to photograph me missing you." I smack his chest again, and he laughs. The warmth of his tenor courses through me, and I laugh with him.

He strokes a piece of unruly hair back from my face and tucks it behind my ear with a knowing smile. He could say it, could give a name to my ugly emotion, again, but he doesn't. He gives me the grace to be jealous without embarrassing me, and for that, I kiss him again. This time, he leans into it, letting his fingers wrap around the back of my neck. His touch is softer than Beck's, his kiss gentler, like a very polite question. It doesn't blind me to my surroundings, but it doesn't leave me feeling breathless with uncertainty either. Declan wears his feelings like the candidates wear their bracelets, for all the world to see. When I'm with him, I know where I stand. Maybe that's not such a bad trade-off? He breaks the kiss, and then kisses the tip of my nose.

"Tell me about your trip," he says, as if I've just been on an extended vacation. My heart thrums in my chest. He doesn't outright ask me about Beck, or CJ, but I feel a dangerous undercurrent in the levity of his words, one that could very well sweep me away.

"I'm not a good sailor," I say. I try to keep my voice light, let him reveal what he knows, or doesn't know. But it does nothing to slow the rapid pounding in my ears.

"You're not?" he asks, a hint of mirth creeping into his playful eyes.

"No sea legs."

He laughs, pulling me into a sweet hug that makes me feel adored, but not held, protected, safe.

"Are they treating you well?" he asks.

"Yeah, just fine. Perfect gentlemen." I decide not to mention the time Kern threw me in the brig, or the time Perlman ripped my clothing to make me look like one of the women in the tavern. Or the time I kissed Beck, and he threw me on a bed. The rest of the time, they have been perfect gentlemen.

"Well, now I know you're lying to me," he says, curling his fingers into the fabric around my waist as I feel the blood rush to my cheeks.

"They're a little rough around the edges, but they're good people."

"How's *he* treating you?" he asks, his gray eyes hardening. There's an edge to his words, and in it, I hear his insecurity. I look at his shirt, hoping I don't give myself away. Beck's treating me well, I suppose, and then not so well. He yells at me one minute, and kisses me the next. But none of that is what Declan needs to hear.

"Fine. He's just fine." I keep my words light and dismissive as I slip my hand up to his cheek. He turns into it, kissing the sensitive skin on my wrist. "You don't trust him." I say it like it's a fact, not a question. And I don't add anything more, because should he? Should I? His nostrils flare, and he shakes his head.

"I trust you," he says. "And I hope you trust me."

"I do," I say, and then chew on the lie, biting the edge of my tongue. "It's just hard to see pictures of you with pretty girls while I'm tossing my lunch off the back of a boat. Especially when the pictures of *me* are not so flattering." He narrows his eyebrows and leans back, but his hands stay firmly planted on my waist.

"What pictures of you?" he asks.

"The poster," I say. He frowns, his confusion evident. "The wanted poster."

His face is stony as he looks at me down the bridge of his nose. He shakes his head. "There is no poster."

"There's not?" I ask, feeling the floor slip out from under me. How in the world are they keeping up the subterfuge of my kidnapping if there's no reward?

"No, I mean, it's been mentioned, but there's no poster. It's been controlled so tightly— Edina has been on top of it actually. She's in our corner."

This surprises me. The dean of the institute never struck me as a fan of mine. I look around, stepping back from him, and on the floor next to the door is the crumpled-up poster. I pick it up and hand it to him. His gray eyes grow wide, and then cloud over as his mouth tightens and he runs his finger over my awful picture.

"So, who then?" I ask.

"I have an idea . . ." he says, folding the paper and shoving it into his back pocket.

"Who?"

"Don't worry about it," he says. "We'll take care of it. I'll make sure no one has to see that picture again."

"Yes, please," I say with a tentative breath. "Though, I can only imagine what I must look like now." I didn't mean to say that out loud, but he grows still, reaching forward with one hand to lift my chin, forcing me to meet his gaze as his eyes soften.

"Your hair is tangled. You have red dust on your cheek, your chin, and your forehead. Your pants are muddy, you have dirt under your fingernails . . ." He sighs, and a sweet smile pulls at the corners of his mouth. "And you're the most beautiful girl I've ever seen."

"I . . . I don't know what to say," I say, chewing on my tongue as heat filters into my cheeks. He's still for a moment, watching me, studying my face, but keeps holding my chin. As the moment stretches, the scrutiny starts to feel uncomfortable. I shift, turning my face away, and he draws his thumb over my cheek, wiping away the dust streak.

"You bring it out in me, I guess. I'm not like this with the others. It's only you, Arden. It's always been you. You know that, right?" he says, the words an echo of the last promise he made before I was spirited off into the night and this whole mess began. And just like that, I'm filled with warm, solid relief. Maybe, after everything, it will all be okay. Maybe I haven't undone his promise. Maybe we can still change the system from the inside out. But then a cold wash of guilt follows: the guilt of three stolen kisses with the wannabe-pirate getting drunk next door, and the ghost of a corpse I'd rather not remember.

Declan kisses me again, and I wish I could trade back those impulsive, reckless kisses with Beck for five more minutes with him, the boy who knows it's always been me. Not the boy who kisses me, and then ignores me, leaving my mind a tangled mess.

"Please trust me," he says again with a heavy sigh. "And be careful of Beck. I know you think you know him, but watch yourself."

"Okay," I say, not wanting to fight. He pulls me against him again, and I press my cheek into his chest, listening for his heartbeat. Maybe it's the room we're in—muffled noise from the surrounding buildings filters through the thin walls in an ever present murmur—but his pulse is weak in my ears. I can't hone in on it, and it leaves me feeling hollow and adrift.

"What are you doing here?" I ask, needing to grab on to something concrete.

"I missed you. Too much," he says. But there's a stiffness to his voice. My core rattles with nerves. He knows. He has doubts. Something is wrong.

"Am I coming back with you?" I ask. He steps back, and there's distance in his eyes.

"Not yet."

"Oh," I say.

"It's become . . . complicated."

"Complicated? Like, Fiona's people from Espancia are negotiating the marriage contract complicated?" I ask, not liking my bitter tone.

"Like there's a body and an eyewitness in Rocky Point, complicated," he says. I feel the color drain from my face, and I think I say something like *oh*, but I don't really hear it. I knew this was coming. I feared it. But I still come up wordless. "Eyewitnesses described two people fleeing from the scene: a bloodied and beaten neanderthal, and a girl with freckles, blue eyes . . . and a tattoo." He cringes on his last words, and his eyes search over me, landing on my hip. I swallow hard as I raise my shirt and lower my waistband, baring my naked hip to him as I once did so long—and yet not so long—ago. The small tattoo of Scio's mountains still itches a little, but his touch is soothing as he examines it. I wonder if he, too, can still feel the ridges of CJ's horrible assault—his initials hidden by ink, but not gone. They'll never be gone.

"Did it hurt?" he asks.

"Not as much . . ." I don't finish my sentence. He moves his mouth like he's going to say something, but then stops. His fingers fall away from my hip, and I readjust my clothes.

"For now, Beck is wanted for your kidnapping. He was seen bloodied and beaten at the scene. Hardly the image of someone incapable of . . ." He trails off again, and then clears his throat.

"Please, just let me explain. He's innocent—"

"Stop," he says, holding up his hand. My heart attempts to comply, but all I can hear is the echo of Beck's words ringing in my head. *Stop it.* "It's better I don't know—I mean, the less I know, the better. But I believe you." I know I should smile. I should feel happy, relieved that he believes me. But he doesn't know what *I've* done. He doesn't want to. He won't let me tell him. So I smile and try to ignore the hollowness that consumes my relief, to say what I'm supposed to say.

"Thank you."

"I need more time to protect you." I nod and stare at my feet. Of course. I couldn't just kill CJ and not expect it to follow me. I close my eyes and hear his voice from my nightmares. *You'll never get rid of me.*

"Obviously, there's history. We can defend it. Call it self-

defense . . . or acting in defense of others, but we need time."
His words are concise and gut me to the core.

"They won't believe me," I say. It's not a question. The only
reason they believed CJ had assaulted me at the State Dinner
was because Declan testified on my behalf. He'd been there,
had seen it with his own eyes, even if he didn't believe what he
was seeing, not the way that Beck had. He hesitated, while
Beck acted. But still, to not believe me then would have been to
call the son of the prime minister a liar. It would have been
political suicide. Who will testify on my behalf this time? And
what will happen to me if no one does?

"We will defend it. You will be safe. I swear to that, Arden."
He takes my hands in his, and he is strong and steady. I want to
believe him. I want to give him that faith, wrapped in a pretty
little box. But I'm honestly not sure if I can.

"Thanks," I say, disappointment weighing down the small
syllable.

"Please trust me. We just need time — to garner support."

"Whose support?"

"For the annual assembly. You'll need support from people
who carry a vote."

"What happens at the annual assembly? Aren't we just
convincing the board at the institute, like last time?"

"Yes . . . and no. For the purposes of the . . . legal situation"
—he clears his throat and diverts his gaze—"you'll need to
convince the Supreme Court. Three of the five justices also sit
on the institute's board. But I'll get you the best advocate money
can buy to articulate your case. It will be clear that it was a case
of self-defense. The charges will be dismissed.

"As for our future," he says. His cheeks flush, and I bite the
smile that threatens to upturn my frown. "We'll need
supporters. At the assembly."

"You need support from the assembly to . . . ?" I don't finish
that sentence, because I'm still on shaky ground. I don't actually

know yet if he wants to be with me, and in what manner. All I know is that, in his mind, we have some sort of future. Together.

"No," he says, suppressing a grin. "I don't need a majority vote to get married."

My stomach flips at the M-word, and it's not entirely pleasant.

"But without support among the assembly, enemies will still lurk in every corner of the estate." I nod. I get it. Without supporters, there's nothing stopping Fiona's Espancian people from targeting the cracks in our foundation. And that doesn't even take into consideration future generations of ambitious benefactors and candidates, much less other enemies of the state.

"So, how do we do that?"

"Garner support?"

"Yes," I say, chewing on the side of my tongue. "But more than that . . . how do we show we have their support?"

"Well, I suppose the simplest way would be to send a bill to the floor for a vote."

Something catches in the back of my brain.

"That's it!" I say, feeling a flush of warm hope in my gut for the first time in . . . well, maybe ever. "Graduates can vote, right? That's what you said."

"Yes, they have the right to vote —"

"So I'll talk to them! Convince them. They'll support my case, don't you think?"

"Arden, they do have a vote," he says, leaning forward, "but the reality is . . . most of them don't."

"Why not?" That seems insane to me. If you had the right to vote on the annual Nordanian assembly, why wouldn't you?

"Many reasons," he says, folding his arms over his chest. "Not a good time of year to travel, too far, too busy with their careers . . . the list goes on." There's an unspoken explanation in his pause, and I don't have to stretch my imagination to know some of their husbands have something to do with it.

"But what if I tried? There must be dozens of graduates. Didn't everyone in the first year graduate? That's eighteen votes right there, if I can just talk to them and get them on my side. I mean, there must be a way," I say, taking Declan's hands into my own. He switches our grip as he shakes his head, pinning my palms between his.

"I wish there was a simple answer. But for now, we need to focus on finding enough support to get you back, so you can graduate."

"But the only way I can do that now is if . . ." I trail off.

"If you left through no fault of your own. Yes," he says. Meaning Beck would have to turn himself in, or be on the run. Maybe forever.

"What about Beck?" I ask. Declan winces, his grip on my hands tightening just enough that I know he expected the question, but didn't want to make promises. "You know he's done nothing wrong. He's not guilty of kidnapping. And—" He holds up a finger before I can say anything else about CJ.

"Once we're married, we can pardon him." His words hang between us, floating, bobbing up and down in front of our eyes like something that could deflate with the wrong response.

"Once we're married?" I ask. The words feel foreign on my tongue, like an unfamiliar dish, or a pudding laced with castor oil. I know he just said he wanted to marry me, but it's one thing to hear his romantic declarations, and another to hear a specific plan. One that will happen sooner—much sooner—than I expected.

"Yes, if you're amenable?" he says, his words tight. I study his handsome face and see the wincing twitch of fear. My heart clenches for a moment, and then the reality of what's happening sinks in. He's proposing. Officially.

It's less a proposal and more a debate, though. I know I

shouldn't be surprised—there's a school literally designed to yield him a wife, and he's told me before—begged me, really—to let him choose me. But the boy who smells of herbs and sunsets just asked me to marry him in the least romantic way possible. Something inside me twists. I know I shouldn't be picky. That I have no right to expect anything else. And maybe, I should just take what I can get. But it feels completely underwhelming, and a small part of me I never even knew existed withers into dust.

"What's wrong?" he asks, frowning.

"Well . . . it occurs to me that this might be the kind of question you only ask once in your life. Is there maybe another way you'd like to phrase that?" I want no doubts, no need for clarification. If I can't have the grand, romantic gesture, I at least deserve that. He holds my hands tighter, bringing them to his lips, and kisses my knuckles.

"Arden Thatcher, marry me."

It's not a question, and my smile grows stiff. But I push through, trying not to overreact, to see it as yet another decision that's been stripped from me. I still have a choice. It's implied, but he's giving me a choice. Isn't he?

"Okay," I say. He grins and kisses me as I hold on to both him and this moment as tightly as I can without crushing either.

"I don't have a ring," he says. "Not with me."

"It's okay," I say. "I don't need one."

"You'll be so good. You can do so much good." His words sound something like hope and pride. It takes me out of the moment, but I force myself to see it for what it is—optimism. About his future—our future. *My future.*

"I don't know about that," I say.

"You can. We can. We can craft a platform that focuses on human dignity—on preventing the sort of situations that you and Zerah faced. Together, we can do anything." My heart swells, filling my chest with a strange warmth I've only ever felt once or twice before. I think . . . this is hope? I take his hands in mine and decide that yes, I want him. I want him *because* I don't need him, and he knows it.

"We just need some support, and we can start our lives together," he says. The romance of the proposal comes to a grinding halt.

"When is the assembly?" I ask, my heart accelerating in my chest. He smiles and steps back, but doesn't drop my hand.

"It's months away. Immediately following graduation. We would need to find people, garner support, secure votes. This kind of campaign takes time. It would become your life's work. Do you see that, Arden? Uniting the alumni—this could be your legacy."

"Legacy?" I repeat, the disappointment clear in my whisper. "But I need to start now. I need to get back there now."

"No one expects you to move mountains on your first try. Be gentle with yourself. Even the biggest task starts with smaller steps. And we can't do anything until we get this little matter of kidnapping and murder cleared up." The euphoria of a new world order fades away as CJ worms his way back into my current world. "Let me manage things in the capital. I'll take care of it. You stay here—stay safe—and then, once it's done, you'll join me, and we can announce our engagement. Then, we can get to work." He smiles sweetly down at me, and I'm fully aware I'm being placated.

"If I came with you, and we announced the engagement now—"

"They won't have it yet. I hate to even mention it, but the institute brings a lot of money into the country, and there are still five women left. Plus you." I step back, pulling my hands free of his. He flinches, but he lets me go just the same. "I have to pick and choose my battles. Right now, my priority is keeping you safe, making sure everything in Rocky Point is managed, lay the groundwork to have *Beck* pardoned." I don't miss the way he spits his name.

I understand what he's saying, but I want to do something. I don't want to wait. I know I'm out of my depth where politics are concerned, but I do, however, know what it's like to be cast aside, and this feels all-too-close to being exactly that. The weight of it settles in my stomach like a stone.

"What if I start the campaign now?" I ask.

"And how would you do that?" he says, smiling. He crosses his arms over his chest.

"Where are the graduates? What if I could meet with them? Start bringing them to my side?"

Declan leans back, looking uneasy. "It's not quite so simple."

"What's not?"

"Finding them."

"What's that supposed to mean?" My heart hammers in my chest. If they can't find the graduates, then what about the girls who don't even get that far? What does this mean for Zerah?

"It means that placing graduates within certain governments doesn't mean we know where they are . . . at present." There's something stilted in his tone.

"So, then, how do we do this? Even after the fact?"

"Well, we wait until graduation, and see who shows up—"

"But you said they don't show up—"

"—and then we talk with them and their partners and plant the seed."

"How many?" I ask, narrowing my eyes at him.

"How many, what?"

"How many graduates come each year? Over all the years, all the women who've graduated from the institute, how many come?"

"Honestly?" he says, brushing the hair from his eyes. "Maybe a handful each year."

"A handful?"

"Yes."

"And let me guess. They're close personal supporters of your parents and will vote however your mother wants them to?"

"I suppose—what does my mother have to do with this?" he asks, and I roll my eyes at the fact that the one thing he takes issue with is that.

"It's not going to work, then. Not that way."

"That's why I said baby steps."

"Well, baby steps might work where you're from, but they mean jack all where I'm from." From somewhere behind me, I swear I hear low, throaty laughter.

"Arden," he says, leaning closer, placing his hands on my upper arms. "I know you want to act. That you want to do something. But right now, you're not exactly safe. It would be dangerous to insert yourself into places where you don't belong." His words ring hollow in my chest, and it must show on my face. He drops his hands, a grimace hovering in the edges of his mouth.

"Where I don't belong?" I repeat. He blows out his cheeks and rubs at the back of his neck.

"You know what I mean—places where people sympathetic to Nordania might want to make a quick buck and return you" —he holds up the crumpled, horrible poster—"and your companion."

"So, we'll be sneaky. Beck is good at sneaky."

"I'll bet he is," Declan says under his breath.

"Stop it," I say, my voice sharp. "You're the one who thought this was a good idea. I'm the one who has to live it. I'm the one stuck on a stinky ship with stinky men and stinky . . . well, it was just really stinky. And then riding across the countryside on a horse—have you ever ridden a horse?"

"Yes—"

"Well, it's not my favorite experience ever, especially while being chased—"

"Chased?" His eyes go wide and concern fills his features.

"Yes. Chased, Declan. And now, here you are, proposing a beautiful, horse-free future that smells like mint and basil and never another stinky ship—"

"I didn't quite say that—" he interrupts, and I level a seething glare at him. He nods and mumbles, "Noted. Never again a stinky ship."

"And then you tell me that I can't come back. That I need support. Well, if I can't come back anyway, let me find some damn support."

He sighs and squints at his long, elegant fingers, giving me a moment to calm down. It felt good, though. To rant and rage and stand up for myself. Standing here, I realize just how long it's been since I've done anything of the sort.

"There is one girl . . . in Nordania. She might help." He looks uncomfortable.

"There's a graduate in Nordania?" I ask. I can't think of any graduates who would have ended up there. That's not the point of the institute.

"Not a graduate," he says, clearing his throat. His cheeks flush, and his jaw tightens. "It's . . ." He trails off and scrubs his face with his hand.

"Who?"

"She was at the institute a few years ago. She left early. But I've been led to understand she's in communication with several graduates."

"What makes you think that?"

He sighs and finally meets my gaze. "She told me."

I blink and take him in. Really take him in. He looks more uncomfortable talking about this than just about any other topic we've ever covered. He continues to stare at my face, his expression careful and guarded, and I wonder whether I should push for the details of his tension around this girl, or if I should just take what I can get and focus on the win.

"You think she would talk to me?"

The corner of his mouth quirks, and his face softens.

"I think she would love you . . . eventually." He chuckles to himself and lets his head hang back.

"So, where is she?" I ask. His mouth goes tight again, and he exhales hard, crossing his arms again.

"I don't know."

"You don't know?"

"I don't know."

"But you've been in communication with her? Enough to know she's in touch with some of the other graduates?"

"Yes," he says, scrubbing his face again.

"So, I'm just supposed to, what? Ask around?"

He shakes his head and looks up, his eyes locking on something behind me. "Beck knows where she is."

My stomach drops. It's the most unpleasant feeling, like the ground I'm walking on has fallen out from underneath me, and a flush of something hot fills my chest.

"Oh," I say, as if there's nothing else. And perhaps there isn't. I've long wondered what the source of vitriol between them is, and now, perhaps, I've found it.

"Will he take me to her?" I ask. Declan shrugs one shoulder, and his eyes shift slowly back to meet mine.

"Only one way to find out, I suppose."

A pounding at the door startles us.

"Time's up, lovebirds," Beck shouts from the other side. "Time to quit yer necking." A familiar, ugly weight settles onto my shoulders as the door creaks open behind me. I turn, and Beck is standing there, holding the door open with one hand. His gaze locks on mine briefly, some sort of question lurking in its depths, and then the facade is back. He wavers where he stands, looking nothing more than the part of a man too deep in his cups. Declan nods at him, then straightens his back, grabbing his coat off the back of the chair and, as only a victor could, crossing the small room to shake Beck's hand. Beck stares at it for a moment, as if waiting for it to do a magic trick.

"What's the plan?" Beck asks, eyes flicking back up to find mine.

"I'm going with you," I say. Something flickers across his gaze, but then he blinks, and it's gone.

"Lucky me," he deadpans.

"Thank you for taking such good care of her," Delcan says. I can just make out the flare of Beck's pupils. He scratches at his beard, and then accepts Declan's hand.

"Well, sure. She's, uh, easy"—he smirks, scratching the side of his nose—"to take care of." If I thought I could manage Hammerhead by myself, I would punch Beck in the kidneys and just leave him here. Declan drops his hand a touch faster than Beck can, but it doesn't matter. Beck won the handshake.

Declan turns to me and kisses me again, harder, pulling me tighter against his body.

"Soon," he whispers, just loud enough that I'm certain Beck can hear. "I'll be the one with the ring." I smile despite the fact that I know exactly what he's doing, and it has very little to do with me. Declan starts to back away, and I pull him back into me, wrapping my arms around his neck.

"I trust you," I whisper in his ear. He grows still, and then squeezes me into him once more, this time with a sharp tenderness that was missing just moments ago.

Then he's gone, pulling on his coat as he goes, once more a faceless stranger in a northern port town.

"Well, that was sweet, wasn't it?" Beck says, arms crossed over his chest, drunken facade once more gone in an instant. His thick eyebrows are curved in skeptical wiggles, and his clear gaze glitters in the low lamplight.

"Don't be an asshole," I say.

"Oh, please don't take that from me . . ." he says. He steps away from the door, and I move to follow him, but he stops, blocking the doorway. He reaches out and slips my scarf back up over my hair, his fingers hot and just a tiny bit hesitant against my cheek. "You look like you just got the runaround. Better watch that neck, Capo," he says.

And just like that, I'm back in Beck's world.

CHAPTER SIXTEEN

*I*f I thought the trip to New Covington was difficult, I was grossly unprepared for the trip inland. We set off at first light, when the sea mist hung heavy in the air, mixing with the stench of fish, spilled beer, and bad decisions. It was the second time we'd slipped out of a port town, but this time, we went the opposite direction. Beck's shoulders seemed heavier, but I never saw him cast a backward glance at the sea. I did, though, wondering if this was the right decision, and if it was the wrong one, would I ever find my way back?

Our horses climb higher and higher, but the compass hanging around my neck remains constant as we travel west by southwest. With each labored breath in the thinning air, I'm reminded of my tattoo and Scio's great mountains. The terrain shifts as we climb, the green-gold, sky-high trees making way for gold-and-brown, drought-tolerant brush.

The air grows crisper, colder, and thinner, requiring that much more work on my part and even more for Sir Squints-a-Lot. We take more breaks for the horses because, as Beck says, "Horses are people, too."

There seems to be no one trailing us, but we take no

chances, leaving behind no trace. Beck even tries to cover some of the horse dung, either relocating it, or burning it for fuel. Suffice it to say, we sleep warm, but we don't smell great.

I'm picking mud from my boots with a stick while we water the horses when he shoves me. I fall, landing on my hands and knees.

"What the hell?" I yell, jumping to my feet. He bats at my shoulder again, pushing a wry smile into his right cheek and exposing his dimple. He removes the orange peel he'd been chewing on and tosses it into the nearby brush.

"You've lost your edge, Capo."

"Excuse me?" I ask.

"You've been out of practice too long. You know what to do. Come on, Capo."

"Okay—enough. You keep calling me that. What's a Capo?" I ask.

"Someone who's lost their edge," he says with a grin. His eyes almost glitter green and gold in the sunlight. He swings at my waist, and I catch his arm.

"That's better," he says. He reaches for my other side, and I block his grab while spinning away from the opposite arm that swings in to get me.

"Better luck next time, grab-hands," I say.

"That's not even an insult," he says. "It's a fact." He lunges toward me, squinting into the light, looking for a vulnerable spot. He swings his leg, reaching for my neck, and I hunch forward, shoving my shoulder into his stomach. I push him back into a tree, and he coughs and laughs, patting me on the back. I take a step back, victory-smile in place.

"You think you're smart there, Capo?" he asks.

"I don't think—" But I don't finish my comeback as my feet fly out beneath me. He sweeps them away, and I fall on my ass. Hard. Pain shoots up from my tailbone, and all I can do is roll onto my hip, laughing to keep from crying. He bends over and offers me a hand. I smack it out of the way and push myself off the hard red earth on my own.

"Don't gloat. It's not ladylike," he says.

"I'm not a lady," I say.

"It's also bad defense." His words are clearer now; I'm meant to learn from this. I arch my back, giving room for my sore butt to relax.

"You're just a sore loser," I say. He coughs a smirk.

"Maybe, but I'm not the one with a broken ass." I shake my head and rub at the tender spot. It's going to be awful to ride on, that's for sure.

"When do we leave?" I ask, hoping he'll say I have some time before I have to get on Sir Squints-a-Lot.

"Soon," he says, scratching at his dark scruff. Glints of gold flash in his dark hair, reflecting the sunlight. "I'm going to go clean off real quick, then we can head out. If we don't dawdle, we should make it there by nightfall. Sooner if the horses are feeling frisky." My stomach twists into molten lead. I'll be immersed in Beck's world then. Surrounded by Beck's people — not just the ones who work for him, but the people who raised him, who made him who he is. If I'm not supposed to trust Beck, what am I to think of his family?

I stare at his back as he walks down the slope to the river, which twists in a long, arching bend not fifty yards from here. He drops his trousers as he walks, kicking them back toward me, and I don't look away quickly enough to not see the curve of his moon-white backside.

"At least buy a guy a drink first!" he yells back, stripping off his shirt. He leaves it on the ground, as well. My cheeks flush, and I check the packs on Hammerhead, tightening the straps to make sure they're secure. The horses and I have brokered a sort of peace — they've come to tolerate my presence, and I don't completely hate them. Or at least, that's how I'm choosing to interpret the fact that Squints hasn't tried to buck me off all day.

Under Hammerhead's suspicious glare, I push a dislodged blanket back into the saddlebag. Something crunches from inside the bag. I remove the thick blanket and unfold it. The brown envelope that'd been hidden inside falls to the ground.

I take a quick look toward the river as I pick it up, but I don't see Beck. There's a little copse of aspens where the river curves—he must be beyond it. Turning so that my back is to the river, I open the envelope. Inside is a fat stack of greenbacks. There must be hundreds of them. Tucked into the front is a small piece of paper. Written in perfect, cursive handwriting, it says:

In consideration of your recent acquisition and continued assistance with our special issue. ~ S.E.L.

Everything goes quiet as blood rushes into my ears. What the hell is Beck doing to get this kind of money? It's not from Declan—but those are Siobhan's initials. If Siobhan knows what we're up to, what is it she's asked Beck to do?

"Find something interesting?" Beck's voice is like ice. I startle and whirl. He's standing right behind me. His eyebrows are low, and with the sun behind his head, there's no light in his eyes, leaving them deadened jade discs.

"What is this?" I ask, hoping he doesn't hear the quiver in my voice.

"None of your business," he says. He swipes it from my hands with very little effort and shoves it back into the saddlebag. His hair drips on me as he takes the blanket from under my arm and shoves it back into the saddlebag, too.

"Who is paying you that kind of money?" I ask, though I know darn well whose handwriting that was. He pulls a rumpled shirt out of the same saddlebag and pulls it on over his head. I hadn't actually noticed he wasn't fully clothed, and my cheeks flush with embarrassed heat. He finishes packing up and unties Hammerhead, his silence frigid and pointed.

"Nobody just gives you that kind of money for nothing.

What have you done?" He ignores me a second time, unties Sir Squints-a-Lot, and hands me the reins. Then he swings himself up onto Hammerhead and clicks his teeth. Sir Squints-a-Lot whinnies, not wanting to be left behind with just me, and I clamber up onto him. Squints hurries to keep up with Beck and Hammerhead, and I lean down into him to keep pace. With every hoofbeat, my butt screams, and I clench my thighs to keep from hitting the saddle more than necessary. It's hard to think around the literal pain in my ass, but the pit in my stomach is growing. Maybe Declan was right. Maybe it is wrong to trust Beck. He's certainly not giving me a reason to right now.

Every time I catch up to him, he clicks his heels into Hammerhead's haunches, and I have to work harder to catch up. The climb is less apparent today, but it's still a workout for the horses. I wait for him to slow down and let the horses rest, but he doesn't. We're getting closer and closer to the behemoth known as the Hildegarden Mountain Range. It looms ahead, its snowy peaks coming into ever greater detail. Behind us, the plain seems to drop off, with nothing but sky beyond it. I have no idea how high we've climbed, but the sky looms larger above us, and I start to feel untethered so far from the ocean. We could be anywhere. I have no idea where we're going, or how to get back. I am completely at his mercy here, and despite the cool breeze, sweat beads along my hairline.

By the time I've caught up with him again, my tailbone is screaming in pain and the river is closer than ever.

"Stop. Now," I say, jerking on Sir Squints-a-Lot's reins. He fights me and bucks.

I cling onto him, but it makes him even madder, and he kicks. I lose my balance and fall off the side. He starts to run, but I grip his reins, and my feet drag in the dirt. He gallops alongside the river, moving closer and closer to the wild rapids. His hooves are too close to the edge, and I pull my feet ahead of me, digging my heels into the earth. We're both kicking up rocks and red dirt, and it's hard to keep my eyes open.

Suddenly, he slows and veers away from the rapids.

"Easy boy," I hear Beck say, and Sir Squints-a-Lot finally slows to a stop. When I open my eyes, Beck is on the ground, whispering to my horse, and I'm inches from going in the river.

"Give me the reins, Capo," he says, and the nickname gets under my skin. I whip them at him, and he walks ten feet down the river with both animals. I get my feet more securely under me, and by the time I've caught my breath, he's back in my face.

"What in Scio's name is wrong with you?" he asks, grabbing me by the arms with enough force to shake me.

"What's wrong with me? What's wrong with you?" I spit back, shoving him off of me.

"Nothing's wrong with me. I'm trying to keep you alive, while you constantly insist on trying to kill yourself. But I've got a wad of cash in my pack, so I'm obviously the villain. You, on the other hand, are a real pain in the ass, *Capo*."

"Why won't you just tell me what that money is for? I know who it's from. Are you doing something dangerous? Something illegal?"

"Obviously!" he shouts, flapping his large hands back and forth between us. "What the fuck do you think is happening here? That we're taking an extended day trip for the hell of it? No, Arden. I'm kidnapping you. And then you fucking killed someone on the way out of town! I'm literally harboring a fugitive, and oh yeah—*you*. Are. A. Fugitive."

Heat rises from my chest, peppering my skin with bursts of flame, working its way up my neck, twisting, pulling tighter and tighter. I suck in air as my throat tightens. The air sticks, like blood coating my lungs, choking me, drowning me.

"Beck, please. What is the money for?" I ask again, my voice a hollow croak, cracking with fear and emotion swelling too fast to control. I attempt to breathe again and can't get it past my neck muscles. He's obviously taking money from Siobhan to do something with me—to me. He's admitted it himself: he's a villain. And we're out here, isolated, alone in the middle of nowhere. He could do anything he wants. The world tilts as I look around me, wild, unfocused and too focused all at once. I can't breathe.

"Arden, calm down," he says, his voice low. He steps toward me, as if he knows I'm onto him. Like he knows I'm about to bolt. I flinch away from him, stumbling back. I try to suck in a breath, but the air is too thin.

"What are you going to do with me?" I'm whispering now. I can't control my voice. I can't control him. I can't even control the land around me as it rises to meet my hands. The river and the terrain get fuzzy. I'm hunched on the ground, curling into myself as if that will keep me intact. I can't feel my face or my hands, or my arms. He's talking, trying to say something, but I can't hear it past the rushing blood in my ears and the gasping wheeze of my overtaxed lungs. Then I'm floating, the ground falling away from my eyes. I close them and whimper, the sound choked and terrifying. I move against the rise and fall of his chest and again, he's telling me something, but I'm not understanding. He carries me to his horse, and I finally hear him tell me to hang on. Then we're climbing into the forest, and there are rocks, and I just want to close my eyes. So I do.

CHAPTER SEVENTEEN

he scent of moldy hay and horse shit assaults my nose as my cheek scratches against a blanket. I push up too fast and see stars as my head spins. My heart feels like it might ignite, it's beating so hard, and I'm already backing away, even before I see him standing across the barn from me. A feral whimper escapes my lips, but then I focus on his legs, on his pants tied at his ankles over his favorite boots, on his square, calloused hands. Beck. Not CJ.

I'm awake. This is real.

"Where?" I try to whisper. My mouth is cottony, and he presses his canteen to my lips.

"Drink," he says.

"I don't want it," I say. My voice is scratchy.

"Drink."

"No," I say. He tips the contents back into his mouth, then holds it down to me. It doesn't smell like spirits, and I realize how thirsty I am. I take it and drink back the rest of the water, feeling it soothe the sharp pain in my throat.

"Where are we?" I ask, finishing my first question.

"Abandoned mine town called Forthweld. About half a days' ride from home."

"Why?"

"Because you can't just attack me, or have a meltdown, or whatever that was out there in the open. In case you haven't noticed, we're wanted criminals, and if someone wants to find us, you just made it real fucking easy, Capo."

"Are we being followed?" I ask. He shakes his head to cover a subtle wince.

"I don't think so . . ." I can hear the invisible *but* hanging there. I take another sip. He stays quiet while I drink and inhale the stink of the barn.

"So, you gonna tell me what that money's for?" I ask.

"It's for kidnapping you." His words are so matter-of-fact, I think I've misheard them.

"What?" I ask, my eyes flying back to his face. His jaw is stony, and his eyes are hard.

"It's from Siobhan. A thank-you for getting you out of there and keeping you out of there."

"Because it was so unsafe for me?" My voice is bitter. We both know she couldn't care less if I was dead or alive. "Does Declan know?" He shakes his head.

"Doubt it."

"But he asked you —"

"Yeah, I know what he asked me. And I'm doing it. I just figured I could maybe make a little money from the situation, if I'm going to be putting my neck on the line."

"So, you're making money off of me," I say, spitting out the bitter words.

"Of course I am."

"Then what's stopping you from selling me to a bounty hunter? I mean, that Buck What's-His-Butt would probably pay a pretty penny for me. You could make twice what Siobhan's paying you."

"He doesn't have that kind of money," he says, his voice flat and humorless.

Is this the moment I find out what I'm worth? After all these years of hearing and internalizing CJ's assessment—that I'm worthless—is this the moment I could actually find out? The mother of the man I'm supposed to marry has apparently decided what I'm worth—and Beck, my only friend, took that money. Beck agrees that this is what I'm worth. He accepted a price on my life. I look at the floor, turning my eyes and whatever they'll likely betray to the ground.

"Well, someone else then?" I say, surprised to hear more venom than pain in my voice. "There's got to be a bigger dog somewhere."

"I'm sure there is."

"If that's all this is, then why not just sell me to the highest bidder?"

"What makes you think I haven't already?" he asks, his voice dangerously low. Cold goosebumps climb my arms, and my eyes lift to his in shock. His neck muscles twitch as he stares back at me, and he blinks too fast. If I didn't know better, I would think that small, broken part of him I saw in New Covington was lurking behind the cracks in his icy facade. *I know you think you know him . . .*

But the thing is, I do. I do know him. Don't I? Part of me trusts the man he's shown me, the one who's saved me from storms and monsters, who soothes and protects, but another part, the part twisted and scarred by CJ, steeped in recent doubt by the boy I'm set to marry—that part screams that those things can't be true. That it's all a lie. That I can't trust him. I can't trust anyone.

I don't say anything. I let him stare me down, let him hurl his anger at me for another moment, until he steps away, shaking his head.

"I should," he says to himself, but still loud enough that I can hear. He keeps his distance, his arms crossed, and he doesn't turn back around.

"How much am I worth?" I ask. Vitriol pumps in my veins, fueled by years of suppressed, invisible scars. Scars he's now laid bare.

"Be serious, Arden," he says, turning his head slightly. All I can see is his profile, and it's unreadable.

"I am. If you're being paid, I want to know my price."

His jaw ticks, but he doesn't turn around. "It's not that simple." He won't look at me, staring at the wall instead, keeping his face in the narrow shadows.

"You're a fucking coward," I say, and he doesn't argue with me.

He rubs his nose with his forefinger and opens his mouth, like he wants to get the last word in. But nothing comes out. He drops his hands, letting them smack against his thighs, and leaves.

The barn is large, but missing slats in too many places, letting in light, but not allowing for air circulation. Who knows how many years of dung and mildew sits composting beneath me. I don't like barns any more than I like sheds. They all smell the same. But I take my time, breathing in the stagnant air, filling my lungs, letting them recuperate from whatever episode I had out there.

Is this why Declan told me not to trust Beck? Maybe Declan knows? Or at least suspected it? Siobhan made no secret of disliking me. I should have expected it. I was foolish not to.

The thing is, I don't blame Beck for wanting to get something out of this. The downside for him is career suicide and maybe even imprisonment. If our roles had been reversed, I'm not sure I would have taken the risk. I just wish he'd told me. If he'd told me, I would have agreed. I would have offered to help. But he didn't give me the choice.

He used me, just like Conrad.

I stand and brush the muck and straw off my clothes, then go out into the fading light. His frame is silhouetted in the open door of a nearby building. The direction of the sun inflates his height into a mountain of rough edges and hard angles. He turns, and the shadows seem to carve away the granite, crumbling the rocky shape. He may have had his reasons for keeping this from me — for using me. But it ends now.

"I want you to take me somewhere," I say.

"You're making demands?" he asks, quirking an eyebrow.

"You want to tell me how much money you think I'm worth?" I spit back, my voice pure acid. He raises his palms in surrender.

"What do you want?"

"Declan said there's a girl —"

"There's always a girl."

"That she used to be at the institute, but she's not anymore."

"This girl got a name?" His tone is cautious, his jaw tight. Something unreadable glints in his eyes.

"No," I say, embarrassed that I didn't think to ask. Maybe I didn't want to know. "But she's in communication with other graduates. And Declan said you know where she is."

Beck stands for a long time, staring off into the distance. Then he scratches his cheek and nods. "I do know where she is."

"You're going to take me to her."

"And if I don't?" Beck asks, though there's an air of amusement in his voice. I open my mouth, but I don't really have a response. I'm not going to turn him in. I'm not going to turn myself in. Even if he is loud and angry and smells annoyingly not unpleasant, I wouldn't do that to him.

"You named my price," I say. "Take me there, or tell me how much I'm worth."

His shoulders fall, and he nods. "Yeah, okay."

"Thank you," I say. He nods, but doesn't say anything else.

"Now, if your family isn't the most magical group of people this side of the mountains, you're giving me half of whatever's in that envelope," I say. He regards me for a moment, and then the corner of his mouth curls up into a smirk.

"We can work out your cut once you've met them."

CHAPTER EIGHTEEN

*T*he farm is just as I imagined, and so much more. It's not so much a farm as a ranch, sprawling over what seems like never-ending acreage of sagebrush and grassland. The farmhouse is the first thing I see—two stories of cardinal-red siding, with white trim around large picture windows. Wooden rocking chairs dot the wraparound porch, and boxes of yellow mums and dahlias perch on the railing. Behind the house, I see a massive barn with a second-story wall of glass. That must be Beck's barn. I watch him as we draw closer, and a little smile creeps into his features, the tension that's lingered between us finally fracturing, shedding off to trail in our wake.

The horses seem to know we're almost there, picking up the pace and closing the distance to their next watering hole with renewed energy. It seems an odd location to hide in, but when I see bodies waiting for us on the porch, it's evident it's an even worse place to attack. Squints's hooves beat in time with my heart as the bodies get bigger and faces come into focus. By the time we're there, the faces are upon us, pulling Beck down from Hammerhead with enthusiastic grins and eager arms.

It's easy to figure out who is who. An older man with a

square jaw and golden hair hanging into his eyes shakes Beck's hand with a wry smile. He rubs the side of his nose and claps him on the back. Beck's father.

"You couldn't call ahead?" he asks.

"You know how it is," Beck says to a woman who can only be described as beautiful. Her ebony hair is woven into a long braid down her back, and her green-gold eyes shine against the almost silky bronze of her skin.

"You should call more," she says.

"Your mother worries," his father adds.

"It's a mother's right," she says, tussling his hair.

"And your mother is never wrong," his father says, before Beck can argue. Beck laughs, shaking his head as he walks over to Sir Squints-a-Lot. He holds the reins so I can slide down.

"That's Arden," he says with no fanfare. I slip on my way down, and he catches me. But then he backs away a touch too quickly, as if suddenly remembering we have an audience, and I bobble on my feet like a newborn egret.

"Welcome, That's Arden," his father repeats with a wide smile, exposing a dimple in his right cheek. He reaches out a hand, and I shake it.

"Just Arden," I say.

"Ammon," he says, and then clarifies, adding, "Senior." The warmth from his smile creeps into the well-worn lines framing the rest of his face.

"Hi," I say, coming up empty for something more eloquent.. His mother squeezes Beck in a hug, forcing him to bend over to fit in her long arms. I'm surprised he has to bend over so much. She seemed so much taller, more imposing. But he folds over, letting her cup the back of his head with her long fingers, and as she holds him, I see more of the boy he once was, the boy she still sees. She pulls away and turns to me. Her eyes slowly move over my face, pausing, analyzing, and I blush under her scrutiny, chewing on the side of my tongue.

"What do you say we head inside for something to drink? You must be exhausted. This one doesn't like to take breaks on the way."

"No, he doesn't," I say. His mother watches me for a moment more before letting her eyes flit back to Beck. A warm smile widens her mouth as she crosses the distance and embraces me in a tight hug.

"I'm Galina," she says, stepping back and holding my upper arms with her long fingers. Up close, she is even more beautiful, and the smattering of freckles across her nose and cheeks make her look far too young to have two grown sons. "The others will be here soon. Let's get a head start on some iced tea." She narrows one eye at me and chuckles to herself, then turns and wraps an arm around Beck, walking him in while Ammon Sr. takes the horses' reins, both of whom go with him without hesitation. I follow Beck and Galina up the steps and through the solid oak front door.

The house is somehow both sparse and rich in decor. The furniture is hand-crafted and functional, while still suiting the space perfectly. In the living room, where I wait alone, leather armchairs flank a large stone fireplace. The thick, raw-edged hardwood mantle displays wooden frames with photographs of two young, dark-haired boys. Bookcases stack on either side of the fireplace, well-worn covers and a few sentimental knickknacks scattered among the shelves. Tucked back in the corner furthest from the fireplace is a piano, and leaning against it is a banjo. I can't picture Beck sitting around playing a banjo. But then, I can, and the image is so playful and perfect, I have to chew on my bottom lip to keep from laughing.

The front door swings open, startling me, and a woman strides in. She wears dark denim pants, a loose green flannel shirt, and a denim jacket. Her long, mahogany hair is swept back into a neat, low ponytail, and her wide brown eyes find me before I can say anything. She smiles softly, in a way that is intimidatingly pretty, and looks over her shoulder as a tall, very handsome man enters.

"Hi," he says, his voice low and shockingly similar to Beck's. "I'm Ammon." He closes the door and shares a wide, wry smile, exposing a neat pair of dimples. His blue eyes are a shock against his bronze skin, and I can see instantly that he takes more after his mother than Beck does. Where Beck is sharp and square, Ammon is long and tall. Actually tall, not just the illusion of tall. He is surprisingly handsome in a way I didn't expect and between the two of them, I feel like a mess.

"Arden . . . Ammon?" I ask, understanding the *senior* his father added earlier.

"The second," he says with an even wider smile. "This is Emlyn." She steps into the room to stand next to him and nods with a warm, but reserved smile. There's something about her that catches my eye, and I find it hard to look away. Something familiar?

"Hi," she says, her voice deeper than I expected based on her fine, delicate features, but as she stands next to Ammon, I can see that she is also long and tall. She extends her hand, and her fingers are impossibly long and calloused. Even her calluses seem pretty.

"You're a friend of Beck's?" Ammon asks, filling the space with a genuine friendliness that seems foreign to my idea of Beck.

"Yes," I say, the word catching in my throat.

"Ah, there they are. I thought I heard them come in," Galina says, walking into the room, running her hand up and down Emlyn's arm as she enters. Beck follows, carrying a tray that holds a white stoneware pitcher and six green glass tumblers.

"There's the old pirate himself," Ammon Jr. says, clapping his brother on the back, forcing him to grip the tray more steadily so as not to spill. The exchanged smile between them tells me Beck expected this, though.

"How you doin', snotrag?" Beck asks, giving his brother a mock-concerned look. "How's he doing?" he asks Emlyn. "Did he tell you about his secret foot condition yet?"

"I think I know all his secrets by now," Emlyn says with a less polite giggle.

"Even the—" Beck nods toward Ammon and makes a squeak, followed by a grunting sound.

"Oh, that?" she says with feigned disgust. "Yes, it was a tough pill to swallow, but we've worked through it, and we're stronger for it."

"You hear that? She loves me anyway." Ammon wraps his arms around Emlyn and kisses the top of her head.

"Well, isn't that sweet," Beck says, setting down the tray and looking over his shoulder at Emlyn. "You do wear a mask, though?"

"Oh, every night," she quips, and we all laugh. I can't stop staring at Emlyn. She's beautiful and funny and quick. And poised. And so familiar . . .

Galina starts pouring the iced tea, and Emlyn sits in a chair, while Ammon leans on the arm. Galina hands me a glass and points to a chair opposite them. I sit. I give the glass a little sniff, and it really is iced tea. I think part of me expected Beck's family to drink nothing but whiskey and rum.

"So, you were just in the neighborhood?" Ammon asks, and I chew on the edge of my tongue. I'm not sure what Beck wants to tell them—or what he's willing to tell them, anyway.

"Something like that," Beck says with his trademark smirk. He's standing off to the side, his arms crossed against his chest, hovering as though preparing himself for an attack. The air in the room is heavy, as if they're all waiting for Beck to drop a bomb.

"How long will you stay?" Galina asks.

"I'm not sure. Somewhere between a bit and a while."

"Very specific," Ammon says.

"I pride myself on my specificity," Beck says. The door opens and Ammon Sr. enters, removing his shoes before he walks into the room.

"Don't mind if I do," he says, reaching for a glass.

"I do," Galina says, blocking him with nothing more than her glare. "Wash your hands first."

"Yes, dear," he says, walking backward into what I assume must be the kitchen.

"Where'd you get the horses?" his brother asks.

"Kern's," Beck says. "Where'd you get the ring?" Emlyn blushes, and Ammon's smile falters, then spreads, making him somehow more beautiful than before. Emlyn curls her long fingers into fists and then lets them relax, exposing a flat copper ring on her left hand.

"We didn't know how to reach you. Didn't want to wait any longer." The room goes still in a way I don't imagine it does often. His words are happy, but concise, his meaning clear to everyone in the room, except me.

"You got married?" I ask, and they suddenly remember me. All eyes turn to me, kind, but daring me to say another word. "Congratulations," I say softly, but it doesn't sound like I mean it.

"Thank you," Emlyn says, just as softly. Ammon squeezes her into his side and kisses her head again. He can hardly say two words without touching her in some way. She smiles up at him, placing her banded hand on his knee.

"Yes, congratulations," Beck says, his voice strained. I don't know why he would be upset by his brother marrying this girl. I thought he liked her. He doesn't seem the sentimental type, to be offended for not receiving a formal invitation.

"What'd I miss?" his father says, coming back into the room.

"Beck's pouting about missing out on the wedding soup," Ammon Jr. says.

"Oh, that soup was damn good," his father says. "And, well, he should figure out a way to call more often."

"Get a phone, and I'll call," Beck says.

"You know the system. You can reach us if you want to," his father says.

"Fine, I'll call the next time you decide to get married," Beck says, his tone as sharp as his smile.

"Fudgling hollyballs, do you want us to reenact it for you?" Ammon asks, taking Emlyn's glass from her and pulling her to her feet. "Okay, it went something like this. Do you?"

"I do. Do you?" she says with a soft giggle.

"I do. Now we—" He kisses her full and soft on the lips, and then twists her into a little dip before he props her back on her feet. "And then there was soup." I try and fail to stifle a laugh.

"And cake," Galina adds.

"You ate cake without me?" Beck says, horrorstruck.

"Meh, it was just honey cake," Ammon says.

"Oh, if it'd been chocolate . . ." Beck says.

"I thought you loved my honey cake?" Emlyn says, looking hurt. I catch Beck's eye. He smirks and one eyebrow twitches up just slightly, and I bite my tongue to keep from laughing at something that was not intended to sound like the filthy joke we're both trying not to laugh at.

"I do love your honey cake. I just don't want anyone else to." They laugh, and Beck and I laugh too hard, our heads still in the gutter. Emlyn and Ammon are so cute, it's almost too much. But somehow, it's not. They're just two pretty people who found each other and fell in love, and there's something so refreshing about being in a room full of people who love them, as well.

"Well, would you two like to get cleaned up? I've got dumplings ready to go for dinner." Beck raises an eyebrow at me, and I bite my tongue again. How in the world do *dumplings* sound dirty? Galina starts to retrieve the empty glasses, but Ammon Sr. stops her, taking charge of the clean-up process.

"That would be nice, but . . ." I say, not sure how to explain that I have no other clothes.

"I'm sure we can dig up something a bit warmer for you, dear. The nights get cold in these parts. I love my son, but he's not very good at planning," she says, giving me an out I very much appreciate.

"Yes, thank you," I say.

"Emlyn, can you help with the linens?"

"Actually," Beck says, moving over to where I'm sitting and setting a too-comfortable hand on my shoulder. "I think we'll stay in the loft."

The room goes quiet, and I swear they can all hear my heart beating through my neck. Apparently, this is what we're doing. We're playing these roles for his family's benefit. Everyone looks from Beck to each other. Everyone but Emlyn, whose wide brown eyes meet mine with a mix of shrewd curiosity and concern — and then hone in on my chest, to where my fingers are fidgeting with Declan's compass hanging around my neck.

"Okay," Galina says, as I drop the compass. A wary smile creeps into the soft folds around her eyes. "At least let the girl use the bathroom upstairs."

"Oh," he says, and I can just hear the blush in his voice. "Sure. I mean, if you like hot water and a shower. I don't know if that's really her thing?"

"It's my thing," I say quickly, and everyone laughs.

"All right, follow Emlyn. She'll get you squared away up there," Galina says.

Emlyn casts a quick look at Ammon, and then rises. I follow her as she leads me out of the room. She says nothing else to me, and I can't help but get the feeling she's made some sort of decision about me that I can't undo. She opens a small closet and pulls out a thick white towel, then opens a door to the bathroom and sets it on the sink.

"I'll get you some clothes," she says with a pinched smile. There's no way her clothes are going to fit me. I'm not short, but I'm certain that if I tried to wear her pants, I would trip all over them. Nor will Beck's mother's clothes fit me. But she returns from a room down the hall with a stack of clothes—denim and wool. I accept them and hope I don't look like a fool. I nod a thank-you and reach to close the bathroom door, but she stands there, watching me, her brown eyes boring into me, dropping to my wrist with the speed of a striking snake. I pull my hand back, covering the bracelet that had been on display, tucking it back up into my sleeve.

"What is it?" I ask. She hesitates for a minute, biting her lower lip.

"You're—" she starts, and then stops. Her eyes drop to my chest again, where I've tucked away the compass beneath my shirt. Beck has told them nothing more than my name. But her eyes see through me. She sees that I'm trouble, that I bring trouble, and that she's been deprived of a choice in the matter.

She clears her throat. "You're going to want to shower quickly. The hot water doesn't last." Her eyes are serious, her words a warning, and even once I'm under the hot water, I can't seem to get warm again.

CHAPTER NINETEEN

*T*he barn is massive. It's also freezing.

The space clearly hasn't been heated recently, and despite what I'm sure must be a stunning view of the valley, the windows aren't particularly well insulated. But being cold isn't for lack of fabric. Draped in the clothes Emlyn loaned me, I feel both over and underdressed. I have so much fabric that I'm stepping on it. I'm not short, but Emlyn is tall. Or at least her legs are.

The space is short on lighting, but Beck builds a fire quickly, and I can make out more of his spartan furnishings. Honestly, though, I just want to go to sleep. Unfortunately, as the room glows more fully into view, that appears to be the first of our problems.

"It's nice," I say, my arms wrapped around my body as I stand as close to the fireplace as possible without setting Emlyn's soft pajamas on fire.

"It'll be nicer in the morning, when you can see out the windows," he says, converting his simple wooden sofa into a bed. I look around the space, and while it is spacious, it is sparsely furnished. This appears to be the only bed.

"Don't worry your head there, Capo," Beck says, crossing the space to a large trunk set against the back wall. He retrieves a stack of pillows and blankets and walks back. "I'll be honorable and give you the bed."

"You don't have to do that," I say. The return of the nickname is bittersweet. It's the first time he's called me that since we left Forthweld, but I still don't know what it means, and I can't help but think it's not flattering.

"I know," he says with a shrug, tossing a pillow directly at my face. I catch it just in time for the pillowcase to hit my forehead.

"Where will you sleep?" I ask, putting the pillow into the pillowcase. It's not that I really want to give up the bed, but it's cold in here, and I definitely don't want him to leave me here by myself.

"Chair is perfectly comfy," he says, nodding at an old, overstuffed chair with a footrest. It doesn't look uncomfortable, but it doesn't look like an ideal place to sleep either.

"Beck," I say, but I don't really know how to finish that sentence. He's been traveling just as long and as hard as I have, and I hate that he might not get a good night's sleep because of me.

"What? You want to take the chair? Or the floor?" he asks with a knowing smirk.

Of course, I don't want to sleep on the floor. But it wouldn't be the worst thing in the world. Honestly, laying on the pine slats next to the fireplace would probably be more comfortable than the threadbare mattresses we slept on at Conrad's. Or the stack of old blankets on the stone floor I slept on in city housing with my mother. It's something I haven't thought of in a long time—the way she used to cuddle me until I fell asleep. The stones were so cold, and she was so warm. A little shudder rolls up my neck.

I shrug. "I've done it before," I say.

He drops a pillow and looks at me—really looks at me. I can't tell what he's thinking, and I worry I've said something wrong. I hug the pillow to my chest, and he nods.

"You'll take the bed."

That's the end of the discussion.

He finishes making the bed for me—insists on it, actually. His brow is furrowed, determination set into the lines around his mouth as he layers blankets over blankets, as if this act of service is his penance. I let him. It seems like he needs to keep busy. And I don't have the energy to fight with him tonight. When he pats the bed, as if to say it's all done, I climb in without another word.

Exhaustion seeps into my arms and legs faster than I can even wonder if I'm sleepy. I'm vaguely aware of him making a bed on the floor next to the fireplace, not six feet away from me, and saying something about chickens. But then I'm gone, and I sleep soundly.

He definitely said something about chickens. That much is clear when I hear the clucking and crowing in the morning. When I open my eyes, he has sandwiched his head between two pillows and is snoring away. The fire is still burning, though it's not roaring. He must have stayed up, stoking the fire.

I don't want to wake him, so I creep out of bed, careful not to make too much noise. When I get past our little makeshift bedroom area, I stop. Ahead of me is a view I wasn't quite prepared for. It feels like I'm looking out across the whole world. Immediately below is an amber field, preternaturally still and reflecting the sun's first warm light. Beyond that is prairie; true, yellow and green grasses, windblown and worn, like a sea on land. Beyond that, trees dot the land until they start to climb and grow thicker, like clumps of broccoli or stalks of sprouts. And then, the mountains.

They're blue and purple and capped with snow that glows rose-gold in the early morning sun. They look like they go on for forever and ever. It would take a mighty quest to cross those, and even from such a distance, I can see why few have ever tried. They're formidable. They're also beautiful.

I think I could stand here all day, just staring at this view, but I hear the chickens again. Since I fell asleep before I could hear what Beck actually had to say about them, I find myself a jacket—it smells like orange, so it's definitely Beck's—and put on my boots to go see whatever there is to see.

The barn smells like a barn, no surprises there. But when I walk outside, everything else smells fresh and crisp. As though the air is so clean, it hurts my nose. It tickles, and I sneeze.

"Bless you," Ammon Sr. says. He stands in the middle of a pen, holding a bag of feed and tossing out a handful.

"Thank you," I say, moving closer to watch the chickens that swarm the ground around him. They're so funny, the way they peck and squawk and edge each other out for the same feed they get every day.

"Want to try?" he asks, offering me the open bag.

"Sure," I say, reaching in for a handful. I lean over the fence and toss the feed. The chickens flock to me, and a small one gets knocked back in the scuffle. I toss it some food behind the others, and it eats it faster than I expected. I laugh.

"You ever raised chickens?" he asks.

"No," I say, reaching into the bag again for more feed. "Never really been around animals. Well, except fish. But they were dead."

When he arches his eyebrows, I add, "I used to run errands around the docks on the peninsula."

"You're from the peninsula?" he asks, pressing his lips

together. "Haven't been there in a long time. That's a massive port. Deep water."

"Yes, it is," I say. I suppose it shouldn't surprise me that he's been there. Beck said his father taught him how to sail. But usually, people who sail into the peninsula port don't also sail the Mittlesee, and Beck grew up sailing the Mittlesee.

"You rode on Beck's boat?" he asks. I press my lips together to keep from grinning, but I wish I could've seen Beck's face when his father called it a boat, and not a ship.

"I did."

"And?"

"I don't think I rode it very well," I say.

He studies me for a moment, and then starts to chuckle. His chuckle builds into a deep, booming laugh, and I laugh along with him.

"I'm sure my son's navigation didn't help things. Likes to attack the waves like they kissed his girl." I feel my cheeks flush, and he chuckles again and waves it off. "Nothing personal."

"No, I know what you mean," I say, remembering my impression of the way he steered his ship—like he took the waves' assault personally.

"Galina's tickled purple to have you here," he says. I've never heard that turn of phrase before, and while it's not up to the same standard as Beck's creative cursing, it still makes me smile.

"She's nice," I say. It doesn't feel like it's enough, but he nods, accepting the words just the same.

"Same for Ammon and Emlyn," he says, though there's a little edge to his voice.

"They seem nice, too," I say, and wait for him to say more. I want to know more about Emlyn. There's something that seems so familiar about her, and she obviously recognized my bracelet, if not the compass hidden against my chest.

"You should make some time to talk to her."

"Emlyn?" I ask. He nods.

"Definitely, uh . . . a girl worth getting to know," he says. He tosses one last handful of feed to the chickens and rolls the top of the bag down, then leans back against the fence. We watch the chickens in companionable silence for a long minute.

"I don't think I'd be a responsible father if I didn't ask what it is you want with my son," he says. His voice is just as calm as before, and he scratches the side of his nose as though he just commented on the weather.

I open my mouth to respond, but nothing comes out. He waves me off again. "I know he puts up a good facade, but you're not going to break him, are yeh?"

"I hope not," I say, my voice softer than I intend. "I can't imagine how he'd steer his boat if that happened."

"Ship." I turn around, and Beck is standing there, hair rumpled, one arm held loosely behind his back. My cheeks feel hot again, and I wonder if he heard us talking. He takes his time walking over, moving with as much swagger as I've ever seen him carry.

"I believe you meant to pronounce it *ship*," he says, but there's a familiar spark in his green eyes.

"Let the girl be," his father says, and I grin. "Sounds like you didn't even make her any coffee."

"Is that what this is all about?" Beck asks. I shrug and he pulls his hand out from behind his back, revealing a tall metal canister that sure seems to smell like coffee.

"Is that for me?" I ask, stepping closer and reaching out as he unscrews the lid.

"Ah, sorry," he says, lifting the container to his lips. "This is for the girl who sailed on my *ship*." And then he keeps walking, all the way to the house. When I turn around, his father is nodding, an appraising look on his face.

"There's more in the kitchen," he says, nodding at the house. "The *boat* coffee is better, anyway."

CHAPTER TWENTY

*E*mlyn is scrubbing potatoes when I walk in the kitchen later that afternoon. The screen door clatters behind me and draws her attention. I stand awkwardly in the doorway as she shuts off the water.

We stare at each other for a long moment, and I don't know what to say. She watches me, her doe-like eyes soft, giving away nothing.

"Sorry," I finally say, feeling stupid. "I didn't know you were —" I stop, because I realize there's probably nothing inherently embarrassing about washing potatoes.

"Do you want to help?" she offers, holding out a yellow potato covered in dirt.

I nod, because apparently, I've become mute. "Yeah," I say, taking the potato and forcing a smile. "Thanks."

She passes me a scrub brush, and we get to work on the day's haul. She's planning to can some for winter and make the others into pancakes for dinner. All of that information is exchanged in about twelve seconds, and then we have nothing else to say. We stand next to the sink, taking turns scrubbing the potatoes under running water. It is so awkward that at one point, I look out the window and see Ammon and Beck walking toward the kitchen. They look up, see us in the window, and turn the opposite direction.

Emlyn chuckles.

"I'm sorry," she says. "This isn't funny, but . . ." And with that, she loses it. She laughs loud and hard, and I'm not sure if I should join her, or call for help.

"Are you okay?" I ask.

"We are so awkward," she says. I laugh, because she's right. But there's still tension between us. I put down the potato I'm working on and dry my hands on my apron as I turn to face her.

"I'm sorry, but do we know each other? You seem so familiar, but I don't know why."

She stops laughing and becomes very still. She curls the potato she's holding into her wrist and presses it against her chest.

"Yes," she says.

"We do?"

"You know me, and I know you."

I blink. "So, we know each other?"

"No," she says, blinking as she stares out the window. "Not exactly."

"I don't follow," I say.

"You're a candidate," she says. My heart pounds in my chest. So, they've figured it out. I bite the side of my tongue and nod.

"I suppose you must get newspapers out here. It was stupid of me not to assume you'd know."

She shakes her head and turns to face me. Her eyes flash down to my collarbone, then back up to my face.

"You're wearing Declan's compass around your neck," she says.

All I hear for a long moment is the pounding of blood between my ears, and her eyes drift down to my chest again, where my hand has betrayed me, pressing his compass into my skin. The institute bracelet is also on full display, and I know she sees both.

"How did you—" I stop when it clicks. "You were a candidate."

She looks back out the window and rinses the potato in her hand. She places the vegetable in the clean bowl and turns around, leaning against the sink.

"Will you tell him I'm here?" she asks. She crosses her arms over her chest, and for the first time, I recognize what it is that's kept her so distant since I arrived. She's afraid.

"No," I say. "He doesn't . . . he doesn't know?" The puzzle pieces start to fall into place, and I realize I'm still tugging on the compass. I let go and press my palms into the lip of the sink. She's the girl. The one I was supposed to find.

"I've communicated a couple of times, but no. He doesn't know where I am."

We stand like that for a long, quiet moment. Emlyn facing the rest of the house, and me facing the mountains.

"And then you arrive, unannounced, wearing his most prized possession."

"Emlyn, he didn't send me," I say. But as the words come out of my mouth, I realize they're not true.

"He didn't?" she asks. I meet her eyes, and she flinches. She chuckles through her nose and squares her shoulders. "What is it that you want?"

"I need help," I say. Her eyes flash down to my chest again, and she snorts.

"It seems you have all the help you need. What could I possibly do?" She turns around and twists the faucet handle, turning it on as she picks up a dirty potato.

"He didn't tell me your name. He said," I start, trying to

remember exactly what Declan did say. "He said that Beck would know where she was. That 'she' might be able to help."

"Help with what?"

"Supporters."

"For what?" Her voice is guarded, and she hasn't looked at me.

"To marry him."

She whips her head to face me, her nostrils flaring. "Then what exactly are you doing with Beck?"

My cheeks flush hot, and this time, I know exactly what the feeling is. Hot, brutal shame.

"We're friends," I say.

"Some friend," she mumbles, going back to the potato.

"He's always been good to me," I say softly, even if his words have hurt at times.

"I'm not talking about him," she says. "Of course, he's been good to you. Beck is the kindest, most pure-hearted man you'll ever meet. I'm talking about you."

"Me?"

"You convince him to help you escape the institute, to put a target on his back, to draw attention to his family home—all so that you can go back and marry Declan? What were you thinking?"

I want to scream, *it wasn't my idea!* To tell her everything. But if I told her that he'd taken money from Siobhan to get me out of there, that Declan asked him to hide me, that coming here was Beck's idea, she would surely tell Ammon. And Ammon might not forgive him.

"I wasn't," I say. "I wasn't safe there. I was attacked and . . ." I stop, because there's no words that will make this better.

"The institute is a vicious place," she says. "Anyone knows that, the candidates especially. I don't know what happened to you there, and I'm sorry it did. But I don't know why you think

I'll help you, when I don't trust you." My chest aches, but I nod. I understand.

"It's not that I want to marry him—I mean . . ." I stop. What *do* I mean? I take a deep breath and pick up another potato, scrubbing it slowly and methodically. "I've had a . . . difficult time. And I can't, in good conscience, not try to make changes. Declan has seen that, and he wants to help. He's agreed that once we're married, we'll work together. But we need support. He thinks . . ." I trail off, because I'm not even sure she cares. I rinse the potato and place it in the clean bowl, then wipe my hands on my apron.

"He thinks, what?" she asks. She's stopped what she's doing and is staring at the potatoes still in the sink.

"He thinks this is something that should happen slowly over time. That it could be my life's work. But I . . . it can't take that long. There are too many other girls, beneficiaries, candidates . . . it can't be slow."

"Okay," she says, pressing her hands into the edge of the sink. "So then, where do I fit in?"

I let out a deep exhale. "There are so many graduates who can vote at the annual assembly."

She wipes her hands on her apron and unties it, her expression tight. This might be my only chance to convince her.

"If I could contact them, bring them to my side—"

"So, you want me to put you in touch with graduates who don't want their locations known? So you can go back to Declan—to the capital—and share that information. So you can bring them back and try to convince them to vote for your vanity project?"

"That's not what this is—"

"Well, then what is it?" she asks, and her glare is made of flint. One wrong word and I'll ignite my only lead, watch it burn in the flames of her rage.

I open my mouth to answer, but the truth is, I don't know.

143

Maybe that is all this is. A little project to make me look like I'm in touch with the people, to make me and Declan more likable, but never intended to do anything. But then something else sticks in my head. The compass.

"You've seen this compass before?" I ask. She blanches and looks down.

"Yes," she says. "He showed it to me."

"When were you a candidate?"

"Three years ago," she says. I do the math, but Declan wouldn't have been of age yet. And suddenly, that last of the pieces slot into place. She's the missing candidate who ran off with someone at the estate.

"I don't know where they are," she says, breaking the pall hanging over the kitchen. "Even if I wanted to help you, even if I trusted you, I couldn't." She looks away as she hangs her apron on its hook, and walks out of the kitchen.

I stay there for a long time, thinking about everything I've seen and heard, all the pieces that led me to this place, and eventually, I start washing the potatoes again. It needs to be done, and the tedium of it is relaxing. At one point, I look out the window, and Beck is watching me from outside. This whole trip has been a bust. He took a risk in bringing me here, even if he did get a payday for it.

But then, he seemed fairly confident that he knew what Declan was talking about. Maybe Emlyn isn't telling me everything? Which means the only question now is: how do I make someone who doesn't trust anyone, trust me?

CHAPTER TWENTY-ONE

$\mathcal{T}$he days are long, but they fly by. It's been a week since we arrived, and nobody else has asked me who I am or where I'm from. Every time the subject comes up, Beck skirts the issue with a joke or an insult. When we're with his family, he is warm and friendly, even bordering on affectionate. But then the day ends, and we return to the loft, and he becomes quiet and sullen. It's confusing, bouncing between these two versions of him. I'm not sure which I prefer. Or which one is real.

I've come to like his father, and I think he likes me. I continue to help him with the chickens in the morning. Chickens might be the first animal that isn't terrified of me, and I don't mind them either. It's a quick job, but it gives us a routine, and a little time to chat. I don't think Beck is any more comfortable with us talking than he was on that first day, and when we're finished, he comes downstairs with coffee for the three of us.

His mother seems cautious around me, but is nothing if not kind and courteous. At meals, she serves me first, and always asks if I've had enough. She makes sure I have a chair in the living room when we gather after dinner in the evenings. But I don't think she trusts me. The longer we stay here, the more I find myself worrying that she thinks I'm sharing a bed with her son, but I also don't make it clear that we're not. And Beck does nothing to dissuade that thinking either. I don't know what he wants them to know, and it seems easier to follow his lead, so I leave it alone despite the growing discomfort.

His brother is another story. I like Ammon. A lot. It's hard not to fall under his spell. He's handsome, charming, funny, kind, and thoughtful. There's something in his manner that I feel myself drawn to. Not in a romantic way, though I think it would be easy to love him; I don't know if I've ever been around a more attractive man in my life. But whenever we find a moment to laugh together, I feel the air around us tighten, as if everyone around us is holding their breath, waiting for something to combust and destroy the whole damn ranch.

Despite that, I like him very much. Which makes Emlyn that much more confounding. She used to be a candidate. She and I should have so much in common, but there are times when I find myself watching her with unkind eyes. I look for her weaknesses, for things Declan might have preferred, for things I have her beat in. I mostly just remind myself she's married to Ammon, but the urge to compete with her is deep-seated and not easily suppressed. Maybe Declan was right. Maybe I am jealous.

Yet she watches me with the same hawkish eyes as Beck whenever I talk to her husband. She doesn't talk to me outside of group settings, and even then, it's only as necessary. But I feel her gaze on me often, more often than I even see her. I thought that maybe we would be kindred spirits. Beck thought she would like me. Declan did, too. But now that I see her, I don't know why they would ever think so. She is obviously an institute type of girl, whereas I am a mistake. She may have made an unorthodox decision to end up here — a story I've not yet been privy to—but she's still of candidate stock, whereas I never fit the mold. So we have little to say to each other, and even less in common than I hoped.

Our routines keep us from having to interact too much, which is a grace. I appreciate not having to make awkward conversation while keeping up with chores. I like the chores. It reminds me of the better parts of living in the peninsula: being outside, accomplishing simple tasks, solving solvable problems. I feed chickens, I hammer nails, I plant bulbs. I do anything and everything that keeps me outside in the fresh air and sunshine. Both the Ammons are tickled to have an extra set of hands, even if they often have to redo whatever it is I've done. They teach me, and I learn, and by the end of my first week, we've gotten into a good routine. Beck flits in and out of my schedule, stopping to watch me flail on occasion and cheering me on even more rarely.

A full week in, I'm helping his father fix the corner of the chicken pen when he convinces me to spar with him.

"You're getting complacent again, Capo," he says.

"I'm not getting complacent," I say, putting my hammer back in his dad's toolbox. "You're bored. Picking a fight won't help your troubled mind."

"It will if you're just being lazy," he says, toeing dirt in my face.

"Oh, lazy, am I?" I ask, and I turn quickly and swing. He dodges my sneak attack and grabs my wrist, tugging me into him.

"Sorry, I guess I meant sloppy," he says with a smirk. He pushes me back, and I get into a fighting stance. It's the most normal I've seen him, and we get back into the habit of sparring and exchanging jabs in the afternoons. A few days in, and we've attracted an audience.

"What's this?" Ammon asks, carrying a fence shovel, his father close on his heels, shoving his hands under his arms. All three of the men have the same thick, bushy dark eyebrows, but at this moment, each is shaped differently: Ammon's are raised; Ammon Sr.'s are low, straight dashes; and Beck crooks one higher than the other.

"Just a little target practice," he says, jabbing his fist into my side. I block it easily. The muscle memory has returned after just a few days of practice.

"Tell him who's the target," I say, feinting left and punching right. He blocks me, and I curse under my breath.

"'Who's the target,'" he repeats like a smartass. He throws a punch and gets my shoulder. I shake it off and reset.

"Just trying to make you look good in front of your family," I say with a sweet smile. He smiles back. I step back. He steps toward me, and before he realizes what he's done, I throw a punch at his kidney and he groans at the impact. Now it's his turn to walk it off.

"You finally bring a girl home, and this is what I walk in on?" Ammon says. I watch a pink flush bloom across Beck's cheeks, and it occurs to me he's never introduced a girlfriend to his family before.

"Aw, is that true, Cupcake?" I ask, taking a swing at his face. He nearly catches a fist in the jaw, but swerves just in time and lands a punch in my stomach, holding back so I don't take the full brunt of it.

"Well, you're not really a girl, Capo," he says, his voice trailing off at the end. The jeering stops for a moment, and I wonder if they actually know what his nickname means. For them to get that quiet, it must be something awful. I swing my back fist up quickly and catch his chin.

"Watch that undercut, powder monkey," Ammon shouts with a barking laugh. It's hard not to join him. His laugh shakes him from the belly and spreads so easily to those around him.

"No comments from the peanut gallery," Beck grumbles

back. He's rubbing the left side of his face, and it leaves him more open on the right.

"Just trying to help out," Ammon yells back.

"Help who?" Beck growls.

"Arden, protect your right side. As long as you protect your right side, he doesn't know what to do." I laugh as I swerve away from Beck's own attempt at an uppercut, and then defend against a swing to my right side.

"Nicely done! Good girl!" Ammon shouts.

"Thanks!" I say with a grin.

"It's not about the way I fight," Beck says, swinging at my left and nearly catching me as I get him in the stomach. He shakes it off and resets.

"Not when you're fighting like that!" Ammon says.

"Back down, son," his father says quietly, and I'm not sure who he's speaking to.

"Thanks for the tips, Ammon," I say, and he winks at me. Beck takes a wide swing before I'm prepared, and his fist nearly collides with my face, but I duck and lean my shoulder into him. He wraps his arms around my waist and flips me upside down.

"That's against the rules!" I yell.

"There are no rules," he says, holding me securely so I can't wriggle out. I swing my heel down and kick him hard in the shoulder. Harder than I should. He launches forward and barely manages to hang on to me as he falls to his knees. My head barely hits the ground, but it's at an awkward angle, and when he does let me go, I fall to my side, landing on my hands and knees. Ammon and his father are laughing mercilessly from the sidelines, and Beck's face is red.

"Hey, I get it," I say under my breath. "There are no rules. I let my guard down. Let's reset." But he doesn't hear me.

"You got something you want to say?" he asks, charging at Ammon.

"What's this now?" Galina says, walking out into the yard, Emlyn's long strides on her heels.

"Ammon is giving a colloquium on sparring," Beck says.

"Ah, don't be like that now—it's charity!"

"Boys, I hate when you do this. Can't you just get drunk and laugh it off like normal people?" Galina says. Beck's nostrils flare, and I can see he's about to cross the line from playful sparring to straight-up fighting.

"Beck—" I start, but before I can get to my feet, Beck headbutts Ammon in the stomach, knocking the wind out of him. He flies backward onto his ass, and Beck falls with him.

"I've been on this planet for twenty-four years, and you've been a pain in my ass for the past twenty-one."

"Is that all?" Beck says with a frown. "I've always been such an overachiever, I'd've thought it felt like more." Ammon jumps to his feet and charges. He swings his fist into Beck's kidney. Beck pulls up lame to his right, and Ammon dances around the other side, back in a sparring stance.

"What? That's it?" Ammon says, panting between laughter.

"Nah, just giving you a chance to get your breath, old man," Beck says, sniffing the air like a feral beast.

"Yeah, thanks. Gives me time to catch you off guard," Ammon says, jumping at him and making Beck flinch, but holding his punch. "Come on, eyes on me. You know you lose when you don't keep your eyes on me." Beck's mouth curls into an ugly sneer, but he forces tension into his shoulders and fakes left, then jabs right, connecting with Ammon's jaw. Ammon doesn't back away, leaning into Beck's left side, just missing as Beck pulls an undercut, getting him in the chest. Ammon grabs Beck's arm and spins him around, holding him awkwardly, and I worry Beck's arm might get snapped off. But Beck shows no signs of giving up.

"Now, who's the best fighter in this family?" Ammon teases, putting Beck into a headlock.

"Suck dill, toadnostril," Beck says between gritted teeth.

"Boys, that's enough," Galina says.

"Nah, we're just having fun, Mom," Beck says.

"Yeah, just a little brotherly love," Ammon says, tweaking Beck's arm again.

"Yeah, we just love each other so much," Beck says. "Giving Ames a chance to fight, instead of running away." Galina curses under her breath as Beck kicks Ammon's knee, trying to knock him off balance. But Ammon anticipates and avoids it, swinging Beck around so that he's kneeling on the ground, still stuck in a headlock.

"Who's the best?" Ammon says, spittle flying.

"Go jerk off with a cactus, you hermit," Beck grimaces. Ammon's nostrils flare, and I can feel the tension amplify.

"Oh, that won't do," Ammon says, turning to face me. "Now, tell Arden you think she's pretty."

Beck slams his knee into Ammon's insole, causing Ammon's knee to buckle. He falls backward. But as he falls, he sweeps his good leg at Beck's back, and Beck goes flying. He lands hard on his stomach, face in the dirt, gasping for air. Ammon straddles his back, pushing his face in the dirt.

"What do you say to that, little brother?" He tugs on Beck's hair, forcing him to lift his chin until his gaze meets mine. "Go ahead, *Cupcake*. Tell Arden you love her!" As he struggles to break Ammon's hold, Beck's eyes meet mine, and I can't move. There's something new in his gaze. Something raw and unfiltered, and I don't know what it means.

"Ammon, enough," Emlyn says. Ammon looks up, startled, and lets go. Beck lays in the dirt for a moment. Ammon offers a hand to help him up, but Beck smacks it aside and pushes himself up on his own. He storms off toward the barn, shoving past me as he goes. Everyone is quiet as we watch him march away, but no one stops him.

Ammon is already walking back to the house, Emlyn's

slender arm around his slouching frame, and Ammon Sr. stands leaning back on his hips, still watching his younger son vanish.

"Arden, why don't you help me with dinner?" Galina says. I follow her into the kitchen, wondering about what just happened, and what exactly is rotting between these two brothers.

CHAPTER TWENTY-TWO

"They're three years apart. You'd think that would be enough to let them be their own person, but rivalry runs strong among the Hermeston men," Galina says, handing me two more potatoes to peel. I lean against the well-loved walnut countertop and slide the knife smoothly over the potato. The kitchen is narrow, but cozy. Dark green, painted cabinets line the opposite walls, broken up only by a window over the large white enamel sink and a cast iron stove. The stove is an older model that reminds me of the one we had at the Laarsworth Estate. That one had a stacked oven, while this only has one, and its legs bow out in sweeping, feminine lines that seem at odds with the spartan materials surrounding it. Still, the stove draws your eye and remains the focal point of the room. I like this room the best, after Beck's loft, and I don't mind spending time in here with Galina. I'm grateful for the busywork that excuses my silence.

"Beck shouldn't have been expected to live up to his brother. But when they were on the boat, that's just the way it was. Everyone's an equal, and if you're not keeping up with the rest of the crew, you're the whipping boy. Beck spent a lot of time being the whipping boy. I tried to protect him some, but I know it made it worse. I never liked that environment." It's hard to imagine Beck being anyone's whipping boy. All I've ever seen is someone who appears completely in control of his destiny.

"So, they haven't always gotten along?" I ask. She cocks her head with a familiar wry smile and shakes her head.

"Goodness no, but they're brothers. Of course, they'll go through spats here and there." She slices into a piece of red meat, trimming off the white bands of fat. "Do you have brothers or sisters?" she asks. Her tone is casual, but she stops slicing for a moment to watch my face. This is the first personal question she's asked.

My mind immediately goes to Carla and Neve. I suppose it should go to the mother who sold me off—for a better life, she said. Maybe she's made a new life for herself? Had another child? Maybe two? But even if she has, I'll never know.

"No," I say, sorry that I don't have more to add. Her eyebrows raise in some sort of understanding.

"You have a benefactor?" she asks as she strikes a match. She leans over and lights a burner on the stovetop. I'm not sure what I'm supposed to say. I'm not sure what they know about me, or if they're supposed to know who I am. If someone comes looking for me, and they know too much, it won't be good.

"It's okay. Beck told me you were recently a candidate. Like Emlyn." There's the comparison again, *like Emlyn*. As if there's some kind of implicit understanding I should be in on. I want to ask what that means. I seem to have nothing else in common with this girl other than the fact that we've walked the same halls. But I also don't want to pry. It's not Galina's story to tell.

"Yes, I had a benefactor," I say, and she doesn't miss my word choice. She seems surprised, but doesn't push for details. She places a large, cast iron pan over the flickering flame and drops in some lard.

"Beck and Ammon have a long, complicated history. Like all

brothers do. They're natural competitors, and when you're competing for resources in a closed universe like a ship, that competition can breed animosity. They fought over bunks, food, girls . . . you name it." I can't picture the two of them fighting over a girl. Or rather, I can't imagine Ammon not winning a fight for a girl, and I immediately feel ashamed for that thought. I look back up at Galina, and she's smiling.

"I know what you're thinking. And it typically went that way. Ammon knows what he has, and Beck had to work harder. Not that Beck doesn't have his own charms, but I suppose I don't have to tell you that." For a moment, I forget that we're pretending, and I feel my cheeks heat as I blush.

"Ammon backed off most of the time," she continues, "but Beck was always playing catch up. The only one who really got between them was Irina."

"Irina?" I ask, the name foreign and sour. She nods and *tsks* her tongue as she pushes perfect cubes of red meat into the pan. It sizzles immediately.

"Beck fell hard one summer in Sudersberg. She's actually Osterstanian. Beautiful girl. I met her once," she says, as if her mind is elsewhere. "Once was enough." She doesn't say it distastefully, just sadly, as if glad to be done with the mess of it.

"And that caused a rift?" I ask, wanting more details, but also really not wanting to know.

"For a bit. Beck thought he loved her, but she loved Ammon. And Ammon loved Emlyn. The moment he met her, he was done. As a parent, you both hope for that and you dread it. You want your child to find someone who can make a world of just the two of them. But then you risk losing your child. And you worry that their world will break, and they'll be left just a broken half. I worried about Emlyn. She was a candidate, and you know that's not easy to come back from."

I nod. I do know what she means, despite the fact that I haven't thought about the institute nearly as much as I probably should, considering I've promised to marry Declan. My cheeks flush with warmth at the thought of Declan, or more specifically, at the fact I haven't thought about Declan in at least a day. I run my fingers across the charm on my bracelet, fiddling with it in an absentminded, but poignant gesture. Galina eyes me carefully, then takes my vegetables and dumps them in the pot.

"Fortunately, Emlyn loves Ammon, and they are a unit. Beck, on the other hand, suffered for Irina—for years. Where Ammon is cautious, Beck is stubborn. Sometimes, he doesn't even know he's being stubborn. He just doesn't know how to quit."

"I can see that," I say, smiling as I lean back against the counter, watching as she works stock into the stew. She sighs and leans back.

"I'm not even sure why he decided to go to the capital when he did. But he did, and now, here you are."

"Oh, I don't . . ." I start, but I'm not even sure what I'm supposed to say to dispel whatever assumption she has made. She holds up a hand and shakes her head.

"I know you're going back," she says, her voice calm and a touch sad. "You have important work to do. And it's about time one of you did it," she says with a note of bitterness, possibly directed at Emlyn?

"What work is that?" I ask, but clearly Beck has told her more than I realized. Her stare levels me, and I shrink in the expectation that I am capable of something important.

"There are just so many of you. You could do so much good, if only you'd talk to each other." I nod in agreement. But if I can't even get Emlyn to talk to me, what hope do I have for anyone else?

"I'm not sure the others want to hear from me," I say, looking up toward the room Emlyn shares with Ammon. Galina folds her slender arms across her chest.

OF WIND AND TIDE

"Keep at it. Make her hear you. She wants this, the same as you — she's just afraid."

I chew on my bottom lip. I'm not sure how to connect with her. But if I can't connect with Emlyn, a girl I've been living with for the past week, then what chance do I have to connect with any of the others?

"Year after year, girls come, and they go, and every year, hope blooms and fades. You're the nation's darlings. You have the ear of the government, a place within it, and nobody thinks you have the right to exercise it."

"A place within it?" I ask. Her eyebrows lower, and she pops a carrot coin into her mouth.

"It's in the charter," she says, and I nod, recalling Declan's words.

"You mean a vote," I say. She nods.

"It's been there since the beginning. It's not a secret. But intimidation is a strong deterrent. I hope you're stronger than most."

"I hope so, too," I say softly. She crosses the kitchen and lifts my chin to meet her eyes.

"From what Beck's had to say, I think you, Arden, are a force."

CHAPTER TWENTY-THREE

*B*eck never does talk to me about that sparring match with his brother. But the next afternoon, he's waiting for me as if nothing happened. From that day on, though, we spar on the backside of the barn, where we aren't seen—or at least, where the others don't bother us. I protect my right side, and he aims harder for my left. I try to ask him about Emlyn, find out what he knows, but he doesn't give me anything.

The days get shorter, the sun dropping below the western hills earlier and earlier. Emlyn remains distant, and the opportunities to talk with her are as slim as her greetings and goodbyes.

Then one morning, I wake to a thin layer of frost on the ground.

Beck stands in front of the wall of windows behind me, his eyes fixed on something in the distance. I wrap my blanket around my shoulders and join him. The floors creak with nothing but cold air from the open barn below beneath them, and my feet ache, stiff against the frigid slats.

"Morning, Capo," he says. He's taken to calling me by the obnoxious nickname more and more. But his frequency has lessened the blow of it, and now, it's merely annoying. I may never know what it means, and honestly, I don't think I really care.

"It's pretty," I say. The sunrise sparkles off the frozen ice crystals that dance on the tips of the tall grasses. I wonder if a touch of winter has come to Declan and the capital, as well. I imagine the estate and its unyielding green dusted in a coat of white. It seems impossible; the last time I was there, it was so warm. It's like we're living in two different worlds.

Beck grunts, not taking his eyes off that spot in the distance. I follow his line of sight to where a black dot bounces on the horizon. We are both so quiet that I can't tell if I'm hearing my own galloping pulse, or the actual sound of approaching hoofbeats. I've been here for weeks now, and it's become so routine, so comfortable, that I've forgotten I'm in hiding. Of course, someone would make their way here one of these days. I step back from the window, and my arm brushes against his. He doesn't move away.

"Relax, Capo," he says without inflection. It's obvious he's not convinced we're in the clear, but I do know that if we were really in danger, we'd be gone by now.

"Who is it?" I ask.

"Dunno," he says. "Maybe the mailman?" His joke falls hollow. His father went into a Highton for the post just yesterday,.

"I don't like this," I say, more to myself than to him. He finally looks away, and his green eyes squint down at me.

"Well, I think it's fantastic," Beck grunts. A wide grin erupts on his face, and I laugh in spite of myself. "Better get into your Sunday best. We've got company."

The rider is close enough to recognize by the time we're inside the farmhouse. It's Helmann Baker, a blacksmith from the nearby town of Highton, where the mail does indeed get delivered. He's brought a delivery of horseshoes for the Hermestons, as well as an invitation.

"My Mabel is getting married," he says to a chorus of congratulations. His oldest daughter, it turns out, is marrying the school teacher's boy. There will be a barn dance Sunday night, the day after tomorrow, and we're all invited.

"Well, how can we say no to that?" Galina says with a warm smile, but the men give their congratulations with stony expressions and mechanical handshakes. Once Helmann is gone, the real preparations begin. Or rather, negotiations. Galina is tense, and Ammon is clearly uncomfortable with the idea, mentioning several times that his parents could go on their own. Beck, for his part, says nothing, and I wait for him to change that decision. Being seen in public sounds like the worst kind of idea, but Ammon Sr. thinks it's not the worst thing in the world.

"It doesn't hurt for you to get to know our neighbors, let them see our faces, learn more about us," his father says.

"They're not our neighbors," Beck quips.

"Not yours. You don't live here unless you're running from something," Ammon snaps back.

"Boys," Galina says.

"We've already given our word," his father says.

"No, Mom did. Mom gave her word. That doesn't require our attendance," Ammon says.

"It's just a wedding party," Galina says. "It's a happy occasion. Why expect the worst?" My eyes find Beck's, and I can tell we're thinking the same thing. *Because it all goes to shit when you're least expecting it.*

I clean the kitchen that night, sending Galina off to bed early so I can focus on the monotony of scrubbing grease from cast iron. It's soothing, a problem that I can solve. It's not a problem that will get me killed, though Meredith, my maid at the institute, would kill me for letting my nails get so bad. And I shudder to think of what Neve would think—if she ever forgives me, that is. Something tells me Declan, however, would be amused. If I do make it through the other side of this and make it back to Declan, I wonder how I'll soothe my nerves. Will they let me in the kitchen to scrub greasy dishes? Will they let me prune the hedge maze? It seems like a lifetime away, too far and too fuzzy to be real. I drain the greasy, dirty dishwater and balance the pot on a rack to air dry for a moment. The sound of voices in the living room floats beneath the swinging door.

"But we can't—" Emlyn's voice carries through the door, and a lower, muffled voice answers. I move closer to the doorway, pushing it slightly so I can hear better.

"We don't know if it's safe," Ammon says. I peek around the edge of the door. He's hovering over her, his hands on his hips.

"We never know if it's safe. We just stay here. All the time. I've never even seen Highton."

"I know, but there's always a risk," he says. I push the door open a touch more, so I can see them both.

"Ammon, we can't live our whole lives in fear. It will eat us whole," Emlyn says, falling into a chair. "It's killing me . . ." He exhales, his posture curling over on itself, and kneels in front of her, placing his hands on her arms.

"I love you so much," she continues with a shaky sigh, "but I can't live my whole life hidden away."

"I will give you anything. You know that. I will do anything to make you happy, Emlyn." She's quiet, looking down at him pleading before her. She lifts his chin with her docile, long fingertips as he slides his hand around her wrist, completely encircling it. But there's no tension in either of their hands.

They hold each other with something much stronger. Something respectful, tender, accepting.

"This is really what you want?" he asks. She nods. He drops his head, as if praying, and lets out a deep sigh. "Then wear something pretty."

She tugs him to his feet and wraps her arms around his shoulders. Ammon buries his face into her neck. I know it's wrong, that this is a private moment, as intimate as they come. But the way they hold each other, the care and the abandon — I can't look away. I've never seen something like this. Complete helplessness that makes two people stronger. I can feel the power of the moment despite the fear and worry. I don't know what this is called, but I feel myself aching for it. This, whatever it is, is not for me, though. This is an exclusive club to which I don't belong.

I'm about to step back when his eyes open and meet mine. He doesn't react, or if he does, he doesn't show it. I close the door and back away, returning to drying the pan. A few minutes later, the sound of the door swinging open and footsteps entering the room interrupts my feigned commitment to the dryness of this pan.

"Need some help?" Ammon asks. I shrug, and he picks up a towel, dries a single fork, and places it neatly in the drawer.

"I'm sorry about that," I say, before he can say anything else. "I heard voices, and . . . I didn't mean to . . ." He doesn't answer right away. Just lifts another fork, dries it, places it in the drawer.

"I spent my whole life looking for something. I didn't know what it was. I looked everywhere. And I mean everywhere. I've been all over the damn world, and never found anything worth slowing down for. And then I did," he says, a faint smile crossing his full pink lips. He lifts a butter knife, dries it, places it in the drawer. "And there's nothing I wouldn't do to keep her. But there's also nothing I wouldn't do for her." I don't fully understand. My pan is completely dry now, but I keep rubbing it with the towel and say nothing, afraid that anything I say will ruin this moment, and he'll stop telling me whatever it is he has to say.

"I guess in the end, I'm just another helpless man." He lifts a fork, dries it, places it in the drawer. "And I wouldn't have it any other way." He takes a deep breath and turns to me.

"Declan is not like that." His words surprise me, and I drop the towel on the floor. He bends over, retrieves the towel, and places it in my hand, his long, cold, calloused fingers brushing against my wrist. "Declan knows what he wants. He knows what he needs. I don't know where you fall, but I'd gander you're a bit of both." He lets out a heavy sigh and levels me with his gaze.

"In the end, Declan will never be helpless." His words are so solid, like a stripe of granite woven along a cliffside. "I don't presume to know what you want, but if you let him, Declan will get what he wants."

"You don't think very highly of Declan," I say, my mouth dry, my voice anemic.

"Maybe not," he says with a sudden chuckle. "But I suspect the feeling is mutual."

"So, what are you saying?" I ask. He turns to face me, leaning his hip into the counter and crossing his arms over his chest, his towel draped loosely over his arm.

"I'm saying that you can only hide so long. Maybe you should go to the party with us?"

"I never said I wasn't," I said.

"You never said you were either."

"Beck never said—"

"Beck might never say," he says. His bright blue eyes meet mine, and he places a hand on my arm, giving it a subtle squeeze.

"Ammon?" I ask, realizing this might be my only chance to ask.

"Yeah?"

"How do I talk to Emlyn?" He lifts his eyebrows, but then a knowing pallor falls over his face and he nods. I continue, "How do I get her to trust me? To hear me? To help?"

"I can't tell you that," he says, scrubbing a hand down his face. "She's been through a lot, and honestly? I don't blame her for being stingy with her faith.

"What I do know is that she has a bigger heart than anyone I've ever known. If you can find your way into it, she'll shift the world for you."

I smile. How can I not? It's not just the way he's described his wife, it's how similar it is to the way she described Beck. He starts to walk out of the room, and then pauses, looking back over his shoulder.

"Emlyn and Mom are putting together a dress from scraps in the attic. If you want something to wear, you'd better get up there sooner than later."

Maybe I should have gone up to the attic first, but I don't. Instead, I find Beck outside the barn. He leans against the main door, one leg bent at the knee, his boot steadied against the wood. His fists are punched down into his coat pockets, and I wonder how long he's been here.

"What are you doing?" I ask, watching my words turn to fog in the cold night.

"Well, I was going to help in the kitchen, but it seems my brother beat me to it," he says. His words are clipped, and he doesn't look at me. There's hurt there, but I'm not sure where it comes from. I think of Galina's words earlier, about Beck working for what he wants and Ammon taking it when he's ready. But I don't know what he could possibly think Ammon has taken from me.

"So . . . Ammon knows Declan," I say. Beck looks at me then, his face mostly hidden in shadows, but I can tell it's not what he expected.

"Is that what he told you?" he asks, looking back at the ground, shifting his feet around to balance on the other.

"Why didn't you tell me?" I ask. "About any of this?"

"It wasn't mine to tell."

"But why not give me a clue of what I was walking into? Why not tell me your brother married a girl who left the institute, and that she's the one with everything I need?"

He shrugs. "Doesn't change the narrative."

"What narrative?" I ask.

"The one where he tells you what to do."

"And what exactly is he supposed to have told me?" I ask.

"Probably the opposite of what you want to do."

We're back to this, then. Fine. If he wants to play this game, I'll bite. I cross my arms over my chest and lift my chin, glaring at him. "And what is it you think I want to do?"

"I don't know," he spits. "But I wasn't going to tell you what to do, and now he has."

"Who says I'm going to listen to him?" I ask.

"It doesn't matter. He's in your head now, and his opinion will weigh in on whatever it is you decide. He's part of it now. He's always a part of it." This isn't about me, I realize. This is about Ammon. About whatever it is that boiled beneath the surface of that sparring match.

"Beck," I say, taking a step closer to him, but he moves, walking along the barn. I run to catch up and block his way around the corner.

"A part of what?" I ask.

His jaw tics, grinding on the words he won't say, and he tries to get around me. I grab his arm, but he blocks me, and I try again. He pushes me away as if we're sparring, and I hold my hands up, surrendering.

"I don't want to fight you. Just talk to me." I reach for him, but let my hand fall to my side before it makes contact with his arm.

His shoulders fall as he huffs out a heavy exhale. I can't see his face in the shadows, but he scratches the side of his nose.

"Fine. Talk. Talk my damn ear off," he says, and I try to ignore the stinging sharpness.

"What did he make himself a part of?" I ask. He digs his foot into the ground and shakes his head.

"Nothing." *Beck might never say.* Ammon's words flash across my mind.

But Beck is right. Ammon is now a part of this, whatever this is. A dog howls in the distance, and I look up at the rich, velvety sky. Half of it is blocked out in shadow. My fingers find my hip, tracing the outline of my tattoo through my clothes, recalling the myth of Scio, who, but for the mountains, would have seen the skies, would have seen her way home.

"Does it still hurt?" he asks, his voice soft. I know he means the tattoo, but all I can feel are the hard ridges of a brand that will never go away. I shake my head.

"No . . . and yes," I admit. We're quiet for another minute, and then I break the spell. "Did you mean what you said? That you didn't want to tell me what to do?"

"Yeah." He spits the word out like it's the most obvious thing, and I remember what he said in New Covington, that he doesn't make my decisions for me. That he never has. I didn't believe it then, but looking through the lens of hindsight, I can see that he's right. He does give me the space to decide for myself, even if I don't always know the answer. I look up at him, standing in the shadows, waiting for me to respond, for me to decide. And there's something in his posture, a slackening in his shoulders, a looseness to his arms. He leans in, but doesn't crowd me. So much like his brother.

"I'd like to go," I say. He's still for a minute. Too still.

"You would?" he asks. His question is toneless, and I can't tell what he's thinking. I nod, letting a cold wind brush my hair across my face.

"Wear something pretty," he says. And then he walks off into the dark and cold, alone.

CHAPTER TWENTY-FOUR

*G*alina and Emlyn have outdone themselves, tearing apart old dresses and crafting new ones for all three of us. Sewing is not something I know much about, beyond the odd repair here and there, and the last time I wore a dress, I had a closet full of gowns perfectly prefit to my proportions. Galina's dress is a patchwork of dark-green floral prints with a coordinating shawl. Emlyn's is a mishmash of a lavender top, with a deep purple skirt that looks somehow effortless and perfectly tailored to her long limbs.

The dress they've made me is a deep mustard gold with little red-and-green flowers on it. The fabric is impossibly soft, and I finally get Galina to admit that it was once a set of sheets. I'm uncertain about it until I try it on and it fits perfectly. The long sleeves keep my arms warm, and the fabric crosses over my chest in a perfectly flattering and concealing way that is somehow both girlish and makes me feel like a woman.

Of course, we don't dress until we've arrived, so as to save the dresses from the mess of the road. We pack up the horses and have just enough, with Emlyn sharing Ammon's horse. I feel guilty, but Beck is only going by the grace of God, or maybe the grace of Galina. I almost say something to him about being pleased he's decided to come, but Galina grabs my arm and gives me a knowing look. So I say nothing, and he gets on Hammerhead and rides. Sir Squints-a-Lot has not missed me and wastes no time expressing his dissatisfaction at having me on his back again. But here I am, here we are, and together, we make the two-hour trek to the tiny mountain hamlet of Highton.

It's a sweet little town, in a picturesque valley, surrounded by mountains. It's not quite as beautiful as the Hermeston farm, but the town itself is lovely and looks exactly like I would picture an old Northern town to look. There's a main street with a general store, a little white church, a millinery and dress shop, a bank, a schoolhouse with a bell on top, and a few other houses spread here and there. The rest of the residential areas climb the foothills around the outskirts of town. We stop in the town itself to briefly water the horses, and then continue on to the Baker farm.

We're early, but hardly the first ones to arrive. People from neighboring ranches have also made the trek for the nuptials. We are given space in the house to change—an awkward endeavor with both Galina and Emlyn in the same room. As I remove my shirt, something clanks against the floor, and I sweep my hand down to retrieve Declan's compass before anyone can ask.

"Don't," Emlyn says as I go to replace it around my neck. I look up at her, and she drops her gaze to the compass in my hand, shaking her head. She's right. The compass is too obvious. Someone might recognize it. Fisting it, I quickly tuck it into my bra. Equally identifiable at a glance, the bracelet soon follows. Emlyn's eyes scrutinize me for a moment, then flit away as Galina helps her with her zipper. I slip into my own dress, and nothing more is said. But I feel exposed.

Once we're dressed, I meet Mable, a plain but sweet girl

with pale skin, white-blonde hair, and clear blue eyes. She looks like a stiff gust of wind could blow her over, but when she's next to her groom, Donald, he steadies her. She looks strong and brave, and together, they look ready to meet anything life hands them. I cheer for them with everyone else when they are joined as husband and wife.

I've never actually been to a wedding. Watching the event unfold, I wonder if the next one I attend will be my own. I know it's tradition to have a church wedding, but I loved their simple ceremony out here, on this piece of God's land, beneath a trellis woven with sweetpea and columbine. I feel eyes on me and turn to meet Ammon's gaze. He smiles briefly, and then Emlyn joins his side, and he kisses her. Beck watches from the rear, close to the barn. I catch his eye, but he shakes his head and retreats into the barn, where the next stage of the festivities are happening. I sigh, accepting that there's a good chance he'll spend the evening pretending to be drunk. Or worse.

I meet more people than I think I've met in my life between the ceremony and the sunset. Ammon Sr. and Galina introduce me as a distant relative, but nobody gets my name or the degree of relation—nor do they ask. By the time it's dark, Beck has made himself at home at a makeshift bar. He's not alone either—his companions for the night are three girls who giggle and bounce every time he says something with a smirk. A petite blonde keeps touching his chest, and I hate the way my own grows hot with emotions I have no right to, and would rather not name. He catches my eye at one point and raises his glass, then whispers into the blonde's ear. She giggles even louder, and I turn away. I try to ignore him after that, but it's nearly impossible.

A four-piece band starts up, playing an old folk song I haven't heard since I was a little girl. The bride and groom dance to the lilting waltz, holding each other like they're so drunk on love, they've forgotten how to move their feet. Others are invited to join in, and the blonde leads Beck to the dance floor. His hands seem to swallow her up, and he grins and cackles as they turn around the dance floor. It looks all wrong and leaves me with a sour feeling in my stomach.

Galina dances with Ammon Sr., and Ammon Jr. sweeps Emlyn in a circle, barely keeping off her toes. She's graceful, though, and if I didn't know better, I'd think she was leading him. As I watch them all dance, happy and healthy and loved, I feel wholly alone. I sit at an empty table, sipping water from a glass jar, as everyone else who has gathered to wish these newlyweds well surrounds them with the example of love.

This is not what my wedding will be like. If I marry Declan —*when*. *When* I marry Declan, we will be surrounded by a room of sycophantic social climbers who want something from one or both of us in return. How will we know how to love each other without an example? I look up, and the crowd clears slightly, revealing Mabel and Donald dancing in the center of everyone: arms around each other, foreheads pressed together, grinning.

This is what I want.

This is not what I will get.

CHAPTER TWENTY-FIVE

It's much colder outside, and the air feels soothing in my lungs. The weight of my future is too much to bear when confronted with the alternative. But even that's not a fair comparison—that's not my alternative. That's never been an option for me. If I hadn't been selected for the institute, my future would have looked something like a decrepit shed and the backside of CJ's hand. I shudder at the thought and squeeze my eyes closed, but even as I stand here in the cold, wide awake, all I can see is the image of his eyes rolling back in his head, his body choking for life one moment and limp the next. I shudder harder and force my eyes open, sliding down the side of the barn, into the shadows.

My dress catches on a splinter, and I curse under my breath. I hope I haven't done too much damage to the dress Galina and Emlyn so thoughtfully made. But I don't have it in me to stand, so I stay crouched against the barn wall, hugging my knees to my chest. The cold night settles like a thin, frosty blanket around me, while just on the other side of this wall, people thrum with warmth. It might as well be another world away.

"Too much party for you, Capo?" Beck asks, stopping about

ten feet from me, his hands fisted into his pockets. "Party's not out here. Not yet, anyway," he says, a looseness to his voice. I remember Slick telling me once: *you'll know when he's drunk—this isn't drunk*. Neither is it the facade he likes to wear when he's playing the part. But he's definitely relaxed from the drink. Or maybe the blonde. I shudder at the thought and hate myself for thinking it. For the rush of ugly heat that chases it through my veins.

"Just needed a breath," I say.

"Yeah," he says, maintaining the distance between us. "It's just awful in there. It's warm, and there's food and music and nice people." I sink to my butt on the ground and hug my knees tighter.

"They sure seem to like you in there," I say, my voice betraying a bitterness I didn't know I harbored.

"Is that jealousy?" A teasing resonance thrums in his baritone voice, moving through me in a way I don't know how to process. He closes the distance between us and stands toe to toe with me. "Aw, Capo. I didn't know you had it in you."

"Shut up," I say, kicking his foot. After another minute, he squats down in front of me, close enough to place his hands on my knees. His hands are warm, and I don't mind the way they feel on my legs.

"I thought you didn't want to come," I say.

"I never said that."

"Actions speak louder than words," I mumble.

"Did you get that from a fortune teller?" His face is alight, like this exchange is the most entertaining part of the night. I suppress a miserable shiver and narrow my eyebrows.

"Stop being an ass."

"What should I be instead? A butterfly? A rock? I'll be anything you want." A joke. Always a joke. But his eyes aren't laughing.

"You're being a real horse's ass right now, and you know how I feel about horses."

"Come on, Capo. What's going on?" he asks. I laugh bitterly and shake my head, looking past him. The sky is inky black, and from this angle, I can barely see any stars for the mountains in the way.

"Why do you call me that?" His gaze tightens, and he frowns.

"Because it suits you." His voice is so soft that only I can hear it. It settles on my knees with a warmth that serves as the perfect antidote to the bone-chilling frost. Then a smile parts his full lips, and I know he's about to say something smart. "Besides, 'sunny disposition' doesn't exactly roll off the tongue." I roll my eyes, but the corner of my mouth betrays me. His hands are still on my knees, and his thumbs drift up and down the tops of my shins in warming paths.

"All right, enough pouting. Talk—*you* wanted to talk. Remember? So talk."

"It's stupid."

"Maybe. But I don't trust your judgment."

"What's that supposed to mean?" I ask.

"Well, you wanted to come to this supposedly fun event, but now you're the one sitting in the cold. In the dirt."

"Touche," I mumble. He squeezes my knees, pressing his lips into a tight line.

"Tell me." I don't know if it's the music, or the wind whistling through the trees, or just the magic of a wedding night, but I let my head fall back against the barn and close my eyes, and I tell him.

"What if I don't get this?"

"What? A wedding? Oh, you'll have that." His voice is tight and careful. I shake my head.

"No, all of this. The way they looked at each other, the way

174

everyone watches them, hoping for the best for them . . ." I trail off, feeling sheepish and silly for saying it all out loud.

"Tell me," he says, like he's making a wish.

"I'm afraid I won't get to be happy," I say, the words fleeing my lungs in a rush. My cheeks heat with embarrassment, and I turn my face away, hoping that he won't see.

"Oh, that," he says, softly. He shifts and sits next to me, his back against the barn, removing his jacket to drape over the front of my body. It smells like leather and cinnamon-laced citrus, with just a tiny hint of salt, even this far from the sea. I breathe it in and let my eyes close, so I don't have to see his expression, see for myself what he really thinks.

"Is that what you want? To be happy?" he asks. It's soft and plain, no hint of joke or pretense.

"I . . ." I start to say, but nothing comes out. I swallow hard around the lump that threatens to burst. "It never occurred to me to want it. But I see Mabel and Donald . . . and I see your parents . . . and your brother . . ." He shifts uncomfortably, and I clear my throat. "I see Ammon and Emlyn. And I see it's possible. To be happy."

The wind rustles across the farm, and in the distance, I hear an owl. I should be colder than I am, but his proximity is keeping me warm. He scrubs at the side of his nose.

"It's also hard," he says, stretching out his legs in front of him. He scratches the side of his nose and lets his head fall back against the barn. "They give up a lot to be happy. They live in isolation, far from the ocean. You ask them, and they'll tell you they don't miss it. But the ocean doesn't leave you. To stay away from it like this, landlocked, like they do—you give up a piece of yourself. Ammon and Emlyn are essentially in hiding here. It's—"

· · ·

"She ran away with Ammon, didn't she?" My words are a whisper, and Beck studies me, his eyes darting back and forth from one part of my face to the next. I wonder what he's trying to learn, what he sees in the lines of my face. Eventually, he nods.

"Declan was too young yet, still a year or two away from being old enough to marry, but when she and Ammon decided to run away . . ." He hesitates, as if trying to decide what words to use next. "Declan was not happy." My stomach drops, and a swell of emotion moves through me. Something that I can't place. It's not jealousy, though. Pity, maybe? For the poor prince stuck behind the hedge maze, watching girl after girl leave him with a pirate boy.

Suddenly, so many things become clear. Declan's distrust of Beck, his venom toward him. The comments Siobhan and he made in my room at the institute, before this whole mess of a nightmare began. The ones he said in the hedge maze. Emlyn was the girl he thought he loved. And I was sent to run away with Beck, Ammon's brother. He had to watch me leave, just like he had to watch her. She was the last time. That's what Siobhan meant that night.

Beck takes my hand in his, and his touch surprises me, startling me out of my thoughts. I don't pull away, though. I let him turn my hand and thread his arm through mine, enclosing my fingers in his.

"Does Declan make you happy?" he asks, plain and simple. I close my eyes and let memories of hedge mazes and rooftop gardens and illicit meetings in backrooms about changing the fabric of the nation weave through my mind. All the while, Beck's hand, strong and rough, tethers me to the present.

"He can give me things that no one else can," I say. "Together, we can change things . . . important, significant things . . ." Galina's word feels heavy and wrong in my mouth, and I know I haven't answered his question—so does he. I close my eyes again and try to picture Declan's sweet smile, his golden-boy good looks and his gray eyes, but they're all a jumble of colors and features I haven't seen in weeks. I can't. All I can see is the carefully curated image of him in the newspaper, smiling at Fiona.

"Come on," he says, standing and tugging gently on my hand. I stand with his help, holding on to his coat, and he catches it and sweeps it around my shoulders. The music is slower now; a fiddle floats on the fragile wind as though, if given the chance, it might just reach the stars.

"What do you say, Capo? How 'bout a dance?" He lifts his thick eyebrows and chews on his bottom lip. He's nervous. I've never seen him be nervous.

With a nod, I place my hand on his shoulder. He places his other hand on my hip, resting his thumb over the spot where my tattoo is. We move slowly to the music, and he is surprisingly good on his feet. He leads me in a small circle, and when the wind picks up, he turns into it so it hits his back and not me. The song ends, but we keep dancing as they start a new one. I close my eyes and lean into the dance, and he slips his hand around the small of my back, his palm warm and strong, anchoring me to him. I feel the scratch of his unshaven cheek against my temple, and he turns his face into my ear.

"Your dress is pretty," he says, and I laugh into his shoulder, letting my forehead fall onto his muscular frame.

"I had very little to do with that," I say, turning into him, letting my cheek rest against his chest.

"Remind me to thank the girls later," he says. His fingers slide up and down my back, moving in time with the rise and fall of our synchronized breaths. The wind blows, carrying the sweet violin and the band away from us, and I feel his heart speed up.

"Hey, Capo?" he asks.

"Yeah, Cupcake?" I reply. He chuckles, and I look up at

ERIN RIHA

him. The warm glow of lantern light from the party casts a
golden haze across his hard features, but he looks so different
than he did standing in Kern's kitchen, telling me we can't do
this. That we have to stop. It was all cold and weather-worn,
then, but now it's sinuous and slippery—warm, gold tones aided
by the lamplight creeping around the side of the barn. There's
nothing in the angles of his face now that says stop. No, this is
the expression I saw in New Covington—genuine, unfiltered,
the tiniest bit of broken hope skirting around the edges. He lets
go of my hand, and I let it fall against his chest as he touches his
fingers to my cheek. A gentle, cold breeze flutters over us,
carrying the sound of a bird whistling. His hand freezes, and his
face hardens, the mask snapping back into place.

"Beck?" I ask. He steps back, and his eyes dart left and
right. The chasm between us is cold and endless, and despite my
better instinct, I reach for him. He takes my wrist and pulls me
along the barn, into the dark.

"What is it?" I ask, as we stop at the back corner of the
barn.

"Shhh," he says, delicately holding both of my wrists with
one hand. He listens, and another birdcall trills on the wind. His
eyes dart around, and then fix on a spot.

"They're here," he says.

"Who?"

"Nobody good."

And then the barn explodes.

CHAPTER TWENTY-SIX

*I*t's too hot. Hot ash floats around us like snow, burning my hand and leaving a tiny hole in the sleeve of Beck's coat. The music has stopped. In its void are screams, the yells of panicked wedding guests. They pour out of the barn in a blur. It smells like firewood and something pungent that I don't recognize—something chemical.

"Your family!" I yell, but Beck takes me by the shoulders and forces me down the hill, running faster than my legs can keep up with. I trip, flying forward, and he catches me around the waist, carrying me over the dry brush. His eyes scan the perimeter, moving us as fast as he can away from the brightness of the veritable tinderbox burning on the hill above us. He stops next to a small stone outbuilding.

"Get in," he says.

"What? No!" I say, moving away from it. He grabs me from behind, and I try to kick away from him. He lets go immediately.

"Arden, please," he says. There's no laughter in his voice and fear grips my throat, threatening to squeeze and never let go.

We're hidden in shadows here, but if someone was looking hard enough for me, they'd find me. Even inside this stupid shed.

"No," I say, my voice shaking on account of my uncontrollable shivering. He reaches for my hand, but doesn't outright take it. He holds his hand suspended between us, palm up, and even in the dark, I can see the helplessness in his features.

"It won't be long. Just until I can get the horses and get us out of here."

"Let me come with you, then," I say, and my voice is wild as I beg. I don't want to go inside this stupid shack. I'll be a sitting duck.

"If they see me, I can run. They'll chase me, and you can get away. If they see you, it's game over."

"What if they do chase you?" I ask.

"Then Ammon will come for you," he says, not even a note of bitterness in his words. Apparently, there's no room for sibling rivalry when there's this much fear.

Over my shoulder, people form an assembly line, passing buckets of water from the well to douse the worst of the fire. But the barn glows red and white hot. He opens the door to the shed, and I smell the rotting hay immediately.

"Please don't make me do this," I say, tears clouding my vision. He grabs my arms and holds me inches from his face, so I have to look at him, I have to hear him.

"He's not here," he says. "Look at me, Capo. He's gone. He won't ever do that to you again. This is not that place, and I will not lock the door. You can leave anytime you want. But please . . ." His voice falters. His hands cup my cheeks, and he forces steely strength into his jaw. "Wait for me to come back." I look at it out of the corner of my eye, but it doesn't look any better than it did before.

I squeeze my eyes shut and repeat his words in my head.

He's not here. I nod. He walks in with me, and my heart skyrockets, but he squeezes my hand.

"Easy, Capo. I've got you." He lifts my hand, then presses it against my chest, where I feel my heart beating surprisingly slower than I expect.

"This. Trust this," he says, tapping my breast bone. I nod, and he backs away from me, leaving me alone in the dark, with just the sound of my own unreliable heart.

I don't dare move. I can't see anything, and I'm not sure what is hidden in this small building. The ceiling is only just taller than my head, and the ground is soft, almost soggy, as if it's covered with fermenting straw. I have no idea if there's a lock, or a handle, or a window, or even ventilation. This last thought gives me pause, and my next breath is labored, flavored by the stink of burning dry rot. Screams make their way through the stone walls, and my body shudders, knocking my teeth together. What if the fire moves down the hill, and I'm stuck in here? I'm standing on hay, and who knows what else is around this building? The stone will only do so much if everything around the building is on fire.

I suck in another ragged breath, and it gets caught in my throat. My lips feel numb, and I scrape my nails against the stone as I grapple at something, anything, for support. If I stay in here, I will hyperventilate—or I will die. I stumble to the door and push through, meeting a wall of thick, stinging smoke. The barn is completely wrapped in flames. From ground to roof, white hot flames lick the dry timber, burning oily hot, disintegrating the building splinter by splinter. I run toward it, looking for signs of Beck, or any of the other Hermestons. I reach the side of the barn and squint into the flames, praying I don't see anyone, but then a voice carries over the crackling fire.

"Mama!" A little girl with white-blonde hair and a pink party dress is trapped behind a burning post. Everyone else is on the other side of the barn, struggling to reach her, but I see a way to get there. I hold Beck's coat over my nose and run into the barn, past the band's platform and over a ceiling beam burning on the ground. It's only a matter of time until the entire roof collapses in. I get past the post blocking the little girl, and a fiery beam plummets from above, missing us by inches.

I wrap the coat around the little girl's face and pick her up, slipping around the plank that nearly took us out. Sweat drips into my eyes, mixed with ash, and my vision blurs. But I can't let her go, can't leave her behind. Carrying her, I stumble around the platform as it careens toward us, lost in a wall of flames. I run, narrowly missing its trajectory. Another plank falls from above, and I feel it slash along the back of my leg, singeing my skin and leaving a scorching cut down the back of my calf. We've only barely left the barn when it squeals its death behind us, collapsing in on itself.

"Are you okay?" I ask. I set the girl down and wipe sooty tears from her cheeks. I don't see any burns on her, though her dress is filthy from the smoke and ash. She nods and hiccups, but says nothing. The fear is still in her eyes, and I squeeze her, murmuring words of reassurance.

"Well, well. If it isn't the girl of the hour," a familiar, smarmy voice says from behind me. A voice I know, but with no face to match. A voice I last heard at the institute, the night I left. This man isn't working for Declan, isn't interested in the payout offered by the institute. This man knew about my scar. Which means that this man was sent by someone worse.

"Run!" I tell the little girl, and thank God, she does. But I don't. I stay put, giving her a head start in case she needs it, and turn just in time for a hand to wrap around my throat, nearly lifting me off the ground.

"Don't you go anywhere. You're a difficult one to find, and even tougher to catch, Arden Thatcher." I don't know this man, but I will never forget his black eyes and yellow teeth, or the thick fold of skin turned in on itself that forms a scar along the underside of his right eyebrow, all the way to his ear. I claw at his hand as it crushes my windpipe. With his free hand, he traps my arms and yanks them behind my back, holding me captive as I struggle for air.

"Now, do as I say, and nobody else gets hurt," he says. "Assuming they's smart enough not to burn to death." He pushes me down the hill, back toward the stone house, and panic rises in my veins. I swing my heel down, landing on his instep, and he buckles in pain. I run, but I don't make it more than three steps before he catches my wrist and drags me back with a hard yank. Something pops in my arm, and searing pain radiates out from my elbow. It shoots like electric shocks into my wrist and up to my shoulder. I scream, and he clamps a filthy hand over my mouth. It tastes like iron and something sour, and I gag. I bare my teeth and try to bite at it, and he yanks my head back against him, applying more pressure to my injured arm. Stars burst before my eyes, and I try a meaningless kick to his groin, only to come up far short.

"A lot of bite for such a dirty little thing." He clears his throat and spits. "Now, let's get you back where you belong." The last time I heard those words, there was a black silk sack over my head. I shudder, and then whimper as the motion ricochets through my injured arm. The man grunts in disgust, then tosses me over his shoulder and easily strides downhill. I kick, and keep kicking, and every time I hit something, he twists my arm again, making me cry out. He plops me down on the ground when we reach the bottom of the hill, and I land hard on my back, knocking the wind from my lungs. I croak for air as he binds my feet with rope.

"Where . . . are you taking me?" I finally get out.

"Well, that's up to you now, isn't it, dearie? Back to your peninsula prison? Maybe somewhere a little nicer? Depends who's willing to pay me better. You're wanted for many things

—murder, whoring, none of it my concern. All depends on whether or not you play nice. Keep thrusting your nasty little legs around, and you might not stay in one piece. The payday on your head is mighty, higher than usual, but I know at least one of your buyers cares little about whether or not you come back to him in one piece." I scream out again, but it does no good. With the fire roaring, and the chaos, my screams are absorbed, lost in the flames, just like everything else. Still, he slaps me hard across the jaw, and I fall back onto my injured arm. My vision flashes white with the pain, and I gasp around it as something ferrous coats my tongue.

"Shut up!" he snarls. I hear footsteps growing closer, and the man seems to relax. "Cordon—what took you so long?"

"Not Cordon," Ammon's voice says. I try to prop myself up, but the process moves my bad arm, and the shooting pain levels me.

"Och, the other runaway brother. I think there's still a reward out there for your side piece, too. Not as much as this one, though. This one's worth more," he says. He fists his hand in my hair and yanks my head back. My arm shifts, and a horrid, feral sound fills my ears. When my vision clears, Ammon is watching me, fear thick in his features, and I realize the sound came from me. Beck and his father emerge from the shadows on two other sides, surrounding the man. All three of them have guns.

"Walk away, and we won't have to kill you," Ammon Sr. says. His face is hard to see, backlit by the orange flames, but he looks intimidating, standing slightly uphill and speaking in a low bass.

"You think three of you are going to outnumber us?" the man hisses.

"No, I think twelve of us will," Beck says, clicking the safety on his gun and raising it lazily to take aim. The man's shoulders tense, and his head turns uphill.

"I think you've got your numbers off," the guy says, but there's a nervous edge to his voice.

"Yeah, well, we've got three bodies up the hill, guarded by four men, and I don't know how many more of you there were, but you're in wolf country, son. You think the three of us are your biggest problem? You've underestimated how hearty this stock is." Beck's father's words are simple, and the man seems to react.

"Forget it," the guy says, dropping me with a heartless chuckle. I catch myself on my good arm, but can barely see through the pulsing ache in my bad one. "Bitch ain't worth all this." He steps backs, and then kicks me in the arm, hard. I let out a low, wild keening sound and fall forward onto myself. Everything around me vanishes in a swirl of stars and pain.

"Hold on, Capo," Beck says. His breath is warm against my ear, but he sounds thin, tinny almost. "Now, what did you go and do here? Did you forget you were supposed to hit back?" I blink up at him. His mouth is screwed into a wry grin, but his eyes avoid mine completely. The barn crackles and pops as Ammon works at the rope around my ankles.

"I . . ." I start to say, but the pain is too much. I just cry instead.

"Watch it, asshole," Beck snaps at Ammon, who moves more gently as he removes the rope from my legs. Somewhere in the back of my mind, I note that it's the least creative curse I've ever heard from his mouth. Beck carefully loops my good arm around his neck. He tries to lift me, but blinding pain shoots up through my arm, and I scream. He says something, but I can't focus on the words. We stay where we are on the ground, and he tries to sit me up, leaning me back against his chest. My arm is stable for the moment, but even breathing is enough to shift it painfully in place. He whispers something into my hair, but I don't hear it. Then a man is there, with kind eyes and firm hands. He moves my arm, and I cry out again. There's a canteen at my lips, and whiskey on my tongue, and I spit it out with a gurgling hiccup-sob. Somewhere, I swear Beck is laughing.

"Trust me, Capo," he says. I turn my head toward his voice. His eyes are so green in the smoky haze. I nod.

He tips the whiskey into my mouth again, and this time, I swallow. It burns going down, and he pours more. On about the sixth sip, I think I say something about needing more women. Then Emlyn is at my side, her hand on my cheek. My other cheek presses into Beck's chest.

I know the barn is crackling, and Emlyn is shushing me, and the doctor is speaking. But all I hear is a soft, fast, *thu-thump*, *thu-thump*. Emlyn tucks strands of my hair behind my ear and tells me something about breathing. The man with the kind eyes is back, telling me what he's going to do. *Thu-thump, thu-thump.* Beck's eyes are so green. The doctor braces me and yanks my arm, and everything around me disappears.

CHAPTER TWENTY-SEVEN

*B*eck smells so good. The way he grunts, I think I may have said it out loud. The doctor reset my arm—shoulder and elbow—after I passed out, which Ammon says made it easier, because I was less fidgety. But now, I'm leaning back against Beck on Hammerhead—at least, I think we're on Hammerhead—and I can smell his leather and salt and a touch of something else. Firewood.

When I close my eyes, I still see the fire, consuming and engulfing the barn; the little girl inside, crying for her mama, who just sold her to a mean man with icy blue eyes and his lecherous son who owns a shed and a filthy knife.

I jolt forward, and Beck pulls me back. My arm is throbbing, but everything is fuzzy around the edges, and I know I'm still under the whiskey's influence. I let myself fall back and feel my body sink into his. He absorbs me, until my blood is his blood, and there's just blood and matter everywhere, and CJ's eyes are all whites in a bed of blood. And then they open. He thrusts a mangled hand for my neck. I cry out, but then I'm back on the horse, and Beck's trying to balance us, but my arm hurts so much that I cry. Then a flask is at my lips again, and I swear I hear Emlyn tell them, "That's enough." But I'm swallowing more whiskey, and then I sleep.

My arm is not the only thing that hurts. I suppose the positive to this hangover is that I'm already in too much other pain to dwell on the splitting headache and the nausea. My calf screams with tight, white-hot pain as I stretch my toes, and the side of my face aches in slow, nauseating throbs. High, midday sun pounds in through the glass walls of Beck's barn, and my head throbs and spins. I know the whiskey and the little bit of food I did eat last night are about to come up, and I try to sit up. I find a bin sitting next to me and heave. It's unpleasant, and the force is enough to remind me of the pain in my arm, but once I get it up, I at least feel a little relief. Then Emlyn is there with white tablets and water. I take them, and she urges me back to sleep, and I do.

When I wake again, it's dark, and I'm grateful for it. My head hurts, but not in the same way. The vomit bin is gone, and Beck is sitting in the chair, his jaw tight and his eyes fixed on me. He doesn't say anything for a long minute, and I wonder if I'm actually dreaming. I push up to sitting with my good arm, waiting for the room to stop spinning.

"Bathroom?" I croak. My voice is raw, from disuse and — judging from the sour taste in my mouth — bile. He stands, mechanically, and supports me under my good arm, helping me to my feet. I walk myself to the bathroom, gingerly, and use the toilet. When I wash my hands, I get a good look at myself. I'm wearing pajamas — so someone did that — and my hair looks like a crow's nest. My face is a smear of dark purple-and-green bruises that run along the left side of my jaw. I brush my teeth and finger comb my hair, twisting it into a low knot that falls out almost immediately as I walk through the door.

Beck stands on the other side of the windows, directly across from me. His forehead is tight, his hands shoved into his pockets. He watches me, but says nothing. My stomach flips, and I look at the floor.

"Thank you," I say. He doesn't move, doesn't speak. "I know you told me to stay put, and I didn't listen. Again. I'm sorry." I dip my chin at my broken body, cringing at the effort. "Is everyone else okay?" I ask. He exhales and nods. I let out a sigh of relief.

"I'm sorry," I say again. Still, he says nothing. I stare at him now, and his face hasn't changed. His hands remain in his pockets, and his shoulders are rigid and unmoved. He has nothing to say to me, and now, anger rises in my belly.

"You know what? Never mind," I say. He lifts his eyebrows, but still doesn't move. "I'm not sorry. Because if I had stayed in that damn shack, I wouldn't have gone back to the barn, and that little girl might not have been saved. So I'm glad I didn't listen to your stupid plan. If I had to do it all over again, I would ignore you then, too. I would never let you talk me into that . . . that . . . shitty shed . . ." I spit the words at him, letting the fear and the pain, the familiarity of the bounty hunter and his terrible scar, wash over me.

Beck walks toward me, closing the distance between us in two long strides. I brace myself—for what, I'm not sure—but he doesn't yell, or fight, or grab me by the arms to shake some sense into me. Instead, he wraps me in a hug, curling himself around me. His hand cups the back of my head as he holds my head to his chest, and I want to step back, to pull away, to yell at him more. But I don't. I hug him back instead, giving in to the root of the fear, the heart of the terror: that I might not have survived the night. I grip his shirt with my good hand, shaking like I'll shatter and fall apart if he lets go, and he rubs his hand up and down my back, holding me tight against him, sheltering me.

He holds me like that through the rest of the night, through fitful, aching sleep, his arms enveloping me, protecting me from everything that isn't in the little bubble we've created for ourselves. And I remain, cheek nestled in the soft valley between his chest and his shoulder. At one point, I must have a nightmare, because he turns onto his side to face me.

"Capo," he whispers, stroking my face.

"Cupcake," I whisper back. He opens his mouth to say something, and then closes it and pulls me into his chest. *Beck might never say.* Ammon's words come back to me, and in this moment, I don't need him to say it. I don't need him to say anything at all. I nestle further into his chest and let him run his fingers through my hair until I fall asleep for good.

CHAPTER TWENTY-EIGHT

*W*hen I wake, Beck is asleep. I've never seen him sleep. The sunlight falls across his cheeks in shafts, deepening the shadows in his growing beard. His forehead is soft, the skin around his eyes relaxed, not a hint of sarcasm or bravado. His arm rests solidly around my hip, his hand flat against my back. There is no tension, no pull in his hold, but I feel safe. I close my eyes and nestle my nose into his shirt, breathing him in. His hand tugs me closer, sliding up and down my back, and I feel guilty for having disturbed him. I reach for him and wince.

"Watch that arm, Capo," he says into the top of my head. I try to bend it, but it's stiff, and I let it stay where it was, lying over his arm, along my side.

"Sorry I woke you," I say.

"The sun is up. We should be up." He groans, but there's resolution in his baritone. I tilt my head up at him, and he looks down at me, carefully cupping my bruised cheek in his hand. For a moment, I think he might kiss me.

"You're killing me, Capo," he says with a groan, and then throws the blanket off us. The air in the loft is cold, and I curl up into him. He groans again, but braces my arms and helps me to a seated position in a way that barely jostles my arm. He goes into the bathroom, and I pick up a sweater that lies on the floor. His sweater. I work it over my head. It smells so good, and somehow still retains remnants of his warmth. He walks out and stops short, seeing me, and then, with a wry grin, he helps me get my other arm through without straightening it.

"Are we safe here?" I ask, sliding the futon back up into couch form with my good arm.

"For the moment," he says, pulling a different sweater over his head and shoving his feet into his dirty boots. "But we should probably move on."

I haven't done what I need to do. I haven't earned Emlyn's trust, haven't gotten any information from her. But I've also brought trouble here to her sanctuary. Literally. They didn't know they'd find her here, judging by the way my attacker talked about her after the wedding. I can't stay. Even if I'm not sure where I want to end up.

"Where will we go?" I ask. A bird flies past the window—large wings, familiar loud squawk, far from home. Too far from home. Beck's eyes follow mine, and he chuckles.

"There's a place inland. About a day's ride west. Past Highton. We can get there without going through Highton, but it's not easy terrain. With your arm . . ." He pauses, as if rethinking the plans.

"I'll be fine," I lie. He raises an eyebrow, and his mouth curls into a half smile, exposing his dimple, but he doesn't call me on it.

"We'll leave as soon as we can get the horses ready," he says. "If anyone's still looking for us around Highton, it will steer them away from here."

"Good," I say. The bounty hunter's words to Ammon last night are sticking with me. They know who he is; they know who Emlyn is. They know there's a reward for her. But something else sticks, stopping me from moving forward with our plan.

"What's that face?" Beck asks, keeping his distance.

"I know who he was. I mean . . . I don't know *who* he was, but I know . . ." I'm not making sense. But Beck nods. He knows, too. Of course, he does. He was there. He got me away from him when he tried to kidnap me at the institute.

"Who . . . who is he working for?" I ask. But I'm already sure I know. The evidence was too heavy in his words for me not to have put it together.

Beck doesn't answer, rubbing the side of his nose as he looks away. I guess part of me still hoped I was wrong, that I had read the situation incorrectly. But Beck's lack of comment confirms it. The man may be willing to collect on what the institute's offering, but that's not the only offer on the table. What happens if Conrad's pockets run deeper? What if he's not the only one with deep pockets?

"I'll get a message to Kern," Beck says, moving toward the door. I look around the space, thinking that I should pack, but I didn't come with anything. As if reading my mind, he says, "Why don't you get the packs ready to go?"

I nod, looking around for my clothes. As I do, I suddenly remember. My good hand flies to my chest, but there's nothing there. No compass, no bracelet.

"Beck?" I ask.

He pauses by the door, turning back to me, and concern tightens the lines around his eyes. "Everything okay, Capo?"

"Yeah," I say, not wanting to ask the man whose bed I just shared about the trinket from the one I'm supposed to marry.

He presses his lips into a thin line and shakes his head. "Try not to dislocate anything else?"

I nod and stand awkwardly, both arms hanging dumb at my sides. He nods one more time and leaves.

It's harder to carry blankets and packs down the steps with one arm, so I end up tossing everything down into the barn, and then climb down after. I try to balance the blankets between my stiff arm and my body, but once I get out into the wind, everything starts to slip from my weak grasp.

"Here, let me help." Emlyn startles me, and I drop everything. Her impossibly shiny hair is braided along her delicate hairline, sweeping it all into a long, mahogany-colored twist. I stand, slightly dumbfounded as she picks up one of the packs and throws it over her shoulder. It settles against the tan of her corduroy jacket, and I pick up the remaining pack and blanket with my good hand and nod my thanks. We walk to the stables, quiet.

Marlbury is squawking in the distance, and I wonder where she ended up landing. She's not in the stables where I expected, so maybe Beck brought her around to the back of the house to grab scraps from the kitchen?

"Hi there, old friend," Emlyn says, stroking Sir Squints-a-Lot's muzzle. He leans into her touch, and I stand aside, watching her cuddle the beast who hates me.

"Figures," I say.

"What's that?" she asks.

"He likes everyone but me," I say. She smiles and keeps rubbing the soft fur between his eyes, as I realize I've said something mean. "I mean, you're nice . . ." I cringe at my gaffe, but she laughs it off and walks over to Hammerhead, deftly attaching the pack she carries.

"I took care of my benefactor's horses," she says. I can't see her beyond Squints, but for as casually as she speaks, her words are clear. *We are more alike than you think.*

"Your benefactor's horses?" I ask, taking the bait.

"I preferred it to housework. I got out of the house that way.

Got some fresh air, a place to hide. I had a little more freedom than the other girls that way, too. It was messy work, but I could exercise the horses."

"I was a glorified errand boy," I say, walking around the front of my horse, setting my pack down on the ground with the blanket. She nods and gives me a weak smile.

"I still had to be there for lessons, mind you," she says. "My benefactor took that seriously. Didn't want to waste any money on us. If we weren't placed well, either in the institute or beyond, it was a loss. He didn't take losses."

"What of the girls who were nominated and not selected?" I ask.

"There were none," she says.

"What do you mean?" I ask, thinking of Neve and the other Unchosen.

"His girls were always picked. He only ever sponsored one for each year and nominated one for each year. This time around, it was his own daughter. He wanted us in there, laying the groundwork for her."

"Fiona?" I ask. She narrows her eyebrows and shakes her head.

"No, not Fiona. A little blonde thing. Doesn't look like much, but was just about the smartest, most scheming teenager I've ever met." I narrow my eyebrows and bite on the side of my tongue. There's only one blonde I can think of, but I wouldn't call her scheming.

"Avery?" I ask, recalling the fair, proper girl who arrived already looking like a princess. She nods, recognition flooding her face.

"That's the one. He wanted us in there, so that by the time it was her turn, there was no question about the quality of his girls. But then I got there, and things changed."

"What happened?" I ask. She's done strapping the pack to Hammerhead and comes back to me to pick up the pack I've laid down. She carries it around Hammerhead, and I can't see her as she attaches it to his other side. I wonder if this is intentional, so I can't see her face.

"Declan . . ." She starts and sighs, staying behind the horse. A familiar weight presses down on my shoulders. "He was still young, but he tried to change the rules."

"What do you mean?" I ask, but after what Beck said the other night, I think I know where this is going.

"He developed a crush. On me," she says, gently. She finishes her work and walks back to Hammerhead's front, nuzzling him gently. I can't blame Declan for falling for her. She's stunningly beautiful, and apparently beloved by horses. That's two things she has that I don't.

"What happened?" I ask, feeling useless without something to do with my hands, or the ability to even pretend to do something useful with them.

"He's sweet . . . and it's easy to fall under his spell," she says, finally looking at me. "But you know that." I smile and feel my cheeks flush. She narrows her eyes at me, and a little smile creeps into them. But she shakes her head, ridding herself of a thought she doesn't share. "He thinks he wants something different from his mother. But he doesn't know what to do with that. I was different. You're different. I'm not saying we're the same . . ." She trails off, but the implication is clear. He doesn't want me. He wants the idea of me. He doesn't want change; he wants the idea of change.

"What did he do?" I ask. Her eyebrows lift in ladylike arcs, and she blinks her long eyelashes a few times too many.

"He wanted to marry me," she says. My stomach drops. I don't know why. I don't really have the right to let it. I just spent the night in another man's arms—the man he charged with protecting me. The man his mother paid to keep me away. I'm not sure who the bigger fool is at this point—him for trusting me, or me for taking the bait. Either way, I feel a seed of jealousy over the fact that the boy I've promised to marry, the boy I'm not sure I actually want to marry, wanted to marry this beautiful woman first.

"What did you say?" I ask. She laughs and shakes her head.

"No, you're not understanding. He wanted to marry me, but we were never romantic. It was a schoolboy crush, and I was naive. I thought that was just the way of political life. You have to understand, he was still underage, and I am two years older. I never looked at him that way. But he offered . . . to help me. Coming from my life, from the way it was, it was hard not to want to listen." Her eyes lock with mine, and in them, I see a familiar web of invisible scars; that skittish, distrusting flicker of trauma. I understand. *We are more alike than you think*.

"It was my benefactor's son," I blurt out. Her stomach pulls in, and a sad smile curls the corners of her full lips.

"My benefactor's brother," she says. "I was one of the lucky ones. He doted on me, never did anything irreversible." Her words come quickly, as if she has to explain away something that will color my view of her. I can explain nothing. I have no excuses. She sees this, and she swallows hard.

"You can understand then," she says, "that when he offered me that life, I was intrigued." I nod. I had the same reaction. Hell, I actually promised to marry him. "It became clear that he was going to petition for the right to propose early.

"His mother was less than enthusiastic. His father even less. They had counted on the economic bump during his coming-of-age year. He suspected they were going to fight him on it, but he had allies in the privy council. He was going to present it for a vote." She stops talking, and her cheeks bloom a pretty rose color as a smile creeps into the corners of her round eyes.

"But then, there was a dinner. And I was not seated at his table. I was seated . . . elsewhere." My heart races with the familiarity of a story I know. *There was a dinner, and I was seated next to a pirate*.

"You were seated next to Ammon?" I ask. She nods and shrugs, running her hand down Hammerhead's nose.

"I fell quick. He fell hard." She smiles and leans in conspiratorially. "He will dispute this, but I fell harder. Anyway, negotiations started for me elsewhere." Her mouth puckers around the word *elsewhere*. I wonder where. "Declan was beside himself and planned to object. It was becoming a scandal. His mother approached me and offered to make it all go away. She would help me out of there, buy me some time, but she didn't know where to send me. I was a fool and told her about Ammon." She shakes her head. "Now, I know that was her intent the entire time. People end up where she wants them, and it's hardly ever in her world."

I open my mouth to disagree, but then close it. Even if this fake-kidnapping mess was Declan and Beck's idea, she paid Beck. She knew where I would end up, and I'm exactly where she wanted me to be.

"So, she made it happen. She gave us some money, and she helped us escape under cover of night. But I wasn't allowed to tell Declan, wasn't even allowed to leave him a note. As we left, she told us we could never return. That officially, I would be a runaway, indebted to my benefactor. It was . . . bittersweet." She wrings her hands and takes a steadying breath.

"Ammon is my person," she says, pressing her lips into a round heart. "I would never give him up for anything. But there was a moment there, however fleeting, that I thought I might change things. Because things *must* change." Her eyes level me, and I realize what she's asking.

"Ammon and I sailed for a bit. It didn't last. There were too many people looking for the runaway girl. And her captor. Rumors fly, and nobody stopped them. People who knew what I was to Declan and thought that they could use me to control him sent hunters after us. We had some trouble around Brandeissland and fled to Sudersberg. Got some help there. Hid with Irina for a bit . . ." She tapers off and makes an unflattering, pinched face. She picks up the last blanket I've left on the ground and carries it back over to Hammerhead, tucking it in the pack.

"Has Beck told you about Irina?" she asks, hiding her face again.

"No," I say. "Galina mentioned her, though."

"Really?" she asks, looking around Hammerhead, her face unreadable. I nod and reach for Squints. To my surprise, he doesn't flinch, but lets me stroke the soft, downy fur above his nose.

"If you can get her on your side, she will be helpful. If not . . ." She raises an eyebrow at me and shakes her head.

"If not, what?"

"Watch out," she says.

"Whose side is she on?" I ask.

"Her own. Always her own." She goes back to tightening the straps on Hammerhead, and then pats his flank once. We are done here. She leads me out of the stable, and we stop just outside.

"But she will know how to find people."

"What do you mean, find people?" I ask.

"While we're at the institute, we're kept apart to a certain degree. Pitted against each other, told we're all in this together, but actually, we're competing for selective appointments. Hell, we're competing for superlatives: the smart one, the exotic one, the pretty one, the virgin, the whore. The underdog." She gives me a little nod after the last one, and my body lengthens, gets taller. "When we graduate, we are sent our separate ways. No two girls go to the same province or kingdom. Ever. Why is that?" she asks. I see Ammon and Beck talking on the porch and meet Ammon's eyes. He keeps Beck engaged. I have no doubt he knows what Emlyn and I are discussing. Beck's words come back to me:

Ammon is a part of this now. But it feels bigger than sibling rivalry.

"I don't know. Happenstance?" I ask, but I feel stupid even suggesting it.

"They tell us we're supposed to further Nordanian interests in our new positions, right? So why wouldn't they want us to talk to each other? To carry the alliances we've formed in our candidacy to the world stage? To band together?" I shrug, and she presses her lips into a firm line before she continues. "I think it's so we don't realize the power we actually have. We go out into the world and spread Nordanian influence . . . but what if we spread something more potent?"

"Like what?" I ask.

"Like hope," she says. She pulls something from her pocket and reaches for my good hand, placing the item on my palm. The cool metal disk quickly warms in my palm, like an ember of hope-tinged regret.

"How did you . . ." I start, and she curls my fingers over the compass.

"I found it in the grass. Thought you might want it back." She gives me a soft, knowing smile, and I feel the prick of tears against the backs of my eyes.

The chain I used to wear it around my neck is gone, so I slip it into my pocket for safekeeping.

"I won't tell you what to do," she says, her voice low and urgent, "but whatever your decision, make it quickly, and make it stick. Beck is . . . he may seem—" Her voice falters as the slam of the front door interrupts our moment. My chest tightens as I realize the option she's giving me: go be what Declan asks of you for the sake of generations of girls to come. But be kind with Beck.

Beck steps off the porch, Ammon and his parents close on his heels.

"You're useless if you don't graduate," she says, too quickly.

"What?" I ask. But my conversation with Declan comes ricocheting back to me. *You and the next generation of candidates will have the power to control the system.*

"If you graduate, you have standing. You have access. If you keep hiding, you'll spend the rest of your life that way." Her eyes are wild and watery now, and I don't doubt she's talking about herself. I lower my eyebrows and chew on the edge of my tongue, and she shakes her head, blinking her long lashes to clear them. "Don't get me wrong. This is the right place for me, but sometimes, I wish I could be more effective. You still can be."

She takes me by the arms, and I wince, but she doesn't let go.

"Talk to Irina," she says. "I wasn't lying before. I don't have what you need, but Irina does. Ask her about Carmen." I blink, and she bites her top lip. "Tell her, 'It's Ammon's wish.'"

She hugs me close, and I hear the crunch of boots closing in behind me.

"Stand up for those of us who are forced to kneel," she whispers, placing a hand on the back of my head. "Give them hell." She pulls back and nods at me, holding my face in her hands. "Follow your heart, and you will never be led astray." I nod back. I'm distracted through the rest of the goodbyes, thinking about what Emlyn has just asked of me.

As we get on the horses, I'm distracted still. It was all so much—too much, really. Somehow, I have the information I need. But it's not what I thought I would get. I suppose I hoped that the person Declan wanted me to talk to would give me an address, or a list of names. This is much less certain. I know very little about Irina, even less of it glowing, but if that's where I have to go, then I suppose, that's what I have to do.

Beck shoots me a concerned glance as we start to head west, and I hear a loud squawk overhead.

"Is that Marlbury?" I ask. He narrows his eyebrows and

nods. "Can you call her back?" He whistles and dismounts Hammerhead. I watch the sea bird return and realize we've made it below the horizon—I can no longer see the farm. A cold wind nips at the back of my neck, and I shiver.

"What's your call, Capo?" he asks, his voice a razor's edge. Emlyn is right—I can't keep running and expect things to change. If Declan really does want change, like he says, then it has to start with me. And I don't have a vote unless I graduate. If I never go back, I'll never have a vote. Yes, things are complicated, with the criminal charges and the fake kidnapping, but I can persuade Declan to move things along. Heck, it's been weeks since I last spoke with him; maybe things have already been worked out. I meet Beck's eyes and wince slightly, knowing that this might strain things between us, that it might pull us apart, and I'm not ready for that. But if there's a chance I can do this—graduate, use my voice for good—then maybe I can make life easier for Beck, too. Or maybe, I could at least make it so he doesn't have to run, and his family doesn't have to hide.

"Tell your crew to get ready to sail." He nods, and I take a deep breath, edging closer to where he pulls paper and a lead pencil from his pack.

"And then tell me everything I need to know about Irina."

His eyes flicker to mine, and he stares for a long moment, his face unreadable as he studies mine, then nods. I'm not running anymore. And I'm not letting the boys fight my battles for me. It's time I face things head on and give them hell.

CHAPTER TWENTY-NINE

"*W*hat did you do to Sir Squints?" Beck asks as we break for water along the river. The sun is high overhead and warms the air more than I expected. My jacket is packed away, and little pellets of sweat line my forehead.

"What do you mean?" I ask. He nods at my hand on Sir Squints-a-Lot's side, his eyes full of concern.

"He's not trying to get rid of you."

"Screw you," I say, but I can't keep a smile from my lips. He leans back against a tree and looks at the ground, scratching at his beard.

"Is that an offer?" he asks, daring a quick look up at me. One eyebrow lifts, and a smirk curls his full lips.

"Is that a come-on?" I ask, hand on my hip. He edges toward me, crossing his arms over his chest. If I didn't know better, I would think he was flexing his biceps.

"You'll know when it's a come-on," he says. My cheeks flush, and I roll my eyes. I know he's joking, but after sharing a bed together, it's a little too on the nose. Emlyn's words come back to me with a sticky wash of shame: *Whatever your decision, make it quickly, and make it stick.* I clear my throat and chew on

ERIN RIHA

the edge of my tongue, putting an end to this little flirtation
before it spirals out of control. To his credit, he doesn't
apologize, or try to talk his way around the snarky comment.
Not to his credit, he instead tosses a stick at me, which spooks
poor Squints, and I have to hold on to his reins with more force
to keep him from bolting. Squints glares at me, and our
newfound friendship is again on the rocks.

"You about ready?" Beck asks, biting his lower lip. "Or do
you need to cool off in the river first?" His eyes rake over my
body, and for a second, I think I might. Thankfully, Squints lifts
his head from the water and stomps his hoof.

"Nope. I'm good," I say. He gives me a business-like nod.

"I want to make it to the campsite before it gets dark. Is
your arm up to a faster pace?" he asks.

"Sure," I say with a shrug, still not looking at him. I try to
pull myself up with one arm, but I lose my grip and slip. Beck is
quickly behind me, one hand on my waist. I don't flinch, but I
don't look at him either.

"Slow," he says. I grip the reins, and his fingers dig into my
waist. I grab the knob on the saddle and hook my left leg in the
stirrup, and he lifts me up. He holds on to my calf, just behind
my knee, a moment too long. As if he's not ready to let go. I
look down and meet his gaze.

"I'm good," I say softly. He nods, a lingering smile hovering
on his lips as he removes his hand. We get up to a decent speed,
faster than before, and it's not comfortable. But I don't want to
bother Beck with my arm. He seems like he has enough on his
mind, and I can see the life coming back to him with every
gallop closer to the ocean.

We make camp just as the sunset turns to dusk, settling into
a space set back into a grove of trees. Beck builds a modest fire,
and I water and feed the horses. His mother packed us
sandwiches, and thankfully, they're delicious. I'd been dreading
more of Kern's mom's meal bars.

The night folds in on us harsh and fast. If we'd stayed much longer, there's a good chance we'd have been stuck in the first real throes of winter. I can smell snow on the air, though the skies above are cloudless.

We chew our sandwiches in precarious quiet. He stares into the fire, like he's going to understand the chemical reaction that sparked it if it kills him. Or maybe like he's trying to avoid a conversation. His shoulders drop, and he looks up at me.

"What do you want to know? About Irina?"

I press my lips together and wrap the second half of my sandwich.

"You've never told me about her."

"I haven't."

"Why not?"

"No reason."

"So, you weren't avoiding talking about her?" I ask. I dislike when he plays this game.

"What do you want me to say?" he asks. There's an edge of irritation tugging at his voice, and he throws something into the fire. It sparks, and he tears into his sandwich, perhaps a little too aggressively.

"I don't know," I say, feeling uncomfortable and guilty for even asking. It's clearly something that makes him uncomfortable, and that, in turn, sends my stomach churning for no reason I'm willing to examine too closely. He stares at me, waiting for me to say something.

"Emlyn told me I need to talk to her."

This surprises him. He sits upright and cocks his head.

"Emlyn said that?"

"Yes."

"*Emlyn* wants you to talk to Irina?"

"She said Irina knows . . . well, that she can tell me what I'm looking for."

"What are you looking for?" His words are a dare, prodding and dangerous. I narrow my eyes.

"For other girls. Graduates who can support me. She says Irina knows where they are." My words sound much more solid than my information feels. Really, all I have to go on is a single name, and that *it's Ammon's wish.* I don't tell him this part, though. It doesn't feel helpful to the situation.

"She won't trust you," he says, finally.

"Why not?"

"Because you're with me." I narrow my eyes and study his face. The corner of his mouth tugs into a strange emotion that I can't decipher.

"Do you think Emlyn's right? That Irina can help?" I ask. His eyes flicker up to me, and then back to the fire.

"Yes," he says. He snorts and finishes the last massive bite of his sandwich.

"But you think she won't."

"I know she won't."

"Because I'm with you."

"Because you're with me," he says, nodding once. "And for about a dozen other reasons."

"Which are?"

"Not worth explaining," he mumbles, poking at the fire with a long, charred stick. The fire sparks, and the embers float into the sky like fireflies. The dynamic has shifted, as if there was a third person present, sitting between us around the fire. I remember his mother's words, that she thought Beck had suffered for Irina for years. Maybe he still is. That thought alone makes my stomach drop, and I clear my throat.

"So, you won't take me to her?"

"I'll take you wherever you want." He meets my eyes, his greens challenging mine, daring me to make a decision.

"But you think it's a bad idea."

"Doesn't really matter what I think," he says. I exhale hard, hating that he won't give me anything to work with. A small part of me wishes he would just tell me no, that he won't take me there, and he won't take me back to Declan; that we'll just hide away, and the rest of the world can go screw itself. My cheeks flush at the thought, and I dig the heel of my boot into the red earth.

"It seems like the only answer I have right now."

"Yeah," he says.

I pack away my sandwich and pull another blanket around me. I can't scoot much closer to the fire without risking burning the blanket. He stokes the fire again, and it puts off a little more heat. I smile at him, grateful for the little burst. It's going to get too cold tonight.

"Thanks," I say, and feel his eyes on me. I can't meet them, though. Not right now. I'm too afraid of what I'll find.

"What else did you and Emlyn talk about?" he asks. When I do look up, he's staring past his feet into the fire.

"She told me about her time at the institute," I say, not sure what he knows and what answer would hurt him less.

"She did?" he asks, but it's not really a question.

"Yeah." I clear my throat and stare around the fire at him. "Is that why Declan doesn't like you?" His eyes flicker to mine. He stares at me for a silent moment, and then laughs. Loud.

"Does he think you're like your brother? That . . ." I stop, because I realize that what I'm actually asking is two different questions, and I don't know if I want the answer to the second one.

"Does he think you're . . . untrustworthy?" I ask, forcing a word that doesn't quite fit. But it's a pointless question. Declan already said as much. The wind rattles the bare branches overhead, and a straggler leaf falls into the fire, sparking, then burning away into nothing.

"Is that the question you want me to answer?" he asks, leaning back on his hands.

I don't really know what I want him to tell me. I already know the answer to my question: it's yes. Yes, Declan doesn't trust Beck. But is it because he's been burned before by Ammon? Is it because Siobhan insisted on seating me next to Beck at a formal dinner? Or is it because of something else?

"I like Emlyn," I say instead.

"I thought you would," he says, leaning forward, propping his forearms on his knees. The fire pops and crackles, and he grabs another piece of wood to add.

"She's not what I expected," I say. "I wish I'd known her better sooner."

"What about Ammon?" he asks, placing the wood into the fire. His voice is cautious, measured—too even. He's asking something deeper.

"I like him," I say, keeping my face neutral. He nods, and then hesitates, as if waiting for something to validate whatever it is he's thinking.

"But he's too tall," I say quickly. Beck smirks. I stare at the fire, and the thought of Declan reemerges. Declan knows Ammon; Declan knows Beck. I wonder if he liked Ammon before this all happened. I also wonder what he actually felt for Emlyn. How close is it to what he thinks he feels for me?

"I don't know what Declan wants with me," I say, my face flushing immediately. I didn't mean to say those words out loud, but they're out there now. I can't take them back, and I suck in my breath. I curl my knees into my chest and lay my cheek against them. The wind whips overhead, colder than before, pushing the fire to my left ever so slightly. Beck's legs come into my line of sight, not two feet away, and then he sits, facing me, his face pulled to the right in sardonic amusement.

"I have a pretty good idea," he says. "I mean, if you want me to paint you a picture . . . "

"Don't be gross," I say, and he grins.

"Oh, well in that case," he says with a shrug, pulling his own blanket tighter around his shoulders. But he keeps his distance.

"Never mind," I say, pressing my forehead into my knees. The wind crackles the fire. I look up, following the embers that spiral toward the stars, watching them dissipate into stardust.

"You're gentle." Beck's voice is soft and precise. "And you're thoughtful. Even when you think you're being careless. You don't make decisions lightly, and you are never selfish. You should maybe be more selfish, but that's neither here nor there. You are smart and brave and so pretty. And there is no one else like you."

I sit straighter and stare at the man who knows all the wrong words, who just found all the right ones. His green eyes dance green and gold and bright as they watch the fire, and the world around me disappears for a minute. I cling to his words, willing them to be true as he continues.

"He needs you. Hell, anyone with a battered spirit needs you," he says, his eyes flicking to mine for the briefest of moments. "You have fire in your blood. Even when the world tries to smother you, you're steadfast. You survive. You're an ember, Capo, a wildfire waiting to burn. You'll change the world, if given the right kind of breeze.

"But more than that," he says, his voice an almost-whisper, "he sees the best version of himself when he's with you." He's still as he stares into the flames, his expression plain and unguarded. *Beck may never say.* But still, I hear him. I hear what he's not saying, the words that match the things dancing, naked and bare, on his face. But I can't say it for him. I don't have the names for those things. He clears his throat and frowns, and just like that, he's back to being guarded.

"You're the person he needs. And you are, perhaps, the person Nordania needs." He shakes his head, but says nothing more. "And if this is really what you want, I will take you to Irina myself and accept the consequences," he says. But he never actually asks the question that instead hangs over the fire smoke. *Is that what you want? Is he what you really want? Can he make you happy?* He shivers, harsh and violent from his core. I don't answer his unasked questions. Instead, I close the distance between us and open my blankets, urging him inside. He drops his blanket and slides in next to me, sliding an arm around my shoulders and wrapping the blankets around us. He lays the third blanket over our legs, and we settle next to each other, neither of us shivering anymore. He kisses my temple, and I fall asleep against his shoulder.

"Arden."

It's too cold, and I sit up quickly, wracked with a full-body shiver. He's rolling up a blanket as he kicks dirt onto the embers. A birdcall jolts me wide awake, and the horses fuss off to our right. I stand and roll up my blanket as I stumble toward Squints. Beck finishes damping the fire and helps hoist me onto Sir Squints-a-Lot, taking the blankets from me. My teeth chatter as I soothe Squints, and I swear I see a flake of snow, though I'm not sure how I could. It's too dark. All the starlight has been snuffed out.

"Follow me." Beck's whisper is urgent in my ear.

Then I hear it.

Hoofbeats. And a cough. Not close enough to attack, but too close for comfort. We walk the horses quietly, slowly, trying not to draw attention. We stay in the tree line until it tapers off, leaving us exposed on the steppe. Beck mounts Hammerhead, and I follow his lead.

The terrain is scrub brush and slopes downhill. Under the cloud cover, the horses can't see well. I can tell Hammerhead is uncomfortable, and Squints is near spooked. A horse neighs behind us. Maybe half a mile. Beck picks up the pace, and we follow, picking up speed on the slope.

Hoofbeats echo behind us, and all I can do is follow Beck. I don't know how he can see anything ahead. But then he pulls up, and I do the same. Squints doesn't panic, but he's spooked. Beck turns left, and the slope gets much steeper. We're on a narrow trail—the first leg of a switchback. There's no room for mistake. I have to trust Squints, and he has to do the same.

"Shh, good boy, careful," I whisper into Squints's neck. I don't know if it's a good idea or a bad idea, but I figure it can't hurt. To my relief, it seems to soothe him, and we continue downhill, curling back in on our path. Then a rock falls, and Hammerhead backs up. Sir Squints-a-Lot whinnies, unhappy and shrill, and I hear shouting uphill. I don't know who's after us, but we're stuck on this narrow path like sitting ducks.

"Faster," Beck calls back, and I hear hoofbeats clattering above us. They've heard us. They know they're closing in. What we're doing is incredibly dangerous. I know it, and so, it seems, does Squints. The clouds part, and the moonlight unveils a series of steep switchbacks and, over the edge, a terrifying canyon of tiny ice crystals floating in the air—and us, for anyone to see.

"Hurry!" yells an awful, familiar voice behind us. There's not enough distance to protect us from someone who really wants to catch us. But in the moonlight, the horses can see better, and they move faster, more sure footed. We curve around a sharp switchback, then the next, and then another. The sound of gravel falling down into the canyon below is nearly paralyzing, and Squints takes a step backward. I tighten my hold on his reins, and he seems to calm, but I'd be lying if I said I wasn't terrified.

We get the technique down to a steady rhythm. When I hear the first blast of gunfire, we've got one more switchback to go. Sir

Squints-a-Lot bucks, and I cling to him with my good arm, but it's not enough. I fly off and land on a rock. To his credit, Sir Squints-a-Lot doesn't run—with Hammerhead blocking his lead, there's nowhere for him to go. He backs up, straight for where I'm stuck on the ground. He can't see anything, and he's panicked. He moves over top of me, and I pull my leg out of his way as he steps over.

"Capo!" Beck calls in a shouting whisper.

"Down here," I shout back, and I stand, reaching soft hands toward Squints's reins.

"Shh, come here, Squints," I whisper, trying to soothe the skittish horse. He hesitates, and I take one side of his bridle. A stone falls from the top of the canyon, hitting the trail just above us, and Squints bucks.

His front hoof knocks my bad shoulder. I cry out, and he skitters backward, slipping off the ledge. It happens both too slowly and too fast: his torso smacks the ground, his hooves scrape slashes into the earth, and his eyes are wide and panicked. Then he's gone, and all that's left is the sound of his scream.

"Now," Beck says, grabbing my good arm.

"Wait!" I cry, not whispering. But he pulls me up using strength I didn't know he had. He sets me on his mount, and I hold on to him as gunfire echoes across the canyon. We lose the moonlight, and he pushes Hammerhead down the last switchback as hoofbeats sound louder on the rock path above.

"Run while you can, Arden Thatcher. It'll make it that much more fun when I get my hands around that pretty little neck of yours." The nasty, familiar voice calls down to us, but we've reached the bottom of the trail, and Beck kicks Hammerhead hard. We take off like a shot. The roar of gunfire follows us, and I bury my face into Beck's back, clinging to him with my good arm and trying to keep the tears from freezing on my cheeks.

We ride hard and fast, and Hammerhead doesn't relent; we have such a narrow window to regain our advantage. We ride through the night, and I steel myself against the tears that threaten to topple me. How could I have let that happen? Squints was my responsibility. He had finally started to trust me —and I failed him. No, worse. I killed him.

Beck keeps us along the tree line as much as possible, which becomes easier as the moon moves westward on the horizon, casting shadows out further and further. Poor Hammerhead must be exhausted, but it's as if he knows how important it is that we keep going. By the time the sun comes up, my eyes burn with frozen tears, and we can just see the lights of New Covington.

"Not far now," Beck says, his voice rough. We ride down Main Street as the sun rises. Kern and his father are, incredibly, already there. I hug him with my good arm and let him cry into my shoulder over Sir Squints-a-Lot. His father hugs me as well, his eyes kind and sympathetic. Slick finds us, and we board and depart within the hour, waving to Kern's father, who stands on the pier. Just as we start to lose sight of New Covington, we see five riders in black line the pier. Even from this distance, I swear I can make out a rider with a long, ugly scar, and something tells me it's not the last we'll see of them.

CHAPTER THIRTY

*O*nce we'd navigated safely out of the harbor, the first thing Beck did was punch Perlman square in the nose.

To be fair, he told him he was going to. His exact words were, "Once you get us out of here, I'm punching that beakish knobrot you call a nose off your face."

Honestly, I had sort of forgotten about the tearing-my-clothes-off-me incident at Madame Celeste's. Apparently, though, he hadn't. I don't think Perlman's nose is actually broken, but his face doesn't look any less beakish or knobrotty.

The waves aren't so disorienting this time. In fact, I find I've missed their rocking movement in a way I didn't expect. Smelling the salt on the wind is soothing, enveloping me in a scent I've come to associate with safety and comfort. I try not to read more into it than that. I don't leave Beck's side, though, following him into the bridge and watching him talk to Shaz in rapid-fire nautical terms. Perlman joins them, a cold compress pressed to his face, and they discuss a route.

"—calm your horses, yeh hercjerker. Still waiting on a response."

"Can't Kern tell that damn bird to hurry up?" Slick grunts.

"You know he can, and you know he won't," Perlman mumbles, his nose whistling on each word. Sleep settles into the corners of my eyes, and I don't know how Beck can be so awake, but he seems to have come alive again since setting foot on his ship. His eyes are bright and alive with renewed energy. He hardly casts me a look, though, which cannot be said for Perlman. His eyes wander over to me nervously every so often.

". . . can wait it out for a while, but eventually . . ."

". . . thank the crudgmusting Gods, skies are clear for now . . ."

". . . twelve knots . . ." Their back and forth is rhythmic, almost like the rocking of the ship, or a fiddle bowing a lullaby, back and forth, side to side. I rest my eyes, just for a moment.

It's dark when I open them again. And I'm not on the bridge anymore. I'm in a bed. I sit up quickly, grabbing at my clothes, finding them firmly where I left them. Even the compass rests, nestled against my chest, hanging from the leather I used to recreate the chain I lost after the barn fire. I look around the room, and it's not mine. Or at least, it's not the room I remember as mine. The bed is bigger; the room is bigger. I've been here before. I open the bottom drawer of the nightstand and find exactly what I expected: rum. But Beck is not here. I pull myself from the bed and note that my arm will bend some now, without excruciating pain. I splash some water on my face in the water closet, and then find my way out onto the deck.

I try to ignore the sinking feeling in my stomach, but as I climb to the deck and look into the bridge, it takes shape, heavy and leaden. Beck is not there. Shaz is at the helm. I want to ask him where Beck is, but my pride stops me. They know who I am and likely expect a certain ending to this story. If Beck is keeping his distance from me, they'll take his side. And I don't want to be told no.

I climb the steep metal steps to the observation deck above the bridge and see a lanky body with bushy red hair staring at the sky. Perlman turns his head as the moonlight catches his sharp, almond-shaped eyes. He gives me a sympathetic smile and turns back to whatever he was doing. Part of me wants to retreat, to find my old bunk below deck and hibernate until it's time to disembark. But I don't. I move one foot after the other, until I'm next to him, staring at the sky. A line of dark, inky-black clouds blooms on the horizon, offset by the otherwise starry sky.

"Pretty night," I say, my words feeling stupid. He nods, and his teeth glint in the moonlight.

"It's the Mittle-lake tonight," he agrees. "Better that than the Mittle-shake. Guess Nordania decided to take the night off, not that I'm complaining. She can be a fickle goddess at times." His nose whistles on each word, and I bite my bottom lip.

"I'm sorry about that punch."

"I'm sorry about your shirt," he says. I nod my thanks. He tilts his head back up toward the sky, and I follow his gaze.

"You navigate by the stars?" I ask. He shakes his head and lets out one small, wheezing chuckle.

"No. I mean, sure. Some. In the dark, you can't follow the sun to know east from west, right? But you know that star right there is due south — see?" He points to his left, and I see a litany of stars.

"Okay," I say and he laughs. He sets down a thermos and puts a hand on my bad shoulder. I wince, and he lifts his hand off quickly.

"Sorry — Beck said . . ." He fumbles around Beck's name, confirmation that they've been given clear instructions regarding how to approach me. "Does it still hurt?"

"It's better, just sore," I say. He nods and places his hand on my shoulder blade instead, pressing his cheek against mine and lifting my good arm straight alongside his. He moves my finger to point.

"Close your left eye," he says, and I do. My finger points to a star centered above the horizon, but clearly in the bottom half of the sky. It isn't the brightest star in the night, but it glows a stunning blue.

"See?" he asks, stepping back, leaving me to point and squint on my own. I nod and smile.

"Yeah," I whisper, opening my other eye and lowering my hand, not losing track of the star.

"As long as you can track that star, you'll never be lost."

"What does it mean?" I ask. "Don't the stars tell stories?"

"It's the southernmost star, so as long as you can find it, you'll always know which direction is due south. It's called—"

"Perlman? You trying to trick her into doing your job for you?" Beck's voice is soft and still. A tentative lightness moves through my neck and shoulder at the sound.

"Something like that," he says with an awkward laugh. I keep staring at the star, curling my fingers around the cold railing. Winter has definitely crept into the sea, teasing the frothy waters into an icy spray. The sky glitters like diamonds scattered across velvet, and the breeze is still welcome.

"I'm out of coffee," Perlman says, sipping from his full cup as he scuttles away. I can't imagine he'd want to stay here, with the heavy tension I'm already feeling. His footsteps clomp down the metal steps, and I stay where I am, listening to the waves lap lazily against the vessel. Beck seems to stay where he is, too. He doesn't enter my periphery. He doesn't say anything, and I can sense exactly what's happening here. It's the same thing as the last time I was on board. We are not friends, and I am not crew. There is no reason for us to communicate unless absolutely necessary.

"Is this how it's going to be?" I ask.

"What's that, Capo?" he asks. I swear I can hear a smirk in his voice, but I don't look at him. I can't bring myself to.

"We're just not going to talk when we're on your boat?"

"Ship."

"I said what I said." I smile, feeling nostalgic for the ease of our banter before everything got confusing. He doesn't return the expression.

"We're talking right now," he says, tucking a piece of orange peel into the side of his cheek. I can hear his amusement, and it stings. I bite the side of my tongue.

"I don't want your cabin," I say, my words sharp and pointy, but poorly aimed. I'm grasping at something, anything, just to get a reaction from him.

"Why not?" he asks. His voice is closer now, but not close enough to touch, to grasp, to punch.

"I don't need it. I'll take my old cabin."

"It's been taken." His words are matter-of-fact, but there's still a levity to them that aggravates me.

"Fine, then I'll take another one."

"Why don't you want my cabin?" he asks again, closer still.

"Because I don't." I am more forceful with my words now.

"But it's fancy. I thought you liked fancy things." His voice is still light, but there's an edge to it that wasn't there a moment ago. I ignore his comment.

"Why don't you use it?" I ask.

"Who says I don't?" His voice is an almost-whisper in my ear now. I turn. He's only about two paces back, but he feels so much farther.

"What?" I ask, losing my balance as the ship rocks just a touch more than it had been.

"We'll take shifts," he says, his mouth curling up to expose his dimple. "You'll take the day shift; I'll take the night shift. We can high five as we cross paths." He's teasing me now, and I want to slap him, not because he's poking fun at me, but because he knows it bothers me.

"You . . . stupid . . . blister pustule . . ." I grumble. He laughs, so loud and shocking that I flinch. I try to suppress a laugh from my own lips, but my burning anger is enough to push it away. He places a hand on my back, and I recoil.

"Arden," he says. His voice is softer now, hovering in the space between us. I tilt my head to meet his gaze. His mask has slipped. He looks unsure, lost even.

"Tell me what to do," he says. His right hand grips the railing, his knuckles white, and the veins create a map of his forearm. A gust hits, and I shudder—I want to pull the sleeves down his arms, rub some warmth into them before he catches cold. But I don't want to make his decisions for him. I don't want him to talk to me just because I demand it. I don't want him to touch me or whisper to me or . . . or anything . . . if he doesn't want to.

"No," I say. He doesn't move, but the distance between us closes, or maybe the air between us just burns up a bit.

"Then tell me what you want," he says. I shake my head and watch him squeeze the railing with the expert technique of someone who has spent his whole life refusing to let go. I don't answer. I don't know what I want. And the little things I think I want, I shouldn't say out loud. Like his touch on my hand, and his breath in my ear.

"Then tell me what you don't want," he says, more urgency in his words. "If you don't want . . . this . . ." He doesn't say *me*, but he may as well. *He might never say.*

"No," I say, with just as much urgency. His grip loosens, and then his hand trails along the railing toward me, settling next to my hand, but not touching. The mere breath between our hands feels cavernous, and I long to close it. The water ripples around us, lapping at the ship's hull, rushing in slightly larger waves as the dark clouds on the horizon rise, obscuring the starlight.

"I know what I've promised. Where we're headed. I have my wits, though, and I know . . ." He takes a ragged breath and lets his pinky touch mine. His touch runs through me like lightning. I feel it in every muscle, every cell, every corner of my body.

"You know what?" I whisper. He laughs, scratching his face, but I don't look at him. I hear the scratch of his nails against his growing beard, which suits him. I like looking at it, at the way it makes his jaw sharper, his eyes greener, his smile brighter.

"I know how this ends," he says, and my will breaks. His eyes fix on mine. We rock back and forth, the natural ebb and flow of a sea upset by rockier waves echoed in the way we move next to each other. He bows, and I bend, and then we swap.

"How does this end?" I ask, my voice catching in my throat. He looks pained, and he pulls his pinky finger away from mine, leaving me colder. But I need to hear it, because right now, and anytime I'm with him anymore, I don't know how this ends. I can't see around it. I know why we're here together, on this ship, bowing and bending. I know what we're trying to do, and where we're going. But then he touches my hand, and I can't see outside of his skin on mine.

"Poetically," he says with the saddest smile. It's not the answer I expect. It implies so much promise, so much more hope and optimism than I expect, because the middle of the poem is the best part, and I know that we are just barely past the start.

"I like poetry," I say, blinking hard. His eyebrows lift, and a disbelieving smile creeps into his eyes.

"I like the ones that rhyme," he says, edging closer.

"Of course you do."

"Gotta rhyme. What's the point if they don't?"

"I just like when it makes me feel something," I say, a flush creeping into my cheeks as I realize just how much I've laid bare. His green eyes narrow and penetrate mine, as if he can see me, as if he can really understand what I'm hiding, buried so deep that I can't even see it. He slips his hand around my waist and pulls me closer, hip to hip.

"Your mind is in the gutter, Capo," he says with a smirk, but then it dissolves, and he lifts his other hand and slips it under my hair, cupping the back of my neck, sliding his thumb along my jaw.

"No . . . and yes . . ." I whisper, and he grins. He understands, even though he might not say. He kisses me, and I kiss him back. Our lips pulse in slow, methodical, lazy strokes, taking our time and absorbing everything. He brushes kisses across my cheekbone, down my jaw, my neck, his beard scratching the sensitive skin along my collarbone, tickling with insatiable delight. I reach for his face and turn his chin back to mine.

"What is it?" he asks. I slowly bend my bad arm in between us and with some effort press my hand against his chest. His breaths are unsteady, and his heart is rocketing. I move his hand to my chest. A smile quirks at his lips, and then he feels the steady rise and fall of my chest, but my heartbeat matches his. His abdomen sucks in, and he presses his forehead against mine. Neither of us says so, but I know we're thinking the same thing. This ending is going to be brutal. Poetic, perhaps, but brutal.

CHAPTER THIRTY-ONE

While we wait for Marlbury to return with news, Perlman navigates us around the treacherous heart of the Mittlesee. The weather is colder, and the waves get choppier by the day, but I learn to move with them better, finding my sea legs in a way I didn't last time. My days fall into a steady routine to numb the anxiety that comes with waiting for Kern's Mollymawk. After I help with breakfast, Kern spends his mornings teaching me to tie knots. I've got the poacher's knot, the double overhand, and the cleat hitch knots down pat, but the alpine butterfly gives me trouble. I keep losing the slack on the ropes because of my injury. My left hand doesn't make my elbow so sore anymore, but my grip is still weak. Suffice it to say, I don't think I have a future in knot-tying.

I bring lunch to Shaz and Beck in the bridge. I can't quite get a read on Shaz, but he's started to warm to me, ever so slightly. His distrust has turned into a hesitant sort of acceptance. Sort of like Sir Squints-a-Lot. I wonder if Beck told him what happened, and he's afraid I'll steer him off a cliff. The ache of driving that horse over the edge is still too fresh and real, and I have to push it down each time I think of him. We might never have truly gotten along, but I didn't mean for him to die. I never wanted it to end that way.

Beck is still withdrawn when we're with Shaz, careful not to touch me, only calling me by my given name. It takes me time to adjust to the name change, since he was so insistent on calling me Capo as often as possible otherwise. I never thought I'd come to like that stupid name, but when he doesn't use it, I miss it.

Perlman usually wakes up after we eat lunch, and I bring extra strong coffee to him in the upper deck. In exchange, he shows me maps of the Mittlesee floor. These are in short supply and difficult to follow, but after several afternoons, I'm starting to understand the changing depth lines of the ocean floor, the great rift down the center, and how he spots some of the valleys where we can anchor and hide for the night.

I help with dinner, and everyone eats in the galley, save for Beck. I've slowly reorganized the kitchen, so I know where everything is. The limited metal cabinets and drawers are no longer a free-for-all. There's an order to things—a silverware drawer, a cabinet for pots and pans, a place for the microplane. Shaz sleeps after lunch, until late in the night, so Beck takes his dinner after everyone else and in the bridge. I bring him a plate, and Kern usually joins us, the three of us laughing and talking while we watch the sun set. I take some time for myself after that, walking the deck in the dark—we haven't seen any ships for as long as we've been sailing, but it doesn't seem like the best idea to walk the deck in broad daylight, especially after we were spotted so easily last time. Once it's dark, however, it feels safer. Nobody outright tells me to do this, but I do, and they don't stop me.

I go to Beck's cabin when I'm tired of walking and sleep

when I'm tired. He never comes to his cabin when I'm still awake. He waits until I'm already in bed to slip beneath the sheets next to me, wrapping a protective hand around my waist. I always fall back into him, and we sleep that way until the sun wakes him, and he leaves before I get up. So each night, I crawl into bed, lights off, and wait. This thing between us feels tenuous, like if I acknowledge it, if I crack the shell of his subterfuge, he might stop.

Tonight is no different. I've come to bed and am just barely settled under the sheets when he tiptoes into the room. I hear him change for bed, and I turn to lay on my side. He lifts the covers, gently, and slides under. Immediately, his warmth fills the bed, and my tired muscles relax into him. He cradles my body, molding his knees behind mine, wrapping an arm around my waist. He presses a kiss to my shoulder, and then replaces the blanket. Then he lays there. I wait for him to fall asleep, but he doesn't. Instead, he spreads his fingers across my stomach and pulls me tighter against him. The heat of his touch is nothing compared to the heat of his body pressed to mine, his rigid muscles crushed against my soft curves. He presses another kiss into my shoulder, and then another one into the back of my neck. Warmth blossoms across my skin, and I want more.

"I was sailing back from Sudersberg," he whispers into my ear. His breath is warm and tickles my skin, and I sink closer, wanting to pop the air bubbles still trapped between us. "We got a message . . . there was precious cargo that needed swift shipment across the Mittlesee. From the capital. A big payday. I was intrigued, but cautious. Precious cargo can be something expensive . . . or . . ." He trails off, tucking a piece of hair behind my ear. "Or something I want no part of." The subterfuge is over. I turn over onto my other side, facing him. His arm settles into the crook of my waist, his fingertips dragging loose, lazy shapes along my spine.

"But you came anyway," I whisper. He nods. The rock of the boat has become second nature, but combined with the sweet cadence of his words, I feel entranced, like I couldn't break this spell even if I wanted to.

"I came anyway. I was invited to dinner, and I was curious. I knew Siobhan was up to something, but I didn't know what. And then I got to my table, and there was this girl . . ." He's quiet for a moment as I remember the first time we met. I recall the moment in surprising detail: the wine, the clatter of clinking glasses, the strange people. The loud, boisterous pirate sitting to my right. *You've got to be kidding me*, he had said.

"Siobhan knew exactly what would happen," he says. His confession sears my skin, and I suck in a breath. "Well, she knew exactly what I would do, anyway." I let my fingers trace a line down his chest, and then back up again. I trace the line again and again, urging him to keep talking, to tell me all his secrets.

"I was supposed to leave the next day, but the shipment got delayed. That's when I figured out what the shipment was."

"What was it?" I ask, sliding my fingers along the hard cut of his collarbone. We only ever sleep when we're together, and I've not had this opportunity before. But after so many days of being held against him, watching him work, my fingers are curious, and being able to explore his cuts and angles more freely is intoxicating.

"Come on, Capo," he says. "You're smarter than that." She paid him money to take me away. I was the shipment. She wanted me gone from the beginning.

"Why don't you call me Capo in front of Shaz?" I ask, changing the subject faster than he's prepared for. His shoulders stiffen, then relax, as he tightens his hold around my waist.

"Because I don't," he says simply. I want to press for more, but I don't want to push him away. So instead, I slip my hand down his side and tuck my fingers under the hem of his threadbare t-shirt. His fingers slip up the back of my own shirt, and his fingertips, roughened from work on the ship, drag across the soft skin along my ribs. An appreciative moan escapes my lips, much to my immediate mortification. I feel my cheeks flush, and when I look at him, he grins. I expect him to tease me, but he says nothing, just keeps his eyes locked with mine, continuing to drag his fingers up and down the base of my back.

My body tenses as I work his shirt up and over his head. I press my mouth to his chest, and his breath hitches. His skin is warm, and the downy hairs on his sternum tickle my upper lip. He lifts my chin to meet his face and kisses me, crushing me against him. His knee pushes between mine, and I hitch my leg around his hip. His tongue tastes my lips, and I yield, letting him deepen the kiss. His hands work up and down my body, sending waves of sensation through my limbs. His hand drifts up the front of my shirt, cupping my breast. I squeeze my eyes shut, tasting the salt on his lips, smelling the faint hint of leather, enjoying his touch—until an unwelcome voice interrupts: *You've sealed me into your skin.*

I open my eyes and see Beck's face—relaxed, calm. Content, even. His eyes are closed, and his mouth slips down my jaw, my neck. He sucks on my earlobe, and my body goes loose beneath him. I close my eyes as he drags his teeth across the sensitive skin on my neck. His heady breath is loud against my ear, and I gasp as a long forgotten memory of CJ makes me feel as if I've fallen back to earth: a dark corner, his mouth in my ear, his hand on my breast, then a hand over my mouth . . .

I push Beck away, and a sob escapes my mouth.

"What? What is it? What did I do?" he asks, sitting up, breathless. My lungs cry for air, and when Beck puts his hand on my back, I recoil. I don't want to be touched. Even here, in this moment shared between just the two of us, CJ has wormed his way in. CJ was the last person to explore my body like this, and the memory is not easily forgotten. He held me down, forced my legs apart, left bruises. It's not the same, and yet it is not so different. My mind has betrayed me, wading into treacherous territory, and it may be enough to destroy me.

"Arden," his voice is low and afraid. I've ruined this. I've ruined this one perfect moment, this moment I wanted so badly, and I might never get it back.

"I'm sorry," I whisper, swallowing hard, pulling my knees into my chest. He touches my back again, and I recoil, shuddering. He's not CJ. He's not.

"I need a minute," I say. I need to not be touched, to just not feel anything against my skin. I shiver, holding my knees to my chest, and let out a shaky breath.

"One thing, Arden," he whispers. "Open your eyes and tell me one thing you see—right now. Something real." I open them. He's on the edge of the bed, far from me. Too far.

"One thing," he repeats.

"Lamp," I whisper. The word sounds strangled, like the fossil of a voice I used to know.

"Good," he says, staying exactly where he is. "I love lamp. Tell me another one."

"Window," I say, nodding at the porthole showing a black night.

"Yes," he says. My skin is clammy, and I stare at my toes, at the blue blanket beneath them, following the line of it to where he still sits at the edge of the bed. He's real. He's here. He reaches for me, brushing a fingertip against my elbow. His touch is hesitant, gentle. But it's too much.

I shudder away from his hand, and I don't have to look at his face to know that I've broken this. Whatever this was, it's done. He stands and backs away from the bed. I don't want him to leave, but I can't tell him to stay. Not now, not like this.

"Get some rest," he says. I hear the click of the door as he lets himself out.

I curl up on myself, under the blankets that smell like him, and hear the faint echo of cruel laughter, and a voice I'll never forget: *You've sealed me into your skin.*

CHAPTER THIRTY-TWO

I wake up alone.

A sinking, untethered sensation rolls up my arms, and I bury my face in Beck's pillow. It's a mistake. It smells of leather and salt, shooting through me like a poisoned dart. I don't know why I feel this way. Beck is always gone when I wake up. It's part of the ritual. Of course, last night, the game changed, and now, it's broken in a way I can't fix by pretending.

But it's so much worse than that. We crossed so many lines last night. I may not know what I want, but I felt close enough to Beck to climb into bed with him. To let him kiss me and hold me, touch me in a way I've never let anyone else touch me. And even in that moment where I lost my head and allowed myself to be completely lost in him, CJ ruined it.

What will happen if I marry Declan?

The door clicks open and shut. I roll over just as Beck sits on the edge of the bed. In the morning light, I can see deep circles under his eyes. I know what he looks like when he's barely slept. This is worse. I did this.

"Hi," I say after a moment.

"Good morning, Capo," he says with a smile, pushing frizzy curls off my forehead. "I've had a busy morning."

"You have?" My throat is dry, my voice hoarse from thirst. He nods earnestly and runs his finger across the bridge of my nose.

"I've been finding constellations in your freckles."

"No, you haven't," I say with a laugh, grateful for the levity. He grins, looking very proud of himself.

"I have."

"Which ones?"

"All of them."

"You've found all of them in my freckles?"

"I have. I'm very capable like that." I laugh harder than I should, and he pushes my hair off my neck.

"Did Perlman teach you?" I ask.

"I should hope not. If he's been navigating based on your freckles, we're all in trouble."

"Just maybe go easy on him this time? The whistling nose trick has lost its novelty," I tease. He smiles, pushing a curl behind my ear.

"I'm sure he couldn't help it. I clearly can't." My lips part ever so slightly, and his smile never fades as he glides his fingers down my shoulder, my arm, and laces his fingers with mine.

"Arden—"

"Aren't you needed on deck?" I say.

He hesitates for a minute, and then sets his brow and nods.

"I mean, if we're headed for the mole on my chin, you might need to save us from impending doom." He smiles and nods, accepting his heroic task.

"Yeah, I should relieve Shazblister." He hesitates a moment, tucking another curl behind my ear, and in spite of myself, I lean into his touch. He sighs, and then leaves. As the door clicks shut behind him, I let a fat tear slide down my nose, drowning at least four constellations in my self-destructive misery.

I can't tie knots with Kern. They won't hold. And I refuse to bring lunch to Beck and Shaz. I persuade Kern to do it instead. I come back to the cabin and rock into a little ball for as long as I can tolerate being alone with my thoughts. Which is both longer than I thought and not long enough. Then I climb to the top deck with Perlman and don't focus when he explains how to coalesce the compass with the horizon and the maps. Something about curvature and longitudinal lines, and then he's telling me a joke about a woman he wants to see from the Port of Pleasure that snaps me out of my own head.

"Sorry," I say.

"No, we were both about to be even sorrier. Once I start telling that story, I have a hard time stopping."

"I thought that's what she said, you moldy beefbasher?" Beck says, cutting into our conversation. My cheeks bloom with a potent combination of embarrassment and anger.

"No, what she said was—"

"Stop. Nobody wants to know what she actually said," Beck says, but I stare at the maps, memorizing the curves of a slender finger of a valley on the page in front of me. "Arden, can I borrow you for a minute?"

I look at Perlman.

"We're kind of in the middle of something here," I say.

"This won't take long," he says, in his captain voice. I nod and walk toward the bridge, climbing down the steps. It's much easier to climb them in broad daylight, but with us actually moving, it's much windier, and much colder, than I'm used to. I shiver almost immediately. Once I'm down, he reaches his hands out to warm my shoulders, and I slip away. It's not that I don't want him to touch me. I want him to hold me, to bury my face into his chest and breathe him in, to be warm and safe. But I saw his face last night when I pushed him away. I saw the look in his eyes this morning when he left. I don't trust my brain anymore, and I don't trust myself not to hurt him.

"I don't want you to hit me," he says, and my eyes go wide.

"Well, that's a killer pickup line."

"I'm afraid I'm going to get this wrong," he says, his voice stronger than I expect. More serious. Whatever this is, he's not joking.

"What?" I ask, sobering as a pit of dread gapes large in my chest.

"What I'm about to say. So if I say it wrong, tell me I said it wrong, instead of getting mad and hitting me. You don't tuck in your nails when you're mad." My lips betray a smile, but my stomach twists.

"I make no promises where you're concerned," I say. His smile fades, but he recovers quickly, smoothing out the worried creases in his forehead. Fear rises in my throat, and I try to swallow it down, but it slips through just the same.

"Marlbury came back today," he says. I grab for the railing. That's not what I was expecting. That's not what I wanted.

"Oh?"

"Irina's not quite ready. But Declan"—his mouth twists violently around his name—"is eager to retrieve you. We can set up a rendezvous whenever you're ready."

I nod. I grip the railing, too tight, my knuckles turning white. The wind rips at me, freezing the tears in my eyes, whipping thin lashes of hair against my cheeks, leaving stinging lines. I don't turn away from the wind. I look right into it, taking the beating.

"We can send back a message, scheduling the rendezvous. Or . . ." He hesitates, and I look back at him.

"Or what?" I ask, my voice levied up into the air, waiting for him to catch it.

"Or we could tell him something else. That there's a delay? Or there will be no rendezvous?" His words pour out too quickly, and he shakes his head and scratches the side of his nose. "Or anything else you want. If you want to stick to the plan . . . or . . . change your mind . . ."

I'm broken. It's a fact that was confirmed last night, when I tried to steal away from the world for a moment with this man who's standing in front of me, offering to outrun the law if I want to change my mind. The thing is, he deserves better than a life on the run, and a girl who can't stand to be touched. Declan does, too, but Declan expects less. He expects a political marriage. I think he will understand.

Beck would understand, too, but I think his understanding would break me over and over again. I can't live with that. Emlyn's words ring hollow in my mind: *make it stick*.

"You want me to tell him I've changed my mind?" I ask. It's a cruel question. I don't know why I ask it. He's not going to answer it. It's just going to force him to admit that he can't give me the answers I want. He might never say it, but maybe I need him to. Maybe that's the problem. Declan will say it, and Beck won't. His faraway eyes give me all the answer I need.

"We're going to be married," I say, my voice numb.

"I know that's the plan, but —"

"He asked, and I said yes." My words are clear and crisp. There is no mistaking them. His hands hang at his sides, fisting into violent angles, but there's no one here to hurt, except me.

"Is that what you want?" he asks, his voice tight.

"I've given him my answer."

"That's not what I asked."

"I don't know what you want me to say," I say. "You knew how this was going to end." He closes the distance between us in two long, heavy strides and takes my arms in his hands. I try to pull away, but he doesn't let go.

"Arden, cut the shit. What do *you* want? Do you want that pretty boy prince who says all the right things and tells you what you want to hear? Is that really what you want?" He shakes me as he talks. Not because he's trying to hurt me, I realize, but because he is shaking. My stupid tears cloud my eyes, and I push him away.

He looks at me like I've slapped him, that small, broken piece of him he keeps so carefully locked away on full display. I can't stand the pain in his eyes, and I look away. He makes an inarticulate sound in his throat, and when I look back up at him, his eyes are hard. I think he might grab for me again. He says something that I think must be truly devastating, but I never hear his words.

An explosion rocks the deck, knocking us both over onto our sides. My hip lands hard on the deck, and we pull ourselves up to face a ship nobody saw coming, about twenty-five knots away.

"Captain!" Kern's flat voice races up to us, and Beck pulls me to my feet, practically throwing me down the steps. We've been spotted.

CHAPTER THIRTY-THREE

"*P*irates." Shaz's word is as heavy as his demeanor.

"You sure?" Beck asks, his voice commanding, and a far cry from where it was just moments before.

"You know something I don't?" Shaz asks, his eyes darting back to me, standing in the doorframe of the bridge.

"Want me to get her out of here?" Perlman asks, pushing Kern at me. My chest gets tight as Beck whips his head around so fast, I'm sure he's injured himself.

"She stays," he growls, daring anyone to challenge his authority. He seems to remember himself then and waves me to Perlman. "Put her to use." Perlman urges me over to join him, and he rolls out another set of maps.

"Whatcha got for me, Shazzblister?" Beck asks.

"Ship off in the distance, closing in at twenty knots. But the explosions are Rumcocks, launched from two smaller boats closing in at ten knots east and west." I don't know how he can see anything, but Perlman snaps his long fingers in my face and forces me to look at the wrinkled maps on the table. He runs his fingers with frenetic precision along thin brown lines demarcating underwater valleys and ridges, then shakes his head, or mutters profanities. I try to follow his fingers and watch them meet dead end after dead end.

"Kern?" Beck says.

"Yeah, boss?"

"Sound the alarm—twice." Kern nods heavily and runs out the door. Moments later, I hear the alarm I've heard before, and then layered on top of it, another one. Men run around the deck below us and start to toss what look like nets over the sides. Slick stands below, barking out orders, and when another explosion bursts in the air due right of the deck, he turns a powerful hose in its direction.

"Are you listening?" Perlman asks, his voice strained with irritation. I nod and return to the maps.

"Where are we?" I ask, studying the brown-and-white, hand-sketched image. It looks nothing like the maps we've been studying. The topography looks different, and the demarcations are strange. It takes me a few minutes to realize they're in another language.

"Osterstani," he mumbles under his breath, though I'm not sure if it's a curse or an answer. I don't have a chance to ask what we're doing with Osterstani nautical maps, though. He puts a finger on a spot between two large reef systems, and I assume that's where we are.

"Looking for a place to hide?" I ask, scanning the various fingerling tributaries sketched out in brown ink.

"A way out," he says, his voice like fingernails on sandpaper.

"Waiting on directions," Shaz yells at Beck, and he looks back at us, his eyebrows low and knit close.

"Continue on course until further notice," Beck says.

"You want me to run?" Shaz says, making it clear that this is not what he would prefer to do.

"Until we have a way out, continue on course." The entire

ship jerks, and I yelp. I have no idea what would have knocked us aside like that, but nobody else seems concerned.

"If we were sinking, you'd know," Perlman says.

"That's comforting," I grumble. He runs his finger along another slot in the map, as I scan the other half. There are at least twelve valleys that look wide enough for us to sail in. Depth is another matter, though from what I can tell, they all seem about right.

"Cancel *Vistock*," Perlman says. It must not be deep enough. I take the valleys to the left, and Perlman scans the ones to the right, following them with our eyes to their natural ends.

"Can't we just stay the course?" I ask.

"For a while. It dead ends, though, and this is wide enough it doesn't require any real skill to navigate, so we lose our advantage." Makes sense. I keep scanning. The first three end in dead ends shortly past the main channel. The fourth is tight and would require extremely focused navigation, so I get excited, but then it splits into three smaller channels that look too small. Two of them dead end, but the third wraps back around to the main channel.

"Here's one," he says, pressing his finger onto the map. I follow it, and it seems to wrap around in too tight coils before it shoots us back north.

"Let me see," Beck says, sliding between me and Perlman. His shoulder touches mine, and he doesn't lean away. He is steady, calm. He's in his element, and I have to remember I'm supposed to do more than just watch. While he scans the route with pinched features, I follow another one at the base of the main rift. It's narrow to start, but widens to a comfortable width and depth. Then, at the southern end of it, it splits into four narrow slots. Three reach dead ends. But the fourth narrows, and then empties out just to the northwest of Sudersberg.

"What about this?" I ask, pointing to the opening. I slide my finger along the path I'm suggesting, and I feel Beck stand straighter as my finger follows the spot where it spills out into the regular trade routes. Another explosion jars our attention, and Beck nods—an ugly, grimacing thing.

"Yes, this could work."

"Show me," Perlman says, and he scrutinizes it, then looks outside.

"It's tight, but—"

"Too tight for their mama ship, but the babies will follow," Perlman says.

"Not at our speed," Beck says.

"How fast are we running this?" Shaz asks. I look outside, to where Slick aims the hose close to the side of the ship. Too close.

"As fast as you can take her," Beck says.

"Tight and fast, just the way I like it. Show me the way, Perlman," Shaz calls back. Perlman carries the map over and starts shouting out coordinates.

"Head southwest at 214 degrees, about ten knots, then I'll guide you from there," he says. Beck hovers behind them, his focus straight ahead. My right hand shakes, and I grip it hard with my bad hand. The pain is mostly gone now, so I squeeze my fleshy forearm harder, evoking a sharp pinch where my forearm meets my elbow. I feel my face pull at the pain, but it calms my nerves, and I breathe into it. Shaz's focus is unyielding. Perlman reads off numbers at a dizzying pace, his head moving quickly between the map, the compass on the instrument panel, and the sky. I try to follow, and once I find the rhythm of his instructions, I start to anticipate, finding the directions for myself. I know what he's going to say before he says it, and when he loses his spot, I help him pick it back up again. When I do chance a look up, the sky is clouded over, and snow is just starting to fall. It would be pretty, if not for the bottles exploding around us.

"One-eighty-two for three knots," Perlman says. I feel

Beck's eyes on me, but he says nothing. Then he takes my hand, his fingers curling around and squeezing hard. It hurts. And I breathe through it. I squeeze back, leaning into the pain, and I watch in horror as a bottle crashes onto the deck and explodes. The flames spread like an oil spill. Slick turns the water cannon on the ship to douse the flames, but with the water focused elsewhere, the damage is done. The ship tilts.

"We got company, guys!" Kern yells up at us. He's assembling something on deck with two other men. I don't know what it is, but it doesn't look like it's going to stave off anyone daring to climb our ship.

"What is that?" I ask.

"Sonic device," Beck says, his words clipped and almost annoyed in his captain's voice. "If he could only remember how to put the damned thing together. Stupid, worthless—" I don't listen to what else he says. Instead, I run out the door.

"Arden! Get back here!" His voice trails after me, but I keep going. I'm worthless standing inside the bridge, but out there, on the deck, my small fingers might be able to help. If Kern needs to assemble something, maybe I can do it. Of course, by the time I reach him, it's apparent that I didn't think before I ran. It's freezing, and snow sticks to my cheeks and eyelashes.

"What are you doing?" Kern asks.

"What are *you* doing?" I ask. He glares at me for a moment, and then hands me a tiny wrench.

"Screw it," he says. At first, I think he's cursing, but then I realize he really does want me to screw a bolt into place. He holds two disks together, and I reach inside. My arm is smaller than Kern's, and I get the job done. The other two men assemble a similar device—they're much further along. But we catch up. We've started piecing the two halves together when Beck catches my arm.

"I gave you an order!"

"And I fixed the damn problem!" I yell back.

"We already have a solution," he barks at me. I turn around and see that Slick has abandoned his water cannon and is assembling a weapon. It has a long shaft and fits heavy over his boulderous shoulders. Someone else helps him load what looks like greasy black honeycombs into the bit over his shoulder.

"You're going to kill them?" I ask, watching in horror.

"What's the alternative?" Beck asks, his jaw set in stony stubbornness. I push away from him, knocking the pieces out of Kern's hands. I nearly slide over the bar next to the water cannon and look down. Five people in a small motor boat sidle up to the ship. They've sliced holes in our nets, and a sixth person already dangles from the side. Just behind them, another small boat waits, setting rags ablaze in rum bottles and launching them at us. I duck as a bomb sails overhead and thankfully cracks on board into a puddle of water, losing its flame. I squint my eyes into the increasing snow at the second boat and make out a familiar, scarred face. I shudder and shout back at Kern.

"You got that thing ready?"

"Two minutes!" he yells back.

"Back down, Arden!" Beck yells, grabbing me around the waist. Slick starts to aim the launcher at the boat just below us.

"They're too close!" Slick shouts. "If I shoot, there's a chance we'll blow, too."

"Dammit!" Beck growls in my ear. I kick Beck's knee, and feel it buckle in the wrong direction. He yelps and drops away from me, and I take hold of the water cannon, releasing the pressure of the seawater and pelting the boat directly below us. Another bomb flies straight at me, and I duck, nearly losing my hold on the hose, but I resume and aim at the man now halfway up the boat. He loses his grip and falls, hitting the icy water. They back off, getting out of my way, and I shift the spray to the boat further out, catching another flying incendiary in its path.

"Back down, Arden!" Beck yells in my ear.

"No! It's working!" I say, clutching the thing with everything I have, feeling my fingernails rip and tear at the pressure of my grip. Beck digs his hands into my forearms, helping me hold the hose despite the immense pressure.

"Ready!" Kern calls.

"Let go!" Beck yells in my ear, pulling me back with all of his weight. We let go of the cannon and land hard on the deck, just in time. A high-pitched noise shoots out over our heads, and laying on the deck, we're reduced to covering our ears. He covers my head with his body, but it's still almost too much. He pulls me to the side, and as we shift out of the funnel of noise, the volume is bearable. He digs his fingers into my bad arm, and I fall into his momentum as he yanks me back and into the bridge. As we walk, I steal a parting glance at our attackers — one ship fades into the snow, the other treads water. In the farther one, an ugly shape stands, hands over their ears, disappearing into the snow.

CHAPTER THIRTY-FOUR

I fall into the bridge, catching myself hard against a table.

"What the hell is wrong with you, Thatcher? Why can't you ever just do as you're told and follow a fucking order?" Beck asks, his nostrils flaring, red patches spreading into his cheeks. I try not to wince at his use of my last name, something that sounds so cold and foreign.

"What's wrong with me? What's wrong with *you*? You were about to kill a boat full of people — many of them just poor suckers stuck following orders — when there was another, perfectly good option."

"I'm sorry, is this your boat?"

"Ship," I spit. I feel several pairs of eyes on me, and the air is tense. I've crossed a line, and now, they expect a bloodbath.

"Excuse me?" he snarls.

"Ship. It's a *ship*." He narrows his eyebrows at me and takes one dangerous stride forward, crowding over me.

"Oh, I beg your pardon, princess. Let me ask again: is this your *ship*?"

"You know it's not," I say, breaking eye contact. He follows me with his face, forcing me to look at him and all his anger.

"So then, these aren't your crew?" His voice is too steady, too loud.

"No, but I understand the value of human—"

"So then, it's not your fucking call." He growls at me, and I feel my chin tremble. I bite down hard on my lower lip to stop it from betraying me, but he's seen it. It's too late.

"If you don't have the stomach for these kinds of calls, then go bury your face in a pillow somewhere and let the grown-ups call the shots."

"You were going to end people," I say, my voice cracking.

"I told you once before: I know what it is to end a life. And fortunately for you, this was not your call. Unfortunately for me, and for this entire ship full of men who know how to follow orders, those turtledicks will live to see another day. And they have seen my ship. *My ship*, Arden!" His voice is so loud, it sends tremors through my bones and leaves me shaken.

"Now, when they find us again—and mark my words, they will find us—they will know exactly what we're working with to fight them, and they'll be prepared. We've lost the element of surprise, and we have no choice but to fight back. If it comes to that, and lives are lost, *that* is on you. So I hope you do understand the value of human life, and not just your own pretty neck." He spits those last words, repeating what the mercenary said.

"That's not fair."

"Fair?" He chuckles, but there's no joy in it. "You want to talk about fair? That's rich, coming from the girl who's been nothing but terrible cargo and worthless dead weight on this stupid, dangerous, life-threatening pleasure cruise. Or did you forget again that this is not some fucking day trip for the hell of it? I mean, come on, Arden. You're asking us to risk our lives, all so you can go back and warm Prince Dunderbulge's bed.

The least you can do is stay out of the fucking way and let us do our damn jobs." For as much as I'm shaking, he is still as stone. I take a step back, and he holds up his hand. I stop and wait for him to do something with it. He shakes his head and drops it to his side.

"You are dismissed."

I turn around and find Slick, Kern, Perlman, and Shaz all staring. They don't look sympathetic, nor do they look surprised. They shuffle out of my way, though, and let me through.

"Kern!" he yells as I'm pushing past the spectators and through the door. It's snowing in earnest now, and I breathe it in quickly as I make my way around the deck to the stairs below. The cold isn't enough to soothe the ice in my chest.

"Arden!" Kern calls after me.

"What?" I spit over my shoulder as I reach the staircase leading down into the galley. He follows me down the stairs, and I stop at the bottom, realizing that I don't know where to go. I hulk for my old room, but when I get there, the door is locked.

"You can't go in there, Arden," he says, apologetically.

"Why not?"

"Because it's someone else's room," he says.

"Whose?" I demand. He's quiet for a moment, and then sighs.

"It's my room."

"Yours?" I ask, the breath sucked from my lungs.

"I have a room now. I got a promotion." He grins. But his smile falters as he remembers that this is not the time for good news.

"Congratulations," I say, but the word sounds more like a sigh.

"Come on." He points me back up the hall and opens the door to Beck's room.

"I am not going in there," I say.

"He won't come," he says quietly. My stomach twists into sharp, inhuman angles, and I curse my body for betraying me again.

"I don't want anything from him," I whisper. Kern toes the floor, and I can see him fighting his instinct to do whatever it is his captain has asked of him. The last time I put him in this position, he locked me in the brig and I knocked myself unconscious. He understands animals. They make sense. A broken animal can be put back together. He didn't understand what it was to reassemble a person as broken as me. But now, he has an idea, and I can see he doesn't want to lock me in a room. I raise my palms to him and go into the cabin. He closes the door behind me, and I hear the latch click, but not lock.

I stand still for a while, not wanting to sit on the bed. Or the chair. I don't want anything of Beck's. I know I'm not innocent in this. He gave me orders—hell, he pleaded with me. I can still hear the fury in his voice when he yelled my name from the bridge. And when they tried to remove me from the bridge in the first place, and he insisted that I stay. There are more people on this ship than just me, but I saw a solution, one that didn't have to cost any more lives, and it was so simple. I could just do it. So I did. I don't regret doing what I did.

But the public flogging—what he said, hurling my own insecurities in my face—was below the belt. Maybe I don't need to know the price Siobhan paid him, the amount they think my life is worth. If that's what he thinks of me, that I'm nothing more than a body meant to warm someone's bed, it can't have been very much at all. I don't know how I could have ever wanted to be close to someone who could humiliate me in front of people who already question my value in the world. Who could throw my own worst fear, that I really am worthless, at me with such callous disregard. Before I met him, I had a world of my own. It was shitty, but it was looking up. I was a candidate. I didn't know what that meant, but now I do, and before he came into my life, things were just fine. Not great. Fine. I was existing. Now, things are confusing, and I don't know up from down. Now, I'm literally in a room full of him. Everything in here smells like him, looks like him, *is* him. I can't get away from him. And it's going to be the end of me. I stalk over to the built-in chest of drawers and yank the top drawer out, expelling its entire contents onto the floor with a huge scream. I breathe heavy with the exertion, but it's not enough damage.

I open the next drawer and empty it. Then the bottom drawer. I find the bottle of rum, nearly full, and with two hands, I heave it at the wall. It shatters, but it's still not enough. I tear through everything I can find until it's all on the floor. I swing my foot into a pile of clothes, sending a spray of pants and shirts in all directions. The destruction is everywhere, but it's still not enough. I grip the back of the chair in the corner and pull it down on itself, screeching with the exertion. The momentum pulls me down onto my knees, and I unleash an angry sob from my throat. I stare at the door, sealed shut ahead of me. I want to throw something at it. Something that will hurt it, and break it, and set it ablaze.

But what's the point? It might be locked; it might not be. Either way, I get through that door, and I'm stuck on a boat in the middle of the sea. The door is just a door, and Beck's boat — his *ship* — is just another barn loft, another room at the institute, another shed on the peninsula. No matter what I do, I will always be trapped in a prison of my own making. I curl myself into a ball on the floor, my face resting on sweaters and long johns that smell of citrus and salt, and I let the tears stream until I fall asleep.

CHAPTER THIRTY-FIVE

y face crushes into something soft as I lay on my belly. I want to stand, to push away and run, but then I remember I can't leave. There's no reason. The sour, metallic scent of blood seeps up from the ground around me, coating my skin, crawling up my nostrils, and I cry, letting the salt of my tears mix with the gummy, drying blood.

"There's no point." CJ's voice rings in both my ears like a gallows bell. "Just give up." The blood is cold and sticky, but still it crawls up my nose. I open my mouth to scream, but then it slides over my tongue, sharp and acidic, burning its way down my throat.

"You know the value of human life, do you? So then, what are you, Arden?" CJ cackles, blood coating his teeth like a toxic candy coating. "You have no value. You are worthless." CJ's words hover around me as his blood suffocates me. I choke, keeping my eyes shut. If it seeps into my eyes, it will win. This thick, viscous worthlessness will seep into my veins like a drug and drown me. I will drown. I let go and let it pull me under. But then a small voice says something . . . something that I can't quite hear . . .

I open my eyes.

Beck sits in his desk chair, leaning straight against the back, slowly rubbing the side of his nose. The room is still dark, thin slivers of wintery moonlight shimmering like eels across the room, casting him in an icy pall. I don't move. Not even to wipe at the tear that falls down my cheek and into the pillow, not even to check to see if it's mixed with CJ's blood.

"Sleep well?" There's a tremor in his voice that makes it clear he knows I did not. I look around the room. It's clean. All traces of my destruction are gone, the drawers returned to their rightful places, the clothing presumably folded and replaced. I don't have words right now. I don't know what to say to make this moment end, or go faster, or whatever it is it needs to do to relieve the suffocating pressure on my chest. Nor do I want him to see that I'm drowning. I don't need a rescue. I don't want him to save me.

"I'm not going to apologize, Arden," he says, his voice quiet. "I am captain of this ship, first and foremost. If I make a mistake, and one of my men gets injured or worse, it's my fault. I'm the one who has to deliver that news to his family." He is so still, stony. I know, in that moment, that he's had to make that sort of delivery before.

"I take that seriously. No matter what you may think of me, I take my job seriously." What does he think I think of him?

"Fine," I say, unyielding. "You're a serious boat captain." His jaw feathers, and he leans forward over his knees.

"But," he says, pinching the skin between his eyebrows. "You were right. We didn't have to kill people to get away. I knew they didn't know the Mittlesee floor. They wouldn't have been able to safely follow us." He looks somehow both older and younger, his eyes fixed on a point on the floor in front of the bed.

"I'm not a horrible person," he says with an uncomfortable smirk. "I told you before I know what it means to end a person. I do. It's not something I relish. It's also not something I thought I could forget. And then, for just a moment, I did."

When his eyes meet mine, they are liquid green and gold. I know what he's going to say before he says it, and I'm filled with equal swells of dread and hope. The emotion of it spills over, flowing down my cheeks, soaking into the pillow, saline to salt.

"I've never been afraid on the water. We've been through some gnarly storms and met some really shitty people who have been much closer to killing us than those fishpuckers today were. I've felt the adrenaline of tense situations, and I've had to make some really difficult calls. But I was never actually scared . . . until today."

I want to touch him. No, I *need* to. I need to feel his skin, to feel that he is real, and this isn't a dream. To place my hand on his and squeeze and tell him that I understand. He's so far—too far. I let out a rasp of air and slip my hand across the sheets toward him. He looks up from under his hand and watches it slide across the bed. He exhales sharply, and then crosses the room in two strides and kneels next to the bed, lifting my palm to his lips, closing my fingers around his kiss. He is real, solid, warm. I reach for his face and cup his cheek in my hand, sliding my thumb back and forth over his stubble. He leans into my hand, and then holds it there.

"I've sent word to Declan," he says, his voice soft and resigned. I pull my hand away.

"Why?" I ask, finally finding my voice.

"Because he can protect you better than I can." His words are a blow, and I can hear the heartbreak in them. I squeeze my eyes shut. The end is in sight, and I can't bear to look. "I'm sorry for what I said before, about you warming Prince Dunderbulge's bed. You didn't deserve that. And you are not worthless. You could never be worthless."

"I don't . . ." I start to say, but I don't know how to finish.

"You should get some more rest," he says, starting to stand. I don't let go, though, and he hesitates.

"No," I whisper.

"No, what?" he asks, his eyebrows pulling down over his eyes.

"Don't go," I say, and I hate the naked, desperate plea cracking in my voice.

"Come on, Capo. You can't go ten minutes without me? Not five hours ago, you were ready to throw me overboard."

"Don't do that," I say.

"Don't do what?" he asks, but he knows very well what I mean.

"Don't pretend like this isn't a big deal."

"Then let's not pretend you aren't going to marry this guy." He swallows hard, and his chin pushes his lips into a pinched purse. My stomach folds in on itself. He stands and takes a step back, pulling his hand from mine. I sit up too quickly, blinking away the stars.

What am I doing? Beck is standing here, right in front of me, having risked *everything* for me. He's offering to take me back to Declan, when it's clearly hurting him. And it's killing me. This could be so simple. I need only to let it be simple.

"Okay, fine," I say, clearing my throat. My voice is clear, strong. I know what I want. "Let's not pretend."

"What?" he asks. He stands frozen between steps: one foot about to walk away, the other still with me.

"I'm not going to marry this guy."

"What?" he repeats, and his voice is stuck in his throat.

"I'm not. End of story." My heart is beating so fast.

"Why not?" he says around a bitter laugh.

"Because I don't love him."

"Then you're a fool," he says over his shoulder, moving for the door.

"Because I . . ." There's a word on the tip of my tongue, unfamiliar and strange. And terrifying. I clear my throat . . . and swallow it back. "Because I can't lose you, you . . . stupid, stubborn flintpustule," I say. He looks back over his shoulder and squints. I flounder, looking for something I can do, something I can say, to convince him. I'm certain. This is what I want. I don't want Declan. I never have. Not really. I told him from the start that I wasn't interested in being married off. I tried to convince myself that it could work, but the truth is, I don't want a future with Declan. I want what Mabel and Donald had. What Emlyn and Ammon have. What I think Beck and I might be able to find.

I lift my chin, feeling more resolute than I've ever felt in my life, my gaze locked on his. Then, with slow, deliberate movements, I reach up and remove Declan's compass, letting it drop to the floor beside the bed.

"You're an even bigger fool than I thought," he says, but the smile in his eyes creeps into his mouth. He presses his fists into his pockets, and his eyes flit back and forth over my face, as if he's trying to memorize every inch of it. *Beck might never say.* I need him to say it. I know I do. But in this moment, watching him struggle for the right words, knowing it's possible to push him until he breaks, I know what I'm willing to sacrifice for him. I move across the bed and sit on my knees next to where he stands. I take his hand and pull him toward me. I see the resistance behind his eyes, in the way his fingers tense against my touch. But he comes closer. He lets me put his hand against my chest, lets me press my hand into his. We anchor each other for four breaths, and then I ask him again.

"Stay?"

He shakes his head, as if he's at war with himself. Then he toes off his shoes, sliding me back onto the bed. He pulls the blankets over us and rests his head in the hollow between my chin and chest. He runs his fingers along my ribs, smoothing, caressing, letting his hand fall down my back and circle my waist, containing me, keeping me his.

"This is going to be a fucking mess," he says into my

collarbone. I shut my eyes and images flash before me: Emlyn and Zerah and Carla. Neve, telling me she'll never forgive me. My stomach turns to lead, feeling the weight of what this would mean, what giving it all up would mean.

"Maybe," I whisper, breathing him in. He sucks in a breath and uses his hand to pull himself tighter into me. "But even if the world burns around us, I have what I want."

"I won't let that happen," he says, kissing the soft slope between my shoulder and chest. "I know . . ." He exhales hard, and I feel his heartbeat accelerate.

"You know what?" I ask, feeling him grapple with whether or not to finish his confession. He slides up my body and turns me into him so our noses are inches apart. He smiles, and I see his hesitation win—this truth will have to wait for another time.

"Why me?" he asks instead. I slide my hand down his arm, running my fingers along the hard ridges of his tricep.

"You're kind," I say, mimicking the words he once gave to me "And you're good. Even when you think you're being a jackass, you're careful with people. You are sensitive despite your bravado and your piratical ennui. You are strong and brave and have the greatest smile I've ever seen. I didn't even know I needed a smile like yours, but I . . . Beck, there's just nobody else like you." He breathes in and out, in and out, then lifts my chin to look at him. He smiles not with his teeth, but with his eyes, his cheeks, his whole being.

"Piratical ennui, eh?" he says. I smile and close the distance, kissing his smile. I don't know how long it takes us to fall asleep, but he doesn't leave me the whole night. I roll over at one point, between dreams that aren't nightmares, and he's still there. Safe and warm. The ship rocks over the swells, and I fall back asleep feeling dangerously close to happy.

CHAPTER THIRTY-SIX

*W*e don't change course. Word has already been sent to Irina, and I need to talk to Declan, tell him I've changed my mind.

Perlman charts our course to safety. Or at least, that's what Beck tells me. Perlman might be the one in charge on this journey, but I see it in their eyes. There's something they're collectively not telling me. Or maybe it's just that they all feel the shift in energy when Beck and I are in the same room now. He no longer keeps his distance from me in public, sitting next to me at breakfast, standing next to me in the bridge, even checking on my navigation lessons with Perlman.

If anyone is surprised or uncomfortable with this shift, they say nothing. Literally, nothing. Whenever I enter a room, people stop talking, and I find it hard to imagine they're talking about something that doesn't have to do with me. I hear mention of Sudersberg, which makes sense, since that's close to where our planned course will take us. But I've not been given much to reassure me.

"Two days, at least," Perlman told Beck, who nodded, his brows knit in some combination of worry and apprehension that

I can't decipher. Though, I have my own mixed feelings about the plans moving forward. No matter where we end up—Sudersberg, or elsewhere—Declan will be there, at some point. We haven't heard back from him since Beck sent Marlbury after the attack. But I know it's only a matter of time.

I feel myself clinging to Beck when we're alone, not wanting to sleep for fear of missing out on what little time we might have together before we're faced with the unknown. We talk in hushed voices until one of us falls asleep. But then the nightmares return. And when I open my eyes, he's awake and watching me.

"Tell me," he whispers once I'm calm. I've never talked about my dreams. I've had them for as long as I've had a benefactor. But these ones stick with me into the day, creeping into my joints, affecting me in a way I can't shake. I don't really want to talk about them, because it makes them that much more real. But not talking about them hasn't helped.

"It's always the same," I say. My breath is my voice, and I don't dare speak louder, lest I solidify the nightmare's grasp on me. He runs his finger along a long curl and gently twists it around his knuckle. "CJ won't let me go. His blood is everywhere . . . it won't go away . . ." He clears his throat and tucks the curl behind my ear, settling his hand on my neck.

"Killing a person is something that doesn't go away. I wish I could tell you it does. It gets easier . . . time makes it easier . . . but there will always be a part of that person whose life you took that sticks." His eyes are sad, and I start to lean away from him, but his hand holds me in place. He expected my reaction, and his prescience gives me pause.

"Guilt is a heavy thing," he says, softly.

"Guilt?" I ask, and I clutch at his wrist, wrapping my fingers as far around it as they'll go. I shake my head. "I don't feel guilty about killing him. He deserved to die. He got off easy."

"You can know his life deserved to end and still feel guilty about ending it. And . . ." He hesitates and runs his thumb along my jaw. "Considering how significant he was in your life, it isn't a surprise you would feel some guilt." His words shatter me — he thinks CJ was significant. No, he thinks I consider CJ significant in my life.

"Significant doesn't have to mean good," he says quickly, but I'm already shaking. Even in his death, his presence continues to grow and fester in the darkest corners of me. I allowed him to take root in me the way he has. "You are allowed to feel guilty and glad and angry and scared and relieved and anything else you want to feel about his death. I'm obviously biased here — but if you hadn't killed him, I wouldn't be alive." The ship is shockingly quiet, and our whispers seem to echo. He must sense it, too, because he pulls the sheets up higher, forming a protective barrier around our most hushed admissions.

"I just wish I could forget," I say, squeezing my eyes shut. "I wish I could close my eyes and not feel his blood. I wish I could sleep and not hear his voice, and . . ." I stop, knowing exactly what else I wish, but I don't dare say it. Not out loud. I wish I could be with Beck, completely, and not think of where CJ has already been.

"It's your mountain," he says, easing me onto my back, sliding my hand down my torso, to where my tattoo hides. Even in the dark, he finds the tattoo, running my fingers over it. I know he sees the mountains, the ink. But I feel only the scars.

"You can't move forward without learning from where you've been. But it doesn't define you. He doesn't tell you what to do. He is gone, forever, and even in your dreams, he can't hurt you."

"I know," I lie.

The days continue and finally, on the fifth day, Perlman and Shaz are agitated enough to approach Beck with their concerns.

"It's been too long. Even if they go the long way around, they could be here soon." Shaz is calmer than Perlman, leaning against the steering wheel in the bridge. We've had a break in the weather, and we sit mercifully still, deep in the narrow tributaries of the southeastern Mittlesee.

"We need supplies. We need a break. We aren't any safer here, than in Sudersberg," he says, and I recognize the tune of an ongoing argument.

Beck stands, arms tense and crossed over his chest, facing it down like a bull in a ring. My eyes drift over Perlman's maps, circling around our location and the direction of the trenches around us. They all direct us to the coast of Sudersberg.

"We're coming up on it, man," Perlman says.

"If we wait much longer, we run an even bigger risk they find us before we get there," Shaz says. Beck sighs and nods.

"Fine. Send word we're coming in," he says. His manner is brusque, his words more clipped than usual, and he leaves me behind with Shaz and Perlman. Perlman wears a goofy smile on his face, and even Shaz looks happy—an expression that doesn't wear well on his features.

" 'Bout damn time," Perlman says, and Shaz punches him in the arm. The expressions they exchange edge on lewd, and my stomach drops.

I leave the bridge, and Beck is nowhere. Other crew members are hard at work, though, and I don't want to cause a scene. So I go below deck and let myself into the kitchen. Kern is there, peeling potatoes. Wordlessly, I help, and together, we go through a full bag in record time. We chop them, and he starts to fry them up.

"Kern, where are we going?" I ask, finally breaking the silence. He looks up, but not at me. I can tell he's been expecting me to ask, but despite knowing that it was coming, he doesn't know how he's supposed to answer.

"Sudersberg," he says quietly. I'm about to ask where in Sudersberg, but then he tells me, unprompted: "Port of Pleasure." Vague recollections of tales from the Port of Pleasure spark anxieties in my brain, and I bite the edge of my tongue.

"Isn't that a brothel?" I ask.

"Yeah," he says, with no pretense. "It's not so bad there, Arden. Beck has friends there. She won't let anything happen to you."

"She?" I ask, my stomach twisting into one of the impossible knots Kern has tried to teach me. But I know even before he says it. I know who *she* is.

"Yeah," he says, finally looking at me. "That's Irina's place." *Irina.* The name slithers around my head, coiling around my heart.

Irina. I knew we were going to see her. I *need* to see her. But I didn't know we were heading for the Port of Pleasure. The woman who wedged a divide between Beck and Ammon; the woman of whom Galina, his own mother, said meeting once was enough; the woman Beck was stubborn enough to keep loving for too long—that woman owns the biggest brothel in all the Mittlesee. That woman could be the key to everything. And I'm the woman he's too stubborn to admit he cares for. But why didn't he just tell me this himself? What exactly does he not want me to know?

CHAPTER THIRTY-SEVEN

*B*eck doesn't say anything about it, and I don't ask. I figure that by the time we get there, he'll have explained something. And I don't want to push him. Our dynamic grows more tenuous by the day, and with every wave we crest, bringing us closer to our destination, I feel him drifting away.

I'm exhausted. I'm not sure how much of it is from not sleeping, and how much is from the toxic cocktail of worry mixed with the effort of fighting a losing battle. I take my time getting ready, washing my hair in the sink and braiding it out of my face. I wish there was a way to get warm again after the cold rinse, but there's not. So I dress, and then hesitate just long enough to decide the warm blankets are a better idea than the cold stares of the crew and the potential to be ignored by Beck.

I lay down and close my eyes, sucking in as much warmth as I can. I don't think I fall asleep, but then he's back, standing next to the door.

"Are you sick?" he asks. His arms hang at his sides, and he leans back against the door.

"I'm fine," I say, sitting up. "What time is it?"

"Almost time," he says, but his voice is careful, cautious.

"Everything okay?" I ask, giving him one more opportunity to tell me something, anything, about Irina or where we're going. He nods, and then seems to decide something and walks to the bed, sitting next to me, not touching me.

"We're about an hour out," he says.

"Okay," I say, running my thumb and finger along the edge of the sheet. He sighs and sticks his hands in his jacket pockets.

"Does she know who I am?" I ask. He lowers his chin.

"Yes . . . and no." He doesn't have to elaborate. I understand. Yes, she knows I'm a candidate, and no, she doesn't know I'm sharing Beck's bed. He doesn't have to explain. I nod and twist my lips to the left, chewing on my tongue.

"Will you tell me about her?" I ask, sitting up and leaning against the wall. His eyebrows lift behind the dark, coarse hair that falls into his face. He shrugs and blows a puff of air out of his lips.

"She's . . ." He shakes his head and soothes his beard with his hand. The catch of his calluses on his scruff is like sandpaper on splintered wood.

"Your old girlfriend?"

"She was never my girlfriend," he says darkly. Galina's words come back to me: *Beck thought he loved her, but she loved Ammon.*

"You loved her?" I ask, and then I wait. I wait for him to deny it. I hold my breath and wait for him to confess he's never loved anyone before me. For him to say the word he's danced around, but never lets past his lips.

"I thought so," he says. "I was determined to." Somehow, this is worse. My neck tightens, and my shoulders tense as I pick lint off the top blanket.

I want to know why he trusts her so much, but it hurts too much to ask. And really, what right do I have to ask him about an old love when I'm still engaged to marry another man? "But you need to know something about Irina."

"Okay . . ."

"She's like a shark in the water. The second she sniffs out your vulnerabilities, you need to watch yourself."

"I thought you said we'd be safe?"

"We will. But she might try to hurt you."

"Hurt me? How?" I ask, not understanding. He turns to me and takes my hands in his.

"Do you trust me?" he asks. His face is plain, his forehead smooth and uncreased, his eyes round and honest. In this moment, the mask is gone. I can see the hope, the plea, the fear behind his request. What it will do to him if I say no.

"Yes," I say. I don't ask him the same question. I don't want to know the answer. I'm not sure which one would hurt me more.

"The best way to deal with Irina is to face things head on. That's what I'm going to do. I'll tell her all about you—about us —once we're there. That should stave things off. But if it doesn't, if she sees it as a challenge . . . I might have to play her game to keep us safe."

"What does that mean?" I ask. He cringes and shakes his head.

"It could mean nothing. It could mean something. She's like a fury riding an eel in a firestorm—tough to predict, tougher to beat, and something you never want on your bad side." He leans forward and cups the back of my neck. His eyes are so green, so sincere, the fear behind them tenuous and real. "Just . . . trust this. Okay? Promise? Whatever happens, Capo, please trust this." I nod, pressing my forehead to his. He takes a deep breath, letting it out slowly, calmly, quietly, like he needs a moment to bottle up everything he's shown me, to be the captain and not the man once more.

Then he leaves.

He keeps his distance as we pull into the massive port. Sleet falls around us, landing on the water like a slushy, dirty crust. The port isn't particularly busy today. There are two other large, commercial fishing boats, unloading their day's haul, and about a handful of small, privately owned operations. Beyond the port, though, is a massive fortress built into a wall of sedimentary rock. It curves around the inlet like a shell, sheltering the port from the rougher trade winds and weather. Jutting out from the bowels of the dark brown stone is a long, narrow, wooden pier. Standing on the end is a group of about twenty people, seemingly all women. They're wrapped in a rainbow of coats and furs for warmth.

At the very end of the pier stands a statuesque woman with bronzed skin and long, white-blonde hair, blowing freely in the wind. She wears a sleeveless, silver chiffon gown, and the tissue-thin layers of her skirt flicker in the breeze like a snake scenting its prey. She stands like a flame in the wind, a candle on the sea. Her eyes are intense, dark brown with even darker brows, and as the boys tie the ship to the dock, they catch mine. A challenging smirk lifts the right corner of her blood-red lips. I look at Beck, but he doesn't take his eyes off her. Not when she raises an unimpressed, perfectly groomed eyebrow at me. Not when she walks up the plank and boards our ship. And certainly not when she takes his face in her hands and kisses him squarely on the lips.

CHAPTER THIRTY-EIGHT

*T*rina's eyes are heavy-lidded and hypnotic. She greets Beck with the intimacy of someone who still stakes a claim. I can't concentrate on anything Beck says to her, or anything she says back. I follow her eyes as she takes in everything around him without ever making it seem as though her attention isn't fully on him. He stands closer to her than I would like, but I can do nothing about it, and it would accomplish even less. Then her eyes meet mine again, and I feel frozen and unforgivably plain beneath her gaze.

Without ever shifting from my eyes, I know she takes in the simple braid I've twisted my unremarkable curls into, following the curve of it around my face and down my shoulder. Her pupils flare, as if in recognition of something she didn't expect. What she could ascertain from a stupid braid, I don't know, but I finally remove my eyes from her gaze and look down, staring at my feet. I don't want to watch her actively judge me or feel up Beck.

The clean, wet scent of snow mingles with the sour odor of fish and sewage. The mix isn't entirely unpleasant, but it's not something I want to get used to. My eyes follow the rock wall to where the fortress has been carved into the rock, climbing at least seven stories in height. Perched atop the highest point in the rock facade appears to be an observation deck of sorts, and women line the railing, watching us. They're too far, too high for me to see any of their features, but my eye catches on one with familiar coloring. I can't imagine I would know anyone here of all places, but there is something so familiar in the way she lifts her hand to her face.

"So this is the *little girl* everyone is making such a fuss over?" Irina's voice is honey sweet, her sharp accent stretching out her consonants and clipping her vowels into a hypnotic rhythm. Her voice is so melodic, I almost miss the insult.

"This is Arden," Beck says, his voice lighter than it's been in days. It catches me off guard. He smiles, pink in his cheeks, crossing his arms over his chest like he's showing off his loot. He looks happy and comfortable.

"Arden," she says, clipping the consonants, making my name sound unbearably ordinary. Her full red lips move into a shallow smile, like she would like nothing more than to spit right in my face as she pushes me from the ship.

"Hi," I say. I do myself no favors in her assessment. She must be freezing, but she shows no signs of it. Her silvery hair glistens and floats around her in the growing breeze, somehow never tangling or mussing. Up close, her dress is even more impressive. Made of layer upon layer of tissue-thin chiffon, it twists and drapes to perfectly flatter her form. She is not dressed for a homecoming; she is dressed for a victory celebration.

"Well, let's not dawdle any more than we must. The storm will come soon, and you must be freezing. Arden." She tacks my name onto the end of her statement with all the grace deserving of a lame animal, as I shiver into the wind. She turns on her heel, and then hesitates for a moment. Beck joins her, and they walk arm in arm all the way to the gates. We follow, more or less in a single file.

"Meow!" Shaz says into my ear, and I shoot him what I hope is a withering glare, but it only makes him laugh uncontrollably. "Madame is out for blood!"

"Madame?" I ask, looking back at him.

"Well, yeah," he says, as if it's the most obvious thing. "She's the one in charge around here."

Madame. That's her title, just like Celeste. And this is a brothel of sorts, Kern had said. I don't have a lot of experience with brothels—more now than I ever expected to have—but I already know the atmosphere here will not be as welcoming to me as Celeste was. We pass through the stone-and-iron gate, and I cross my arms over my stomach. I may be out of my depth here.

Beck goes one direction with Irina, and they don't invite me. Instead, I'm whisked off in another. A girl dressed in menswear leads me up too many winding staircases to count, though I do try to pay attention to which direction they curve. Left, right, right, right, left. I am out of breath by the time we get to a wooden door that she opens with zero fanfare. I enter, and immediately stop short.

"Well, you look positively royal," Neve says, standing in the middle of a large, richly appointed bedroom.

"Neve?" I say, but I don't wait for her response before I crush my friend and roommate from the peninsula into a hug. She resists at first, always more refined and dignified than me. But then she relents and squeezes me back.

She looks the same, but different. Her dark, ebony hair flows in free waves, framing her oval-shaped face and making her copper skin glow. She smells different. Spicier. At the estate, she was obsessed with anything that smelled like a baked good. She was always trying to sneak vanilla and almond extracts from the kitchen to put into her bath oils. Now, her soft, dark hair smells like unfamiliar spices and rich stone fruits. I lean back and cup her face in my hands. It's hard to believe it's only been a few months since I last saw her. She has aged, or maybe just grown up, especially around the eyes. Her hazel gaze looks harder, colder, despite her soft smile.

"How are you here?" I ask. Her gaze goes far away for a moment, and then she returns, strong and hard against my question.

"That's a story for another time. Let's get you into something more comfortable," she says, casting an eye down at my oilskin pants and heavy sweater. Until I saw Irina in her dress, it didn't occur to me that I should wear anything else. Neve is dressed impeccably, as well. She wears a form-fitting, long, icy-blue skirt with a crisp white blouse tucked into it. Her makeup is done simply, but it's clear she is wearing it, accentuating her full cheeks and making her eyes pop. Her gentle elegance is in stark contrast to the decor—all lavish materials, but garish in overdone maroons and blacks that threaten to swallow us in opulent sexuality. If Irina could have put me in a more overtly sexy room, I wouldn't want to see it.

She helps me into a pair of impossibly soft black pants and an equally soft and warm cream-colored turtleneck sweater. I wonder where these clothes came from, but they are so warm and comfortable, I don't question it. She reaches up to untwist my braid, but then stops mid-reach and leaves it. When she reaches for her makeup kit, I stop her, and she laughs, the first genuine Neve thing I've heard yet.

"What are you doing here?" I finally ask, when she leads me out the door to hunt down some food.

"I left the peninsula, and this is where I ended up," she says. There's something stilted in her words that extends to her posture, and I wonder about the story behind her non-answer. The hallway we walk down is narrow and low-ceilinged, lined with door after door. We walk past one, and I look inside, to where a woman who looks at least ten years older than us massages an older man's naked arm. She sees me staring and winks. I look away quickly, feeling my cheeks flush.

"I'd have thought you'd have grown a thicker skin, considering everything," Neve says with an amused arch to her brow. My stomach clenches as I wait for her to explain, or to get in her punchline. "You were just on a ship full of men. So many penises."

"Neve!" I gasp to mask my embarrassed laugh. It seems she too has grown a thicker skin. We walk down a half-story staircase ahead, and then turn right down a hall that is lined with windows overlooking the port. Another door opens ahead, and a man exits, calling something back into the room he exits in a language I don't understand. But I do understand the look of satisfaction on his face. A chill runs down my spine, and I keep my mouth shut again until we pass into a large dining room.

Neve seats me at a table and promises to return. It's a decent-sized space that strangely reminds me of the dining hall at the institute. It's currently empty, but there are six round tables with six chairs each and small windows that look out over the water, as well, letting in the bare minimum light to illuminate the space. This is not a space for guests, but it is nice.

"This will have to do," she says. "It's not salted fish, but it is edible." She gives me a tight smile, delivering a plate of cheese, bread, and small, dark-brown dried fruits. I take a piece of cheese and nibble at the corner of the salty, briny wedge. It's delicious. I didn't realize how hungry I was until this moment. She's quiet while I eat, and then, once my hunger is sated, I can't hold off any longer.

"Neve, what are you really doing here?" I ask. She raises an eyebrow and gives me the smile that tells me she still thinks being two months older than me entitles her to more secrets.

"I could ask the same of you," she says, and I sink into my old posture, letting my spine curve back against the chair.

"It's a long story," I say.

"So is mine." Her words are crisp, and only just mask the hurt I see beneath the surface. Her last words to me were: *I will never forgive you for this.*

"Neve, you have to know, I didn't know he—" I swallow hard. Funny how much time I can spend thinking about CJ, but actually talking about him being alive is what catches in my throat. "I had no idea."

"You could have turned it down," she says, but she can't hold my eyes. I couldn't have turned it down, and she damn well knows it. It would have guaranteed me a life in hell, and it would have done nothing for her.

"If I had known, I would have told you." I pick at a piece of bread, tearing the meat from the crust.

"I know," she says, softly. She's had months to go over this in her own head. She knows every way around it.

"But you got out," I say.

"I had to. I couldn't stay. There was nothing for me there," she says.

"What about Carla?" I ask. She looks away, and her face grows dark.

"She'll be okay," she says, as if convincing herself. "Another story for another time."

"Okay," I say, looking around the space again. "But what are you doing *here*? I mean, you're not . . ."

"Not what?" she asks, challenge in her bright eyes. After everything I went through on the peninsula, it's hard to believe she really didn't know what CJ was doing to me. But Neve has always been good at focusing on what she needs to do to survive. Still, I can't imagine she's whoring herself for her freedom.

"What? You think I'm selling my body?" she asks, but there's no hint of scandal in her inflection. No shock, no shame. That alone surprises me more than anything else.

"Isn't this a brothel?" I ask. She smiles and nods.

"Yes, it is."

We walk down another hallway, and then reach an exterior vestibule of sorts. It almost reminds me of a street of shops I've seen in other towns. But a glass ceiling hangs overhead, letting in light filtered through the falling snow. There is a natural air flow, a bustle, an energy. It's mostly men that swarm the streets, all three stories of them. Above the main thoroughfare, two more stories of store fronts tower above from suspended steel walkways.

"In Sudersberg, like most of the Mittle Continent, women are prohibited from opening their own businesses. Irina calls it codified poverty. But in Sudersberg, there's a loophole. Prostitution is legal. If a woman wants to open and run a functioning brothel, it is allowed."

"I don't understand," I say, looking into the window full of small bottles of oils. "This is part of the brothel?"

"Legally defined, a brothel is a conglomerate of independently contracting women selling their services to customers under the supervision of a madame. As long as we sell a *service*, it's legal." I look through another window, where a woman fixes another woman's hair with a litany of beads and feathers.

"What do you sell?" I ask. She presses her lips into a proud smile.

"Makeup," she says.

"Makeup?" I ask, wondering how that's a service.

"I make my own products, and I apply them for my clients."

"You make your own makeup?" I ask, letting a relieved smile move into my cheeks. She laughs, and I can see the pride glitter in her eyes under her copper eyeshadow.

"I do," she says, then flutters her eyelids. "Do you like it?"

"I do! Neve, that—that is so cool!" She grins, and then reaches for a door handle and opens it, letting me follow as she goes inside. She flips on the lights, and I find myself inside a small boutique with two folding chairs and four shelves displaying small boxes in pretty wrapping paper in a veritable rainbow of colors. Pink and gold paper lanterns hang throughout the shop, and everything feels expensive.

"You make a living this way?" I ask. She shrugs and sits down in one of the chairs.

"Enough," she says. "I'm not rich or anything, but I can afford my rent, and as long as we pay rent, we have a place to sleep." She points upstairs and makes a little face. "It's dorms up there until you can really turn a profit, but then you can rent something bigger. There are some loud snorers up there, though, so I mostly sleep in the back room. It's technically against the rules, but as long as I'm paying my rent, she doesn't seem to care." I stare at my friend as she sits in the chair she owns, in a business that she runs. I am humbled and more than a little embarrassed I haven't accomplished more than learning how to knee a man in the groin.

"So, there's not actually any sex selling around here?" I ask.

"Why? Are you interested?" she asks, raising a voyeuristic eyebrow.

"No," I say quickly. She chuckles under her breath.

"Doesn't seem like you have any problems in that department," she says with a knowing smile.

"What?" I ask, the color draining from my face. I know Beck said he would talk to Irina about me, but I didn't think he would betray such intimacies. Or that the walls might literally have ears.

"I mean, it's all over the news."

"What is?" I ask. She raises her index finger and gets up, walking through a door in the back wall. I try to peek around the door, but see nothing. When she returns, she hands me a newspaper. On the cover is a photo of me kissing Declan on the main lawn.

"Where did they . . ." I start to say out loud, but then I remember. That day I got mad, and we were out on the lawn, and he kissed me. In front of all the prying eyes. Well, we were definitely seen. It's actually a really pretty picture; we both look beautiful and happy. The headline reads, *The Institution of Marriage Alive and Well: Bachelor Bags a Bride! But Where is She?*

"Oh," I say, my stomach dropping. *Marriage*. He's told the papers he wants to marry me—but I've made other plans. Plans that involve a man hidden away from me, somewhere in this earthen brothel, with his childhood love.

"Well, that's not the reaction I expected from the girl who stole my spot . . ." She doesn't continue, but I know what she's thinking. Her spot, her man, her life. Neve is not my friend right now. Neve is someone who could sell me out—to her boss, no less. I have to be careful. I force an embarrassed smile and nod.

"I just didn't know he was going to say something before I had the ring," I say quietly. Her eyebrows rise into perfectly plucked half moons.

"So this is true?" she asks.

"More or less," I say in a near whisper. If this is in the papers today, it's surely come after he received Beck's message. I have no idea what that message said, but if this is the official reaction to it, I can only imagine it said one thing: *She's yours. Come get her.*

But that was before everything that happened, before the

late-night confessions — before I gave it all up by choosing Beck. He was right. This is going to be a mess. *Whatever happens, Capo, please trust this.* I cling to Beck's words, forcing the doubt from my mind. It's real. He's real. I just have to believe in that.

"Oh, honey!" She pulls me into a hug, and then leans back and wipes away a tear I didn't know had snuck down my cheek.

"Happy," I whisper, and she grabs a tissue for me.

"I know I'm supposed to hate you for the rest of your life, and that feeling might return, but . . ." She takes a deep breath. "You did it. You came from even less than me. I know I don't admit it, but it's true. And you beat the odds. You made it. Like, you really did it. It's incredible."

"Yeah, incredible," I say. I did it. I really did it. Too bad that I don't want it.

CHAPTER THIRTY-NINE

$\mathcal{W}$ e leave Neve's boutique a short while later and explore floor after floor of makeshift shops, where women peddle their services and wares. They vary widely, both in quality and type: from simple, paper-made accessories attached loosely to existing apparel to metal-worked earrings pierced into new locations. There's a lot of competition for oils of all varieties, and there are many types of massage and skin services. Neve introduces me to a tall woman with fiery orange hair—the only person in all the brothel who should be allowed to touch anyone's skin. Other than Neve and her makeup, of course.

Even more impressive is the sheer number of men and even women shopping through the wares. People could shop anywhere, Neve says, but they come here because the prices are more reasonable, and they believe in the cause. I'm not sure I believe how staunchly these people support that cause, though, especially when I watch a man ogle a woman's chest as she rubs oil into his forearm. But it is both foreign and exciting to see women succeeding in this way. As far as I know, I've not seen something like this before.

"How do you find your way around here?"

"You learn—there's even more paths in this maze than anyone realizes," she says. I wonder what sorts of places lie beyond the walls I've seen thus far.

"It's pretty amazing what we can do when we work together, instead of competing," Neve says. Her words are so flippant, something she's clearly heard and possibly repeated a thousand times, but they are striking nonetheless.

"What did you say?" I ask, turning away from the window display that had caught my eye.

"What?" she asks, narrowing her eyebrows, as if she can't believe I would question her observation. "Just that when we stop competing against each other—like men want us to—it's incredible what we can achieve together. This couldn't be done on our own. Irina really was a trailblazer in seeing the potential here."

"She was?" I ask, swallowing hard. I don't like the thought of her, but I'm finding it harder and harder to not respect her.

"Before she turned this place around, it was a two-bit brothel in the traditional sense. She took it over when the original madame died, and she gave it legitimacy. It used to just be sailors and pirates who came here. Now, you have reputable men whose wives send them here for specific products." *Sailors and pirates.* A creeping sensation flows down my arms at the thought that Beck came here for less than legitimate purposes prior to it becoming what it is now.

"We should get you back, so you can get some rest before we Storychat tonight," she says.

"Storychat?" I ask.

"Yeah, it's something we do whenever old friends return. It's fun. Dinner, drinks, a fire, and we all talk and sing. It's cozy . . . it probably sounds dumb, but . . ."

"No, I get it. It sounds nice. I'd love to go to story talk with you," I say.

"Storychat," she says with a teasing smile. I nod, and a little meanness creeps into the corner of her eye. "From here, we could take the shortcut to your room, but it's . . . shall we say, a less savory part of the town?"

"What do you mean?" I ask. She makes the decision for me, and I follow her down a hall and through a set of dark double doors.

Once through, the temperature increases by at least ten degrees, and it gets darker. The hall is wide and low-ceilinged, and all the doors are closed along our route. The air is heavy and smells of strong incense and musky cologne. But occasionally, noises escape that make me walk a little faster, a blush rising to heat my face and chest. Neve is enjoying my reaction entirely too much.

"I thought you said this wasn't like other brothels?" I ask, as we reach the end of the hall.

"It's not, strictly speaking. But a girl's gotta do what she's gotta do to survive. We can't all have powerful men paying our way," she says. I bite down on my tongue and play with the tip of my braid, choosing to let that barb slide past unrequited. We pass through another set of double doors, and the air on the other side is fresher, cleaner.

"Why would people do that if they don't have to?" I ask, staring at the stone floor as I walk.

"I don't know, and I don't ask. They're grown women entitled to decide for themselves how they want to make a living. They're taken care of and well compensated. If they want to do something else, they have the capacity to do so." Her tone is harsh, and her eyes dare me to challenge her assertion. I don't believe her, though. I don't believe there are that many women who feel they have to do that, and feel free to step away from it if they don't want to. But I don't say anything.

"Do you know a lot of the girls here, then?"

"The women?" Neve asks, her tone harsh.

"Yes, the women. Have you met them?" I wonder if she could tell me about Carmen . . . assuming there isn't more than one, of course.

"Sure, you could say that." She slows her pace slightly and looks back over her shoulder. "Why do you ask?"

This is my chance. I should just ask. Maybe I can avoid having to talk to Irina at all, if Neve can introduce me to Carmen.

"Do you know — ?" But something stops me. It seems too easy. I should just trust Neve, but there's something off about this. I don't know what, or why, but I feel uneasy. "I mean, is there anyone here . . . that I should meet?"

She quirks the corner of her mouth and shrugs. "Plenty," she says.

We turn another corner and reach another set of double doors. Neve knocks, and then opens the door, not waiting for an answer. We enter a luxurious sitting room, elevated by fluffy area rugs, silky drapes, and satin furniture in shades of lavender, black, and white. Through a wall of leaded glass windows, I watch the snow fall on the bay, the waves lapping in a thick blanket of white. Neve indicates that I should stay where I am, and then knocks on another door to the right.

"Where are we?" I ask. As if in answer, Irina emerges from behind the door, wearing a lavender silk robe that slips off her bronzed shoulder. Her eyes lock with mine, and I fight the urge to flinch. She says something soft to Neve, stroking her cheek, and Neve nods, walking out the double doors without so much as a backward glance, leaving me in the lion's den.

"Arden," Irina says, closing the door behind her and tying the belt on her robe. She looks mussed, less put together than before, and the lead pit in my stomach gapes wider. The last time I saw her, not more than a few hours ago, she was dressed to kill. Now, it seems she's succeeded.

"I understand Neve gave you the grand tour?" she says,

walking to a gold-framed cart in front of the windows and pouring herself a glass of clear liquid. She offers me one, and I shake my head. Apparently, I don't talk around her. She shrugs and pours herself a little more. She slinks along the windows to a black satin settee and sits, leaning against the arm too casually. This is her den, and I am her prey. She's comfortable, and I do not belong.

"So, what do you think of my business?" she asks, her words lilting into the rhythmic cadence of her accent.

"I'm impressed," I say softly, but I sound closer to a child who has to admit she's wrong.

"Why, thank you. That means a lot," she says, tucking her feet beneath her hips. The robe parts slightly, exposing the creamy golden skin of her thigh, and she smiles as she catches my glance.

"And tell me, what did you think of Beck's ship?" She sips her drink, but her eyes never deviate from my face, nor do they lessen in their intensity. She's looking for a specific answer here, and I'm not sure what that is. I do know I don't want to get this wrong. Something tells me that the wrong answer will rescind any good will she has toward me. But I also get the feeling that if I back down, she will walk all over me.

"It was . . . comfortable," I say. Her eyes widen briefly.

"Hmmm," she purrs. "In my experience, men bore of comfort." She sips her drink again and lets her eyes slide down my body with a lazy, obvious gleam. They hover around my breasts, and she purses her lips shrewdly.

"A girl with your skill set would do well here," she says.

"Excuse me?" I ask, crossing my arms over my chest. Her head flies back, and her mouth springs open with a laugh that fills the room.

"Oh, don't be so incensed. I think you could sell salt to a sailor. I think maybe, you already have," she says, her words constricting, growing tighter and lower. She runs her fingers through her shiny hair and doesn't even bother to look at me. Something tells me she knows I'm burning from within. She doesn't have to look up to see my cheeks are on fire.

"Thank you for your hospitality," I say, pushing my feet into the floor for strength. "If you don't mind, I'm tired from the journey and would like to rest." Her eyes jerk back to my face, and her too-dark eyebrows rise into perfect crescent moons.

"Actually, I do mind. You are my guest, and from what I understand," she says, nodding her head back toward the closed door behind her, "you may have brought mercenaries to my doorstep. Even worse, the Nordanian government is likely on its way." I look at her door before I can stop myself, and she watches my gaze with hungry victory.

"I'm sorry," I say, and hate myself for the apology.

"It's nothing," she says, waving me off as she stands. Her robe swirls around her as she walks back to her bar cart, pouring more of that clear liquid into her glass. "It wasn't actually your doing, after all."

"It wasn't?" I ask. She whips her head around, sending her hair flying over the other shoulder.

"There's only one person who comes here when he's in trouble." I gulp at her words, and she smiles, victorious. "Oh, don't feel badly, dear. This is his pattern. He does what he does, gets into trouble, whatever, but he always ends up here. He will always come back here." Galina's voice fills my head: *he just doesn't know how to quit.*

"He comes back, because I know what he needs," she says, sauntering closer. "Just ask him. He'll tell you." I don't want to believe her. I close my eyes for a moment and try to remember Beck's face before we got off the boat. His eyes were earnest; I want to believe in the memory of them. *She's like a shark in the water . . . she will try to hurt you.*

"If you say so," I say. When I open my eyes again, her eyes are fiery gold embers.

"I'm not playing games here, *little girl*," she says, and the way she curls her mouth around the *R* in *girl* feels like a scythe, a deadly weapon of its own leveled straight for my throat. "I know what he needs, and more importantly, I know what he doesn't need. You will be the *death* of him. Of this, I am certain." My heart races, galloping at full speed like it must either launch forward or risk falling backward and off a cliff to its death. I want to tell her she's wrong, to fight her off. But I am in her house. I must play along.

"I appreciate your concern," I say, speaking slowly to keep my voice as even as possible. "And I appreciate you opening your gates to me and the trouble that I bring." She looks like she wants to spit in my face, but instead, she steps closer, so she's within arm's reach, and sips her drink.

"I will fix this, as I always do. And then you will be gone, and he will be safe, and after that, I want you to stay away. From me, from my business, and from my family."

"Beck is your family?" I ask, unable to mask the laugh that catches in my throat.

"He's more than family," she says, running her tongue over her lower lip to catch a drop of liquor.

"Funny," I say, feeling adrenaline pump through my veins, but not anxiety. As if I'm not in my own body. "That's not how his family talks about you." Her eyes go round with surprise. I've hit her where it hurts, but then her smile returns, curling her lips up in lethal curves. Her palm connects with my cheek, fast and hard, sending a searing pain through my cheekbones and a ringing in my ear. I touch my fingertips to the stinging slap, and when I look back at her, she's chuckling.

"You are such a waste of flesh," she says, shaking her head. She walks over to a small table and lifts a newspaper. "But very photogenic." It's a different paper than the one Neve had. My cheeks burn, and I bite down hard on the edge of my tongue, trying to keep the tears back. I can't cry in front of this woman. It would hand her the victory she seeks.

"And I quote, *The heir to the Nordanian Conservative Party has allegedly left the capital to collect the woman he's allegedly proposed to. Sources from within the capital tell us, under condition of anonymity, that 'Arden Thatcher captured his heart swiftly and completely, and prior to her sudden departure, he proposed marriage. She accepted, and he has now gone to collect her.' As for the circumstances around her departure, the capital is tight-lipped, though insiders say the First Lady—once a candidate herself, and a staunch advocate for the girls who attend the program—is 'on a tear' and hungry for blood. "If it is true that she was kidnapped by someone within the First Family's circle of trust, she's determined to bring down the swift hammer of justice." As for the engaged couple, sources say Declan is eager to marry as soon as she returns, if not sooner, which, according to the charter for the Nordanian Women's Institute, would forfeit her candidacy."* She drags the last word, over-enunciating the soft *C*'s. *"While it is always a disappointment to see a candidate fail to graduate, the same source expresses optimism for her platform moving forward. 'Both she and Declan are ready to hit the floor running and effect change across the realm.' End quote,"* she says, with an ugly lip smack.

"What?" I ask, a near whisper. She folds the paper in quarters and hands it to me like a birthday present. I take it and scan the blurring text. There it is, clear as day. *Declan is eager to marry as soon as she returns, if not sooner, which, according to the charter for the Nordanian Women's Institute, would forfeit her candidacy.*

I won't graduate.

But only graduates have a vote.

"Looks like you're an even bigger fool than I thought," she says, her tone almost sympathetic. Declan is silencing me? If I go back, if I marry him, I lose any chance I had to create change. It doesn't matter what the paper says, what this "anonymous source" told them. I know what it means. There's no way his mother is in favor of this marriage, so maybe this is the compromise they struck? But I thought Declan wanted to change things. That's what he said: *you and the next generation of candidates will have the power to control the system*. He included me in that. But then he also said we had to take small steps. My face is hot as I stare at the newspaper in my hands, and not just where Irina slapped me. I no longer feel as guilty about ditching Declan's compass, or about choosing Beck instead.

"Oh, *little girl*, how you have made a mess of things," she says, tsking her tongue as she reclines back on the settee. "Like I said, what a waste of flesh. You could have really made something." Her face is serious, tired, her voice tinged in disappointment. I don't know why I ask it, but she seems like the only person who might give me a straight answer.

"What do I do?" I ask.

"Why would I help you?" she asks. It's a good question. One that I don't have an answer to. I shake my head and shrug.

"Because Ammon is asking you to. 'It's Ammon's wish.'"

Her nostrils flare, and every shred of pretense slips from her face.

"Go get some sleep, *little girl*," she says, waving a hand at me. I've been dismissed. As if on cue, her door opens. Neve is there, waiting for me to follow. I trail behind her to my room — to the room Irina lets me borrow — and collapse in a heap on the bed, feeling somehow more trapped and alone than ever.

CHAPTER FORTY

*N*eve doesn't follow me into the room. She closes the door, and I'm left alone in the first tacky room I've seen that looks like it belongs somewhere between a brothel and a circus. The bed I'm lying on is piled high with too many pillows, but they muffle the sound of my frustrated scream. I don't even realize it's my voice until my throat is raw from the exertion. My hand clutches the newspaper I forgot I was still holding, and I throw it hard against the door. It hits the floor with a disappointing, muffled thud.

I should have seen it coming. I made the decision to trust Declan — once in the capital, and then again, in New Covington. But why? Why did I trust him? He said he wanted to keep me safe, and then he sent me off with a fake pirate. He came to check on me, told me that I shouldn't trust Beck, and then left with promises to return with a ring. It all seems so obvious now. Ammon was right. Declan gets what Declan wants. And he's decided that what he wants is me. He was just telling me what I needed to hear. I knew I was being placated, but I thought there was something complicit, that there was an understanding between us. Now, I know better.

He said we were going to make changes. He said graduates have a vote, and that we could use *my* vote to make those changes real. But clearly, he decided I didn't need my own voice. Because of course, he would. The system exists to bolster rulers—no, *men*—like him, and having a peer with a voice of her own doesn't support that.

It would be so easy to just blame Siobhan or his father for this. It certainly reeks of Siobhan—agreeing to give her son what he wants, so long as I get nothing in return. I know I bring nothing to the table. I have no valuable connections, nothing of significance to offer; I'm not like Avery or Fiona, girls who were literally born to marry him, to govern placid and domestic at his side. I ruin whatever ambitions she has for Declan, so why shouldn't I be left resigned to a life of quiet subjugation?

Good thing I'd already decided not to return. But still, knowing that I was so close to a future that would have mattered, and that it was all a lie, hurts in a way I probably should have expected. Of course, I was never meant to be anything more than what I am. How could I be? CJ and Conrad made sure of that.

A mean smile peers out at me from an inside page of the crumpled paper, and my curiosity gets the best of me. I pick it up and unfold it, finding Fiona's cruel eyes staring back. *Daughter of Well-Respected Nordanian Family Rejects Position With Brandeiss Delegation.* Fiona was offered a spot with the Brandeiss people and turned it down? I didn't know that that was something that was done.

Sources close to the candidate say that she was displeased with the implication that she would have to leave prior to graduation from the program. She attempted to negotiate a later enactment date, but the Brandeiss delegation refused her proposed terms, and we have exclusive confirmation that this offer has now been rescinded. It is not the first time a candidate has rejected an offer, but it is the first time one has been rejected so publicly.

It doesn't seem unreasonable to assume that Fiona had her eyes set on Declan, and now that Declan has declared his intention for me, the institute would try to place her. But it does seem odd that it would fizzle out on negotiations around her graduation. There have been plenty of other agreements in the past that have allowed, even encouraged, the women involved to graduate. I recall two years ago, there was a girl who was forced to graduate before her placement would take effect. It may have even been from Brandeissland. So, why don't they want Fiona to graduate?

I stare at her face in the black-and-white, grainy newsprint, at her mean smirk, her eyes slightly narrowed like she's about to say something really cutting and smart. It's a pretty picture, and I doubt that anyone who doesn't know her would think anything of the photo. But I do know her. I know what she looks like when she's plotting and playing a winning game. This isn't that. Is it possible Nordania is the one attempting to force her out early? That they're doing the same thing to her they're trying to do to me?

A knock on the door distracts me, and my heart flutters. My cheeks flush red, embarrassed at my hope for Beck to be on the other side. I let out a deep breath and chomp down on the side of my tongue to brace my face as I pull open the door.

"Well, aren't you fancy?" Kern says, his eyes looking past me into the room beyond.

"Shut up," I say, retreating into the room. He follows, and I hear the door click shut behind him.

"You should see where I'm staying," he says with a whistle. "You'd be much happier with your suite. Trust me."

"Where are you sleeping?" I ask.

"Oh, I don't plan to sleep there."

"Where will you sleep, then?" I regret the question as soon as I've asked.

"Not where I'm staying," he says with a roguish grin. I laugh, marveling at his optimism.

"I would look for another option," I say, "but I'm pretty sure it doesn't exist." I hope he knows I'm talking about the room and not, well . . .

"Yeah, probably not," Kern says with a smile. "Irina really hates you."

"Thanks," I mumble, glaring at him. It doesn't surprise me — I already know she hates me — but his confirmation feels like the final dagger in the dying corpse of my hope.

"I mean, I've never seen her dislike someone so intensely. She's usually the one yelling at the other women to not be so mean to other girls. 'Stop competing — support each other!'" He drags his vowels and clips his consonants in an impression of Irina's accent that is equal parts hilarious and perfectly on point. "You must've really pushed one of her buttons." He stares at me under his heavy brow, and I realize this is a question he desperately wants answered. What did I do to crack Irina's stony facade?

"I don't know what you want me to say." I shrug, walking to the sitting area and plopping down on an armchair. It's not cozy, and I don't want to linger, but he settles into the identical chair opposite me; it hugs him perfectly. He looks comfortable in a way I will never be. He has no enemies here, no worries. I wonder if anyone has ever considered him competition, or even an enemy. I'm envious. And then I'm ashamed for having even entertained that thought.

"She's rattled by you. What did she say?"

"Nothing," I say, not willing to repeat her words. *You will be the death of him. What a waste of flesh.* I know there's a good chance she was just trying to hurt me, just like I was when I told her Beck's family thinks so little of her, but I can't help but cling to the glimmer of truth in her words. I knew enough to know that mention of Ammon would wound her pride. It would be foolish to think she wouldn't use exactly the same strategy against me. I don't want to give her words that power, but neither can I bring myself to tell Kern what she said. Part of me thinks he wouldn't disagree. And then it really would be true.

"You're not on losing ground here, you know?" he says, and I look at him in surprise, wondering if he could hear my thoughts.

"What does that mean?"

"You don't have to hide. You haven't lost. If anything, you're on equal footing. She only wins if you let her."

"Isn't it a bad idea for you to be here like this? I mean, what if she finds out you told me to fight her?"

"Who's going to tell her?" he asks with a lazy chuckle. I shake my head and look around.

"Something tells me the walls have eyes."

"So what if they do?" he says with a shrug. "You really going to let the walls tell you what to do?"

"I don't know. What am I supposed to do?" I ask. My voice sounds sullen and defeated, even to my ears.

"Come to Talk Story. Show your face. Beck will be there."

"Hmmph," I mumble and lean back into my chair. "I don't think he cares whether I come or not. He's made his feelings about this situation perfectly clear."

"And how exactly did he do that?" Kern asks, tilting his head.

"He's done nothing to stop her."

"What would you have him do? This is Irina's fortress. She controls everything that happens here, most of all what happens to him," he says, standing suddenly.

"What if she's right?" I ask. "About me?"

He stands still, his short fingers tapping rhythmically against his thighs.

"Then she's right," he says with a shrug. "But that doesn't mean you should give up. You came here for a purpose. Don't stop just because she hates you." He nods and walks toward the door. "I guess I just always saw you as a fighter. Never occurred to me you wouldn't try."

He leaves then, having said what he came to say.

I stay in my chair, feeling the walls' eyes bore into my skin, deciding whether to let the current of Irina's judgment sink me, or if I want to fight my way to the surface and win.

CHAPTER FORTY-ONE

*K*ern's words sting more than I expect, and I carry them with me as I leave my borrowed room and step out into the hall. He's not entirely wrong, though. We left Beck's family planning to hide, until Emlyn convinced me that I shouldn't. That I should fight back. I told Beck I wanted to fight. And now, at the first sign of trouble, I'm cowering. Irina is a formidable opponent, but she doesn't exactly have the backing of an entire nation—though it sure feels that way as I lose myself in the labyrinthine halls of her fortress, looking for the location of Storychat.

I wonder if this is intentional. Maybe she wants me to get lost, and nobody will ever find me, least of all Beck. His absence stirs a discomfort in me that I can't quite put into words. It's part fear, part dread, part sadness and resignation. I'm not afraid for his well-being; I know he will always land on his feet. But the sense of dread, the idea that I was finally brave enough to go after what I wanted, and that I may have taken that leap of faith on my own, is overwhelming. I don't want to know what I'm missing in his absence. But when I hear his booming laughter through a set of closed wooden doors, I hesitate. I tug my sweater into place, smoothing it over my leggings, and put a hand to my chest, stilling the rise and fall of my breath.

Composed—on the outside, at least—I push through the door and find myself in a large room, with four deep sofas arranged in a square around a large round fireplace. The only light in the room comes from the fire, casting orangey-gold shadows and giving the room's inhabitants warm, heady glows. There are about a dozen people scattered around the fire, and a couple more tucked away in the farthest corners. I hear Beck's laugh again, but I don't see him. Nobody notices me at first, and it gives me a chance to take in the space in more detail.

Rugs woven in intricate designs and patterns are layered beneath the sofas, all upholstered in the softest velvet. The firelight casts a warm glow over everything. Tapestries hang from the walls, and there's almost no stone exposed, except for the area around the three large windows along the back wall. Two of them sit flush with the room, but the third, on the far left, is set back into an alcove, where there's a bench with at least a dozen pillows.

I see all the familiar faces I expected: Kern sits between two pretty girls who are dressed in less than seems comfortable to me, but they seem happy enough with him next to the fireplace. Shaz sits with a red-headed woman who giggles too loudly, and Slick sits in the corner with a man he seems very cozy with. Perlman sits dangerously close to Neve, and while she says nothing, something tells me she knows I'm here.

I walk around the fire toward the window seat—it feels like a place I can hide. As I turn the corner, I see Beck, sitting back on the far couch, his arm along the back of the sofa. Irina leans into his side, her hand resting securely on his chest. I freeze for a moment, feeling the rotting stink of jealousy rise in my throat. I swallow it back and feel Irina's gaze on me as I retreat further into the window seat.

"Looks like we've been graced with royalty," her mean voice quips, and a chorus of hollow laughter follows.

"Long live the princess!" Shaz's special friend squeals. To his credit, he leans away from her and shakes his head. I feel familiar warmth creep into my cheeks, and I can't take my eyes off Beck. He doesn't move, his shoulders rigid and his grin tight.

"How about a toast?" Irina says, raising her glass of clear liquid.

"Here, here!" The redhead tosses her glass into the air, too, almost losing it in the process.

"To the health of the realm. May the heiress to the throne accomplish everything she set out to do, and may she want for nothing." She looks straight into my eyes as she drinks—her meaning clear: leave Beck, and go back to where you're supposed to be.

"Cheers!" The redhead squeals again, and a few of the other women oblige the toast as well, but the men are quiet, happily sipping their drinks.

"Well, you'd think people don't want the last candidate standing to succeed," Irina says, to dubious laughter.

"Can we just get back to the story?" Neve asks, her eyes back on Perlman. I can't see his face, but he leans into her with a posture I've not seen on him.

"Haven't we all heard this story a million times?" Redhead complains, turning to Shaz. "I'm bored."

"Then get another drink," Shaz says, ignoring her. She pouts, but leans back against him, refocused on Perlman.

"So, Liberius goes fishing, and while he's gone, Alijord, the God of the In-Between, who has pierced the veil to the land of the living, convinces his sister Nordania, the Goddess of the Winds and Tides, to blow him off course. He gets lost, because he never learned the basics of celestial navigation, which really makes this whole story his own damn fault, because—"

"Stick to the story, compass-boffer," Slick says, to the sound of laughter and some clapping.

"Well, while he's lost, Alijord returns to Liberius's home to persuade his beloved—" Someone coughs loudly, blocking out Perlman's words, but I can't focus on his story.

Instead, I look out the window at the sweeping view beyond. The snow has stopped, and the moon glistens blue and silver on the soft waves in the bay, as whitecaps break against the rocky cliffs in brilliant whites. The window panes are thick and somewhat warp the view, casting an otherworldly look on the scene. I settle back into the corner, against the wall, and hug a pillow to my chest.

I don't know why I came. I don't belong here. I don't care what Kern said. This is not the place for me, and I have no way to battle Irina when I'm so clearly in her world. All I can do is hide and wait it out, but when I look back at the group of cozy people listening to cozy stories, I can't quite bring myself to watch Beck be with her. I know he asked me to trust him, but so did Declan. And look how that played out. So I stay trapped inside my alcove, staring out the window, surrounded by people, but alone.

"Blanket?" I'm not sure how long I've been sitting when the familiar voice intrudes. I look up, and Beck is standing just outside the alcove. I'm shivering, I realize. I'm not sure how long that's been happening either. The firelight is lower now, glowing in passionate reds, and the low murmur of Perlman and the others continues. I nod and accept the fur-lined throw he offers. It immediately warms me from within, and I return my gaze to the outside.

"You don't look like you're having much fun, Capo," he says.

"Don't," I say quietly, not looking at him. I hear him sigh, and then he is sitting at my feet.

"Arden, I told you this would be . . . I asked you to trust me," he says softly.

"You know how well I follow orders." My voice is as cold as the picturesque view laid out before me.

I hear him laugh softly. "Couldn't even follow that one, eh?"

"Yeah, fine. You told me. That makes it all okay. Thanks for the blanket," I say, watching the boats rock gently in the harbor below.

"Can you look at me?" he asks, a sharp undercurrent extending from his words and up through my legs. I don't want to. I don't want him to explain his relationship with Irina. I don't want him to ask me about Declan and how I got hoodwinked. I don't want him to look at me with those green eyes that see right through me and diagnose me and coddle me and send me to bed with little more than a good night. But I do. I look, anyway. I look, because I can't not.

"What do you want me to say?" I ask. His eyes glint gold back at me, and it hurts. It hurts that I don't want to look away, that I want him to be something he might not be capable of—something that he might just not want to be. Because if he did, if he wanted to be that person, he would have been by my side today. He would have fought harder. He wouldn't have left me alone in a strange place with people who wish me ill.

"I don't . . . I don't know. Are you okay?" he asks. His eyes flit back and forth from one side of my face to the other.

"I—" I start, but then I choke on something I don't want to expose. I swallow hard and chomp on the side of my tongue. "She hates me, Beck. Like, really hates me."

"Of course, she does," he says.

"Thanks?" He smiles and takes my startled expression as a sign to sit closer. I want to push him away, but apparently not enough, because I let him raise the blanket, let him lift my legs and stretch them across his lap. He keeps his hands on top of the blanket, but holds his palms firmly over my shins.

"You're a threat to her. Of course, she doesn't like you. But she also won't hurt you."

"How do you know?" I ask. I don't specify which thing I'm asking about. He lets his head fall back against the window, his thick, dark waves shrouded in a hypnotic blend of shadows. His eyes skate so easily over my face, and the easygoing pirate, the mask he likes to hide behind, is gone, replaced by the sincere man who has become my friend. And maybe more?

"Because she cares about me. If she hurts you, it will kill me, and she'd never do that to me." It's not a great answer, but I hear the honesty in it. *You will be the death of him. Of this, I am certain.* That's what she said. My eyes drift toward the fire and find Irina, angled in such a way that her eyes meet mine, burning coals. I look away, afraid of getting burned.

"You trust her that much?" I ask. He eyes me carefully, and then nods.

"Yes," he says. He turns away and strokes my leg gently through the blanket, watching his fingers work in gentle circles. "We have a complicated relationship. It's been different things at different times. But I've come to depend on her. She won't hurt you. I've asked her not to. I've explained why it's important . . ."

"What did you say?" I whisper. A little smile curls the corner of his lips, cutting a shadow across his scruffy cheek, emphasizing the hard cut of his jaw. My stomach flutters in appreciation of his beauty, and my cheeks flush.

"That you're an ember in waiting. That all you need is the right breeze, and you'll ignite the world. I told her that you're going to change things. That you're going to do what must be done—not for yourself, but for other women." He swallows hard, and the smile curls into something ugly and wry. Her words come hurtling back to me like the newspaper I threw at my door. *What a waste of flesh you are.* Beck clearly hasn't seen the newspaper yet, hasn't read the announcement. She knows he's asked for her help with a losing cause. And I am going to lose, if I haven't lost already. I let my head fall back against the tapestry behind me, hitting the hard stone behind it, and close my eyes tight.

"That sounds like you want me to go back to the institute." I swallow around the lump in my throat. I don't say the other part of that statement—to go back to Declan. He knows as well as I do that any chance I had to be the person he described is tied to a road that leads to marriage. And I don't understand. I don't understand what's changed. I chose him. I still choose him. But now, it sounds like he's ending this before it even starts. Before he's even given it a chance.

"It's not about what I want," he says, his voice tight, as if he's repeating something he's heard. His jaw is slack, though, his expression earnest and utterly heartbreaking. My heart sinks, and I find it hard to suck in a full breath. It doesn't take a great stretch of the imagination to realize this is the result of his time with Irina—that she planted this seed. She tried to convince him of something. But I didn't come this far, to what feels remarkably like enemy territory, to let another man make another decision for me. Especially one that seems capable of shattering us both.

"That doesn't sound very piratical," I say, trying to lighten the moment, to fight back against his declaration. His lips curl in a smile that doesn't reach his deep green eyes. But he doesn't say anything more.

"So, that's what you told her? That I'm leaving?" I ask, but it's less a question and more a surrender.

"Yes," he says. He's quiet, looking down, wearing that same naked expression I saw beside a different campfire. He means these words, just as he meant the ones then, and the dread I was feeling implodes, ricocheting through my chest, leaving nothing but pain and sorrow in its wake. That's it, then. I've lost. Irina's won. People laugh around the fireplace, a warm, heady sound that makes me feel slightly intoxicated, but my sadness tempers it, keeps me focused on his hand as it slowly creeps across the blanket and curls around my fingers.

"I also told her that you're important . . . to me." He stumbles over his last words, and his jaw tightens. I look at his face and see him battling with the words that sit perched on the tip of his tongue, biting them back, deciding whether or not to say. He ultimately decides not to, and he looks back down at my hand, clinging to his. I want him to tell me what that means. To push him, just enough that he'll say what he's been so careful to keep hidden away. But he won't look at me, and I can sense that if I push right now, he'll go over the edge, and I might not be able to catch him.

"And so every night"—Perlman's voice floats across the room, telling the happy ending to his fairy story—"if you watch the sky long enough, you can watch Liberius reaching for his long lost love through the veil in the sky, and once a month, as the dawn breaks, they seem to merge, becoming one, a beacon of hope that shines four times brighter together than alone."

"That's lovely," Neve says, brushing her fingers through Perlman's bushy hair. As if on cue, the fire is down to nothing but embers, and even under the blanket, with the warmth of both our bodies combined, the room fades into the cold reality of a beautiful night ended. Irina is gone, vanquished. By unspoken agreement, everyone starts to leave, coupled off—all except Kern, who leaves with a drunken look in his eyes and a lady on each arm. Beck and I are left alone, shivering in the window seat. I don't want to leave him, not again, not here. But then he stands and wraps the blanket around my shoulders, and walks me back to my room.

CHAPTER FORTY-TWO

"*T*hanks again, for the blanket," I say stupidly, as we reach my room. I couldn't remember the way, but he knows. Of course, he knows. Just one more reminder that he belongs in this world, while I do not. He laughs and rubs his palms up and down my arms quickly, warming me with friction. His hands are strong, and his touch is firm, but not heavy.

"Well, it's not technically mine to give." He lets go of my arms and scratches the side of his nose, drawing attention to his heavy-lidded eyes.

"Aren't you a pirate? Isn't that what you do?"

"That's what they say." He smirks, and a familiar fire sparks in his gaze, suggesting exactly which direction he expects this conversation to go. But the flirty banter feels nice. I don't want it to end. I don't want us to end. I'm not ready for this to be over.

"I mean, it would be in character to gift your lady something, even if it wasn't yours to gift." My cheeks get hot with blooms of blush as I realize what I've said.

"My lady?" he asks, his full lips twitching. "I thought you weren't a lady."

"Sometimes I am. Sometimes I'm not," I say, leaning in ever so slightly.

"Do I get to choose?" he asks, stroking his fingers along my arms.

"If you want," I say, touching my fingertips to his taut stomach. He sucks in a quick breath, and his pupils dilate. I don't know this expression. I'm not sure what it means. He's quiet as he watches me, a turbulent storm of unspoken emotions swirling in his gaze. He runs his fingertips up and down my arms, teasing and soft. I want him to tell me what he's thinking, what he wants, but he doesn't. Instead, he says:

"Keep talking like that, and you might attract other suitors. Or worse — Perlman."

I huff out a laugh and drop my gaze. "I thought it was a pretty good come-on," I mumble, my cheeks blazing with embarrassment.

He leans in, close to my ear. "We talked about this. When it's a come-on, you'll know."

His hands are slowing down, but not stopping. He presses his lips to my forehead, then pulls back, looking down at me with that soft, unfiltered gaze. "You do me in, Capo."

I snort, and he doesn't pull away, but he doesn't lean in either. It feels like goodbye. Too soon.

"Beck," I whisper, and he smiles. I push up on my toes and touch my lips to his, kissing his lower lip. He leans into it, and his lips part. I suck on his lower lip as he wraps his arms around me, holding me tight, yet tenderly. His fingers find their way up my neck to my jaw, and then his thumbs press back on me ever so slightly, breaking the kiss.

"Good night," he whispers, his eyes still closed. There's a strange sort of resignation in the lines of his face, and my heart speeds up as he steps back. I reach for his hand, knocking the blanket off me, and a shiver wracks my body.

"Don't," I say, so quietly that only he can hear. He pauses, but doesn't look at me, as if just looking at me will break his resolve.

But in this moment, I know what I want.

"Arden," he whispers, leaning away, but not letting go of my hand.

"Stay with me," I whisper, and he breaks. His eyes find mine, and there is a fire in them I've not seen before, tempered by something much softer that I know I'll let myself sink into, if only he'll stay. His hand trembles in mine, and then he comes back to me and presses his lips against mine, firmer. I fall back against the door as his hands slide down my waist, wrapping around the small of my back and pulling my hips into his. All I know is the salt on his skin, the scratch of his cheeks against mine, and the momentum of his kisses. He pulls back, panting. The space is too much, too far. I've felt glimmers of this before, but never in such an aching way. In this moment, with nothing but our ragged breaths between us, I know what it is to need another person.

"Please," I whisper. He's still, too still, and I think he might say no. But then his arms wrap around me, holding me to him, and he nods.

"Always," he says. His mouth presses against mine as he slides his hands down my body, gripping under my thighs and lifting me off the ground. I wrap my legs around his hips, hooking my ankles along the curve of his back. I am vaguely aware of the door yielding and closing as he carries me across the threshold, his mouth tracing an aggressive line along my neck and collarbone, alternating between lips, tongue, and teeth. I thread my fingers through his wavy, silky hair, and kiss him with more hunger than I've ever felt.

The room is cool and dark, but his hands are feverish, and as they slide my sweater over my head, I feel his heat through my core. He drops me on the bed and takes his time unpeeling my pants, letting his fingers graze the soft skin they reveal.

Then he tucks me under the feather-soft blankets, stepping back to undress himself.

I watch him remove his pants first, and then his sweater, exposing a form that has grown sharp and angular with the rigors of both ranching and sailing. He catches my appreciative stare and quirks a smile, lifting one eyebrow as if in a dare. Heat flushes into my face from my chest, and I watch him get into bed next to me. He wastes no time pressing me against the length of his hardened form, letting his mouth kiss and nibble the length of my body; my shoulder, my stomach, my hip.

His fingers find my tattoo, and he presses a long, reverent kiss to it as I run my fingers through his hair, savoring a much deeper swell of emotion that emanates from his kiss. He slides back up my curves and removes my bra. I let myself remember what happened the last time he touched me like this, the bitter intrusion of CJ in my head. I keep waiting for the crawling sensation to hit, the feeling that I don't want anyone touching me. But it doesn't come. All I feel is this deep-seated need, and in this moment, under his tender kisses, I forget myself.

I slide my hands over his ridges and planes, an excited participant, exploring the contradictions of his body and his touch: the hard and the soft, the fervent and the gentle. I exalt in the hard curves of his triceps, the flex of his stomach, the strain of his muscles that leaves me aching, wanting deeply and completely. I need more, and I tell him so. He pulls back for a moment, and I can see the strain in his face.

"Are you sure?" he asks, hesitant to forge ahead without my confirmation. But I am. I'm sure in a way I've never felt before. I need him, I want him, and I tell him so. He lays me on my back gently, kissing my forehead. A gasp slips between my lips, and a low rumbling vibrates in his throat as I give him a part of me I thought I'd never be able to give to anyone. My head tilts back, and he kisses my exposed throat, his teeth grazing my prone, sensitive skin. It's too much, and not enough, all at once.

I feel his rhythm and move to meet him. I close my eyes and focus on the sensation. The tension within me constricts, tighter and tighter. I arch my back, wanting more and more, wanting to give him as much as I'm taking. The tension climbs, until it is so much, I feel like I will burst.

"Go ahead," he whispers, hoarse with restraint. I let go and feel him do the same, and for a moment, we are unhinged together, selfish in our climax, but devoted to the other's needs. When it's over, he remains still for a moment, until our breathing slows, burying his face into my neck. The pressure of his weight is grounding, and when he rolls to my side, I feel adrift. But then he curls around me and presses soft, chaste kisses to the sensitive skin on the back of my neck. I shiver, and he pulls the blankets up over my shoulders as he strokes my arms, my ribs, my hips, without want or desire, but with care and tenderness.

So this is what it can be like. It's not all power and want and selfishness. It's give and take and compassion and need. It's tender touches interspersed with vulnerability and always, always patience and selflessness.

I thought I knew what sex was. With CJ, it was a violent, selfish manipulation of power. I feared it, and rightly so. But as I lay wrapped up in the man who still kisses the back of my neck, whose hands still trace the curves of my body with patience and need, I see that it can be something entirely different indeed.

CHAPTER FORTY-THREE

*F*or a moment, I think I've had a nightmare. I hear an urgent rapping in a strange pattern. Then the bed is empty, and when I sit up, I forget that I'm not clothed, and Irina's eyes are on my naked breasts. Beck narrows the door's angle, and I shrink into the sheets. I look at his form, smiling when I see he's holding a pillow in front of his groin. His voice is hushed. Hers is urgent, and mostly absorbed by the door and his broad shoulders. I strain to hear what they're talking about, but then the door is shut, the pillow is dropped, and Beck is back in bed.

As he closes the door, I get a quick glimpse of her face. It's stony, all sharp angles and something squishier, like fear. As my eyes readjust to the dim light, I can see the amused smile twitching Beck's jaw.

"What was it?" I ask. He pulls me against him, and I find it hard to focus, feeling a new, yet familiar ache again so soon.

"She wanted me to tell you something," he says, slipping his hand across my stomach.

"What's that?" I ask.

"Nice tits." I groan and push my forehead into his chest. His soft laugh fills the room, and he rolls onto his back, pulling me with him. I rest my chin on his chest, looking up at him as he grins.

"She's not wrong," he says, squeezing my breast faster than I can get away. I curl up on myself, laughing as he chuckles and presses a long, sweet kiss to my shoulder.

"What time is it?" I ask.

"Late. Or early. Depends how you look at it."

"Can we call it late?" I ask, not wanting to consider this morning yet. Something about the morning coming feels like an ending I'm not ready to face. Hopefully not a poetic one, anyway.

"Yes," he says, stroking loose hair back from my forehead. The curl he pushes back falls forward again, and he continues to press it back behind my ear in a gentle cycle.

"She came here in the middle of the night to tell you to tell me I have nice tits?" His answer comes in the form of avoiding my gaze. "So, what then?" I ask. He presses his lips into a thin line.

"Don't worry about it," he says, pushing the curl back again and holding it in place. I push up, and his eyes travel to my chest. I pull the sheet against me for a little modesty.

"I am worried about it. I don't think she'd come to my room in the middle of the night if she didn't want something. What did she want with me?" I ask, looking around for my clothes that were discarded in such a rush.

"She didn't want anything with you. Don't worry about it." I freeze. His fingers trace the curve of my spine as I understand his meaning.

"She came here looking for you?" He sighs and sits up.

"Really, don't worry about it."

"What did she think was going to happen? That she would entice you to leave me?" I ask, my jaw quivering. From anger or sadness, I don't know.

"No, she knows better than that." His face darkens, and I feel a shift in the air. He's moving farther away from me, practically flying, and I can do nothing to stop it.

"What's happening?" I ask, my voice a near whisper. His jaw is hard, and he sighs, then scratches the side of his nose and pulls me against him, holding a kiss against the top of my head.

"You worry too much, Capo. Nothing is happening. We're going back to sleep, and in the morning . . ."

"In the morning, what?" I ask, still feeling that hint of distance between us.

"Did we decide it's too late, or too early? Can it be too early?" he asks, sliding a hand down to my butt and squeezing. I pull away, and he smiles devilishly.

"It's too late," I say, but he kisses me, and I feel myself melt into him.

"Oh, Capo, it's never too late. I promise you that," he says, his voice soft and sweet. I don't know if that's true, but tonight, under the darkness of night, it's not too late.

CHAPTER FORTY-FOUR

This time, I do wake to a nightmare. Beck is out of bed, dressing, trying to tell me something, but the bells are too loud. They pulse through the stone walls, rattling my bones, and in my sleepy haze, I don't understand. Then he's fully dressed and trying to put my bra on me. The ridiculousness of the moment sends me into a nervous laughing fit, and he takes me by the shoulders and shakes me.

"Arden, focus!" he says. He's using his captain's voice again, and I flinch, sobering instantly. "The alarms. We have to go." They're not bells. They're alarms, and they're for us. The light coming in the window is just tinged with the first silvery-blue threads of predawn. How long ago was Irina here? She was trying to tell us something. No, telling Beck something. Not me. Beck.

"What did she want?" I blurt, not bothering to specify who I mean.

"Arden! You have to focus. Get dressed. We need to go, now." I fasten my bra, and he hands me my sweater, then my pants, then my socks and boots. As he ties the laces of his own boots, I listen to the screaming pulse of the alarms, and reality finally sets in. The bounty hunters are here. They've found us. Again.

"Ready?" he asks, waiting at the door. I join him, and he hesitates. He turns, taking my face in his hands. "Whatever happens, Capo," he says, and there's something I can't read in his gaze. "Promise you'll remember." I nod once, my confusion plain. His fingers press in, as if trying to memorize the sensation of my skin, the slope of my cheeks. He kisses me long and hard, enveloping me in his tender warmth. My fingers curl into his sweater, pulling him tighter against me, but then a new alarm sounds, and the kiss ends, and we're in the hall with dozens of other panicked people.

He pulls me to the right, and we go in a familiar direction against the flow of traffic, curling left, then right, another right. I quickly lose track. But then we reach a set of fancy double doors I don't want to see.

"No," I say, but he squeezes my hand and pulls me forward. He doesn't even knock, just enters as though he's done it a thousand times. His fingers lace with mine, and he pulls me in behind him, kicking the door shut with his foot. It's like Irina said: *he always ends up here.*

"*Now* you listen . . ." she says, focused on something on a table not facing us.

"Are you going to help us or not?" Beck growls.

"Us?" she asks, turning around, her fingers focused on putting a gold earring in her ear. Her catlike eyes meet mine, travel to my chest with a smirk, and then settle on my hand intertwined with Beck's. She sighs, a bored wisp of a thing, and nods.

"I tried to help this morning. You're fools, and you'll be damned, the both of you," she says over her shoulder as she walks to the door in the wall that must lead to her private chambers. She nods, and we follow into a long, narrow room with an impressive four-poster bed draped in heavy lavender brocade and gauzy white chiffon. Beck helps her push the bed away from the wall. She squeezes between the furniture and disappears into the stone. Beck motions for me to follow her, and I do, with him trailing close behind me. I hear wood scraping, and when I turn around, I see him attempting to pull the bed closer to the door. Then he shuts the door and turns. I guess if someone gets into her room and sees the bed pulled from the wall, they'll look for a door, but any little bit of time helps.

We wind through the darkest, most narrow stairwell I've ever seen in my life, and my chest pinches tight, like a vice grip is pulsing the life from it. Beck touches the small of my back and leans in close.

"Slow breaths, Capo," he says. Irina stops in front of me, and I can just see the glare she shoots at Beck in the black shadows.

"Don't talk," she says, but her voice is strained, and she slows her pace. If Beck is worried about the slower pace, he doesn't let on, though his touch against my skin feels slightly stiffer. I squint to make out Irina's sinewy silhouette. My hand runs along the wall, gripping the crumbling ledge of stone that serves as a railing. My feet somehow find each step, and through my boots, I feel more and more gravel the lower we get.

The air changes, too. It gets colder, damper, and a chill sinks into my bones. I can hear the water before we reach it, and my legs feel like jelly. It takes everything I have to hold my own weight, and I lean into the wall.

"This is the hard part," she says, shifting to the side. A little light reflects off the water that laps the walls of the stairwell below, and I can just see a line of liquid, but I'm not sure what I'm looking at.

"Where now?" I ask, my voice shivering.

"We have to go under. It's high tide. This tunnel floods twice a day. We'll have to go under, and then climb out."

"What?" I ask, my voice thin and reedy with growing panic. I lean back into Beck, but he places both hands on my shoulders and holds me in place.

"Couldn't have taken us another way?" he asks.

"Not if you want to find out who has infiltrated my home." Her words are clipped, her meaning clear: you brought this on yourselves; this is what you deserve.

"How far?" he asks.

"Not far. Six yards? Then the ceiling lifts, and you can get up. Whoever gets there first can light the torch—will make it easier to see for the remaining two." I dip my toe into the water, and the shock of cold on my toe is overwhelming.

"This is insane," I say, the tremor in my voice wild and unforgiving.

"This is your choice," she says quickly. My eyes are not good in this much darkness, but I swear she's looking at Beck. He clears his throat and lets go of me, rolling up his sleeves.

"I'll go first," he says.

"No, wait," I say, but he silences me with a kiss. He leans into my ear.

"I'll get the light. You'll be able to see your way. I will wait for you." Then he's gone, splashing through the water. I hear a sharp hiss as he inhales, and then he splashes again, and the sound of his body working through the water dissipates to nothing far too soon.

"I told you this would happen," Irina says, her voice low and even.

"What?"

"You will be the death of him," she says.

"What's down there?" I ask. "Where did you send him?" I move toward her, but trip and fall on my knees in the icy water. It's too cold, and I stand quickly, but the iciness creeps into my veins. I don't know how he'll make it out on the other side. Fear coupled with the water soaks through my veins, and I gasp. It's a long moment as we both stare at the water for a sign of Beck's success or failure.

"I thought you wanted to help other women—that's what everyone says."

She regards me. "Depends on the woman, I suppose—*little girl*."

Then a light shines through the murky saltwater, highlighting the depth and the line of the ceiling.

"You're such a fool. So easily manipulated. Of course, the path is true. I would never put him in harm's way," she says, her tone somehow colder than the water. It provides just enough angry heat to fuel me forward.

"I'll go," I say, taking a step down into the water, but a strong arm stops me at my waist.

"No, I'll go. You really think I'm giving you the chance to leave me behind?"

"Why should I believe you're not going to try to ditch me?" I ask. In the shimmering light, I can just see her raise an eyebrow.

"I guess you're going to have to trust that Beck is the man you think he is." She slides into the water too easily, as if she's rehearsed this route for sport and the cold does nothing for her. Or maybe she's just cold-blooded and the cold water doesn't shock her. I watch as her long, lithe form disappears under the ceiling, leaving me to stand alone in a flooded tunnel.

The alarms from above echo in strange patterns down here, bent and shaped into something even stranger by the water. I've never been a fan of small, enclosed spaces, but this one takes the cake. The light flashes, and I have to believe it's Beck signaling that the route is clear. A swell of panic climbs into my chest, and I swallow back a sob that wants to break me. Then I take a deep breath and plunge into the water.

It's a mistake. The water is too cold. My lungs and muscles seize up. I resurface for another suck of air, but my diaphragm won't expand. I get as much as I can, my lungs making a strange, stilted choking sound, and then I float down as quickly as I can. I force my eyes open, and the water stings a little, but at least I can see. She said the tunnel was six yards, but it looks so much longer. I pull myself along the wall as my lungs burn. My sweater is heavy and drags in the water, making me have to work even harder. The path stretches out in front of me, and I think I can just see a pair of shoes standing at the end of the tunnel.

I let out a little exhale in relief, and it is a critical mistake. My lungs scream for air, and my heart pounds slowly, too slowly, in my ears. My arms stop bending at the elbows, and I have to reach forward with stick-straight arms. I move slower, inching along, certain that both Beck and Irina made it through the tunnel much, much faster. My eyelids grow heavy, and the cold starts to lessen. I can't feel the sharp, unfinished ridges of the stone beneath my touch. I close my eyes and let the current sweep me where it will. I just need to rest. I don't feel the ceiling when I float up into it, bumping my head against it. And I don't feel Beck's hands on my wrists as he pulls me back through the end of the tunnel.

I emerge into the somehow colder air, and a loud, croaking, guttural sound escapes my throat as a firm hand claps against my back. My body aches with violent tremors, and I have to remind my lungs to keep functioning.

"Were you going for a record, perhaps?" Irina asks, standing in her coordinating bra and underwear, suddenly bald. I blink and watch her unroll a sleek bob of coppery-brown hair as she chucks the swath of white-blonde into the shadows. She pulls a pair of pants from a destroyed crate and puts them on. They seem to fit her perfectly. Swaths of fabric drape around the splintered wood, and the faint smell of oranges cuts into the mildew of the tunnel.

"You okay?" Beck asks, his breath raspy as his eyebrows draw together. He stands, stripped down to his underwear, having just been swimming like that to get me.

"Yaaaa—" I try to say yes, but my voice won't work in conjunction with my jaw.

"Beck, clothes, now," Irina says. He carries me up the steps and pulls my sweater off over my head. Every muscle tightens and aches. He rubs his rough hands up and down my arms, then reaches into the crate and quickly pushes a sweater down over my head. It's wool, too scratchy, and too big. But it's okay. Irina looks at me as I shiver, unsympathetic, and I peel my pants off my legs.

"Where did these come from?" My teeth chatter violently around my words, making it so I can barely get them out.

"It's dry," she says, folding her arms over her chest as Beck dresses himself in a matching black sweater and denim pants. He gives me a pair of pants that are too big.

"This way," Irina says, starting up the stairs without us.

"You okay?" he asks again, scratching at his cheek.

"Yeah," I say, narrowing my eyes on Irina's disappearing shape. "Let's go."

We follow Irina up the stairs, and the climb is harder from the swim. My lungs ache, and I keep coughing, as if there's still murky water filling them I can't expel. Beck tries to persuade Irina to slow down, but she doesn't. If anything, she goes faster. Then we level off and approach the end of a hall. There's a door there, and Irina tells us to wait. She presses through the door, and a sliver of bright light slips through into the stairwell. Her hands go limp, and then she rolls her shoulders back, lifting her head into a regal posture.

"Gentlemen," she says, her voice muffled by the wall. "To what do we owe this pleasure?"

"I assume you're bringing us what we asked for?" a familiar, ugly voice says. I freeze. Beck's hands find my shoulders, pulling me back toward him, but he's not fast enough. A long arm grabs for me from the other side, using my surprise to pull me through the door, bringing me face to face with an ugly scar.

CHAPTER FORTY-FIVE

His fingers tug at my clothing, and I hear a feral growl behind me. I kick at him, and then his hand is on my hip, feeling for the ridges of the scar beneath my tattoo.

"There you are, sweetheart. Right on time, Irina." The mercenary holds me against his hulking figure, both wrists twisted behind my back, my bad arm still tender under his familiar grip. He laughs in my ear, and it's an acidic, stinking, pulsing thing. "Aw, don't worry. I won't hurt yeh . . . much." He puts a little more weight on my arm, and I lean into it, almost toppling over in an attempt to ease the remembered pain, and he laughs again.

"Careful," Irina says, her eyes trained on him, careful to avoid mine. I don't see Beck, but I hear him grunt somewhere behind me, followed by the smack of bone on flesh.

"I said, careful," Irina says again, her voice tighter, and the men behind me laugh.

"Pity, was just fixing up his face a bit, yeah?" one of them says.

"Yeah, only one needs back in one piece is this piece," the

man holding me says, brushing wet hair off my neck. I hear Beck growl behind me again, and then more fist to flesh.

"Mikyll, she is not a piece of anything," Irina says, her eyes blazing. Then, she seems to think better of fighting this battle. "Keep her better than in one piece, or she'll be worthless." My heart drops as Mikyll, the hunter whose sour fish breath spews across my neck, laughs and holds me out from him, leaving a precious few inches of space between us.

"As for him, while I appreciate that your instructions are merely for his body, I will gladly make it worth your while to keep him alive," she says, her tone flippant.

"And why's that, dearie?" Mikyll hisses in my ear, his tongue dangerously close. "He's been keeping yer bed warm?" I hear the thumps of physical assault, and Beck's stifled groans.

"No," she says, her shoulders tenser than her flippant words.

"Ahhh," Mikyll says, pulling me against him again, wrapping a predatory arm around my stomach. "I know the stink of jealousy when I hear it. Ye're telling me he's been getting a little taste of the future First Lady herself, eh?" I swing my leg back into him, but he dodges, and I topple forward. He catches me around the waist, his hips against my backside, and laughs again. "Ah, I see what she likes."

"You'll see nothing, Mikyll. Eyes on the prize. You get her out of my house, and forget the trumped-up debt." Irina's voice is cold, her consonants clipped, too crisp to be completely calm.

"Now, see? There's a little problem with that," he says. His voice has a heavy tread, the vowels floating in a clipped, guttural valley between the heavy, grounded consonants. I haven't noticed it before, and I can't place where he's from.

"Problem?" she asks. If she's rattled, it doesn't show, but nobody moves.

"Yeah, see, all my people want is the girl. She can be useful.

But this guy? He's dead weight. Better we just drop him overboard, somewhere along the central reefs."

"That's not the deal," she says, crossing her long arms over her chest. A shudder goes through me.

"Well, deal's not done yet, dearie. I think we're gonna need a little extra cash to keep this one alive. Hungry mouths to feed and whatnot."

"Muleshit," she says, nearly spitting at him. "I know just as well as you that you won't feed him."

"Well, that's just cruel. I don't know what kind of operation you're running here, but in Swendenland, we happen to believe in a little something called human dignity."

"So, what? You want me to pay you to arrest this man, who is nothing to either of us, just for the sake of keeping him alive?"

"Yeah, see that's the thing. I don't think he's nothing to at least one of us here. Maybe more than one of us." He hisses in my ear, and I flop my head forward to get away from him. He cackles and pets the back of my hair. One of his lackeys steps forward next to me, moving in toward Irina.

"One false move, Mikyll, and I can hold you up just enough that you'll miss your chance."

"I don't believe you. And there's more of us than you, so . . ." The lackey grabs her on the left, and she tries to take a swing at him, but another lackey grabs her on the right. My heart plummets, and I try to veer around Mikyll to see Beck, but he holds me firm.

"So, what? You're going to take me now, too? What good does that do anyone?"

"Oh, no, we've no use for you. You're useful here, in your 'home,' as it were. I know you're not stupid enough to have the money on you. Take us to wherever you keep it. You'll pay us, and then you'll do nothing to interfere with our business here. And you'll let us out, or we'll attack."

"Good luck," she spits. "This place hasn't fallen to insurgents in a millennia. You really think you and your piddly rowboat can take it down?"

"Well, yeah, once you take into account all the devices we planted on our way in."

"You're lying," she says, but there's a question to it. She didn't see them enter. She was busy trying to distract me and Beck, leading me straight to her comrades in arms.

"Maybe," he says, a shrug in his voice. Then he pulls me back against him again, and I feel his stink of sweat press into the back of my sweater. A chill rushes through my bones; I feel like I just got out of the frigid water. "But maybe not?" He laughs again, and I bite the edge of my tongue.

"Do we have a deal?" he asks. Irina breathes heavy, her chest heaving high and proud, but her eyes flicker.

"Fine."

"Oh, goody!" he says. "Please, do lead the way." He pulls me along with him, and I finally get to see Beck as we turn toward the door. Beck's eyes aren't on me, though. They're on him, Mikyll, his gaze murderous. Then I'm forced to walk past him, one foot after the other—toward what? I have no idea.

CHAPTER FORTY-SIX

*A*s it turns out, Mikyll keeps all three of us intact—or mostly intact. We fill the tight cell he's thrown us into, each to a corner, and nobody talks. They walked us down to the vault, and Irina opened it. She was then unceremoniously removed from the room, and we were all locked together in this cell—a stone room with no warmth and actual bars along the front. It wasn't meant to hold three people for more than a few hours, though I don't think they intend for us to be here any longer than that.

I stand, my arms wrapped tight around my waist, trying not to let the shivering take over and damage my teeth. Irina stands in the opposite corner, eerily still. She doesn't look cold, doesn't look flustered. She stands calm as she was on the pier, the first time I saw her, like she knows she'll get out of this somehow. I want to shake her. Beck sits in a heap of folded legs and wounded slouch. He won't let either of us touch him, so I know it's bad. He's hurt. But he won't look at me, and he'll barely look at Irina.

Each look he shares with her slices into me, though, adding to the bruises and scars that won't ever heal. To her credit, she doesn't gloat, but she doesn't have to. Even after we shared a bed, he still returns to her when he's in trouble, just like she said. I try to ignore the deadly sting of it and fail. I can't help it. He ignores me, just like he did when I first arrived on his ship. That time, we'd shared nothing more than a kiss. We shared so much more than that a few short hours ago, and now, he sits in the opposite corner of a tiny cell, sharing thoughts and looks with his first love like I don't even exist. Like I'm not standing right in front of him. Like I mean nothing.

"Dammit, Irina!" Beck's voice is a low growl, and it startles me. I've heard him scared. I've heard him angry and fighting. But never this. This is something much more terrifying.

"Shut up, Sobeck," Irina says, over-enunciating the consonants of his given name like a curse. A name I've never spoken. He launches up, leaning over his left side.

"This is your fault."

"No," she says, flying at him. Neither backs down, and their eyes blaze. I can see why they didn't work. But my stomach sinks as I imagine the ways they probably did.

"No?" he says, ragged laughter under his breath.

"What? Did I not tell you this would happen?" she asks. My chest tightens, a veritable vice grip constricting my heart and its syncopated rhythm. "Did I not warn you she would bring disaster to us all?"

"Beck?" I ask, but my voice barely breaks the pall of the cell. Their shared energy is impenetrable, like kindling next to a stack of dynamite. Beck doesn't say anything. His eyes widen briefly, and his breath goes shaggy. I know he heard me.

"I told you to stay away from her. But you couldn't do it. We talked about all the reasons to keep your distance, but you wouldn't listen. Thinking with the wrong head, perhaps?" she says with an amused little chuckle. His fingers curl into stony fists.

"Irina," he croaks, in a way that makes me shudder.

"And then, I gave you one more chance. I knew where to find you. You know, I didn't even have to go searching. I knew exactly where you'd be."

"Of course, you did. I told you how I felt," he says, his voice low enough that it's hard for me to hear. But his words give me something small to cling to, something to send a warm flush into my cheeks despite the frigid stone.

"So predictable. Clinging to the one girl you can never have," she says, her words like acid. He flinches, and then sneers back at her.

"And look at you. I didn't think you had it in you to be jealous of a girl who actually has a heart." She winces and pulls her hand back to strike him. Something stops her, though, some internal struggle I can't even begin to decipher. She clutches her own wrist, holding it back, and spins around. They stand like that, shaking, him looking past her shoulder, her looking at the wall. She's still remarkably calm, given the circumstances.

"Irina?" I ask. Her face whips to mine, and her stony glare guts me.

"What?"

"How much money?" I ask.

"What?" she asks, her face screwed up in confusion. I swallow hard.

"How much money did they take? Perhaps I could . . . perhaps there's a way I could pay you back, if Declan—" Her pupils flare, and she cackles, her laugh cutting off my words, filling the space like a mean audio attack. I feel Beck's eyes on me, but don't dare look away from Irina and the vitriolic acid pulling at her features.

"Oh, that's rich. The poor girl wants to reimburse my stores. You know what, honey? You do that. I'll send you a bill." She turns away from me and stares out through the bars. Beck still hasn't moved, and the weight of Declan's name bears down on my heart like lead.

"Well, well, well." Mikyll returns with his two lackeys. "I have to say, I am very happy to do business with you, Madame. Please!" I stare at the floor as I feel his lecherous gaze on me. He cackles. "No sense of humor, this one. I'll never understand what the better half sees in their women. I see some of it, but . . ." His eyes trail down my body, and I fold in on myself.

"Have you gotten what you wanted?" Irina asks, her voice clipped and businesslike.

"Yes," he says, and even without turning around, I can hear the grin. "And now, we'd like to take the gentleman first."

"Why?" Irina asks, not bothering to mask her panic. I whip around and watch Beck, who doesn't react. He keeps his eyes trained on Irina's legs, and his avoidance, his deliberate refusal to even look at me feels pointed and cruel. Mikyll laughs, a mean-hearted burst of bravado.

"Because I'm not taking more than one of you at a time. And because I can." He unlocks the door and part of me wants to fling myself at Beck, to grab onto him, to fight off Mikyll and his lackeys. But I don't, and neither does Irina. There's no point. They take him from us, and I watch the back of his head vanish around the corner of the room. He doesn't say goodbye—he doesn't even look at me. Mikyll leaves us with a little bow, and then it's just me and Irina, locked together in a cell. I crouch, pulling my knees into my face, and try not to cry.

CHAPTER FORTY-SEVEN

*W*e don't speak. We don't share a glance, sideways, head on, or otherwise. We sit on opposite sides of the cell, her with her legs stretched out before her, me with my knees hugged tight to my chest. I try hard not to breathe her ration of air. But I still feel her eyes on me, and I know she feels mine. She's calm. I'm frantic. But my breath is under control as I let my steady pulse center me and set the rhythm.

I have to focus on her. On the things that are real, just like Beck showed me. One real thing at a time. The temperature: bone-chilling. The walls: chipped and in need of paint. The dim light fading into the free space outside the bars in front of us. The hatred spewing off Irina, toward me. Hatred for violating her space, for touching Beck.

"Why do you hate me?" I ask, before I think better of it.

"What?" she asks, her voice violent and targeted. I wince. She has good aim.

"Nothing," I mumble, curling into myself against the impossibly cold wall.

"Don't lie to me. You obviously have something to say. Just say it." She doesn't waver, her eyes penetrating my skin, leaving me feeling raw and threadbare. I bite the edge of my tongue and look away.

"Do you love him?" she asks, the question sharp. And there it is. The word I've been edging around in the haziest recesses of my mind since the night of the barn fire. But it's more than that, too. It stretches back to the closet in my room at the institute. Back further to our sparring session where he pushed me into a tree, and I froze, and he pulled me out of my head and wouldn't let me continue. It takes me all the way back to CJ drugging my wine. To CJ taking me from the party. To the smell of Beck before anything truly awful could happen.

"Of course, I do," I say, my voice unsteady. It feels so inadequate, though. Not enough. But she nods, lowering her chin ever so slightly.

"You can do so much good, though . . ." She trails off, not finishing the thought I've processed so many times.

"What do you want with him?" I ask.

Her nostrils flare, and she tilts her head, letting her actual hair fall over her slender shoulder.

"He is not the person he pretends to be. He is not a pirate. That's bravado. He is tightly wound and complicated and—"

"I know," I say. Her pupils dilate, and her jaw slackens. "He's protective and insecure and intelligent, and—"

"I know." Her eyes hold mine, and I think I must be hallucinating when I see them glass over. She turns her gaze back to the wall as the imaginary glass between us shatters.

"Is he good to you? Declan, I mean?"

"Yes." My voice is softer, but no less sure.

"I don't envy you," she says.

"What will you do?" I ask. "After this?"

"Business as usual," she mumbles.

"Glad you have a plan," I say, because it feels like the right thing to say, and I can't come up with anything better.

"What will you do?" she asks, not facing me. I'm grateful she doesn't turn in time to see whatever it is my face surely reveals. I have no pretense about what my fate might be. I can only hope Mikyll decides the payday from the institute is more worth his time than whatever it is Conrad will pay him.

"I don't know," I say, my voice giving me away. She crosses her slender arms over her chest, thrumming her small fingers against her forearm. Her eyes flicker from the floor up to mine.

"My whole life," I say, taking a deep breath, "I've been used by one man or another." My head flits from Conrad, who bought me from my mother, to CJ, who took me into his shed and used me to release his own stressors. To Declan, who supposedly wants to help me change things, though I'm not sure why. To this—to Mikyll, who obviously wants to use me to line his pockets and pad his profit margin. And then there's Beck. He doesn't want to use me. At least, I don't think he does. Not really. Yes, he took money from Siobhan, but he's the only person who's ever given me the space to make my own decisions, even when I thought he didn't. And now . . . *you will be the death of him.* Maybe Irina was right.

"Aren't you sick of it?" she asks, her voice cautious. "Sick of them using you?"

I shrug. "Aren't you?"

"Men don't use me. Not anymore. I use them."

"And yet you're locked up, same as me," I say. Her mouth tightens, and she flexes her hand, but replaces it against her stomach, tucked firmly under the other. Her eyes hold mine, and they are marred with suspicion, but I catch something else in their depths—a glimmer of something like kinship.

"One of these days, I'll actually be in control of my fate," I say, with a well-timed snort.

She presses her full lips into a thin line.

"You do realize the power you wield, yes? That's the problem with you candidate girls. You're all the same. You play the games, competing with each other, and for what?" She shakes her head, and then sets her brow. "Women like us could upend the world, if only we took the chance. So many of you . . . can you imagine what we could do if we stopped competing against each other?" She leans her head back against the wall and stares down her nose. "There is no competition. Not really. They just force us into their mold. We're more manageable that way. But if we could get past that—past these imaginary divisions they've created, if we could stop battling each other and work together . . . I mean . . . things could actually change."

She looks at me then, her gaze impassioned. Here, then, is the person Neve spoke of, the woman Kern said fought for compassion among other women. Her conviction erupts her face into something I could absolutely see Beck falling in love with. My heart pinches, and I let out a shaky breath around the tug.

"And you, *Arden*"—she chuckles to herself, enjoying a brief inside joke—"you have the potential to change it all." My chest warms, feeling the weight of her words. "Don't squander it."

"I won't."

She gives an elegant snort and looks away. "You already are. Who's going to listen to a runaway bride?"

Her words make me cringe. No one will. I know that, and I will have to live with it the rest of my life if things go the way I want, the way I've promised Beck. But if they don't go the way I want, then . . . she's wrong. I'm not going to waste the opportunity to do something good. To make my life matter, even if it never truly heals. Even if I don't get to be happy.

"Irina," I say, hoping she hears the pleading in my voice for what it is: honesty.

She arches an eyebrow.

"Did you mean it? The Nordanians are on their way?" She nods in a quick, curt dip.

"Sunrise," she says. Past her shoulder, dim blue light filters in through a window somewhere. I think back to her warning that Mikyll might miss his chance.

"Is there any way to get them a message?"

"Why?" She watches me with a careful, assessing gaze. She doesn't say any more, as if she's testing me to see what I might reveal next. Something vibrates within—a frenetic, pulsing beat.

"Because they can help us. I can help us. Send me back to Declan."

"Why should I trust you?" she hisses. But that's all it is, air between her lips. There's no cruelty to it. She wants me to give her a reason.

"Because I've been on the bottom, my face smashed into the ground, living in my own hell. And I don't want that for anyone else—ever again, if I can help it. If I can make a difference. But I need help. I need supporters."

"And you'll make that sacrifice?" she asks, disbelief clouding her eyes. "You'll give it all up, for them?" She looks sad. And I feel it. Because I feel what she's actually asking. Would I give up Beck to live this life of service? I swallow hard and close my eyes. Because there's a very loud part of my heart screaming at me to stop all this, to be selfish for once and just listen to it. But I also know that I can't.

"Yes," I say. It comes out small, but resolute. I would give it all up. If it will save Beck, if it will free girls from what I had to live through—from what Emlyn had to live through—then yes, I would make that sacrifice. I would bear that pain. She studies me for a moment, and her eyes widen. She sucks on her cheeks, and something like anger hardens her expression.

She gives me a curt nod, rising. Then she crosses the cell, taking me by the shoulders.

"Will you keep him safe? Keep him alive?" she asks, allowing her eyes to round in deep-seated worry. I nod.

"With my life." Her eyebrows rise, and I see something like respect creep into her gaze as she studies the resolve in mine. She nods, accepting my words. Then she lets go, rapping a familiar rhythm on the wall. The wall shifts, revealing a door — and a girl with hazel eyes and unbreakable drive.

"Neve?" I ask, but she doesn't get the chance to answer as Irina pushes me in, letting the darkness consume the three of us, along with the familiar musty smell of hidden stairways.

CHAPTER FORTY-EIGHT

*W*e wind through darkened stairwells at a breakneck speed, or at least, that's what it seems like. It's so dark, so cold, and there are so many turns. I'm almost dizzy by the time the alarm bells ring anew, echoing in the cavernous tunnels like a harbinger of misfortune. We keep running, one foot after another, up and down, left and right. I have no idea where we are and no idea how Irina or Neve do either. For a moment, I wonder whether they are intentionally trying to confuse me, if they want to lose me so I will remain lost, trapped in the bowels of Irina's fortress in a mountain for the rest of my days.

Then a door opens, and bright yellow light spills in, momentarily blinding me. Sunrise.

"Keep close," Irina says, and we funnel into the busy marketplace, full of bodies but not vendors. I try to stay close, but throngs of panicked people pulse against us, threatening to disrupt our plans. Two women cling to each other and shove between me and Irina, knocking me into a shuttered stall. I push myself back up and try to make up the lost ground, fixing my eyes on Irina's dark bob. But then, there's a commotion. Irina is knocked to the opposite side of the hall.

I lose sight of Irina, but Neve's shiny head moves up ahead on the edge of a larger altercation. A woman and a man exchange sharp words in another language. The alarm doubles in volume, and the mob shrinks around them, a current of people both ahead and behind me pushing in. I follow Neve's hair and watch as it sinks below the crowd.

"Neve!" I cry, pushing past the two women ahead of me. I try to wedge between a man, a woman, a child—I gasp at the sight of the little boy, not even five years old, clutching his mother's hand. The frantic energy seeps into my legs, and claustrophobia tightens my chest. A hand grips my wrist, too hard. On instinct, I pull away, but the grasp doesn't budge. I look at the hand, following the arm behind smashed bodies, and eventually, Irina emerges.

"Neve?" she asks. I nod in the direction I saw her last, and her eyebrows flatten into a grim line. We charge ahead.

We find Neve on the ground, another person fallen on top of her. In the many years I've known Neve, her strongest quality has always been her ability to remain nonplussed. Right now, she is anything but. And rightly so. Her eyes are wide and wild, and her mouth hangs open, gasping for air like a fish suddenly beached. But there's no time for talk, no time to confirm she's not injured.

The arcade erupts in gunfire, and around us, everyone ducks—everyone, except us. We're expecting it, and it highlights exactly where we are. It also makes it both easier and harder to run. People move out of our way, and we sprint as the gunfire continues. Stone and dust bursts from the walls to the left and right. We turn a corner and flee into an empty hall, leaving us completely exposed.

"Run!" Irina says, and we do. Neve is slow, and we have to

pull her along with us. By the time the gunshots ricochet off the walls around us, we're nearly at the opposite end—a dead end, or so it would seem, but I know better than to think Irina has led us to an end she can't escape. She struggles with a hidden panel on the right. She dislodges it, and I sink my fingers into the lip of the door, pulling the heavy stone toward us. We get it open just enough that I can squeeze through. I hear a scream behind me, and Irina comes through.

"Where's Neve?" I ask, but she doesn't answer, just lugs an awkward body through the hole in the wall.

"Help me!" she barks, and I do, wrapping my fingers around the lip of the door and pulling it shut. "Watch out!" she says, just as my fingers get smashed between the stone seal. I'm able to pull them out as she wedges it back in place and lowers a stone bar to lock it. The sharp bite of bullets in the door echoes throughout the chamber, but then I hear Neve panting.

"Neve? Are you okay?" I ask, crouching down to where she clutches her calf. I reach down to check her and feel wet, thick warmth. Blood. It seeps into my skin, and I want to wipe it on her clothes, to get it off of me. I cannot have her blood on my hands.

"I'll survive," she says, gritting her teeth.

"You better," I say, but I am shaken. She flashes a sharp grin, and I know she will.

"Well said," Irina says, and together, we support her as we walk through yet another dark hall. This one is touched by the light of the new day from somewhere, and I hear the splash of water up ahead. My stomach drops at the thought that we might have to swim again. As if she's anticipating my thoughts, Irina says:

"It's a back way directly to the docks. No swimming this time."

"Thank Scio," I say, and she snorts. But there's no room for laughter. We barge ahead, moving down, down, down. It's not the fastest escape and certainly not the smoothest. Neve won't admit it, but her leg is bleeding more and more, and she gets quieter and heavier the further we go. We have to support more of her weight with every step. The stairwell is meant for single file, and we are three across. It's a slog.

We finally reach the sandy bottom, and Irina pushes open a creaking metal gate. Icy wind thick with salt and snow whips our faces. I grit my teeth into it, forcing myself to keep moving. We're on a small bridge, and we're climbing. We climb step after step, moving into the wind, and then, I see sails. We keep going, closer and closer, higher and higher, and Neve gasps.

Directly ahead are the official blues of the Nordanian Government, and standing at the end of the pier, golden hair whipping in the wind, is Declan.

Even in wintery weather, his gray eyes pierce mine, and a relieved smile fills his cheeks, shifting into the corners of his eyes. He moves forward, with purpose, and then breaks into a run. I don't dare let go of Neve, but I feel myself move faster. If I can just get us to him, he'll protect us.

And then he's here, and his arms pull me away from Neve. I feel her lurch slightly as his arms wrap around my back, and he lifts me off the ground, holding me tighter than I ever imagined he knew how, refusing to set me down, even when I ask.

"Neve," I say. "Help Neve." But then he does, and the wind is so loud and harsh, and I'm so confused, I can't formulate the words I need to say. Or ask for the words I need to hear: the words that will settle me and reassure my fears. Neve is carried away, Declan shouting instructions. Irina talks to someone whose face I can't see, and we are on the main pier. I'm draped in a heavy fur coat, and then I see those bright green eyes, and everything stops.

They watch me as they walk past, his hands tied behind his back. I feel Declan's arm around my shoulders, and Beck's eyes drift to his hand on my arm. I see the pinch in his features, the flaw in his armor, the mask slipping for the span of a heartbeat.

But then he smirks.

And just like that, he is gone, led into the belly of the ship — Declan's ship. I am here. He is here. But we are anything but safe.

CHAPTER FORTY-NINE

I'm fine. That's what I keep telling everyone who buzzes around me. There must be three hundred of them. Or four. But their faces blur together in a mix of concern and problem solving. I tell them there's nothing to fix, that I'm not injured. Beck is injured. Fix Beck. Neve, too. And take me to him. But they don't respond. They ignore my pleas, so I stop asking and just tell them I'm fine. Over and over again, on repeat. Then they tuck me into a bed and turn off the overhead light. But daylight still streams in through the portholes, and I let it keep me awake.

My body aches, but the bed is surprisingly soft. The linens are even softer and reek of cotton and dead plants. It would be so easy to let myself go, to give in to the sleep that beckons from the pillows, from the absence of adrenaline, to the subtle rocking. Left, right. Left right. It's too subtle. This boat is too big. Ship. It's a ship. This ship is too big. I will my eyes to stay open, watching the light change from sweet yellows to cold whites, to warmer oranges.

When the door opens sometime later, I know I shouldn't be

shocked. But I sit upright too fast. Stars blur my view of Declan in a heavy blue peacoat.

"I'm fine," I say.

"I heard," he says, with a sweet hint of a smile. He stays close to the door, his hands in his pockets. His posture is so good. It always has been, but after months of being around Beck and his sea-legged slouch, Declan seems so much more upright. His wavy blonde hair is darker for lack of sunshine, and I swear the weather has worn thin lines around his eyes. He looks older. Tired. I'm sure I do, too.

"I want you to know there are no charges being drawn against you — or anyone — for CJ's death," he says.

"Thank you," I say. I should feel relieved. But the heaviness of taking his life with the swing of my hand still sits like lead in my bones. I suppose it will always be there.

"It took some work . . . we found a witness. He testified . . ." He hesitates, working his mouth into a tight pucker around words he doesn't want to use. "He attacked you?" I watch him watch me, and I can guess what he wants to know.

"Beck stopped him," I say, and he presses his lips together, his eyes hardening. He lifts his chin ever so slightly, and then closes his eyes. "Then I stopped him from killing Beck." His eyes open, and he takes me in anew. He exhales, his shoulders drooping, shortening him. This is not what he wanted to hear. His witness must have led him to believe I killed him while protecting myself. My renewed virtue, perhaps, or what shredded remains of it were left intact. Instead, I was protecting Beck. The person he doesn't want me to trust.

Perhaps he was right. Trusting him led me to his bed.

"I'm glad you're safe," he says, still keeping his distance.

"It was touch and go as recently as today," I say, nodding in the direction — or what I think is the direction — of Irina's place. He stays where he is, and I don't know what to do either. The last time we spoke, we made promises to each other, and now, we're like two strangers. I wonder if he feels the distance the same way I do.

"We should discuss next steps," he says, finding his voice again.

"Yes, I think we should," I say. This is where I tell him what I want and what I don't want. That I want Beck, and I don't want to marry him. But something heavier, harsher, sits in my chest and instead, I spit out, "I read that we are to be married as soon as possible?"

"Yes, that's the general idea," he says. He doesn't look at me, and I can see the fight in him.

"So, I'm not meant to graduate?"

"Arden," he says, a near whisper.

"I'm just meant to be your wife, to never have my own voice?" I ask, clenching my hands into fists.

"It's not like that."

"Then what is it like? Because the last time I saw you, you told me that I had the power to change the system. Me and the other graduates. And now, we're going to marry so fast that I can't possibly graduate?"

"Arden, I had to pull strings to make this happen. I had to make some compromises."

"So you compromised my autonomy? You sacrificed my voice? That is not what I signed on for."

"Well, let's be honest: you haven't signed on for anything yet."

"I told you—" I stop myself, realizing that I'm about to argue that we are, in fact, engaged to be married. Which is the exact thing I came here to stop. He takes a step toward the bed and stops, still a step away.

"You are not an advantageous prospect. You are unpredictable, and you can't be easily controlled. You are not what they counted on. I had to twist the situation to get them on board."

"So you bargained away the only thing I had for myself? Something I have earned?"

"Well, hold on there. You haven't earned it," he says, and his voice is businesslike again.

"What?" I ask.

"You've been gone. You've missed too much. It would be impossible at this point for you to make up the workload in time for graduation exams." My stomach drops.

"I left because you told me to—"

"I know. Because I thought it was the best option. But I didn't anticipate needing so long . . . I guess my mother was one step ahead of me there, as well." His face darkens, and his eyes avert.

"So, let me try. Let me sit for the exam."

"You could, but if you fail, it will be made public. You may lose whatever goodwill you've garnered through this ordeal. And in the meantime, we still have to explain your absence."

"Right," I say, losing track of the argument as Beck comes into the crisis conversation.

"For now, the only way you can return is if you left for legitimate personal reasons or against your will."

"Well, I did leave for legitimate personal reasons. I was being attacked. I was almost kidnapped."

"That's not legitimate," he says, edging his words with caution. "The capital is safe, impenetrable by malicious forces." My stomach drops.

"So, we have to go with . . . but he didn't—"

"You were kidnapped, held against your will."

"And Beck . . ."

"Is under arrest for a capital offense." To his credit, Declan does look sorry. But it lands hollow in my chest.

"So, what do we do? We both know he was only helping." A cringe works into his jawline.

"There's not much we can do, for now. At least, not until

we're married . . ." He swallows around the word, as if just the act of saying it will launch me away from him. It almost does. "Until after we have a mandate to make some changes. I think . . ." He edges closer, and to my surprise, he sits on the end of the bed. The bed feels so small. Too small.

"Changes will be made, Arden, and they will be sweeping. You are already seen as the people's candidate. It's a good thing. There is sympathy with you for rising above your station." I bite my bottom lip. I don't think he means to sound so condescending, but also, I suppose he's right.

"When we call for new measures, we'll have to make an announcement explaining them. There are obviously other stories you could tell about how the system is broken . . ." He clears his throat as I feel an angry, embarrassed flush move around my ears. "But I think it would be better used on this. Tell them that once you became independent, stopped playing into the old system, the old world attacked you and led you to flee the capital, seeking refuge at sea with a transport I personally approved of. Beck is innocent, you were not kidnapped, but by that point, we're already married and it doesn't matter."

It's not a bad strategy. It exposes the truth of the system on a high level. But it still ends with me having to sacrifice my voice. My vote. I didn't realize just how much my vote mattered to me until I knew I had lost it. I will lose my vote, my independence. I will lose Beck. Everything I told Irina will be gone. I'll be nothing. Worthless on a pretty pedestal, but still worthless. My hands tremble, and I fold them together to steady myself.

"What about my vote?" I ask, clutching to the simplest question.

"I don't know," he says, shaking his head. "Maybe . . ." He seems to be chewing over something in his head. "Maybe we could get you a tutor? Try to catch you up until we return?"

"How long until we return?" I ask.

"I don't think it's safe. Not yet," he says.

"When?" I ask. He shrugs. If we have to spend the winter here at Irina's Pleasure Palace, I might be willing to take my chances alone at sea.

"You aren't officially in the protection of the capital guard until we're married."

"So, we really do have to get married that soon? Just for me to be safe?" I ask. My heart feels like it's stopped working. My arms go cold.

"Just the reaction every guy wants when the girl he wants to marry thinks about the wedding day," he says with a self-deprecating smile. But I see the cracks in the edges of his impeccably smiling facade.

"Well, it sounds like that's what has to happen for everyone to get out of this alive," I say. "Either that, or we tell the truth, and then . . ." But I don't finish, because there's no reason to. If I don't marry him, this all goes away. The current shifts away from progress, and it would be all my fault.

"No, Arden. You don't have to marry me to be safe. You can also leave. In fact, if that's the only reason . . ." He trails off, leaning over his knees and looking at the floor. "If that's the only reason you said yes, then don't marry me. I know it seems silly, given the nature of this whole charade of an institute, but I do want to end up with someone who wants to be my wife. Not someone who just wants to stay alive and sees me as the only way to do that."

"Then you're a fool," I whisper words I've heard too recently, feeling them deep in my gut.

"What?" he asks, not lifting his eyes.

"That is the position I've ended up in. And I thank you for sending me off with Beck . . ." I swallow hard. "I was safe with him, away from the institute. But now, I have bounty hunters and mercenaries from Swendenland trying to kidnap me for real, and it seems my only options are to either disappear into nothing, where I have no choice but to come work someplace like this—" I gesture toward where I think Irina's brothel is. "Or I marry you, and maybe get to amount to something more than what everyone has told me I would."

"So, you're saying it's a choice about survival? That there is no room for—no possibility of . . . emotions . . ." He flushes a deep red, no doubt colored by frustration and embarrassment.

"No, I'm saying that is my reality, and you don't see it because you've never had to make a decision that keeps you alive." My voice shakes now, the admission taking on a life of its own. He is still bent over his knees, but he at least looks up at me, and I continue.

"I have made impossible decisions since I was twelve years old, sometimes on a daily basis. Decisions that no person should ever have to make, ever. Decisions that have kept me alive, decisions that have compromised my dignity, have made me question whether life is really so much better than the alternative. So yeah, emotions are lovely and nice, but the reality of this decision is that I can follow my heart, but one decision will keep me alive, and the other may not."

It is clear he has never considered this before. His eyes are narrow squints, trying to find the right words. But he hangs his head, scratching the windblown hair on the back of his neck. Then he sinks to his knees on the floor and moves along the bed, so he's sitting low on his knees next to me.

"You're right," he says. "I don't know what it's like to think of my own survival. I'm lucky in that regard, very lucky. God has blessed me with a fortunate life, and I've been ignorant. Perhaps willfully so." I grit my teeth and try not to shake.

"But am I so wrong to want the woman who agrees to be my wife to actually like me?" Once again, he looks like the hopeful, charming boy who made me feel things I wasn't sure I would ever be capable of feeling.

"I like you fine, Declan," I whisper. He laughs, and I hear the stifled sadness in his voice.

"Is it wrong of me to want more than that?"

I shake my head. It's not wrong, because I want more than that, too. I want to be cherished and trusted and uplifted and challenged. I know that's what I want, because I've found it. And right now, the person who made me feel those things is tied up, probably in the lower bowels of this ship, waiting to be tried for my kidnapping. I don't know what's keeping me from just going and getting him now, from walking away from this stupid institute and all of its grand and hollow plans.

Except, I do know. It's the girls like Neve and Carla and Zerah and Emlyn. The girls who are younger than me, and the women who are older than me, who have never had a fair shot in their life. Women who have never held the advantage a single day of their lives. And if I could just make my voice heard, maybe I could change things for them. Without me, Declan will end up with another version of Siobhan, and the next generation will be suffocated under the weight of the patriarchy, because that's the way it's always been, and the CJ's of the world will continue to rise. But I can't do anything if I'm only someone's wife. I can't just tell people this is the way it should be. I have to be able to show them.

"Is it wrong of me to want to be more than just your wife?" I ask, avoiding his question. He flinches slightly, but nods. This is it. This is when I tell him what I want. Maybe he'll understand? He'll respect that I love Beck, and he loves me, and he'll still want to fight for what's right. Maybe?

A knock at the door breaks us apart, and he turns to answer it. As he speaks softly with a guard, I wipe the wet cowardice from my eyes with my sleeve. When I look up again, he's turned around, but the door remains open, the guard waiting in the hall.

"I know I've asked a lot of you, but I need you to come with me," he says. I nod and follow him wordlessly through the shiny white hallways of a ship at least double the size of Beck's. His posture is too perfect, too careful. I don't trust it, and I definitely don't trust the direction we're going, deeper and deeper into the bowels of the ship. After the third stairwell, my stomach drops in understanding.

"Just . . ." He takes my arms in his, forcing me to look at him as we pause outside our destination. "Please don't hate me," he says. I push past him through the door next to us and find Beck bound to a chair.

CHAPTER FIFTY

"Oh goody, it's the boy wonder again," Beck says as Declan steps in behind me, moving to stand by my side. I try not to wince at the fact he didn't bother to greet me, or the way he keeps his eyes turned away, refusing to look at my face. Declan's face is twisted into something hardened and commanding. I can't picture him in battle, but I imagine it would look something like this. His eyebrows are a straight line over his stony gray eyes, and his jaw adds harsh, angular ridges to his boyish curves.

"Beck," I say, taking a step closer. I reach toward him, but he turns his face away from me, and my hands turn icy. "Are you okay?"

"Yeah, just perfect. But don't worry, darlin'," he says with a snide whistle. "Your dreamboat over there isn't gonna treat me for injuries sustained while I was protecting the damsel in distress."

His words sting, and my brow furrows. I don't know what game he's playing, but I don't like it.

"Beck, what's wrong with you?" I ask, moving closer. "Why are you being like this?"

"Well, for one, I'm starting to lose feeling in my arms," he says.

"Can we untie him?" I ask, looking at Declan.

"Not while you're here," Declan says, his voice firm. Beck scoffs.

"Oh yeah, protect her from the big bad pirate. She might get *kidnapped* again."

"Beck, stop. You know what happened. You don't have to do this," I say, taking another step closer. "We don't have to do this." Beck's eyes meet mine. The gold is almost nonexistent in the cold, dim lighting, and he breaks the connection.

"It's not that simple, Capo," he says. The return of my nickname should be reassuring, but something about the way he says it does the opposite. It sits in my chest like a warning.

"What's not?" I ask.

"Tell her," Declan says. He wears anger on his features with regret.

"Tell me what?" I ask, elongating my words so they sound calm, though the effect is anything but. Beck won't meet my eyes, but a wry grin lifts his lips.

"Your boyfriend over there wants me to tell you about the money his mother paid me."

"I know about that, though," I say. The smile on his face fades, and I swear I see a hint of shame creep into his eyes. But then it's gone, and he's back to being the pirate.

"You knew that I was paid. You didn't know what I did to keep it."

"What did you do to keep it?" I ask, and time slows down. Even before he says the words, it's as if I know what he's going to say. I know he's going to lie. But I don't anticipate how much it's going to hurt.

"I had to keep you away from the boy wonder. That's what the money was for. Just like she paid Ammon. It was easy enough for a while. But then, there were bounty hunters, and you got so pouty about things, and I knew I needed a more convincing way to keep you with me . . ."

Ice shoots through my veins, and my jaw tightens. *No. No. Don't say it. It's not true.* His jaw twitches, but his eyes are cold and dark.

"So I said some pretty words. I touched your face. I caught your eye across crowded rooms," he says with a cruel laugh. "It was so easy to pretend. You're such a fool. So easily manipulated." Irina's words are repeated on his lips, and they feel like a stab to the gut. I recoil, feeling the attack, trying to understand what's happening. *Whatever happens, Capo, please trust this. Promise you'll remember.* Those were his words, the words he made me promise to. And for once, I decide to listen.

"No," I say, my voice low and shaky. His eyes shift up to mine, taking in my denial with detached interest.

"I'm sorry it came to that. It was just the easiest option. So much easier than tying you up every night, though that would have had its own perks." He winks at Declan, and I hear Declan take a step closer. I hold a hand back to stop him.

"Stop it," I whisper.

"So, I played the hero a few times. I danced with a pretty girl for a night. I told her things she wanted to hear. And I got paid. A lot. Even more than Ammon got for Emlyn — his mother must *really* hate you!"

"*Stop it.*" I'm shaking, and there is nothing in this room but me and Beck and his hateful lies. Lies that come so easily . . . too easily . . .

"And that was just the first half. I could've asked for more. Siobhan was so desperate to get rid of you. Knew you'd ruin everything. But I didn't. Negotiating is so messy — it just didn't seem worth it." He eyes land on me then, cold and hard as he delivers the fatal blow.

My stomach is lead as I stare at him, and my cheeks are cold. *You could never be worthless*, that's what he said to me. And he's right. He knows exactly what I'm worth, and apparently, it's half of what the woman who hates me most was willing to pay. I knew he took the money, but she was willing to pay more, and he didn't think it was worth the hassle. *I* wasn't worth it. He's the one who decided the value of my life. Not Siobhan. He used me, after all.

I feel my bottom lip quiver and bite down on it. But it's too late. He's already seen.

"Oh, come on, Arden. I'm an asshole. You know that. You were an easy mark. Didn't take long to figure you out, and it wasn't all bad. I mean, you're a hell of a kisser. Have fun with that, pretty boy." I slap him across the face. Hard. He takes the full brunt of it, letting it snap his head to the wall. And I hate that I know it hurts me more than him. I feel the bruise on my palm immediately. It almost distracts me from the stabbing ache in my chest. His pupils flare, and then his eyes go back to being cold, hard coals.

"You're not a pirate, you're a coward." I feel Declan's eyes on the back of my head, and I can't bear to look at them. To see the hurt or the pity. Instead, I keep staring at Beck, willing him to snap out of it, to just *look at me*, to give me a sign that this is all a ruse to placate Declan. But he blows raspberries through his full lips with a wry smile, face still turned to the wall.

"You really do pack a punch, Capo. Never saw it coming." His voice is hard and rigid, and he doesn't turn his face back around, doesn't give me the chance to stare him down. I glare at the side of his head for another moment, and then I can't anymore. Everything feels wrong. My skin is cold, and my clothes aren't right; they're not mine. Beck's eyes are cold, too cold. He watches me with a distant disconnection that makes me shake from deep in my belly.

It's as if something has taken over, some creature has consumed him, filling the cavities of his body, and it's watching me with mild curiosity. There's nothing of the man I've grown to trust, no remnants of the man I love so deeply it burns me up inside. His hands won't find my body, won't wrap me up in his, won't press kisses to the back of my neck, won't push the hair from my eyes. I thought I knew this man sitting in front of me, but whoever it was I knew is gone.

I feel the sick rise in my throat before I can respond. I clutch a hand over my mouth, holding the sour acid in my mouth until I can get out of the room. Beck's still watching me, and for just a second, his expression softens, breaking around the edges. The bravado cracks, and I see something else waiting underneath. It's only there for the span of a heartbeat, but that's enough. It's too late. I don't know what to trust anymore. Was any of it real? Or is that just another mask he's used to manipulate me? To make sure he gets every penny of what little I was worth?

My stomach lurches, and I stumble from the room, losing the battle and the contents of my stomach just on the other side of the door. I fall to my hands and knees, landing in the vomit. Maybe it will slide up my arms and burn me through. The pain of it would hurt less than Beck's words. His words that cut like glass.

I am vaguely aware of a door closing behind me, and then a towel to the left of my face. I take it and wipe off my hands and face. A hand is there, and I take it. Declan is there, his eyes hidden in shadow, but their meaning plain. He is sorry. He's sorry for putting me in this situation, where I could be so easily manipulated and hurt. But he is also sorry that I love someone else. Someone who doesn't actually exist.

He walks me upstairs, and Neve waits for me in my room. Neve, my sweet friend from the peninsula, whose eyes widen slightly at the sight of Declan, but then soften on me as she folds me into a hug, even though I'm covered in my own sick. Neve, who helps me bathe and change into pretty clothes and makes up my face with creams that smell like lavender and summer days. Whose life I stole. Oh, but I wish I could give it back.

CHAPTER FIFTY-ONE

*D*eclan's cabin is bright. The light that streams through the wall of windows is just tinted with the first oranges of sunset. It flatters his complexion, making him seem less strained, less tired, returning just enough of the gold to his hair and cheeks. But his eyes give him away.

"You look pretty," he says, but he winces at the word *pretty*. I look down at the white wool pants and Nordanian-blue sweater. Neve outdid herself, even with her new limp we both pretend not to notice. She pinked up my cheeks, and put copper powder on my eyes, after lining the top lids with a dark kohl. The combination of makeup and sweater gives the illusion that my eyes are a perfect Nordanian blue. She tamed my hair into long, tame curls. Curls that will surely get windblown as soon as we go outside for whatever it is they're planning on the deck. But it's a smart outfit. The pants are clean, pristine, pure. The blue is the stuff of Nordanian lore. I don't know where she found the sweater, but she mumbled something about calling in a favor and told me not to ask again.

The suede boots she shoved my feet into are another story. They have a high, pointy heel that is very pretty to look at, but not so pretty to walk on. Beck would laugh at them, and then poke fun at me until I took them off.

No. He wouldn't. I don't know what he would do. The person I knew doesn't actually exist. That person was a ruse, an illusion. A carefully constructed lie in service of a paycheck. A fresh round of sick threatens to ruin my outfit, and I swallow it down and force a little smile.

"Thank you," I say.

"There are people outside. Reporters. We need to appease them."

"Okay," I say. I guess we've come to an unspoken understanding that we should be seen together by someone.

"But we need to decide what we're telling them?"

"What we're telling them?" I ask.

"Yeah. With our farewell."

"I don't understand," I say. He keeps his distance, as if his stepping any closer might change my decision. "Will we be interviewed?"

"No, nothing like that," he says, leaning against a window. I don't know how he can stand to do so. It must be so cold. I can't seem to stop shivering. "We will be photographed. People will be able to guess what our reunion was like based on how we look in the photographs. I know it sounds silly, but people spend entirely too much time scrutinizing the photographs of people like us." I recall the newspaper at Kern's parents' house that sent me into an insecure fit, and the one at Irina's—the photo of Fiona that made me think way too long about a girl who has never spent a second thinking about me.

"I believe it." He smiles, surely recalling my accusations about him and Fiona from the first newspaper.

"If we hold hands, it might be perceived as friendly, or forced. If I put an arm around your shoulder, it could be seen as supportive or brotherly. You can imagine there are a litany of perceptions based on body cues."

"This is something you've spent a lot of time thinking about?"

"This is what I've been raised to think about," he says, a sad twitch to his mouth, as if he finally recognizes that we have led very different lives. But there is common ground between us — we've both spent a good amount of time concerned with our appearances. He wants people to find him trustworthy and likable; I wanted to mask bruises and scars, both visible and unseen.

"What do you propose?" I ask, cringing at my use of the word. He shoves his hands into his pockets, so much like Beck, and looks across the room.

"Can we be honest with each other?" he asks. I sigh and look at my hands. I dig my thumbnails into my middle fingers. *Honest*. Yes, I want honesty. But I've had a lot of *honesty* for one day. Maybe too much.

"I hope so," I say.

"It's okay," he says, his voice impossibly quiet. I'm not even sure I heard him right, but then, he repeats himself. "It's okay that you have feelings for him. I understand." I squeeze my eyes shut.

"I don't . . ." I start, and then shudder away the lie. "I thought I understood . . . I am a fool." Irina's words come barreling back at me. *You're an even bigger fool than I thought*. She knew. Of course, she knew. Anger pulses the tears down my cheeks, and when I open my eyes, Declan hasn't moved. But he leans toward me slightly, as if he will be at my side the moment I allow him.

"You're not," he says. His voice is so sure, I almost believe it.

"There were reasons to doubt . . . you warned me yourself. It's like he said, he told me what I wanted to hear. No less, no more . . ." *He might never say*. Ammon's words have a whole new meaning. Of course, he would never say. Everything gets murky under the harsh light of the truth. How could I have been so wrong?

Declan crosses to me and takes my hands in his. I look at him, his face a blur, and he pulls me softly into his chest. He is gentler than Beck, his arms longer and looser, but no less secure. They don't crowd me, don't constrict me. They contain me, and give me space to breathe.

"It's okay," he says again, and I wipe at my eyes again.

"It's not. It's not fair to you."

"No, probably not," he says with a little chuckle. "But fair isn't real."

"You deserve better," I say.

"Maybe. But the problem is I want you."

"Why?" I ask. He chuckles, low and deep, the sound resonating through me.

"Because you're smart. You challenge me. You make me see the world as it is, and the world as it could be. You make me see my own potential to make things better. And you make me want to be better." His voice shakes, and I feel the courage it must have taken him to confess this to a girl crying over another man.

"I want to be better for you. I know I'm supposed to want to be better for my country, but it's for you, Arden. You're everything I've ever wanted, and so much more. You're what I want, *and* what I need. And if I could wake up to your face, your *beautiful* face, for the rest of my life, I would spend every single one of those days working my ass off to be better, to make a better world—for all of us, but especially for you." The air between us stills, and I worry that if I so much as breathe into it, it will shatter. But then I breathe, and it holds. It doesn't dissipate. It remains: surefooted, solid, steady.

"I want to be that person for you—the person you think I am . . . so much," I say. I feel his chest still with the implication. But he presses forward.

"Is there any chance you could be? Do you think . . ." He hesitates and pulls back. I look up at him and see the fear in his eyes. The heartbreaking, gut-churning fear.

"What? What is it?"

"Do you think you could ever love me?" he asks. I close my eyes and let my forehead fall into his chest. Even here, on a ship, worlds away from his gardens, I smell them on him. The earth, the mint, a hint of basil. It grounds me, roots me to the planks beneath my feet.

"I'm not actually sure I know what love is, or if I'm capable . . ." I admit, my voice small and tight. "But if I'm going to try, then I'd like to think I could imagine trying it with you." His arms fold over me just a touch tighter, still leaving me room to breathe, and I look up at him.

"I can live with that," he says, a small smile spreading across his lips. A knock distracts us, but we don't break apart. He lets the person on the other side of the door interrupt us without breaking the moment, lets him tell us it's time, and then asks for a moment, so he can lean down and kiss my cheek, his soft lips pressing warm sweetness into my skin. It's not the same as it was with Beck. With Beck, it was something completely different, something that transcended the actual physical touch. But it wasn't real. This is real. So I put my hand in Declan's and walk with him, side by side.

CHAPTER FIFTY-TWO

We wait inside the ship while more photographers fill in the docks, finding the angle they want. As we stand, I feel something press into my hand—a small disk of brass I thought I might not see again.

"I understand you kept this on your person until very recently." Declan's words are soft, sly whispers against my ear. I smile in spite of myself, curling my fingers around his compass. The chain has been replaced. "It was found on Beck's ship. Just returning it where it belongs."

"Thank you," I say, running my thumb over the latch.

"May I?" he asks, waiting for my permission. I nod, and he clasps the necklace behind my neck, his fingers lingering on the clasp so lightly. I wonder if he worries he'll break me. Funny that he can't see it's too late—I'm already broken.

"Ready?" asks the official I don't know.

"Hang on." Neve is there, brushes in hand, and she applies a light dusting of powder to my cheeks, telling me to keep my hair out of my face. I promise I will, and then walk outside into the wind and the flashbulbs. Declan laces his fingers with mine. I'm sure this is something he's planned. And I get it. If our hands are held tight, it might look unfeeling. If our fingers are laced, it looks intimate. It feels more intimate, too.

The wind whips at us, and I suck in a breath. He grins and wraps his arms around me as we approach the end of the deck, laughing as he rubs his hands up and down my arms. He is wearing a jacket and a scarf. I'm wearing a sweater. It was prettier than my coat. I need to be pretty right now. The things I have to consider now are really not so different than before, just less practical.

"Are you nervous?" he asks.

"Yes," I say, and we both laugh. "Can they hear us?"

"No, I don't think so. But some might read our lips."

"Really?" I ask, looking out from our perch on the second deck, across the lower deck, to the pier, where no less than thirty photographers snap photo after photo of us. It seems like such a waste of film, but as I take in the ragged state of some of their clothes, I decide that if a photograph of me will feed some hungry bellies, I'll be more than happy to smile away.

"We're almost done," he says, pulling me into his side and waving at the throngs of people who aren't behind cameras, but who have also started to gather. They're predominantly women, and some of them look on with curious eyes. Curious about Declan, or his massive ship? Curious about me? The girl who came from nothing and rose to be held in his arms, to be photographed by every camera in the city?

He says I have the support of the nation. That I'm the underdog. But that superlative comes from somewhere else, somewhere unofficial. Maybe not the old-world bureaucracy, but something deeper, less stable, threatening to explode. My whole life, I've been used by one man or another. I don't want to be in the business of being used, nor do I want to be in the business of using another person to my own gain. Yet, here I stand, with a man who has the world at his fingertips — not just that, but the power to change the world, and the motivation, the will, the desire to do it. Because of me. The port is full of women watching us, some empowered like Neve and Irina, others less so. And in Nordania, where I was abused and neglected, and nobody thought twice about it, there are even fewer who are empowered.

I stand on the precipice of an uncharted voyage. One that Declan is ready and willing to make. One that needs a few tweaks, a few adjustments along the way, but as I feel the steadiness of the man pressed into my side, I trust that we can do it together. I don't know if we will ever grow to love each other, but in him, I feel a comrade in arms. Someone who wants to be more than what is expected of him. I look up at him, and he looks down at me. I smile, and he smiles back.

"Kiss me," I say. His eyes get wide, and his cheeks flush pink. I see the pull of something soft and sad at the corners of his eyes, something wrestling within him, talking sense into him, but then he smiles wider and leans in, pressing his lips to mine. They're familiar and soft and nothing but appropriate in front of the people all around us. He slides his arms around my back and holds me against him with such a soft touch, I think I might float away.

I want to lose myself in him, but all I can think of is the last person I kissed. *Whatever happens, Capo, please trust this*. But Beck wasn't real. None of it was. My heart pinches where a piece of it is deadened and black. But I keep kissing Declan as the crowd cheers.

I pull back, and his smile grows a little sadder as he cups my cheeks and wipes away my tears. He knows they're not for him. But it'll still make a pretty picture. We turn and wave at the masses again, and then he leads me back inside. We walk straight to his room, and once the door is closed, he eyes me carefully.

"That was quite the body language." He laughs, and so do I, but we're both cautious.

"Was it okay?" I ask.

"It depends. Why did you do it?" he asks.

"Because . . ." I think for a second. "Because I wanted to. I wanted to give you what you need for the photos. I wanted to show people that we are real, that we're not going away." He presses a hand against the window, and wrestles with my answer that didn't really answer his question.

"Did you mean it, though?" he asks. I press my lips together and bite on the edge of my tongue.

"I wanted to . . ."

"But?" he asks. I search for the right words, honest words that won't sting.

"But there were so many people . . . it was so strange," I say. A laugh bursts from his throat, and he squeezes my hand.

"It is beyond strange. I don't think I've ever done that in front of people before. Not intentionally, anyway," he says with a blush of a smile. I match it. "I can't wait for people to pick apart our technique."

"Oh, great," I say, groaning.

"Don't worry. We'll work on it." My stomach flips at the thought of kissing him again, at the thought of his hands on me. I bite my tongue to suppress the shudder, the panic. But then I look at his even smile, his steady eyes. He's so calm. His hands hold mine, and it's hard not to believe him, though I'm still not sure I'm ready to try.

I watch the port disappear into the darkness from inside the door to the deck where we officially waved goodbye. I don't see Beck's ship as we disembark. I hope Kern and Perlman and Shaz and Slick are safe. I try not to think too hard about what they did or didn't know.

Evening lights blink to life, and I can just make out the

shadow of the crowds that haven't dissipated. We are just starting to hit the ocean waters, and the ship rocks, but not enough. Not as much as Beck's ship, anyway. Several floors down, Beck sits in a cell. I know I should want him to be hurting. But it doesn't come. I hope he knows what a rotten excuse for a human he is. If he's not lying.

I don't trust anything anymore—not him, and certainly not myself. I hate him for making me believe him, for making me doubt everything else, for making me not know what it is I'm feeling, or what it is to trust my own instincts. I hate him. And I hope he's not too cold.

"I didn't know you had it in you." Neve's voice is smooth as silk.

"What?" I ask.

"I knew that you were strong. I knew you could survive. Hell, I've seen you survive so much worse." My face blanches, and a hint of guilt droops the corners of her eyes. It's the first time she's ever even hinted at knowing that CJ wasn't just "doting" on me. "I honestly didn't think you'd last there. At the institute, I mean. But you're smart—smarter than me. In ways I wouldn't have survived. And Beck . . ." There's a real note of sadness there.

"What about him?" I ask. My voice is too quick, too harsh. Her eyebrows bend into sad curves, but she shakes her head. She presses a folded-up piece of parchment into my hand, then looks out the window at the disappearing port. If I didn't know better, I would think she looked sad to see it go.

"What's this?" I ask. She doesn't answer, and I carefully unfold the warm paper. Written in tight, slanting script, is something that makes me smile.

Don't fuck this up, little girl.
43-15-12 S 124-49-23 E

"You can do this. I really believe that. And I want to be

there when you do," Neve says, solid as always. She pulls her eyes from the window and looks right through me.

"Do what?" I ask.

"Win." My heart flutters, and I am about to tell her it's not about Declan. But her eyes are fiery and hard, and I know that what she means is so much bigger than one privileged man.

"Oh, that?" She laughs, and I laugh with her.

"How are you going to do it?" she asks. I shrug, pressing the paper into my pocket, against my tattoo. Together, we look out the window, watching the cove block us off from the port.

"How anyone else trying to upset the norm would do it." She narrows her eyes at me, and I smile. "We're gonna have to break some damn rules."

ACKNOWLEDGMENTS

There are too many people to thank who helped along the way, especially in the season this book took to come to print, where we experienced a global pandemic and our world turned upside down. For everyone who asked how it was going, who told me about their favorite part, and who have read to this page in the book: from the bottom of my heart, thank you.

To Kisa Whipkey, for being the best editor I could ask for. For pushing me to find the most authentic versions of every character and nudging me into that place where the story transcends what even I thought possible.

To Ash Ruggirello, who created another stunning cover and rolled with it when I asked if something was too blue.

Thank you to Chris Winkelaar for yet another beautiful map of Nordania. And for gifting his family farm as inspiration for Beck's family's home.

To my fellow Wingnuts, Mari, Desiree, Heather, and Jefna, for jumping into this bottle with me and indulging my rants. To my LoveSwords, Kira, Jessica (J-Lo), Jessica (JP), Kaila, Meredith, and Air, thank you for your unceasing enthusiasm for all things Beck (and all things cheetah-print).

To Elliott and Walt, for being mature beyond their years and understanding that Mom has a weird job, and sometimes COVID-school has to wait so she can just "get that down real quick."

And to Chris, my North Star, for being the most supportive and encouraging partner I could ask for.

ABOUT THE AUTHOR

Erin Riha writes young adult fantasy novels about ambitious girls who don't know they're not supposed to exceed expectations. She lives in Portland, Oregon, with her husband and two very noisy boys.

www.ingramcontent.com/pod-product-compliance
Lightning Source LLC
Chambersburg PA
CBHW030810260626
47169CB00001B/265